CW00504406

Ghost of
a Stranger

Deborah Twelves

First Edition 2021 Fortis Publishing

Copyright © Fortis Publishing under exclusive licence from Deborah Twelves.

The rights of Deborah Twelves have been asserted in accordance with the Copyright, Designs and Patents Act 1998.
No part of this book may be reprinted or reproduced or utilised in any form or by any electronic, mechanical, or other means, now known or hereafter invented, including photocopying and recording, or in any information storage or retrieval system, without permission in writing from the publishers.

ISBN-13: 978-1-913822-16-3

Fortis Publishing
Kemp House
160 City Road
London
EC1V 2NX

Although this story is based on real events, it is a work of fiction. Some characters and events have been added for creative purposes and are entirely a product of the author's imagination.

About the author

Deborah Twelves was born in Sheffield, but raised in Ponteland, Northumberland. She studied French and Spanish at Edinburgh University and taught languages for some years while living in France, Spain and Northern Quebec. She now divides her time between her home in Pwllheli, on the Llyn Peninsula of North Wales and her family home in Northumberland but often travels abroad. She has a black Labrador called Nala and a black Lusitano horse called Recurso (Ric), who take up a lot of her spare time, although yacht racing, which she began at an early age with her father, remains her great passion.

Deborah has written many articles for the sailing press over the years.
Ghost of a Stranger is her second novel, based on true events in her life. It is also the second book in *The Stranger Trilogy*.

The Stranger Trilogy
Book 1 - *Twenty Years a Stranger*
Book 2 – *Ghost of a Stranger*
Book 3 - *The Boy Stranger* (available in 2022)

For Ruth:

My best friend, my soul sister.

True friends shine bright like diamonds: beautiful, precious, valuable and always in style.

Acknowledgements

My heartfelt thanks go to the following people:

Ken Scott, my wonderful book coach and mentor, for inspiring me, encouraging me and always believing in me.

Reinette Visser and the team at Fortis Publishing, especially my editor Joan Elliott for her invaluable efforts.

Ruth Lloyd-Williams and all at Network She, who have done so much to support and promote me as an author

My friends Sir John Aird and Barbara Shooter, for taking the time to proof read for me.

My wonderful Madagascar Rally family, who opened up a whole new world to me and inspired many of the characters and events in this book:

John and Sarah of Bespoke Rallies
Toby and Finella
Reg, Don and Frank
Barbara, George and Henry
Jose and Maria
Roger and Gillian
Peter and Jane
Geoff and Penny
John and Fen
Roger and Maggie
Nicholas and Lesley
Norman and Liza
Andrew and Diana

To all those of you out there who read and enjoyed my first novel, Twenty Years a Stranger, and gave such wonderful reviews, your words of encouragement meant the world to me and gave me the confidence to continue my journey as an author. I really hope you enjoy the next part of the story in Ghost of a Stranger.

Last, but most definitely not least, I am grateful beyond words for my wonderful family and friends who continue to support me in everything I do. I count myself very lucky to have you all in my life and wouldn't be where I am today without you. I hope you know how much I truly love and value you.

Prologue

10 years earlier

Sophie

Kate Ryan stood by the graveside and watched in silence as they gently lowered the coffin into the ground. Anger bubbled up inside her at the thought of the person who lay inside it. The man who, only a couple of weeks earlier, had laughed and joked with them, full of life as they all made plans for the future they had so carelessly taken for granted. At thirty-five years old this was not how it was supposed to be. She wiped the back of her hand across her face, determined to stay strong as a tear slid down her cheek. An unspoken bond tied her forever to the four other people standing by her side.

The day everything changed, Kate was awakened by the slapping of water against the hull as the Beneteau charter yacht rocked gently in the wake of another boat heading out of the harbour. She was uncomfortable in the cramped rear cabin and her arm was numb from being squashed against the side of the boat by her partner Michael, who remained dead to the world beside her. Kate tried unsuccessfully to turn over, banging first her elbow, then her head before she gave up, squeezing her eyes tightly shut against the early morning light filtering in through the little cabin window and wishing she hadn't drunk quite so much the previous evening. She already had the makings of the mother of all hangovers and, what with Michael's snoring and the annoying slapping noise of the water, she knew there was precious little chance of sleeping it off. She realised she was going to have to make a more determined effort to get out of the bunk to go in search of water and Alka Seltzer, her tried and tested remedy. Unzipping her sleeping bag, she crawled out of the cabin and quickly located the miracle cure in her toilet bag. She found a half-empty bottle of water and dropped two tablets straight in, staring at them and yawning as they fizzed comfortingly. There was no sign of life from any of the others so, feeling decidedly nauseous, she opted to go up onto the deck for some fresh air, grabbing a fleece as she went. She realised in dismay that they had left all the seat cushions out, which meant they would be wet from the overnight dew, but just as quickly she decided she really didn't care and flopped down on the nearest bench, pulling the fleece over her head. The very sight of the empty bottles and cans littering the cockpit made her want to vomit, so she closed her eyes to blot out the offending images. She remembered being told that if someone felt seasick they should lie on their stomach with their face down on their hands. Assuming the principle applied to any kind of nausea, she decided to give it a try and mercifully drifted off to sleep.

The sound that snapped her sharply back into consciousness was a low guttural howl, more animal than human. For a moment she was completely disorientated, with no idea where she was, but she quickly came to her senses and realised that the piercing screams that had replaced the howl were coming from one of the cabins below.

"What the fuck...?" Michael yelled as he emerged from his drunken slumber and staggered clumsily out of their cabin. Kate half stumbled and half fell down the wooden steps in her haste to work out what was happening, while the deafening shrieks continued and chaos reigned below.

"What the hell is going on?" shouted Jerry, emerging from the other rear cabin, as his girlfriend Roisin pushed past him to get out and see what the crisis was.

"Not me," said Kate, holding up her hands and already heading for the door of the front cabin, which had been commandeered by Sophie and Craig.

The noise stopped abruptly as Kate entered the cabin to find Sophie huddled in a corner, as though she was trying to get as far away from her fiancé Craig as possible. The wild look of anguish and terror on her face made Kate shudder. Scrambling across the bunk on all fours to reach her friend, she put her hands on Sophie's shoulders and shook her. Hard.

"Sophie, look at me. Look. At. Me."

Kate spoke sharply to get her attention as Sophie dissolved into tears and began to whimper like a beaten dog.

"It's okay. You're okay," she said, in an attempt to restore order.

Kate resisted the temptation to slap her face hard and instead began to stroke her hair in reassurance.

"You need to calm down and tell me what's happened. Are you hurt?"

The whimpering continued, but still there were no words of explanation and Kate was aware that the others had gathered behind them in the doorway of the cabin, staring in bewildered silence.

"Please Sophie, you're scaring me. We'll help you, whatever it is, but you need to talk to us."

Around that moment it occurred to Kate that, in all the commotion, Craig had not moved a muscle. Not stirred at all in fact. As she stared at the motionless shape of his body in his sleeping bag, she was overcome by a new feeling of dread, which quickly turned to panic as she realised her rookie error as a first aider. It was always the quiet ones you should be worried about in these situations. Of course, she knew that.

"Craig! Craig!" she screamed as she pounced on him and desperately began to shake him, knowing almost immediately there was no point. The chalky pallor of his complexion, the half-open eyes and the blue tinge to his lips that she noted as she rolled him over onto his back would haunt her for the rest of her days. Kate knew instinctively that she had to remain calm and somehow managed to do all the right things, like checking his pulse and putting her ear to his mouth, hoping and praying for some sign of life, however slight.

There was none.

"Call an ambulance," she said sharply, turning to the others. "And the Guards. I think Craig's dead." The words sounded hollow and strangely lacking in emotion, as if they were spoken by someone else. "And for Christ's sake get Sophie out of here and up on deck."

Kate shoved the other woman towards the cabin door, suddenly irritated that she was the only one who seemed capable of doing anything useful. There was a commotion as the others backed away to make room, falling over each other in their haste and confusion. Roisin grabbed Sophie's hand and pulled her through the cabin, while Jerry climbed in beside Kate.

"Are you sure he's dead?" he asked, apparently unwilling to believe what was happening.

"Of course I'm fucking sure. Look at him, for Christ's sake," she shouted, tears springing to her eyes.

She suddenly felt a wave of nausea come over her and was overwhelmed by the need to get out of the cabin, away from the suffocating smell of death and into the fresh air.

"I need to get out of here Jerry," she said, already beginning to retch, her whole body shaking in delayed shock.

She hated leaving Craig alone like that, but it was obvious there was nothing more either of them could do for him. He was gone.

Up on deck, the five of them sat huddled together in stunned silence, save for the occasional whimpering from one of the girls, waiting for the Guards and the ambulance crew to arrive. They didn't speak, because they had absolutely no idea what to say to each other. There were no words. This was supposed to have been a fun weekend, a party for Christ's sake. They had chartered the boat to celebrate Roisin's new career as a fully-fledged clinical psychologist, the perfect excuse for a reunion of old friends. Yet now here they were, waiting for one of their best friends to be carted off to the morgue. It made no sense.

Two weeks later, after numerous conversations with both the Guards and Craig's family, going over and over the same thing, it still made no sense. Nobody could offer any explanation as to why a healthy young man in the prime of his life had suffered a massive and catastrophic stroke in his sleep that he had no chance of surviving. True, they had all been drinking that night, but no more than usual on a night out and Craig never really overdid it anyway. He was one of those people who just couldn't take his drink and he always suffered the most horrendous and debilitating migraines the next day. As a result, he had concluded over the years that it simply wasn't worth it.

The tight-knit group of friends began blaming first themselves and then each other, wondering if one of them could have been stupid enough to spike his coke, or if he had just picked up the wrong drink and had some sort of bad reaction to the alcohol. Then they began to question whether Sophie and Craig had taken something else in the cabin that night. Maybe Craig preferred to get wasted on something other than alcohol... They were all looking for someone to blame in their desire to make sense of what had happened. Suspicion seemed to fall naturally on Sophie, always a bit of an outsider and, more importantly, the last person to see him alive.

The Coroner's report put paid to all that. The amount of alcohol in his bloodstream was negligible and there were no traces of any other substances, legal or illegal. Apparently, it was an unthinkable, tragic accident that no one could have predicted or prevented. The only thing they had to be grateful for was the fact that his death was instantaneous and he would not have suffered any pain or indeed known anything about it. Sophie, together with everyone else on the

5

boat that night, was exonerated from any responsibility for his death.

Kate's thoughts were interrupted as a handful of earth landed on the coffin with a gentle thump and she stole a look at Sophie, wondering where her family were and why they were not there with her, supporting her. She realised suddenly that she had no idea if she even had any family, as she never talked about them or her childhood and had always avoided questions about the past.

Sophie stared straight ahead, her face impassive, feeling numb and strangely detached from the whole proceedings. She knew she was expected to cry, that people would think it strange if she didn't, but somehow the tears wouldn't come. It was happening again. Just like before. It was only a matter of time until tongues started to wag and people started to blame her, despite the coroner's report, just because her face didn't fit. She had already seen it in the expressions of the very people who were supposed to be her friends. It had been that way all her life.

Sophie still vividly remembered the unhappiness of her school days in Bradford as if it were yesterday. She was known as Megan back then. The taunts and the bullying had gone on for years and no one, not even the teachers or her parents, ever did anything to stop it. She had never fitted in, never been one of the 'cool kids'. Her mother had a lot to answer for there, she thought with a scowl, always insisting on the 'sensible and practical' option for clothing and shoes, which meant that Megan stood out as being a bit of a geek and was ridiculed by the other girls. She was desperate to fit in, but no matter what she did she was always the outsider. She wanted to scream in their faces that none of them had any idea what her life was really like, but she never did.

If they had known about all the trouble with her father, maybe they wouldn't have been so quick to judge. After that all came out, it was impossible for her and her mother to stay where they were, so they moved away to Colchester for a fresh start, where nobody knew what had happened. Or at least that was the idea. She even changed her name to Sophie Flaherty. When she started at her new school she thought things might improve, but of course, someone found out. How could they not when it had been plastered all over the papers? The whole circus began again, with her teachers and even her own mother labelling her as a 'strange girl' and 'a loner'. They said she was unable to connect with people, describing her as a deeply troubled child. She was promptly referred to the Educational Psychologist and forced to attend weekly appointments in an effort to help her interact better with her peers, but nothing ever changed. Not until the day she found herself alone on the stairs with one of her tormentors and took matters into her own hands. The other girl sneered at her spitefully as they crossed paths, muttering the word 'nutter' under her breath. The next thing she knew, the girl was lying at the bottom of the stairs, with injuries serious enough to keep her off Sophie's case for the foreseeable future. One of the other kids swore to the Head she had witnessed the incident and seen Sophie shove the girl so hard in the back that her feet actually left the ground as she crashed down the unforgiving metal steps, arms and legs flailing. Sophie vehemently denied doing any such thing, but of course, no one was interested in her side of the story and it was clear both the school and the other parents wanted her gone. They got their way and the rest of her education was delivered in a school for children with special educational needs like hers. The 'Ed Psych' remained a permanent feature in her life, having declared her to have worrying behavioural traits and serious anger management issues.

Sophie hated her school days, but she was bright and had no trouble getting the qualifications necessary to secure a place studying nursing. That would be her ticket to a new life. She couldn't wait to get away, so the sudden, untimely death of her mother just as she finished her training seemed like the perfect opportunity to cut all ties with the past and reinvent herself in a place where nobody knew her story. She took up her new job in Dublin, full of hope for the future.

Everything worked out well for a while and she even found some people she could call friends, which was a new experience for her, but like everything else good in her life, it didn't last. When she met Craig through her friend from work, Kate, it seemed like she had found the missing piece of the jigsaw to make her life complete. She knew immediately that he was perfect for her and was without question the best thing that had ever happened to her. He made her feel special and promised he would always look after her. It was their destiny to be together forever.

Until he cheated on her of course.

She wanted to die when she first found out, but the self-pity turned quickly to anger and she could still see the fear in his face as the venomous recriminations, foul language and threats poured from her mouth, describing not only what she would do to herself, but also to him if he tried to leave her. Those threats were immediately followed by sobbing pleas for him to stay with her and declarations of undying love. It was a terrible time, but somehow they got through it. She generously agreed to forgive and forget and assured him they would be stronger as a couple because of it. She even believed it herself for a while, but in reality, she knew she would never truly be able to trust him again. If only his love for her could have been as true and as pure as hers for him. If only he had stayed faithful to her. Things could have been so different. But in the end, he had turned out to be just another massive disappointment, letting her down like everyone else in her life had always done. She could not allow him to treat her as a doormat like her father had done with her mother, or make a fool of her like the girls at school, laughing at her behind her back and making her life a misery. She was not that tortured little girl anymore. The new Sophie knew exactly how to deal with people who disappointed her and let her down.

Someone nudged her on the arm, jolting her back into the present and she realised the service was coming to an end. Sophie's face remained expressionless as she stepped forward and dropped a single white rose onto the coffin of her beloved Craig, her head full of bitter thoughts that this was not how their story should have ended.

The day after Craig's funeral, with a distinct feeling of déjà vu, Sophie walked into a hairdressing salon in Blackrock and stared at herself in the mirror as the stylist held up a handful of her long auburn hair.

"Are you sure about this? You have such beautiful hair," the girl said with an envious expression.

"I'm absolutely sure. I want a completely new look," she answered, looking the girl straight in the eye, with an air of finality that she hoped communicated a clear instruction to her to get on with her job and stop poking her nose in where it was not wanted.

Two hours later Sophie stood up and looked admiringly at the face staring back at her in the mirror, framed with a sleek dark brown bob and choppy fringe. She smiled happily as she left the salon, feeling like a new person, as if a huge weight had been lifted from her shoulders. Turning the music up loud in the car, she headed out of town in the direction of Baltimore. The further away Sophie Flaherty drove from Dublin, the more optimistic she began to feel about the future. The old Sophie died that night on the boat with Craig. She was gone forever, together with all the baggage she had been dragging along with her for so long.

It was time for Caitlin Branagh to make a new start and she would most definitely not be looking back.

Of course, Kate and Roisin reported their friend missing and tried everything they could think of to track her down, but nobody from that ill-fated boat trip ever heard from her again. If they were honest with themselves they felt guilty about the way they had been so quick to turn on her and were keen to make amends, but despite all their best efforts to find her, she had vanished without a trace, her face added to the long list of missing persons on file with the Garda. As time went by, life began to return to normal for them and they had no choice but to get on with their own lives, in the way people inevitably do when they lose someone. Sophie was consigned to their memories and became just someone they once knew. Someone who would have been a constant reminder of an event in their lives they all preferred to forget.

Part I

The New Order

au ro ra

Aurora was the beautiful Roman goddess of the sunrise, whose tears turned into the morning dew. The name symbolizes optimism and new beginnings.

Best Kept Secrets

Two may keep a secret, if one of them is dead.

Present Day

Grace

I thought my worst nightmares had already come true, that the universe had done its worst and thrown all it had at me, but I was wrong. An impending sense of doom hangs over me like a black storm cloud as I sit alone at the kitchen table, stomach churning, waiting for the police to arrive. Their second visit in less than twenty-four hours.

They turned up on my doorstep last night out of the blue, a young woman in uniform and a man in a suit, holding out their identification for me and asking me if they could step inside for a moment. It was blindingly obvious from their body language that they did not come bearing good news, but nothing could have prepared me for just how bad it was going to be. A few carefully chosen words was all it took to plunge me right back into the middle of all the chaos and pain of the last few years that I thought I had put behind me forever.

The silence in the room is deafening and I think about my dad in an attempt to calm my nerves. What would he have made of all this? I would give anything to feel his arms wrapped tightly around me and hear him telling me everything will be all right. I will never have that again, but I know he walks beside me in spirit, my guardian angel, always there to guide me, protect me and give me strength when I need it most.

I find it comforting to believe in ghosts, the guardian angel type, but there are evil spirits out there as well. Tortured souls of people who did terrible things during their time on earth or who perhaps conversely suffered terrible things at the hands of others. Ghosts of those who can never rest in peace, condemned to wander among us for eternity, trapped in the misery of limbo between this life and the Afterlife.

Ghosts like Daniel, with unfinished business to settle.

I feel suddenly cold, despite the warmth of the room, and force myself to focus on the present. By way of a distraction while I wait, I pick up a photo I found last night when I embarked on a frenzied clear-out of the loft after the police had delivered their bombshell and left. The photo is of a young woman in a white bikini, standing behind the wheel of a yacht, laughing as she looks ahead and up to see the set of the sails. Her body is tanned and toned and she stands comfortably with one hand on the wheel, the other up to her face, shielding her eyes from the glare of the sun. Her long dark hair is wet and tousled as if she has just been swimming and there is a mask and snorkel on a towel beside her. She looks happy; like she hasn't got a care in the world. The water sparkles, a beautiful turquoise blue against the white sails. The woman is me. And Daniel is the one taking the photo, making me laugh on our honeymoon in the Seychelles. In my mind's eye, I can see his face behind the camera as clearly as if it were yesterday. He always loved taking photos.

"What happened to you, Daniel?" I whisper to myself, suddenly overcome with a crushing sadness, which turns just as quickly to anger, as an unwelcome memory of all the other photos and videos I found on his computer backup device creeps into my mind. Photos and videos I was never meant to see. Photos of numerous other women engaged in a variety of lewd sex acts with *my* husband. Once seen, never forgotten, unfortunately for me.

I trace the shape of the woman in the photo with my finger, trying hard to remember happier times. A time when I truly believed we were in love. Inseparable. Soulmates with a dazzling future ahead of us. How could I have known there were already too many secrets lurking in the shadows, wrapping themselves around us like invisible spectres, waiting to drag us down to a dark and sinister underworld that would ultimately destroy us?

There are too many memories thrashing around in my head and I find I can no longer trust any of them. Truth versus lies, fact versus fiction. Impossible to disentangle them all and come up with a truthful version of my past. A random conversation pops into my head and I remember that Daniel was not a confident swimmer and would never under any circumstances put his head below the water voluntarily, not even to go snorkelling with me. I can hear his voice as clearly as if he were sitting next to me.

"I love the water Grace," he said, "but I love being on it, not in it."

He went on to tell me the story of how he almost drowned once as a child, trapped for far too long under a capsized dinghy, struggling for air, certain he was going to die. I remember feeling a surge of compassion at his vulnerability as he explained how the fear had always stayed with him, causing him to have a panic attack if his head was submerged. I believed every word he said back then. Why wouldn't I? But Daniel told me a lot of things over the years, not many of them true as it turned out.

I fantasised many times about his death after I received the email from Lorraine, but when it actually happened, I had to admit it did not bring me the peace I hoped for. The truth is, I was haunted by what happened that night on the boat, tortured by the thought of

Daniel's fear and panic as the waves crashed relentlessly over his head and the currents dragged him down. I could have helped him, but instead I let him die.

I used to lie in the bath at night in the dark, thinking about what it was like to drown, allowing myself to slip slowly under the surface and holding my breath, just to have an idea of what it would actually feel like. I would force myself to stay submerged, holding my breath until I felt the acute pain in my chest, the stabbing sensation behind my eyes, the pounding in my head. But when I emerged, gasping frantically and drawing greedy gulps of fresh air down into my lungs, I always knew I was kidding myself, because the warm, soothing bath water was a far cry indeed from the turbulent, ice-cold waves of the Irish Sea.

I became morbidly obsessed with the subject of drowning. Apparently, a body only remains submerged until enough gas builds up inside it from bacterial decomposition to make it buoyant. Once that happens it rises to the surface again. However long that takes, the science is indisputable and the body will inevitably one day be discovered.

The same applies to secrets. But secrets only have power over us while we are trying to keep them hidden from the world. As soon as they are out there in the open, their power dissolves. There are always consequences to be faced, but with exposure comes a certain sense of relief. I think that was how Daniel must have felt after we all received the email and his life unravelled in the most spectacular fashion, although obviously I will never know for sure on that score.

I drag my muddled thoughts back to the present and look at the clock again. I had all the time in the world to go over everything in my mind last night because sleep was never an option. Not even for a few minutes. When the police appeared on my doorstep I was convinced it was my day of reckoning. My time to set the record straight and tell the truth about what I did. A chance to lay my ghosts to rest.

The thing is though, they didn't want to talk to me about that night on the boat. They had a different agenda, one I could not have predicted in my wildest dreams.

A Door Opens

Two years earlier

Caitlin

Caitlin paused for a moment to wind her scarf a little tighter around her neck and bent down to pick up the ball that had been deposited hopefully at her feet by Bentley, her beloved golden retriever. She turned and hurled the ball back along the beach, watching it travel an impressively long distance, picked up by the wind, as Bentley bounded happily after it. This was a game he never got sick of and she smiled to herself as he appeared again in front of her just moments later. It was hard to believe it was the middle of summer, given that the temperature was only just in double figures and heavy storm clouds were gathering overhead, threatening to unleash a torrential downpour at any moment. There was a mighty crash every few seconds as the waves broke onto the pebbly beach, followed by a loud hiss as they retreated, sucking seaweed, shells and stones with them. She never tired of listening to that sound as she lay in bed in her cottage and, if she got up in the night as she so often did, unable to sleep, she could see the warning light flashing for sailors off the island of Cape Clara.

That was when she felt closest to Aidan.

Caitlin loved days like this and she could be found there on the beach every morning without fail, come rain or shine, winter or summer. The little fishing village of Clearpoint, just a few miles along from Baltimore, on the beautiful southwest coast of Ireland, was the place she called home now. She had rented a cottage there one summer after she upped sticks and left the city in an attempt to escape the unhappiness and tragedy that had clouded her old life in Dublin. She had no idea where she was headed when she set off, but she knew she had to get away. A mile from the nearest village, set on a headland overlooking the little island of Cape Clara, the traditional stone cottage with its wood-burning range cooker and open fire in the lounge seemed as good a place as any to make a fresh start.

After what happened in Dublin, Caitlin told herself firmly that she had done with men and vowed to remain single for the rest of her days. That was until she met Aidan, with his piercing blue eyes, mischievous smile and a mop of unruly, sandy-coloured hair that she couldn't help wanting to run her fingers through. She had most certainly not gone to Clearpoint looking for love, but when Aidan turned up at his aunt's rental cottage to fix the hot water and offered to take her out to the nearby island of Cape Clara on his uncle's fishing boat, she found herself blushing like a love-struck teenager and felt the familiar fluttering of butterflies in her stomach every time he so much as looked in her direction. Caitlin did not make friends easily and was not naturally flirtatious, but she smiled as she remembered how she had felt that electric shock of attraction every time he spoke to her or allowed his hand to brush against hers. He was keen not to push things too fast, but it was as if some greater force were involved and they both soon realized that they had to be together. It seemed the most natural thing in the world for Caitlin to stay there in Clearpoint and so she made the impetuous decision to rent the cottage for six months, determined to seize the second chance at happiness she had so unexpectedly been offered. After all, she had well and truly burned her bridges in Dublin when she left. What was stopping her?

Caitlin threw the ball for Bentley again and thought how much her life had changed since that fateful decision. When Aidan proposed, she thought she was finally getting the fairy tale ending she deserved and their wedding day, a mere six months after they had first clapped eyes on each other, was perfect. Just a handful of people, close friends and family, gathered in the little church in the village, followed by a party for what seemed to be everyone from miles around in one of the barns at his aunt and uncle's farmhouse. They travelled a whole eight miles on the little ferry from Baltimore to Cape Clara for their honeymoon, neither of them keen on flying or drawn to the idea of exotic locations. Five days later they returned home to the cottage his aunt had generously gifted Aidan as a wedding present. After all, she said, it would be coming to him sooner or later, given that she had no children of her own. It was a dream come true. They had each other and everything they needed right there for the rest of their lives.

Not anymore, she thought to herself, as tears sprang to her eyes. She wondered miserably for the hundredth time why everything always had to go wrong for her. It was as if she had some sort of reverse Midas touch.

"Bentley!" she shouted, as the dog shot past her legs, abandoning his ball in favour of a new prize further down the beach. She squinted against the wind, trying to work out what he had found in the rock pools ahead. He sniffed at something, then jumped back, barking with increasingly determined insistence.

"What have you found then?" she asked, excitement in her voice to humour him, running along the beach to see for herself. She stopped short a few metres from him and her hand flew to her mouth in disbelief. It was a man, lying face down in the sand. His head was over to the side, resting on the back of his hand and he had one knee bent up at right angles, almost as if someone had placed him in the recovery position.

"Aidan!" she screamed as she ran up to the man, dropping to her knees in the sand and lifting his head to cradle it in her arms, resting her cheek against his wet hair. For a few moments, the relief and hope that coursed through every fibre of her being were powerful enough to banish the horror of that awful night, when the Guards came knocking at her door. She knew why they were there before they spoke a word. They came to tell her that the inshore lifeboat had run into trouble in horrendous conditions and two of the crew, one of whom was her beloved husband, were still missing. That was the night her whole life fell apart. Again. She refused point blank to believe Aidan was dead and continued to hold onto the irrational hope that one day he would come back to her, having made his way home from some distant shore he was washed up on. They had never actually found his body and so consequently she had gone on living in some strange kind of limbo; hoping, waiting, trapped in a surreal half-life.

Every rational bone in her body was telling her that the man she was clinging to could not possibly be Aidan. It was over three months since the terrible tragedy when he answered his lifeboat pager and headed off into the night to help a stricken yacht in danger of being grounded on the rocks. Caitlin knew that, if Aidan really had washed up on the beach after all that time, it would be a hideous, ghoulish version of her husband that she would now be clinging to, one that would haunt her days and nights forever. But still, she wanted so desperately to believe in miracles.

The man in her arms groaned and she forced herself to release his head and look properly at his face. As she did so, all hope left her and she began to sob uncontrollably, recoiling from him in horror and staring at him in renewed despair and grief. He looked nothing like her Aidan. Granted, he was a similar height and build, but his eyes were brown and his hair grey. There was no mischievous smile playing on his lips, no twinkle in his eye and definitely no butterflies in her stomach.

How could I have been so stupid? she chided herself.

The stranger was coming round. He groaned again and seemed to be trying to sit up. Caitlin came to her senses abruptly and moved closer to help him. He may not be her Aidan, but he had clearly endured some terrible ordeal of his own and deserved at the very least some compassion from her. She had been powerless to do anything to help Aidan that dreadful night, but she could help this man now and maybe even in some way atone for not having been able to save her husband from the clutches of the sea.

Caitlin supported the man into a sitting position, helping him to lean back against a rock so that he would feel more comfortable. She opened her little daypack and gave him a bottle of water, which he gulped down greedily, obviously dehydrated. Rummaging deeper, she found a couple of energy protein bars, which she hastily ripped the wrappers off and gave to him. He managed a weak smile in return.

"Thank you," he said, in a barely audible voice.

"What's your name?" she asked tentatively, not sure what to do or say next.

He seemed confused and stared at her without answering, a blank expression on his face. What was she thinking? The poor man was obviously in shock and needed medical attention.

"Don't worry, you're going to be okay. I'm going to call an ambulance so we can get you to hospital. I'm Caitlin, by the way. I'm a nurse."

She reached for her bag again to find her mobile, praying she would have a signal, but before she could make the call he lurched forward, grabbing her arm with a surprisingly strong grip.

"No!" he shouted, with an air of authority that stopped her in her tracks. "No hospitals. I'm fine. I just need a bit of time to come round properly and maybe some help to find a dry set of clothes," he added with a smile, releasing his grip on her arm and softening his tone as he noted the fear and shock on her face. "Do you think you could help me with that?"

"I don't…maybe…," she mumbled, unsettled by his apparent aversion to any medical intervention. "I just really think you should be checked out by a doctor."

"The thing is Caitlin, I know for a fact I have no broken limbs and I'm absolutely certain there's nothing wrong with me that a hot drink, some food and maybe a good night's sleep wouldn't cure. You said you're a nurse…surely you can help me? Please?"

He was looking at her with what could only be described as desperation in his eyes and before she knew it she found herself offering to take him home with her, just for one night, despite being unable to shake off a feeling of foreboding that something was very wrong here.

"Can you at least tell me what happened to you?" She tried again. "It's not every day you find someone washed up on the beach in these conditions…not alive, anyway."

She thought again of Aidan, thrown from the safety of the lifeboat into the terrifying ferocity of the sea, into the clawing arms of the waves that were intent on dragging him away from her, pulling him down to a watery grave…. She realised in a flash of clarity that she had to help this man, whatever his story was.

"I'll tell you everything I can remember, I promise," he continued, seeing her soften towards him. "Only please, I'm begging you, help me get somewhere dry and warm before I actually die of hypothermia out here. That would be ironic, don't you think?"

He had begun to shiver and she forced herself to focus on what was immediately important, like the practicalities of the current situation. She decided at that moment that everything else could wait, pulling off her jacket as she spoke and wrapping it around his shoulders.

"Can you walk? If you can just make it off the beach and up to the lane, I'll fetch my car. I don't live far from here. I can be back for you in about ten minutes."

To her amazement, the stranger from the sea did indeed manage to summon the strength to crawl up the dunes with her half supporting and half dragging him. When they reached the top he slumped down against a large rock with his eyes closed, exhausted from the effort. Caitlin looked around her furtively, but there was no one in sight and little likelihood of any passing traffic on the rough track, which was only really accessible to the most robust of

4x4s. She was scared to leave him alone, but there was no alternative.

"Are you sure you'll be okay on your own? Just stay here and I'll be back as quickly as I can."

He managed a vague attempt at a smile.

"Don't worry, I'm not planning on going anywhere. Just remember…please Caitlin…no one can know I'm here. Not yet. I promise I'll explain…I know it's a big ask, but trust me. Please?"

Trust me.

She stared at him and, just for a moment, all she saw was Aidan's eyes burning into her own, as he held her face in his hands that night and kissed her, before walking out into the storm.

"I'll be back before you know it. Trust me. I love you."

But he had never come back to her. He had left her like all the others.

Caitlin shoved the memories to the back of her mind, put a hand on the man's shoulder in reassurance and set off running down the track towards home, with Bentley at her heels.

Against the wind, it took her a little over five minutes at a steady jog to reach the cottage, where she let the dog into the kitchen, gave him some biscuits, then grabbed her car keys. Hesitating for a moment, she put one of Aidan's heavy outdoor coats over her arm. Everything of Aidan's was exactly where he had left it, ready for him when he came back to her, as she knew he would one day. The wind snatched the door from her grip and it slammed shut behind her, seeming to shake the very foundations of the cottage. The rain had started and she felt the panic rising up in her as she wondered whether the man she had left by the roadside would still be there…whether he would still be alive.

Aidan's battered, but reliable Defender was more than man enough to tackle the rough track down to the headland and, in the distance, she could make out the huddled shape of the stranger, his back turned against the onslaught of the wind. She pulled up beside him and helped him unsteadily to his feet, wrapping the precious

24

coat around his shoulders on top of her own coat as she manoeuvred him into the passenger seat and closed the door for him. For whatever reason, the sea had chosen to spare this man and deliver him up to her for sanctuary. She suddenly felt fiercely protective of him.

Once in the house, Caitlin guided him up the narrow wooden stairs and into the spare bedroom, handing him Aidan's dressing gown and instructing him to get undressed while she ran him a bath. She gave him the pyjamas she had bought for her husband last Christmas, the ones he had never had the chance to wear, telling herself that Aidan wouldn't mind at all and would have done the same thing himself. She waited till the man (she still didn't know his name) was out of the hot bath, to make sure he did not pass out from exhaustion and drown, then helped him under the duvet in the spare room and left him to sleep, busying herself in the kitchen downstairs by making a casserole for later.

She checked on him every half hour, but he was clearly exhausted and slept for a full five hours before coming down to join her by the fire in the lounge. He was wearing the clothes she had put out for him: Aidan's chunky, navy blue fisherman's jumper over a white polo shirt, a pair of faded jeans and thick, wool socks. He hesitated awkwardly in the doorway and, in the dim glow of the firelight and the candles, she could almost believe it was the man she loved standing there. Almost.

"Power cut," she explained with a shy smile. "It often happens when there's a storm. You get used to it out here."

She gestured to him to sit down in the chair in front of the fire.

"I guess I owe you an explanation," he began in a quiet voice.

"Why don't we have something to eat first?" she cut in before he could say any more. "You must be starving. Then you can tell me everything in your own time. There's no rush."

For some reason she could not explain to herself, she was not ready to hear his story yet. She wanted the two of them to remain there in their little pretend bubble of alternative reality for a while

25

longer. She needed to keep him with her and she was already enjoying playing house, remembering what life had been like as part of a perfect couple, back then before everything was snatched away from her.

"You really are an amazing woman. Thank you from the bottom of my heart for taking me in and trusting me." He paused a moment and cleared his throat before continuing.

"I wanted to ask…won't your husband mind me wearing his clothes?"

"Erm, no, he really wouldn't." She hesitated briefly and looked into the fire. "He's away for a while."

The man seemed relieved and smiled a knowing smile, clearly drawing all the wrong conclusions, as he stood up to follow her into the kitchen.

"I'm Patrick, by the way," he added, extending his right hand towards her. "Patrick Salenden."

"Caitlin Flynn," she replied, shaking his hand and laughing self-consciously at the bizarre situation they found themselves in. Now that he was rested, she couldn't help noticing how the man exuded an air of confidence and familiarity that she found slightly unnerving.

Someone should have reminded Caitlin about Little Red Riding Hood because then she might have realized she had just invited the wolf into her house.

Look to the Future

When your past calls, don't answer. It has nothing to say.

Grace

"So what do you think? Are you definitely in?"

Samantha looked at me, eyebrows raised in question as she pushed the flyer entitled 'Magical Madagascar' across the table towards me.

"Yes, yes yes! One hundred percent. Let's do this," I laughed, clinking my glass against hers to seal the deal. She had told me about the trip a few months ago, but it all seemed like a pipe dream until now, when suddenly it was becoming a reality.

"Just one thing though," Sam added. She held my gaze and her voice took on a more serious tone. "This is a huge commitment. The trip is not until next year, so we both have to promise that, if either of us meets a new man, it changes nothing. This is an adventure for the two of us and no man can get in the way of that."

"No worries on that score," I replied, pulling a face. "You do remember my husband Daniel?" I asked, my voice laden with irony. "Thanks to him, I won't be going anywhere near another man for a very, very long time. Here's to 'Magical Madagascar' and our adventure of a lifetime. This is exactly what we need; something incredible to look forward to and plan for. And what's more, it starts on my birthday. Clearly a sign from God that we should do it."

I laughed as I raised my glass to Sam's again and we knew instinctively that this moment marked a new chapter in both of our lives, albeit for different reasons.

"I can't believe we're actually doing this!" I screamed, stamping my feet in excitement like a five-year-old, my imagination already transporting me to the distant shores of the world's oldest island, 'magical' Madagascar. The land that time forgot.

The trip in question was a 4x4 car rally organised by a company called Venture Rallies. For four weeks, our group of twelve cars would tour the island, discovering the beauty and diversity of its wildlife, landscape and people, from the rainforests of the east, through the incredible highlands and mountains of the centre, on to the stunning white sand beaches and Baobab forests of the west coast. We would cover a total of nearly five thousand kilometres, driving on anything from tarmac to dry river beds and sand tracks. This was truly the stuff dreams were made of.

"Are you absolutely sure about the money?" I asked, looking Sam straight in the eye and feeling compelled to confront the elephant in the room.

I was still smarting from the fallout of Daniel's bankruptcy, but it appeared now that his untimely death had put me once again in the unenviable position of the 'path of least resistance'. Vanessa Harding of Miller Laidlaw, Trustee in Bankruptcy for the estate of Daniel Matthew John Callaghan, was now sniffing around for information about our race boat 'Mistress', clearly not one to open her jaws easily once she had locked onto her victim.

"Absolutely positive!" replied Sam, without the slightest hint of hesitation. "Look, Grace, Charles already had the money set aside in our rally account and he was desperate to do this trip. He would have agreed you are the perfect person for me to do it with now and

28

I know for sure we have his blessing. I'm paying for the rally out of that account and that's the end of the matter. I was also thinking we should maybe add on a week at the end in a resort somewhere, just pure relaxation for the two of us. Nothing too flash; we'll stick to a budget. What do you think? These rallies can be pretty tough going and there aren't many rest days if you look at the itinerary. It'll be amazing, but there's a hell of a lot of miles to cover."

"That sounds like a great idea. I've got some money saved from the sale of the boat and I can't think of a better way to spend it. I've earmarked it as my 'making amazing new memories at Daniel's expense' fund. It seems only right that he should compensate me for all that happened, so he can start by paying for that holiday," I laughed, pushing the disturbing image of Daniel's face disappearing into the blackness of the sea firmly out of my mind. "And thank you, Sam. For everything," I added. "I'll start doing some research. It'll give me something positive to focus on instead of all the relentless questions and bickering with that bitch Vanessa Harding and her cronies. I promise you when this is all over I'll make it up to you."

Obviously, I meant the last bit, but I had absolutely no idea how I was going to achieve it. If anything, Daniel's demise had only served to make things worse and, in his absence, all eyes appeared to have refocused on me, in spite of the agreement I had signed with the Trustee. It seemed he was still trying to screw my life up, even from beyond the grave. One thing was certain though, there was no way the lovely Vanessa and her sidekick Corinne Burns were getting their hands on the boat or any proceeds from its sale. I had enough friends and contacts in the sailing world to ensure I had a cash buyer pretty much as soon as we docked in Ireland after Daniel's tragic accident. Better still, the guy who bought her was French and was planning a full re-fit and re-spray in his home port somewhere near La Rochelle. In short, 'Mistress' was long gone and good luck to anyone trying to trace her or to prove I had seen any money out of her. I was suddenly struck by the realisation of just how much I had learned over the years from the master of devious practices, aka my husband. It was a small victory, but it made me feel stronger. The thought fleetingly crossed my mind that, if Vanessa knew what had really happened to Daniel, she might concentrate on watching her back rather than risk pushing me too far.

Sam came over to give me a hug.

"Forget the money. If we've learned anything in the last couple of years, surely it's that money is not the most important thing in life. I can't do the rally without you. You are literally the only person I would want to do it with. And for heaven's sake, stop worrying about what happened to Daniel. I know it still bothers you, but it's been nearly three months now. It was an accident, it wasn't your fault and he doesn't deserve so much as a nanosecond of your thought time. Let's face it, Grace, he had it coming. Big time."

That wasn't strictly true of course, about it not being my fault. But Sam didn't know that. Only two people knew the truth about what happened that night on the boat. One of them was me and, as for the other one, he certainly wasn't going to be doing any whistle-blowing anytime soon. I shivered involuntarily as I remembered that night. It seemed so clear-cut and simple at the time, but I was tormented by the memory of what I did. I had somehow justified my actions in my own mind by convincing myself I was ridding the world of a monster, but the harsh reality as I saw it now was that I had robbed two children of their father, however dysfunctional he may have been. I truly believed they were ultimately better off without him, but I couldn't help worrying about the karma that could well be heading my way.

"Grace…?"

Sam was looking at me strangely.

"Snap out of it," she said, a sharp edge to her tone. "This is supposed to be a happy time, a new beginning. You've got so much to look forward to. 'Dickhead Daniel' robbed you of a huge part of your life and I do get how bitter you must still be feeling, I really do, but don't let him take any more from you. You need to move on. Seriously, it's time to let it go, for your own sanity."

I sniggered at her term of endearment for Daniel, pushing the dark thoughts firmly to the back of my mind.

"You're right," I agreed, reaching for the Champagne bottle and reminding myself there was no going back. I had made my bed and I now had to lie in it. Regret was a wasted emotion. And besides, Sam had a point, I really did have a lot to look forward to. I had sold the house in Conwy after the divorce, as there were too many memories of Daniel associated with it, opting for a smaller semi-detached property in the northeast, nearer to Mum and the rest of my family. I had managed to find a place close to Marsden beach with fantastic views out over the water. I could walk out of the house, across the road and straight down the steps by the Grotto to the beach with Lola and, most importantly, I could hear the waves and smell the sea from my new home. I remembered going there often as a child, scrambling up onto the rocks and staring out to sea, imagining I was on the bow of a ship, setting sail to find adventure on distant, exotic shores. Not for the first time, I found myself wishing someone had invented time travel and I could skip back to those days of innocence.

My beloved horse Valentino had moved with me of course and was now on a yard about fifteen minutes away. The yard manager, Ellie, was the daughter of an old school friend and had immediately fallen in love with him, treating him like royalty. It was great to finally be able to spend more time with my very own Black Beauty, instead of running around the country playing detectives. Maybe I could even start taking him out to some of the shows again. I was getting on with my new life and I had to admit it felt good.

"Anyway, we have more immediate problems to worry about," I joked, changing the subject. "Like what the baggage allowance is for the skiing trip."

"Good point," Sam laughed. "I got stung for fifty quid when mine was over the weight last time. I'm not getting caught like that again. It's those bloody ski boots that weigh a ton!"

In a couple of months, we would be back on the slopes of Lech, just the two of us for the first time ever. We had thought long and hard about the choice of resort, given that we had been there so often as a foursome with Charles and Daniel, but we loved the place and knew the runs like the back of our hand. Why should we allow Daniel to spoil it for us? We had opted to stay in the town itself this time, rather than in the hotel in Oberlech we always used to go to. We had found a great last-minute deal in a lovely catered chalet for twelve people, privately run by the owners themselves and members of their family, perfectly located at the edge of the slopes. It was picture-postcard pretty, built in the traditional Austrian style with hot tub, rooms with balconies overlooking the village, the works.

Sam and I had made a sort of pact, agreeing that the best way to get through the trauma of Charles' death and the 'Daniel business' was to have things to look forward to and dates in the diary. Skiing and Madagascar were the big ones of course, but we were also doing pretty well with the smaller things and, all in all, I felt we were to be congratulated on our efforts so far. That particular weekend we were heading to Liverpool for a Mike and the Mechanics concert. I had to admit that, when we booked the tickets I had trouble naming any of their songs, but as the brilliant music and poignant lyrics flowed over me, it all came flooding back and I found I could sing along to pretty much every one. I was transported back to the eighties; my era, my carefree days, before Daniel began to suck the life out of my dreams without me even realising it. Sam and I were quick to embrace the whole experience and were up in the aisle dancing with a number of other die-hard groupies, all of us keen to relive our youth. The words of the song 'Taken in' could have been written for me:

Taken in, taken in again
Caught up in the promises
Left out in the end

As the song continued, I could have sworn Mike Rutherford was looking straight into my eyes from that stage, as if he knew all about me and what I had been through.

No pride, taken for a ride
You say I'm the only one
When I look in your eyes
I want to believe you
But you know how to lie

In the interval, we both signed up immediately for the new album and vowed to give it pride of place on our Madagascar road trip playlist, which I was responsible for. 'Out of the blue' was one of the new songs, all about finding love when you least expected it and, as the music worked its powerful magic, I was suddenly filled with optimism and hope. I refused to allow what Daniel had done to taint my view of the male species in general and ruin my future. I would not be the embittered 'wronged woman', who had a cynical take on everything and trusted no one. I was too young for that and I had too much to give. One day, when the time was right, I would meet someone who would truly love me, respect me and want to be with me. And, most importantly, I would be enough for him. Just me. I would have my fairy tale ending one day, I was certain of it.

The concert wound up with one of the old favourites, 'Another cup of coffee' and, as the entire audience got to their feet and chanted the final chorus over and over again, I felt certain that Fate had brought me to this concert for a reason. Everything and everyone around me melted away and Mike was singing to me alone, telling me what I knew I had to do.

Don't look back
Don't give up
Pour yourself another cup

There was a whole big world out there, full of amazing things to see and wonderful new people to meet and I intended to seize every opportunity that came my way with both hands.

When Daniel wormed his way into my dreams yet again that night, I realised I could no longer see his face as he disappeared into the blackness, no longer recall the features of the man who had been such a huge part of my life for so many years.

Little by little I was exorcising the ghost of my husband.

Ghosts Laid to Rest

10 years earlier

Caitlin

Caitlin was nothing if not pragmatic. Her life experience up to that point had taught her there was nothing to be gained from trying to hang onto the past. Draw a line and move on. That was the rule she lived by and it had served her well enough so far.

Just three weeks after Caitlin's startling discovery of the stranger on the beach, another body washed up on the shore around ten miles further along. The main difference was that the second body was no longer alive. In fact it was barely even recognizable as human. Her prayers had been answered and Aidan had indeed been delivered back to her, but it was not the joyful reunion she had conjured up in her imagination. There were no passionate embraces and no tears of happiness as they clung to each other. Instead, she found herself standing at his graveside, totally numb, watching in silence as they lowered his coffin into the ground and shovelled dirt on top of it.

History repeating itself.

In her heart of hearts, she had always known this day would come, but now that it had, she felt strangely detached, unable to shed any more tears. After all, it wasn't the first time she had buried the love of her life.

Caitlin had truly believed things would be different with Aidan, that she would finally get her happy ending but, after a couple of years, the tell-tale signs were there all over again. Did he really think she wouldn't notice how he looked at that slapper Sinead from the village post office and flirted with her? Suddenly she found herself right back at square one, with all the familiar insecurities bubbling up to the surface again, intensified by the fact that Aidan was five years younger than her. There was no way she was going to allow him to leave her and ruin the perfect little life she had so painstakingly built for herself, so she took matters into her own hands and came up with a plan that would get things back on track.

A baby.

Aidan was desperate to have children, the more the merrier he said, but Caitlin had no intention of ever going down that route. She did not want her body mutilated and distorted by the torture of childbirth like her own mother's had been, nor did she relish the idea of playing second fiddle to a baby in her husband's eyes. Besides, she was already pushing forty, which meant she would be classed as a 'geriatric pregnancy'. How fucking insulting was that? No, in her opinion they were perfectly fine as they were, just the two of them. But that didn't mean she couldn't pretend; for the sake of her marriage.

When she announced to Aidan one evening that he was going to be a daddy, he was so overjoyed with the news that for a moment she almost wished it were true. He was like a child on Christmas morning, chattering incessantly about how he was going to do up a room for the nursery, what plans he had for 'the bump', what names he liked….

As a nurse, Caitlin knew exactly how to play it and it had been a piece of cake for her to obtain someone else's urine sample for the pregnancy test, but even she had been surprised to find out just how easy it was to fake the scan. Whoever would have imagined there were such websites as 'fakeababy.com' and 'fakeultrasounds.net'? It was even possible to personalize them, for God's sake. So she did. And all of a sudden, Aidan was looking at her through new eyes, all thoughts of Post Office Girl banished from his mind.

For a while, all was rosy in the garden but then, at fourteen weeks, tragedy struck. Aidan was away on a two-day fishing trip and returned home to find a distraught Caitlin sobbing in the kitchen with her head in her hands.

She looked up at him with her tear-stained face and he knew instantly.

"I'm so sorry, I'm so sorry," she repeated, shaking her head. "I lost our baby. Our *daughter*," she blurted out, dissolving once again into heart-wrenching sobs.

The sight of her blaming herself broke Aidan's heart, even more so than losing the baby. He dropped to his knees by her side, arms enveloping her, head buried in her lap, as they cried tears of sorrow together, united in their grief.

Except his grief was the real deal.

"It's not your fault, really it isn't. These things can happen. Our little one just wasn't meant to stay here on earth with us," he said, trying to soothe his wife.

He clutched her hands between his, desperate to find the words to somehow make this better.

"We'll get through this, my love, I promise you. We'll get through this together. Shh, please don't cry," he pleaded.

Caitlin stopped sobbing for a moment and looked him straight in the eyes as she delivered the bombshell.

"I can never go through the pain of this again, Aidan, never. I mean it. I feel like my heart has been ripped out of my body."

"Of course you feel like that now, of course you do. The idea of another baby is unthinkable at the moment. But there will come a time, in the future, when you'll want to try again, I know there will," he said, his voice gentle and sincere. "Lots of women have babies in their forties. It's common these days."

Her face hardened and her tone had an air of finality.

"I can't. I just can't."

Of course he had gone on living in the hope that one day she would change her mind, one day she would indeed be ready to try again, but it was never going to happen. He was devoted to her, showering her with affection and giving her the love and attention she craved, but every time he broached the subject of another baby, she became detached and withdrawn, so gradually he stopped pushing and accepted the way things were, for her sake. Caitlin felt the occasional pang of guilt about deceiving him, but she knew in her heart of hearts she was being cruel to be kind. Things were back to the way they had been in the beginning and, now that the baby issue had been put to bed with the avoidance of any nasty arguments and falling out, they could get on with living the fun and happy life they were destined for, as a child-free, married couple. Balance, at least in Caitlin's world, had been restored. Aidan would thank her eventually.

What she had not bargained for of course was that Life was about to throw her another curve ball. Despite her best efforts, her beloved Aidan left her anyway in the end and there was not a damn thing she could do about it. All of a sudden, out of the blue, everything was taken out of her control and she found herself catapulted once again into the role of grieving widow, forced to bury the man she adored.

Finding Patrick had been an absolute godsend. It was almost as if he had been sent to her by some higher power. She knew very little about him, but he seemed happy enough to stick around and repay the favour of her saving his ass on the beach that day by being there for her in her time of need. How true it was that Fate worked in mysterious ways.

When the time came for the funeral, she went alone. No one from the village knew Patrick was staying there with her and the last thing she needed was the guaranteed looks of reproach and recrimination from Aidan's family if they found out she had moved another man into their home so soon. His aunt Eilish in particular had been suspicious of Caitlin from the start and always treated her as an outsider. She was constantly poking her nose into their business, asking tricky questions about her past and her family that she had no intention of answering. Aidan had been brought up in the village by his aunt after he lost both his parents in a car crash as a young child and she made no secret of the fact she thought the sun shone out of his backside. Caitlin was pretty sure Eilish resented her having the cottage now he was dead, but that was just too bad. She had gifted it to her nephew as a wedding present, so she would just have to get used to the fact that it belonged to Caitlin now. She was Aidan's widow, so all that had been his was now hers; including the cottage and a fair bit more besides, once the life insurance company paid up.

Caitlin got through the funeral and the subsequent wake in a trance-like state, maintaining an air of serene dignity. The role of tragic heroine was one that suited her well, she felt. The coffin bearers were his fellow crew members from the RNLI and maroons were fired in tribute. Aidan was popular in the village and the surrounding area and a lot of people turned out to pay their respects, but Caitlin felt only resentment at their intrusion. She couldn't get away from the wake fast enough and made her excuses as soon as she considered it was decently possible. Everyone seemed to assume that it was all just too much for her and put her lack of any outward show of emotion down to shock. Not that she really cared what anyone thought.

When she arrived back at the house, Patrick immediately came over to her, looking anxiously into her eyes.

"Are you okay?" he asked, concerned. "Stupid question I suppose...," he added, his voice trailing off.

"I'm fine. Really I am. Everything was exactly as I expected it to be. It just feels so strange being here without him."

"So why stay here then?" Patrick asked; a puzzled look on his face.

"Because I actually really like it here," she said with a sad little smile. "It's my home now and it's the first place in a long time where I have felt truly happy and at peace with myself. I belong here."

Caitlin sat down at the kitchen table and realised that she felt entirely at ease with this man, who had come into her life so unexpectedly. He remained her biggest secret yet, kept safely behind closed doors in the cottage, hidden from prying eyes and wandering around in her dead husband's clothes. She was well aware of the fact that other people would find their situation weird, which was why it was best no one knew about it for the moment, but that couldn't last forever. When Aidan first went missing, Caitlin had shunned the concerned offers of help and support from people, refusing to accept the worst-case scenario and stating categorically that she simply wanted to carry on as normal until he came home; business as usual. The locals had respected her privacy, but all that had changed now that Aidan was definitely dead. It was only a matter of time before visitors began appearing at the door to snoop, armed with their well-meaning offerings of consolation in the form of a casserole or an apple pie. She knew she had to come up with an acceptable story for them, one that would curb the inevitable tongue-wagging.

"I can't imagine any of Aidan's family or friends will be particularly happy about me being here," said Patrick, pulling a face and apparently reading her mind.

"I don't care what they think," she said, a steely edge to her voice. "Aidan is gone and nothing can ever change that, but I'm still alive and I can do what I want with whoever I want. People will just have to accept that. Anyway, I'll tell them you are an old friend of the family, staying with me to recuperate in the sea air after a long illness," she concluded, with a determined nod of her head to indicate the matter was settled. "You know what? Right now, what I really need is a drink. And definitely something stronger than tea," she announced, changing the subject abruptly.

Patrick laughed and walked over to the fridge.

"I think you deserve that. Anyway, it's after five o'clock and the sun's over the yard arm somewhere," he said, returning with a bottle of fizz and two glasses. "Let's drink to the future, whatever it may hold. And new beginnings for both of us."

Caitlin remained silent for a moment, before replying.

"Yes, here's to new beginnings. Speaking of which, I think now would be as good a time as any for you to tell me about yourself and why you are so keen to keep your survival a secret. Surely there are people out there who will be missing you?"

The question hung in the air for a moment, as she held his gaze and said simply:

"I'm ready to hear your story. All of it."

Patrick had known from the start that this was coming and had prepared for it, launching straight in without missing a beat.

"Of course you deserve to know all about me, but I'll warn you, it's a very long story."

He paused for dramatic effect before continuing, a weary, but earnest look on his face. Staring directly into her eyes without flinching, he began.

"I married my first wife when we were both very young, too young really. We wanted to start a family as soon as possible, so I was over the moon when she got pregnant almost straight away. Everything seemed to go well with the pregnancy, which made it all the more tragic and inexplicable when our baby daughter was still-born."

"Oh my God, that's terrible. You must have been devastated," Caitlin interrupted, remembering her own imaginary baby and Aidan's reaction to the 'miscarriage'. The apparent shock on her face was exactly the reaction Patrick had anticipated.

"Yes, we both were, but the doctors said there was no reason we wouldn't have a healthy baby in the future. In time, I thought we would get over our loss and try again, but she just sank deeper and deeper into the depths of depression and no amount of professional counselling or sympathy from me could help her. After two failed

41

attempts to kill herself with pills and alcohol, she walked out of the house one day and threw herself under a train to do the job properly. She was just twenty five years old."

Caitlin gasped and instinctively took hold of his hand. She hadn't seen that one coming.

"You really have been through it, haven't you? You don't have to tell me any more if you don't want to," she added quickly. "No, I want to. I *need* to tell you everything. So that you can understand."

Patrick Salenden, the man formerly known as Daniel Callaghan, had learnt over the years that the best, most convincing lies are the ones hidden within the truth, mixed up and tangled until they are inseparable, indistinguishable. He took a long slug of his drink and continued.

"Of course it was a long time before I could even think about being with another woman, but eventually, when I least expected it, I fell in love again. Grace. The love of my life, or so I thought. When we got married, I honestly believed it was forever, that we would spend the rest of our lives together. But it wasn't to be," he said, shaking his head sadly. "I don't even know when it all started going wrong, but she clearly had some deep-rooted psychological issues. She just couldn't bring herself to trust me about anything and I think it drove her completely crazy in the end. She started accusing me all the time of having affairs when all I was doing was working every hour God sends to keep her in the lifestyle she always wanted. One minute she'd be threatening suicide, the next she'd be attacking me with a kitchen knife or hurling something across the room at me. I swear I thought she was going to kill me on more than one occasion. She was like a woman possessed when she got like that. It sounds ridiculous to say it out loud and it makes me feel stupid and ashamed, but looking back on it all now, I think I was a victim of domestic abuse."

Patrick stopped and waited for all that to sink in. He was pleased to note from Caitlin's horrified face that she was totally in his corner on this one. She shook her head slowly and squeezed his hand tighter, but said nothing, so he continued.

"I think the straw that broke the camel's back was that she was desperate to have kids, but sadly was unable to get pregnant. We tried everything of course, including two rounds of IVF, but her body didn't react well to it at all and she became so ill the doctors advised us it would be dangerous for her to continue. She was convinced I was going to leave her for another woman who could give me children, but the truth was I didn't care about that. I adored her and she was more than enough for me, but she never believed that and seemed to have some sort of self-destruct button she was determined to press. I tried everything, I really did, but it got to the point where I was terrified each night of what I was coming home to, of what she was going to do, either to herself or to me. I came to the conclusion we'd be better off apart, but if I so much as mentioned separation or divorce she went wild. I stuck it out for the best part of twenty years because I loved her in spite of everything and I always believed she could change. And also out of some sort of misplaced loyalty I guess. Can you believe that?"

Patrick rubbed a hand over his face and sat back with a weary sigh.

"One day it finally became too much and I realised I couldn't go on anymore with things as they were. I came over to Ireland on the ferry secretly and took a trip down to the south coast, which I've always loved, to have a couple of days on my own and try to clear my head. I walked across the dunes, down to the beach and just stood there, looking out to sea, kind of mesmerized by the waves. Then all of a sudden I found myself walking straight ahead and into the water. At the time, it seemed the most logical and natural thing to do in the world. I hadn't planned it, but somehow it felt right. The perfect way out. When I think about it now, all I feel is ashamed that I was so weak."

Patrick stopped and lowered his head, unable to look Caitlin in the eye.

"No!" she said, determined to show him she understood. "You have nothing to be ashamed of. You were clearly pushed to the absolute limit of what any person could stand. I am just so glad I went walking on the beach that day. If I hadn't found you...well, it doesn't bear thinking about."

Patrick took a deep breath and pressed on.

"The thing is Caitlin, I feel like I've been thrown a lifeline here, in more ways than one. I feel like it was my destiny to survive, to be washed up on that beach and for you to find me. This is my chance to be someone else, to reinvent myself. To leave all that heartache and unhappiness behind me. My wife will be okay; more than okay in fact. She'll have the house and there's plenty of money left in our joint account. I even wrote her a note saying I was going away for a while to give us both some space, so the police won't be interested. She won't have a clue where to start looking and, in the end, she'll have no choice but to forget about me."

Caitlin lifted her hand to his cheek and spoke in a tender voice.

"You have been to Hell and back. I totally understand now why you didn't want to talk about all this before. But you can trust me, I promise. We're going to work it all out together. You deserve a second chance and I'm going to help you."

He looked at her with a mixture of gratitude and disbelief.

"Why on earth would you want to help me any more than you already have done? You barely know me and you owe me nothing."

"It's strange, but I really feel there is a connection between us. I can't explain it, but I feel like I've known you for years and could talk to you about anything. Fate brought us together, Patrick. Two lost souls. We will save each other."

Saint Caitlin, champion of lost causes, had found a new purpose to her life.

"I know exactly what you mean, but I didn't dare to hope that you might feel the same."

Patrick hesitated a moment, then took her hand.

"I want to be completely honest with you, so there's just one more thing you should know. Patrick Salenden wasn't always my name. But that's who I am now and you have to trust me when I say that it's better for you if you don't know any more details about the old me. I can never go back there. Never. My future is here now. With you."

Patrick could almost hear the resounding applause in his head for the Oscar-winning performance he had just delivered. He waited calmly for Caitlin's response, which did not disappoint.

"So far as I'm concerned, Patrick, the man that walked into the sea that day, whoever he was, he drowned. He's gone forever."

She looked at him thoughtfully for a moment, then smiled and added:

"The name Patrick suits you by the way."

It was a good job Pinocchio was a fairy tale character because if what happened to him had been true, Daniel's nose would already have been a good two feet longer. As would the lovely Caitlin's.

A Daughter's Love

Mothers hold their children's hands for a short time,
but their hearts forever.

Grace

Tears rolled down my cheeks as I stood helplessly at the end of the hospital bed and the doctor's words seemed to drift in from very far away.

"Your mother is stable at the moment and the signs are all good, but unfortunately she has suffered a serious stroke. We won't know for a while how she will be affected in the long term, so we're keeping her sedated for the moment while we monitor things. There's every possibility she could make a good recovery, but only time will tell, I'm afraid."

I turned to my brother for reassurance, but there was no mistaking the worry on his face as he put an arm around me and hugged me tightly.

Less than twenty-four hours earlier I had been away in Dun Laoghaire with Sam, for the National Yacht Club dinner and prize giving. I had only done a couple of the races that year on a friend's boat, because of everything else that was going on, but that was enough to qualify for the annual dinner, which was something of an institution. It was a black tie event, providing the perfect excuse to get dressed up for a change and party in style with some of the old sailing crowd. Then on the Sunday we borrowed bikes from the hotel and cycled up to Finnegan's pub in Dalkey in the vague hope of bumping into Bono, who was apparently a regular there. Unfortunately, it turned out Bono was otherwise engaged, but we drank Guinness, raised a glass in his honour and enjoyed a late lunch with cocktails. I was beginning to feel like my old self again and it was a great weekend, full of fun and laughter, but I suppose I should have known from experience just how fragile happiness is.

I got the phone call on the train journey home, having said goodbye to Sam in Chester. The caller display showed it was Mum and I assumed she just couldn't wait to find out how our weekend had gone, but when I answered, all I heard from her was nonsensical, jumbled noises that sent a chill right through me. I could sense her confusion and frustration as she kept trying again and again to tell me something and I knew instinctively I had to act fast.

"Mum, I need you to sit down, stay where you are and wait. I'm putting the phone down now because I have to call an ambulance and as soon as I've done that I'll call you back. Try to stay calm. Someone will be there to help you soon."

I cut her off and made the 999 call immediately, then called my brother in a blind panic, knowing he would take charge of this latest nightmare. Three hours later, I made it to Mum's bedside, trying to stay calm and wondering what the hell I had done wrong in a previous life to deserve all that was being thrown at me now. It was as if the universe itself was conspiring against me, determined to crush me every time I thought I was finally making progress. Maybe this was the karma I had feared, a clear sign from the universe that every action has a consequence.

It was two days before they brought her round and the confusion and fear in her eyes when they did almost broke my heart. The cruel reality of what had happened meant that she was trapped in her own little world, unable to speak or communicate even the most basic yes or no information. I couldn't begin to imagine the horror of what she was going through, but I realised instinctively that our roles were reversed and it was my turn to be strong for her, to reassure her that she could get through this, to help her. More than anything, I had to truly believe in her ability to do it, because if I lost faith in her, I knew she would give up.

Over the next few weeks, Jeremy and I took turns to make sure we were at the hospital for every visiting session, determined not to let her down. Aphasia was apparently what we were dealing with after the stroke. I had never even heard of that word before, but after talking to Jeremy about it and trawling the internet extensively, I soon understood it was a condition that affected a person's ability to speak, process information and even swallow properly in some cases. The isolation and loneliness that inevitably accompanied that inability to communicate were terrifying.

I talked at length to the speech therapists for advice and decided to approach it like teaching a child, going right back to the basics of thumbs up, thumbs down for yes and no. We clearly had a mountain to climb and the hardest thing was seeing Mum's frustration as she desperately tried to find the words she wanted to say. I could see it was all there in her head, but she just couldn't get the words out. According to the therapists, it was almost as if her brain had to be rewired to bypass the damaged circuits and find new pathways for speech. I spent hours researching the subject and read that singing could sometimes help, so we sat together in her little room, singing nursery rhymes, children's songs, counting songs, alphabet songs, Christmas carols…you name it, we tried it and little by little, I saw an improvement. Tiny things became major achievements to be celebrated, like the day I walked in to find her upbeat and enthusiastic, desperate to show me that she could count to ten by herself and I almost cried for joy. She would hang on my every word and repeat words after me over and over again, determined to get them right and copying the exaggerated shapes I made with my mouth as I showed her how to form the sounds of the letters. We read children's books together, did speech therapy exercises relentlessly and throughout it all, amazingly, Mum managed not to lose her sense of humour. Of course she had her down days, but the doctors were full of praise for her dogged determination to succeed and classed her recovery as nothing short of remarkable, given her age and the severity of the stroke. When they finally discharged her a few weeks before Christmas, happy that she could safely return to her own home, I thought to myself what an incredible woman she was and how lucky I was to call her Mum.

I had to admit I was not looking forward to my first Christmas as a divorcee, a club I had definitely not planned on being a member of, but I was determined to put on a brave face for everyone else's sake. I always used to love Christmas Day, when all our family traditionally gathered at Jeremy and Phoebe's house, but it was also Daniel's birthday, so he had even managed to taint that for me and I couldn't help but think of him. In the general hustle and bustle of the day, it was easy to forget for a while, but as we sat around the table for dinner, I felt suddenly very alone, sad for the family of my own I had never had and envious of the love and easy camaraderie between Jeremy, Phoebe and their children.

By the end of the festive period I had well and truly had enough of all the romantic films, the 'happy couples' who seemed to be in my face everywhere I looked and the 'smug marrieds' who never hesitated to tell me how much better off I was on my own. I knew I was being unreasonable and they all meant well, but I just couldn't wait to get away from it all. Thank God Sam and I were going skiing the day before New Year's Eve. Naturally, I felt guilty about leaving Mum, but Jeremy was adamant I should go, promising to keep a close eye on her while I was away and even agreeing to look after the adorable but delinquent Lola Labrador. Mum made her own feelings very clear.

"The last thing I need is for you to put your life on hold for me. I just want you to be happy and enjoy yourself, now you've got rid of *him*."

I smiled at her look of utter disgust at the mere thought of Daniel and thought what a tough cookie she was.

"I'll ring you every day and you have to promise you'll ring Jeremy straight away if you need anything at all," I told her.

She nodded, with a look on her face that said: "Stop treating me like a child."

I knew I couldn't live life going from one holiday to the next forever, but for now, distraction and escapism were my ways of coping. A new start to a new year with my best friend. It had to be all about looking forward now.

It was snowing hard when Sam and I landed in Innsbruck and it felt as if we had been transported into a different, magical world, where everything was picture-postcard perfect. We only just made it into the resort in our snow-chained taxi before they closed the Arlberg Pass due to the amount of snow falling. Not good for the roads, but fantastic for the skiers. Mateus, the chalet owner's son, met us at the airport and explained in his faultless English that he ran the chalet with his partner Dani and he would also be our ski guide for the week. We thought we knew the slopes pretty well already, but he had the advantage of having grown up there and made sure we were always on the best runs at the right time of day, in the best mountain chalets for gluhweins and lunch and, most importantly, in the best bars at the end of the day for the legendary resort apres-ski.

I loved the feeling of physical exhaustion after a hard day's skiing and always pushed myself to the limit, forgetting about anything else as I concentrated on picking the best route down the slopes. My happiest times were always in the mountains or on the sea and I thought back to the carefree years I spent in the French Alps as a student and in Canada as an exchange teacher. I was making new memories now and there would be many more good times to come, I was sure of it. It was impossible not to feel positive when you were literally on top of the world.

Towards the end of the week, we headed out for the day on the first chairlift and I was filled with a sense of calmness and well-being as I gazed at the stunning mountains all around me, bathed in the glow of the early morning sunshine.

"God, I wish I didn't have to go back home to real life," I sighed.

Mateus laughed.

"What's so bad about real life then?" he asked, turning to me with raised eyebrows and pushing his goggles up onto his helmet.

So I told him. The potted version of course. His eyes widened.

"Wow, that is some story. No wonder you don't want to go back home. But it just so happens that I have the perfect solution to your problems. So here's my suggestion…why don't you stay here till the end of the season?" he asked, making it sound somehow so simple. "Be spontaneous."

I laughed out loud at the absurd idea.

"What do you think, Sam? Shall we just stay here?"

"Why not? Nothing stopping either of us," she joked.

"I'm not joking," Mateus continued, a determined look on his face. "At least hear me out before you dismiss the idea. My family has another chalet in the resort and the hosts have just walked out in a massive huff, after some complaints from guests. To be fair, it's not really a bad thing, as they were pretty useless, but it has left us in the lurch a bit. My mother is furious, as it means she will have to step in herself and she really doesn't want to do that. So, my big idea is that you two stay on here and run it for us till the end of the season! You're both great with people and know the sort of standards the guests expect…you could easily do the job and I know you'd be amazing. Just think about it, please…even if it's only for a couple of weeks until we can get someone else."

I looked at his face and realised he was actually serious.

"You make it all sound great, but the harsh truth is that neither of us knows anything about running a chalet. And I have to say, we're really not great at cooking either," I added with a wry laugh, remembering a meal I once cooked for a new boyfriend years ago. I decided on lasagne, confident that nothing could go wrong with that, but I somehow missed the bit of the instructions that said I needed to soak the sheets of pasta before cooking. As a result, we ended up looking at each other awkwardly across the table, trying to put a brave face on things while chewing through something akin to cardboard. There was no second date.

Those were the halcyon days at the start of my career when I was the only female teacher at Fenchurch Boys' School in Essex. A lifetime ago. The headmaster's parties were legendary and I saw myself in my mind's eye as a newly qualified teacher, sitting on the sofa in Mr Holden's living room next to Philip the maths teacher, who wouldn't stop surreptitiously pinging the top of my suspender belt to make me laugh as I tried to have a polite and sensible conversation with my boss. Two years after I left the school, I found out that Philip was Philippa at weekends and hadn't been quite so interested in me as I thought. I remembered the stuff I had found in Daniel's bedsit and decided there was clearly a recurring theme in the story of my life.

"You wouldn't need to cook," Mateus continued, his voice dragging me away from the ghosts of the past. "We already have a chef to take care of that side of things. It would really just be overseeing things to make sure everything runs smoothly. A bit of cleaning, general hosting and sorting out any problems for the guests. The pay's not great, but you get a bit of pocket money, free board and lodging and a ski pass; it's all about the lifestyle at the end of the day. Think about it and we'll talk after dinner. You'd have a great time, I promise you."

He laughed again, presumably at my stunned expression, but I had to admit I was already beginning to give the suggestion some serious consideration and making hypothetical plans in my head. Surely this was what it was all about, seizing every opportunity and acting on impulse to live my best possible life? My brain was working overtime as I tried to work out how I could make it all happen, my head telling me I had responsibilities back home, while my heart told me to take a leap of faith and just do it. That evening, after a number of frantic phone calls home, it was decided that Lola would go back to stay with Mum and Jeremy promised to keep a close eye on the pair of them. He surprised me by being far more positive about the idea than I thought he would be and I realised how much I had come to rely on his support and advice. Valentino was already settled on full livery in his new five-star home and I was pretty sure Ellie, who loved him like her own, would jump at the chance to exercise him for me. In short, there was nothing to stop us. In a matter of hours, the decision was made and I discovered just how easy it was to change your plans and the path of your life if you really wanted to.

The following day, instead of getting in a taxi to the airport, Sam and I headed over to the other chalet with Mateus, eager to embrace our new career as chalet hosts. I knew in my heart of hearts I was running away from things again, but I also knew I had to get through this in whatever way worked for me.

Carpe diem and all that.

The Man Behind the Mask

Daniel

Patrick James Salenden.

The name was growing on him. As was the neatly trimmed beard and moustache he was now sporting, in keeping with Patrick's recently updated passport photograph. A pair of black-rimmed glasses completed the image and gave him an air of authority he rather liked.

He had been with Caitlin for almost four months now and considered his feet to be well and truly under the table. Naturally, part of the fun had been making her believe that him staying was all her idea, but in the end it had been almost too easy. Manipulation was his speciality after all.

He made his winning move a couple of weeks after she had fallen hook, line and sinker for his sob story about trying to kill himself because of his crazy wife back in the UK. Portraying himself as the victim in an abusive relationship had been a stroke of genius in his opinion and he felt he had played the part magnificently. Mind you, the bit about the crazy wife wasn't entirely a lie. He still found it difficult to come to terms with the fact that his bitch of an ex-wife Grace had actually left him for dead in the sea. Worse than that, she had engineered him falling into the water in the first place. Fucking psychopath! He shuddered at the memory of the shock as he hit the icy waves, felt the pain of the salt water entering his lungs and the raw fear as he truly believed he was going under for the last time. She had pulled some stunts during the whole divorce fiasco, but he never thought for a second she was capable of anything like that. He sighed, imagining for a moment what a formidable team they could have made. If only she hadn't double-crossed him.

Caitlin was a completely different kettle of fish to Grace. Thank God. The last thing he needed was another bunny boiler like Grace in his life. To be honest, he still couldn't believe his luck where Caitlin was concerned. Not only had he survived the near-drowning experience and been found by the perfect person to facilitate his reincarnation, but he had also managed to wipe the slate clean and get rid of all that baggage he had accumulated over the last twenty years in one fell swoop. No more kids and their demanding mothers bleeding him dry every five minutes. No more tax man hounding him. He could concentrate on the important stuff. Like creating his new perfect life.

And of course, making Grace pay.

If she thought she was going to get off scot-free with what she had done, she had another think coming. He fully intended to make it his mission in life to ensure she paid the price for her actions and to become the very personification of Karma where she was concerned. No need to rush though. Better to let her think she was safe, then begin the game when *he* was ready. Her guard was down now and, blissfully unaware of his continued existence, she was happily telling the world about everything she was doing on Facebook, all privacy settings open. He, and anyone else who cared to do so, could easily stalk her every move and that was exactly what he intended to do. Daniel had always despised Facebook and all other social media in the past, preferring to stay well and truly under the radar, but he had to admit it was coming in pretty useful now. He would make sure Grace knew pain she could never even imagine and he already knew exactly how he was going to do it. It just wouldn't necessarily be *her* pain. At least not at the beginning.

Daniel had taken care to choose his new name wisely. The 'real' Patrick Salenden was in fact a scammer in America, a lying scumbag who had cheated him out of almost forty thousand dollars a couple of years ago, by selling him a classic car that didn't even exist. Daniel had flown into a blind rage when he discovered the scam, but even the most persistent and unscrupulous Private Eye he could find had been unable to track the man down and Daniel had decided in the end that it would be unwise to draw further attention to his own activities by getting the authorities involved. The scammer had gone to great lengths to provide false ID documents for the transaction, including a driver's licence and a signed bill of sale, notorised by a solicitor, who also turned out not to exist. Daniel thought long and hard at the time about how to deal with the situation, but it was only when he locked horns with the Trustee in Bankruptcy following his divorce that he managed to come up with what he considered was a truly inspired plan to turn things around to his own advantage.

The Trustee was hounding him relentlessly for proof of the existence of any other directors of Jupiter Holdings, so the ideal solution as he saw it was for Patrick Salenden, complete with his fake ID, to become a bona fide director of his Delaware-based company. Delaware was the state of choice for foreigners looking to set up a business with very little documentation required, known for having no obligation per se for companies to provide financial statements or indeed any information at all about the directors of a company, all of which suited Daniel just fine. Secrecy and discretion guaranteed. The added fact that it was famed as a tax haven made it just about as perfect a location as you could get. The elusive Patrick Salenden had proved to be extremely effective in keeping the Trustee in Bankruptcy at bay with regard to Jupiter Holdings, despite Grace's best efforts to stir things up by banging on about the ID documents he had provided them with being fake. Daniel knew it would take them years to prove anything and, more importantly, with the involvement of other directors (even pretend ones like Patrick), it suddenly became a whole lot trickier for the Trustee and her henchmen to get their hands on anything to do with his company or touch any of the assets 'owned' by said company and directors.

Having tested the water, so to speak, Daniel felt emboldened by the success of his latest deception and decided to take things a step further. A bit of searching on the dark web, a few phone calls to the right people and 'Patrick' soon had his own US passport and a whole host of other related documentation such as utility bills and a birth certificate. Daniel used his own photograph for the ID, but with the addition of spectacles and a rather fetching beard from a fancy dress shop. As a director of Jupiter Holdings, Patrick already had his own debit and credit cards with access to the company bank account, but he could now open further personal accounts without a problem. The world was his oyster. It cost thirteen thousand dollars for the privilege, but it had already proved to be an invaluable investment.

The thing was, Daniel had known for some time before Lorraine's email crashed into his inbox that he needed to get his money out of the UK if he was going to keep it away from the grasping hands of the tax man. He had effectively run rings around those idiots at HMRC for years, but the odds were finally beginning to stack up against him and he had decided it was time to think about making a move. Time in fact for Daniel Callaghan to do a runner and lie low for as long as necessary, while his alter ego Patrick Salenden got out and about a bit more. His plan should have been failsafe and he was well on the way to getting everything in order to be able to make his move when Lorraine almost spoilt everything with her poison pen antics. Almost. Then Grace jumped on the band wagon and things began to turn really sticky when it transpired that she had both a backbone and some brains. Who would have thought it? Daniel had to admit he had been well and truly caught with his pants down, but none of his women had been a match for him in the end and they were deluding themselves if they believed otherwise.

Daniel's mood darkened as he thought about Grace. The stupid bitch clearly thought she had won, but what she didn't know when she left him for dead that night was that he was carrying all the documents for his reincarnation strapped to his torso in an Aquapac waterproof pouch, ready for a quick exit if needs be. It had always been part of his grand plan to disappear soon after that boat trip, but obviously it was supposed to have been on *his* terms. Having his hand forced by Grace was most certainly not part of that plan and he had lost far more than he should have done as a result. Daniel was not one to forgive and forget, but he could afford to be patient. The real beauty in this new twist of fate was that Grace truly believed she was safe and would not be looking over her shoulder anymore. When he eventually made his big move, she would not see it coming. He clenched his teeth and felt the familiar stirrings of arousal at the power he now had over her.

He was fucking invincible.

Daniel's musings were interrupted as the door opened and Bentley leaped out of his basket to go and greet Caitlin returning from work. He got to his feet dutifully and walked over to give her a hug as she stood up from fussing the dog.

"How was your day?" he asked, forcing a smile and trying his best to look interested.

"Oh, you know, fairly routine. Blood tests, health checks, injections…the usual."

She lost him at 'fairly routine'. He had no idea what 'the usual' was and had no desire to find out in any further detail.

"I've got to go up to Dublin for a few days tomorrow. Work stuff," he announced, keeping it vague with a weary sigh and a roll of the eyes for good measure.

Caitlin looked crestfallen.

"Oh Patrick, that's such a shame. I've got a day off on Thursday, so I thought we could do something together. We hardly seem to have any time for each other these days."

"I know and I'm sorry. I'll make it up to you, I promise. It's just hard trying to build up my consultancy work from scratch and I really need to follow up every contact I can get," he said, as sincerely as he could manage. "I don't want to be sponging off you all the time. I need to pay my way."

Of course, Daniel wasn't really sorry and he had never had any qualms whatsoever about sponging off the women in his life. However, he was desperate to get away for a bit, before Caitlin drove him round the bend. Staying with her was undoubtedly convenient in a number of ways, but she was a bit of a strange one and he was struggling to get the measure of her. First, she had invited him into her home after finding him on the beach, no questions asked, then she had dressed him in her dead husband's clothes and insisted he stay there with her to recuperate. It was only a matter of days before she invited him into the marital bed. Even by his standards that was quick work from the grieving widow, not that he was complaining of course.

Caitlin continued to look crestfallen, but resigned herself to the situation.

"Of course you must go. I'm the one who's sorry for being so selfish. Just promise you'll hurry back," she added, planting a chaste kiss on his cheek.

"I'll be back before you know it. Now, what's for dinner?" he asked, keen to change the subject.

Daniel had to admit that Caitlin was a top scorer in the culinary prowess category and there was always a tasty home-cooked meal to look forward to in the evening. It also worked to his advantage that she wanted him to keep a low profile for the moment and insisted on doing all the shopping as a result. He had even resurrected his infamous spreadsheet, adding Caitlin's name to the others for comparison and evaluation purposes. There would be a test for her in the form of a big pile of dirty laundry when he headed off to Dublin, but from what he had seen so far he had high hopes for her on that score.

Two days later at six o'clock in the evening, punctual as ever, Patrick Salenden walked through the doors of The Porterhouse in Temple Bar and immediately began scanning the room. A woman with long dark hair in a ponytail, seated alone at one of the little tables, smiled in his direction and shyly raised a hand to her shoulder in greeting. His first impression was favourable, given that she looked exactly like her profile picture on the dating app. He strode confidently over to the table.

"Roisin?" he inquired, then bent to kiss her on each cheek in a continental-style greeting he felt was appropriate, without bothering to wait for a reply.

"That's me. And you must be Patrick," she replied with a nervous laugh, slightly taken aback by his confident over-familiarity.

"Patrick James, at your service. Can I get you a drink?" he asked immediately.

"Gin and slimline please. Bombay Sapphire."

Daniel observed her slyly from the bar as he waited to be served. She was in her late forties, he guessed, reasonable looking, although seemed a bit uptight. Probably come straight from the office, judging by the dark suit and hairstyle. He noted she was carrying a few extra pounds, but in his experience, that tended to make women of a certain age all the more grateful for male attention. He already knew from her social media that she had been divorced for five years and had no kids to get in the way of anything. Perfect.

He returned to the table with their drinks and was soon regaling her with tales of sailing adventures on the high seas and of course his helicopter flying days, sadly cut short following a near-fatal accident. She seemed suitably impressed and giggled when he gave her a cheeky wink and offered to 'show her his scars later if she liked'.

Two hours and a couple of gins later, he decided to move things along and suggested they go to get something to eat, but to his intense irritation, she announced she already had plans for dinner. Daniel was less than happy at having to spend the night in a Travelodge when he had fully expected to be invited to go back home with Roisin. In his experience, women on those dating sites were usually more than game for a hook-up on the first meeting. It had certainly been like that with Jane and Lorraine. Even straight-laced Anita had been happy enough to put out with a little gentle persuasion. When Roisin texted later to say how much she had enjoyed his company and suggested meeting up the following evening, he thought petulantly about ignoring her and moving on to the next one from his list of matches, but he didn't like losing and felt he should give it one more shot.

Daniel decided to push the boat out and booked a table at a Parisian-style bistro called Pichet on Trinity Street in a determined effort to impress. He was prepared to speculate to accumulate if he had to, but he took a calculated risk that, as a modern woman, she would insist on going Dutch and he wouldn't be landed with paying for the lot. The grilled pineapple margarita at the cocktail bar afterwards seemed to clinch the deal and, after splitting the bill (boom!), they finally headed back to her apartment overlooking Dun Laoghaire harbour, much more Daniel's kind of place than the austere setting of the Travelodge he had been forced to endure the previous night. Roisin may have been a slow starter, but she was clearly gagging for it once they were back at her apartment. Daniel smiled to himself as she straddled him and took charge, apparently happy to do all the hard work. His trusty little blue pills had ensured he did not disappoint her with a half-hearted erection and, judging by her enthusiasm, he reckoned his Dublin accommodation was in the bag from now on.

Caitlin was willing enough in the bedroom, but conventional sex bored Daniel. In fact, it had to be said that sex with the same partner, male or female, simply did not cut it for him. It was high time he got some excitement back into his life and Caitlin only had herself to blame if he had to go looking elsewhere for fun. Her little cottage in the south suited him as the perfect hideaway for the moment, but he was pretty sure he would be scheduling regular business meetings in Dublin over the coming months.

As Daniel drifted off to sleep that night, he wondered casually whether Roisin's underwear would fit him. He wouldn't mind betting she was the sort that would be up for a bit of experimentation and a more alternative approach to sex. Why couldn't people understand that high-flying entrepreneurs like him needed variety and risks to keep their attention? There was one thing for sure, he had no thoughts of 'learning from his mistakes', as that old fart of a judge had suggested to him in the divorce court. He sniggered quietly to himself as he remembered their earlier conversation over dinner when Roisin had told him she was a clinical psychologist and proudly handed him her business card. He had nearly choked on his food and struggled to keep a straight face at that point.

"I bet that sounds pretty boring to you," she said, wrinkling her nose.

On the contrary, it sounded anything *but* boring to Daniel, whose interest in her had just been heightened by about a hundred and fifty percent. The challenge of deceiving a medical professional, one who was trained to spot complex personality disorders such as the one he had been told he suffered from, appealed immensely to his warped sense of humour. Seducing a clinical psychologist. It didn't get any better than that. He felt himself begin to grow hard again as he thought about it. What an incredible coup that would be if he could pull it off.

Roisin had unwittingly thrown down the gauntlet the second the words 'clinical psychologist' left her mouth. The game was on again for Daniel Callaghan, aka Patrick Salenden, and he could only begin to imagine the fun he was going to have with it.

The Last Run of the Day

*When life gives you good reason to cry, always remember
that there are a hundred more reasons to smile.*

Grace

I heard the crack before I felt it. But seconds later, when I did feel it, the pain was indescribable.

Just thirty seconds earlier my life had been perfect. It was the end of a fantastic day skiing with Mateus and we were on our way back to the chalet to prepare for the guests in the evening. My routine with Sam for the last five days had been hectic, but fun: get up early, oversee breakfast, chat to the guests and make sure everyone was happy before waving them off for their day on the slopes. As soon as they were all out, we went through the chalet like a tornado, cleaning the rooms, tidying the breakfast stuff away and setting out everything for afternoon tea. Then we were free to head up into the mountains for a few hours ourselves.

Sam was tired that afternoon and had gone back a bit earlier, but the snow conditions were perfect and the sun was out, so Mateus and I skied until the very last minute, cutting down from the last run onto the little winding track that would take us directly home to the chalet. It was a simple enough track, but if you didn't keep up a

63

reasonable amount of speed, you would end up poling it for a good ten minutes. What I didn't expect to see as I rounded a bend was a wall of people, all of whom had clearly run out of speed and were completely blocking the path. With a steep drop to the outside and a cliff face to the inside, I chose the inside, realising the error of my ways as I hit the unforgiving icy ridges on the path far too fast, losing control completely and flying through the air before landing hard in a tangled mess of skis and limbs.

Mateus, who was a little way ahead waiting for me to catch up, was powerless to do anything other than watch the disaster unfold. As I screamed out in agony and clutched at my leg, I knew in an instant that my new chalet host career was over as quickly as it had begun. With one look at my lower leg, ski still attached and twisted at an alarmingly unnatural angle, my worst fears were confirmed.

Being carted down the mountain on the blood wagon had not been top on my bucket list of things to experience, but sadly it was unavoidable. As I lay on the stretcher, waiting for the x-rays to determine just how bad the damage was, I noticed miserably that everyone else in the clinic had someone with them and I dissolved into floods of tears, overcome by a wave of self-pity. I didn't blame anyone of course and I knew Mateus had to get back to the chalet to tell Sam what had happened and help her with the guests, but still I cried, engulfed in self-pity, wishing I had someone there to put their arms around me and comfort me.

When the doctor came in to explain the results of the x-rays to me, he didn't know quite what to make of the gibbering wreck before him. Naturally, he assumed I was crying tears of pain and gave me an extra shot of morphine, then sat down next to me and held my hand as he talked. That simple act of kindness made me even worse. What he did not understand was that the tears were not just on account of the physical pain. They were tears for all I had lost with Daniel and tears of frustration at the fact I was being knocked back down yet again, just as I thought I was actually getting somewhere in the long and difficult process of rebuilding my life.

After the third shot of morphine, I finally managed to regain my composure enough to take in what the doctor, who reminded me more than a little of the kindly Judge Barraclough, was telling me. Having first ascertained that I had adequate medical insurance, the best option in his opinion was to transfer me to the private clinic in the neighbouring town of St Anton, where the renowned Doktor Franz Bergmann would operate on my knee that very evening. I was just happy that someone else was taking charge of the situation and nodded gratefully in agreement. As the morphine began to take full effect, I drifted in and out of consciousness, but was vaguely aware of being loaded into a little ambulance on the stretcher, then wheeled off again and through some glass doors that slid open automatically, with the sign Bergmann Unfallsanatorium above them. My first impression was that it was more like a five-star hotel than a hospital. People, presumably nurses, glided past silently, all dressed in pure white, and it seemed to me in my dazed state like all the beautiful people of the entire region had gathered there to work. None of them looked a day older than thirty-five and they were all slim, tanned and immaculately groomed. Doktor Bergmann himself was no exception when he came to see me for a brief pre-op chat and I thought for a moment Robbie Williams had taken up orthopaedic surgery on the sly.

"So here we are in the tibia head room," he announced in impeccable English, addressing me from the doorway, as I stared back at him through a drugged haze.

"The good news is, I can fix your leg. The bad news is, you will have a big scar."

He paused for a moment.

"But hey, scars are sexy," he added, with a little laugh.

"Will I be able to ski again?" I asked nervously, not sure whether I wanted to hear the answer.

"Sure, but maybe not this season. And only if you stop fucking with your knee," he added, wagging his finger in my direction. "See you in theatre."

On that note, he breezed out with a casual wave of his hand and I was left wondering if I had just imagined the entire conversation. Doctors didn't actually speak like that, did they? Apparently, this one did. He exuded confidence, with just the right amount of arrogance to make him incredibly sexy and elevate him to hero status in my eyes. All I really cared about were the words: "I can fix your leg." It was going to involve metal pins and plates and a bone graft, which didn't sound particularly encouraging to me, but I was happy to place my trust in Doktor Superhero.

The nurse who turned up next to prep me for theatre was a different kettle of fish entirely and did not fulfil any of the requirements needed to work in that place so far as I could see. Goodness knows how she had slipped through the net. She reminded me immediately of Rosa Klebb in the James Bond film 'From Russia with Love' and had a similar no-nonsense, borderline sadistic attitude, as she plonked a bed pan down beside me and folded her arms crossly in response to my bleating that I wanted to get off the bed and use the toilet. She was clearly having none of that, so I admitted defeat and gave in to the humiliation that was the bed pan. I was pretty sure it all started to go wrong when she first came in and asked brusquely:

"Sprechen Sie Deutsch?"

Her question was met with a pathetic grin and a shrug of the shoulders. It was not that she couldn't speak perfect English, she just clearly thought I should be making more of an effort as a visitor in her country. Under normal circumstances, I would have agreed with her and made a brave attempt to dredge up something of my A-level German from years ago, but the morphine put paid to that. A couple of injections and several signatures later, on what I assumed was a consent form she shoved at me, I headed off to theatre for my reunion with Doktor Bergmann.

When I came round the following day, it took me a few moments to comprehend where I was, then I realised I could not move my leg and it all came flooding back to me. Sunlight streamed in through the large, floor-to-ceiling window at the end of the room and I gazed out wistfully at the beautiful Austrian mountains, with the first early bird skiers already zigzagging down the slopes. Twenty-four hours ago, I would have been one of them. Thankfully, Nurse Klebb appeared to have gone off duty and I felt far more reassured by her replacement, who came in with pain killers and a restaurant-style menu for lunch and dinner, which she kindly helped me to understand. This was clearly not going to be the usual calibre of hospital food and I began to perk up a bit.

I perked up even more when a youngish man, who looked like an Italian model with his dark hair and moody features, introduced himself as The Physiotherapist and proceeded to strap my leg into a metal contraption that gently bent and straightened it for around twenty minutes, without any effort at all on my part. It was all starting to feel very surreal, but I was also beginning to get anxious about what would happen next, conscious of the mayhem my accident must have caused for an awful lot of people. Right on cue, Doktor Bergmann appeared and perched himself on the chest of drawers opposite my bed to deliver what I hoped would be good news of a speedy recovery, but it was not to be. His message was short and to the point.

"The operation went well and your leg is straight again. You will need crutches when you leave here and you will be non-weight bearing on that leg for ten weeks."

"Ten weeks?" I repeated, incredulously, unable to hide my horror.

"Yes, that's right. Two and a half months," he clarified as if I was a bit simple. "That is if you want your leg to heal properly. After ten weeks, you may start gradually to put weight on it and you will of course need intensive physiotherapy in order to get back the maximum range of movement. Any more questions?"

I shook my head, trying desperately not to start crying again.

"Okay, good. We keep you here for two days."

He waited a moment, probably to see whether I was going to come up with any more stupid questions, then he was gone, leaving me to digest the information and weigh up my somewhat limited options.

Sam managed to get in to visit me just before lunch, as soon as she had done everything in the chalet. This was not at all the fun-packed few weeks we had envisaged and I was consumed with guilt, knowing it was all down to me and my stupid recklessness.

"Jeez Grace, you don't do things by halves, do you?" she said, marching up to the bed and giving me a hug. "I've brought you some stuff."

She put the overnight bag on the bed and opened it to show me. Most importantly, I noticed immediately that there was chocolate, several bars of it in fact, together with my phone charger, my toilet bag, a couple of pairs of knickers and a change of clothes.

"I brought you leggings to wear, but judging by the size of your leg in that bandage, you might need to cut one leg off to get them on!"

"Oh God, I'm so sorry. What a bloody mess," I sighed.

"Look, what's done is done, so there's no point moaning about it. It's not like you did this deliberately. I've spoken to the insurance company this morning and they're arranging flights home for us as soon as possible. Mateus has contacted a couple of his mates in the UK, who have agreed to fly out and run the chalet for the rest of the season, so it's all sorted, everything's cool."

"I feel so guilty, I've ruined everything for you as well as myself," I said, feeling the familiar tears well up in my eyes.

"Don't be ridiculous. These things happen and, to be fair, it was more your dream than mine. I'm already knackered," she laughed. "I have to say though, what the hell were you thinking with your bindings?" she added, her face a mixture of reproach and incomprehension.

"What do you mean?"

"Mateus brought your skis home after the accident and he said he just couldn't understand why your bindings didn't release when you went flying. He had a good look over your skis and you had the DIN settings tuned high enough for a person twice your size and weight and probably Olympic downhill standard. Not ideal, obviously."

"That's ridiculous. I always have the bindings set so that they will release if they need to. I get them done by the technicians when they service them each year and I don't touch them. I know they were done properly."

"Well, I don't know, I'm just telling you what he said. I do know one thing though, you can't afford to do any more damage to yourself after this, not before the Madagascar Rally. A bubble wrap suit maybe?" she joked. "Seriously Grace, it's five months away. No more accidents. I need to get off now, but I'll be back to pick you up tomorrow, just let me know what time."

After Sam left, I had all the time in the world to lay there thinking about what she had said. It didn't make sense to me, as I knew I always erred on the side of caution with my bindings. Then I remembered Daniel's face when he came to drop off my skis for me after the house got sold. The knowing smirk that reminded me of the way he was when he saw me that day before my car was set on fire. A seemingly innocent little comment, loaded with menace:

"The car looks great, by the way. You're obviously looking after it."

It had been the same with the skis:

"You always did ski so well with these. They were a good present, weren't they?"

I had left my skis behind in the house by mistake when we cleared everything out and naturally, Daniel had taken them, just because he could. I assumed that would be the last I saw of them, but in an uncharacteristic moment of helpfulness he had dropped them off at the house in Conwy for me shortly before the fateful delivery trip on 'Mistress', saying he had taken them to help me out, to avoid the Trustee's henchmen disappearing with them. I remembered thinking maybe he did have some tiny pangs of conscience and decency after all, but I wasn't so sure now.

I thought again of his cryptic little comments. It was as if he wanted me to know that he knew something I didn't. His way of letting me know he was still in control. Taunting me. Except he was no longer in control of anything, I reminded myself.

When I spoke to Sam about my theory the following day, she was sceptical.

"To be honest, I think you're being a bit paranoid Grace. Even if he did mess with the bindings, how could he possibly have known you would have an accident? He couldn't have engineered that, so I don't really see why he would have bothered. It all seems a bit far-fetched."

"That's the whole point, Sam. It's all part of the game with him. It might cause me harm, it might not. Like Russian roulette. Part of the fun for him is not being certain how it will all pan out. I promise you he would have been getting a kick out of knowing I was in danger because of him and he would love it even more that I had no clue about it. It's all about the power with him. He gets off on it, I'm telling you."

Sam rolled her eyes and shook her head.

"Enough of the amateur psychology, especially where that arse-hole is concerned. I think the morphine has affected your brain," she laughed. "How many times do I have to say it? Forget about him. He's gone."

Alone in my hospital bed that night, I couldn't sleep. I kept turning things over and over in my head, aware that I was irrationally building Daniel up into some hideous, vengeful spectre, intent on destroying me. But in spite of the voice of reason telling me he was gone for ever, I was unable to rid myself of the thought that, even in death, he had the ability to screw up my life.

The Homecoming

Daniel

When Patrick strutted through the door at around six-thirty in the evening, he was struck immediately by the delicious smells of a roast dinner coming from the kitchen.

"Something smells good," he said, keen to reward Caitlin's efforts in the kitchen.

She ran to the door with her customary eagerness and threw her arms around his neck, closely followed by the ever-enthusiastic Bentley. These full-on displays of affection always made him squirm uncomfortably, but he tried not to show it, disentangling himself as quickly as possible from her clutches.

"Put me down," he said, attempting to sound jokey.

Caitlin appeared to be in good humour as usual and he thought for a moment how people so often look like their dogs. She was certainly as easily pleased as Bentley and had a similar intellect and temperament so far as he could see.

"I missed you so much," she continued, taking hold of his hand. "Come and sit in the kitchen while I finish dinner. I've made your favourite, roast beef, and I even managed to get a bottle of Mount Gay. That was the one you asked for, wasn't it?"

"You are an angel. What did I do to deserve you?"

He was already hoping she didn't expect sex later. The 'one for the road' Roisin had suggested before he set off for home had just about finished him off.

"I've got a couple of emails to do, then I'm all yours."

Patrick disappeared into the other room and opened his laptop. First, he sent Roisin a lewd message, referring to his sex flashbacks and how he couldn't wait to do it all over again, then he set about his regular task of social media stalking to check up on Grace's activities.

A couple of minutes later a broad smile spread across his features and he began to chuckle, unable to resist a quiet "Yesss!" accompanied by a little fist pump in the air.

"Good news?" came Caitlin's voice from the kitchen.

"Yes, a deal I've been waiting to hear about has come off for one of my clients. More commission for me," he lied, without the slightest hint of hesitation.

He had been extremely irritated by Grace's posts about her latest venture, apparently living the dream in Lech with that cow Samantha. More like living the nightmare now, he thought to himself as he looked with satisfaction at the pictures showing her swollen leg in a cumbersome black brace and a pair of red crutches at the side. He hoped it was painful and she ended up with an ugly scar and a limp. Why should she get to swan around enjoying herself after what she had done to him? Mind you, in a weird kind of way, he had to admit that Grace had done him a favour when she engineered his 'death'.

In his old life, when Daniel Callaghan set up the Big Sexy Superstore in Stainsford and then branched out with his bespoke parties, one of his best clients was the head of an organisation not best renowned for its legitimate business practices. Before long, money was being rinsed through the store for 'Mister X', who seemed to think he was Stainsford's answer to The Godfather. Daniel had been arrogant enough to think he could run rings round 'Mister X', in much the same way as he had done with HMRC, proceeding to syphon off large chunks of the money for himself. Unfortunately for Daniel, however, 'Mister X' was not the thick lout he took him for and it quickly became apparent that he did not take kindly at all to being swindled out of his hard-earned cash. Even

Daniel was astute enough to realise he was messing with the wrong people. Not content with simply getting his money back, the gang boss had started to demand ridiculous amounts in compensation and Daniel had latterly been finding it increasingly difficult to dodge both him and his thugs. It would be fair to say that relations had broken down irreparably and it was getting to the stage where Daniel was certain they did not have his best interests at heart. In fact, he was fairly sure it was only a matter of time before he found himself at the bottom of the nearest canal with a concrete brick attached to his ankle, as retribution for having messed them around. In pre-empting what would undoubtedly be their next move, Grace had unwittingly done something to help him for once. He must find a way of thanking her properly.

"Dinner's ready," shouted Caitlin from the kitchen, interrupting his thoughts.

Patrick closed his laptop and wandered through to find she had already placed his meal on the table and opened a bottle of Rioja to let it breathe, just as he had trained her.

"Wow, this looks amazing. You really are a great cook, you know."

Caitlin beamed happily at his words of praise and poured the wine before sitting down opposite him.

"How was Dublin?" she asked.

"Oh, you know. Pretty boring really. I'm not keen on the city at the best of times, especially when I'm there for work. I've definitely signed up the guy I met as a new client, so that's good news, but he's pretty demanding, unfortunately. He's already insisting on weekly progress meetings as part of the contract. Obviously, that's a massive pain, as I'll have to be away from home more, but with the money he's paying I'll have no problem making it up to you. That's a promise."

Caitlin could not hide her obvious disappointment.

"Well, I suppose they do say that absence makes the heart grow fonder, so we'll just have to prove that's right. And it's great that you're building up your reputation in the consultancy business," she conceded.

Caitlin was not entirely sure she believed the 'absence makes the heart grow fonder' thing and she had already detected more than a faint whiff of bullshit in the air. She had never asked for any more details about Patrick's past, as he had made it clear it was all far too painful to talk about. He was with her now and their future together was bright, he had assured her. Why spoil it all by focusing on things and people that had no relevance to them? Somehow though, she wasn't quite buying it and her naturally suspicious nature led her to believe that there was considerably more to his whole story than she had been favoured with. What she knew for sure was that 'knowledge is power'. Consequently, while Patrick was away in Dublin, Caitlin made the most of her time alone to do some digging and try to find out more about the man she now called her partner. Who was he before he became Patrick Salenden? It was high time she got to the bottom of things, but to do that she needed a name.

She began by systematically going through all his clothes, searching every pocket of every item he had left in the cottage, trying to find something that had his old name on it. Having drawn a blank there, she turned to the internet and spent hours on the computer, going down rabbit hole after rabbit hole, all to no avail. She googled 'tragic wife throws herself under a train', 'man mourns wife who took her own life in railway tragedy' and a whole host of other combinations, adding a date of around twenty years ago. Surely the newspapers would have reported that? But despite her best efforts, she learned precisely nothing.

Not surprising really, given that he had told her a pack of lies.

There was nothing on 'Patrick Salenden' either. She knew it was his adopted name but had half hoped there may be some kind of link there, like maybe he was a dead relative or something? Again, she hit the post and reluctantly had to admit defeat for the time being. She was determined to find out his real name somehow and, when she did, it would lead her to everything else she wanted to know, she was sure of it.

Caitlin looked across the table at Patrick, tucking into the meal she had prepared and wondered again why she always had to spoil things for herself. Fate had delivered her a wonderful new partner to share her life with, but all she could do was fixate on poking around in his past, basically looking for trouble. Patrick immediately clocked her wistful gaze and knew exactly what to say.

"So where would you like me to take you on holiday then? I said I'd make it up to you for having to be away a lot more and I meant it."

Caitlin smiled and considered for a moment, before replying:

"I've always wanted to go to Barbados," she said shyly, wondering what he would think of that suggestion.

"Great idea! I think that would be perfect for us. You know what, I like to think I've travelled a lot over the years, but I've never been there, so it'd be our special place," he lied, remembering several holidays there with Grace and how much she loved the island. They visited the Mount Gay factory every time they went there, on a kind of pilgrimage to the home of his favourite rum, and always stocked up on bottles of the stuff to take home with them. The first year they went they hired a little mini moke and toured all around the island, spending time on the rugged east coast, visiting sugar cane plantations and eating in the fashionable restaurants favoured by celebs on the west coast. The Cliff had been the best and he thought of the New Year's Eve they had spent there, when Grace had treated him to dinner as a surprise, at an extortionate cost…he would have to drop a few subtle hints to Caitlin.

"Why don't you start doing a bit of research on the internet and see what you can come up with? Probably best to aim for later in the year, after hurricane season, maybe even Christmas. If you find something you like, just book it and I'll sort the money out with you afterwards. It'll be nice to have something to look forward to," he said, raising his glass to hers, before adding:

"I have heard from friends who've been there that The Cliff is amazing, but all the best restaurants on the west coast do get booked up weeks, if not months ahead at Christmas and New Year, so it would be an idea to get some reservations in if we decide to go at that time."

Caitlin nodded enthusiastically, ready to accept the challenge. She felt that, on the balance of things, she was due a bit of fun in her life. She loved the fact that Patrick was wanting to plan a holiday at the end of the year, which proved he saw his future with her. Maybe she was overthinking things and should trust him after all. She really didn't know what to believe anymore.

Later that night, as she lay in bed with Patrick snoring loudly beside her, the familiar ghosts were never far away from her thoughts. She felt an overwhelming sense of doom flood over her as she remembered all too vividly the crushing disappointment of discovering time and again that every new man of her dreams was in fact just as mediocre and weak as all the rest. And it wasn't only the men in her life who let her down. Throughout her whole life, the people she trusted and relied on the most had repeatedly betrayed her trust. As a result, she had learned over the years to get in first and make sure she threw the first punch.

Caitlin's childhood memories were not ones of happy family days out to the seaside, loving cuddles, smiling faces, excited squeals on Christmas morning. The things she remembered were tears, cries of pain, her mother cowering in terror from the drunken fists of her father. Megan, as she was known then, had watched it all from her hiding place at the top of the stairs, like a scene from a horror movie unfolding before her eyes, powerless to do anything. Then one day he turned on her, without any warning, just because there was no milk in the fridge. The blow from the back of his hand sent her flying to the floor, then as she scrambled frantically to get away, he helped her on her way with his boot up her backside. Old beyond her years and recognising the sign of things to come, Megan decided in that moment that she would be ready for him next time.

She did not have long to wait. A matter of a few hours in fact. And then it was all over.

By the time the ambulance crew and police arrived on the scene that night, her father was beyond help. They burst in to find the teenage Megan sitting alone on the sofa, staring blankly ahead and covered in blood, while her mother knelt by her husband's body, screaming hysterically. Having gone first to the girl and ascertained that the blood was not in fact *her* blood, they turned their attention to her father, pronouncing him dead at the scene from his horrific injuries, caused by a frenzied attack with a serrated kitchen knife.

Megan had indeed been ready for him when he came in from the pub that night and, despite her inferior height, weight and strength, she had the element of surprise on her side and of course the advantage of a clear head. The first blow to the neck would have done the job well enough, having severed his carotid artery, but the girl just kept lashing out, until her horrified mother, screaming like a banshee, eventually managed to pull her off.

Caitlin had never told anyone about this part of her past. All the sordid domestic violence stuff came out in court of course and the Judge ruled that it had been a desperate act of self-defence by a young and troubled thirteen-year-old girl, in fear of her own life as well as that of her mother. They moved away after the court case, in an attempt to erase the past and build a new life, but despite what they had endured together, she and her mother were not close. In fact, Caitlin despised her mother and vowed never to be the pathetic victim she had been for so many years. Not that it ever seemed to do her any good standing up for herself. When it all kicked off at school and she pushed that vindictive little cow down the stairs, no one was interested in her side of the story. *She* was the one who ended up being punished and sent to a Special School, better equipped to deal with her 'anger issues'. No wonder she had taken herself as far away as possible to start a new life on her own the second she was old enough to do so.

But of course that all went wrong as well.

Patrick grunted and turned towards her in his sleep, dragging her away from her dark thoughts of the past and back into the present. As she looked at him she immediately began to feel calmer. He would never let her down. He owed her. She had saved his life and now it was his turn to repay the debt.

This time things would be different for her. She would make sure of it.

Set the World on Fire

The man crouched in the shadows, watching, waiting, knowing there could be no mistakes. His reputation had been built on his willingness to do the things no one else wanted to do and his professionalism in getting the job done, both of which meant he could charge top dollar for his services. The client on this occasion was one of his regulars, although no names had ever been exchanged. Everything had been planned meticulously, as the man was a big fan of the so-called five Ps: "Planning Prevents Piss Poor Performance"; at least that was his version of the saying.

Everything was in darkness and there was no sound except the occasional rustling of hay and the muffled snorts of the animals. It was time. Creeping silently across the concrete yard, constantly aware of every tiny detail of his surroundings, the man reached the little wooden chalet. In his hand he carried a can of kerosene, which he now opened and placed on its side, allowing a trail of liquid to spill out from the side of the chalet to the barn. Moving quickly, he went up the two steps and found the key to the door exactly where he had been told it would be, hanging on a piece of string on the inside of the left-hand bottom window, invisible unless you knew it was there. The window was shut but not locked and it took just a few seconds to retrieve the key and untie it from the string. Once inside, the kerosene heater was immediately visible, apparently used for emergencies when the power went off, as it so often did in rural areas. The man, who was a stickler for precision, order and cleanliness in his own life, wrinkled his nose at the smell of the place, noting in disgust that it was a tip. He wasted no time in moving the heater close to the curtains and a pile of dirty horse rugs discarded on the floor. Lighting it first, he pushed it over onto its side to facilitate the inevitable.

Whoops, he thought to himself, retracing his steps, locking the door and replacing the key exactly where he had found it. Then he retreated into the shadows to watch, knowing he wouldn't have long to wait. Judging by the state of the place, he was doing them a favour. He waited just long enough to see the orange glow from the windows, then the flames tearing through the wooden wall of the chalet and picking up the trail of fuel leading to the barn.

His work there was done.

Up to Heaven

*The enemy you must fear the most will not enter your life
wielding a sword, but offering the hand of friendship.*

Grace

I sat on my white leather sofa with the patio windows wide open,
gazing out over the waters of Marsden Bay and its iconic rock. I
never grew tired of that view and felt a wonderful sense of calmness
and well-being as I watched the waves gently breaking on the shore
and heard the hiss of the water as it receded, sucking the pebbles
with it. The long three months on crutches was finally over and I
was home, able to drive my car and even manage walks on the
beach, albeit very slowly.

Mum had insisted I go and live with her after my enforced
repatriation from Austria so that she could look after me. I had
resisted the idea initially, mainly because I felt she had enough
problems of her own to cope with, but gave in when I realized she
was actually looking forward to me being there with her. In a funny
kind of way, it seemed to help her to recover from the stroke, as she
made it her mission to focus all her attention on doing things for her
temporarily crippled and very irritable daughter. I was not a good
patient and hated being cooped up indoors, unable to do all the

things I loved, but somehow we got through it together and I was finally able to go back home on my own two feet.

Sam had come to stay for a few days and was just returning from a more rigorous walk on the beach than I could manage, together with Lola, who was dripping wet and carrying her beloved ball in her mouth. My phone pinged and I couldn't resist a little laugh at the message:

Hope you're behaving yourself now you're off those crutches…actually, I really hope you're not and you're going to tell me all about it! (Winking emoji) xx

"Who's put a smile on your face then," asked Sam, sitting down beside me. "Lola's in her basket in the kitchen drying off, by the way," she added.

"Oh, it's just that Aidan guy I told you about," I said, casually.

"Err, what Aidan guy?" demanded Sam, with raised eyebrows. "You most certainly did not tell me about him."

"Really? I thought I did," I lied, knowing she would have disapproved. "He sent me a friend request after my accident. I checked out his profile and thought he seemed okay, so I accepted it and we've been messaging on and off ever since."

Sam rolled her eyes and sighed.

"Did you have any mutual friends?"

"Yes actually, a few. And like I said, I checked his profile out and he seems like a genuinely nice guy," I said, a touch defensively.

"Grace, I can't believe you are so naïve sometimes. You do realise half the people sending these random requests are weirdos, don't you? Why did he pick you out of the blue I wonder?"

"I suppose I must have come up on his profile at some point, you know how it suggests people you might know, friends of friends? He's from Ireland, so maybe there's a link with all the sailing I did over there? I don't know to be honest. Anyway, it's just a bit of fun and quite nice to have some flirty male attention, even though we both know it's going nowhere."

I laughed and showed her his profile picture.

"Aidan Flynn...solid Irish name he's got there. He's certainly easy on the eye, I'll give you that. If that's actually him of course," she added, suspiciously. "Have you googled him?"

"Yes I have as a matter of fact," I replied proudly. "Not much came up. Just a couple of press articles about lifeboat rescues he was involved in and a thing about a business award...he's in the building trade apparently, renovation and property development."

From the look on Sam's face, she was not convinced.

"Don't worry. I'm not planning on marrying him! Like I said, I'm just having a bit of a laugh and I'm sure it's the same for him."

I had to admit, I didn't entirely trust Aidan either and wondered if maybe the reason he had not suggested meeting up in person was that he already had a girlfriend. Or a wife.

It all started soon after I got back from Austria when I was feeling particularly low about the way things had turned out and my leg was killing me. I put a few posts on Facebook of my leg in the brace with my shiny red crutches next to me and a sad face emoji to elicit the sympathy vote from all my pals. When Aidan sent me a friend request, I just assumed he must know me from somewhere, probably sailing, given that his profile picture was a photo of him on a boat. As soon as I accepted, he followed it up with a light-hearted message of encouragement:

Good luck with those crutches! Remember it's up to Heaven with the good leg, down to Hell with the bad. Been there, done that! X

I hated that phrase, having heard it countless times before, trotted out glibly by Daniel after his helicopter crash, when he was finally able to try walking again on his crutches. Aidan had no way of knowing that of course, so I could hardly hold it against him.

Sam stopped scrolling through the Facebook profile and handed me back my phone.

"Well, he looks okay I suppose, but I'd still be very careful how much you tell him about yourself."

"Oh, believe me, I am. It's all very light-hearted, just a bit of banter to relieve the boredom at the moment, nothing more. Anyway, stop sounding like my mum and go get the paperwork for the rally. Let's see what we need to be doing," I said, anxious to change the subject.

It was still almost three months until our trip to Madagascar, but there were some things we had to get sorted well in advance, mainly an international driving permit, adequate travel insurance, vaccinations and malaria tablets. And of course, team T-shirts. After extensive trawling of the internet, we eventually settled on black ones, with 'Girls just wanna have fun' written across the front in bright pink and a logo of a jeep with pink flames coming from the wheels. Perfect.

I had to admit I knew almost nothing about Madagascar, except that it was an island off the east coast of Africa and someone had made a very successful animated film about it. 'Penguins of Madagascar' also rang a bell, but I was pretty sure that was some kind of joke and there were no actual penguins on the island. I started doing some research and the more I read, the more captivated and fascinated I became. I learned that there were apparently over one hundred species of lemur on Madagascar, many of them sadly endangered today and that the island was once roamed by the now extinct giant lemurs, similar in size to a male gorilla. I looked at photos on Instagram of the tropical rain forests, the vast mountain ranges, the stunning beaches with desert islands dotted around in the turquoise blue waters, the prehistoric rock formations, the baobab forests… and I fell in love with it. Madagascar looked like everything I had ever dreamed of and more.

"Oh wow, have you seen how cute this is?" I asked, leaning over to show Sam a close up of a lemur's face, looking straight into the camera. "It's like a gorgeous little teddy bear. Do you think we'll see them in the wild?"

"We'll be there for nearly five weeks, so I'm guessing they can't all hide from us," Sam laughed, then groaned as my phone pinged again.

"Is it that bloody Aidan again?" she asked. "His behaviour is a bit too much 'crazy stalker' for my liking. I'd be getting rid if I were you."

"Yeah, you might be right. I'll ignore him for the moment," I replied, resisting the temptation to check the message. The thing was with Aidan, there would be days of radio silence until I had pretty much forgotten all about him, then all of a sudden there would be a flurry of flirty messages from him. It wasn't like I was obsessing about him or desperate to hear from him exactly, but when he did get in touch he always made me laugh and I suppose I couldn't help being flattered by the attention.

As I drifted off to sleep that night, there was no room for Daniel in my head. My dreams were happy ones of white sand beaches, crystal clear seas and giant lemurs, until I was jolted awake at three in the morning by a noise like a pneumatic drill beside my head. I was thrown into a panic as I recognized my phone ring tone and fumbled to answer it with clumsy fingers. One thing was certain, anyone who called at that time was not calling with good news and I immediately assumed the worst. But to my surprise, the name on the caller display was neither Mum nor my brother. It was Ellie.

"Ellie, what is it? Are you okay?" I asked, guilty at the relief I felt when I realised it was not bad news about my own family.

"Grace, you need to get over to the yard. There's been a fire," she blurted out without preamble.

"What?"

My brain struggled to process what she had just said.

"Oh shit, no! No! Is Valentino ok? Ellie, please tell me he's ok," I pleaded, desperate for her not to say the words I was dreading.

"I think so, yes. He got out of the stable somehow, but we're not sure where he is. He must have panicked and run off, but I haven't had a chance to look for him yet...I had to try to help here first. Grace, this is the worst thing I've ever seen in my life. It's like a scene from Hell..." she trailed off, clearly in shock.

"I'm on my way now," I said, leaping out of bed as fast as my injured leg would allow and dragging on my clothes from the previous day. Sam was already in the doorway, a concerned look on her face.

"What's happened? Is it your mum?"

"No, there's been a fire at the yard. Ellie thinks Valentino got out somehow, but she didn't say anything about the others. I need to get over there."

"Oh dear God, that's horrific. Give me five minutes."

We arrived at the yard within fifteen minutes, to find the fire brigade had responded quickly and had already got the fire under control, but the scene of devastation and despair that remained was utterly heart breaking. The acrid smell of charred wood hung in the air and the whole place was shrouded in an eerie cloud of thick smoke. Owners, yard staff and helpers were all wandering around the place in a daze, tending to the rest of the horses, who had been let out into the paddocks to give them the best chance of survival if the fire spread further. Others were just staring at the wreckage in disbelief and horror, clinging to each other in the hope of some kind of comfort as they watched the fire crew at work.

Juliet, the yard owner, had been awakened by the noise of horses kicking at their stable doors, but by the time she raised the alarm the blaze had already taken hold in the wooden chalet that was used as an office. It quickly spread to the front stable block and barn where Valentino and five other horses lived, the flames ripping unchecked through the wooden barn, full of hay and straw. In the few minutes it took Juliet and her husband Mike to get there, the centre of the barn looked like a volcano and the whole roof was ablaze. The frantic squeals and wild kicking of the horses that were still alive and desperately trying to get out of there would undoubtedly haunt them for the rest of time. Incredibly, they managed to half saw, half smash through a section of the back wall, blindfold two of the terrified geldings and drag them to safety. They were badly burned, traumatised and suffering from smoke inhalation, but they were alive and that was all that mattered. The three nearest the chalet, where it looked like the fire had started, were not so lucky. I began to shake uncontrollably and tears streamed down my face as I relived the time I was trapped in a burning car, fighting for my life, running out of strength and choking to death. I couldn't breathe and the terror I felt was as real as it had been that day.

"Grace," said Sam gently. "Grace, come on. You have to pull yourself together or you'll be no use here. You have to stay strong."

She was right. The sight that greeted us was indeed grim, but at least I could cling to the hope that Ellie was right and Valentino had somehow escaped the inferno. She came straight over when she saw me, eyes bloodshot from the smoke and dirt-stained face streaked with tears.

"We've lost Simba, Rio and Tarin," she stated flatly, seeming to stare right through me. "I just can't believe this is happening. They must have been so scared, trapped in their stables. We tried, we really did, but there was nothing we could do to help them...I'll never forgive myself," she finished, before dissolving once again into tears.

"Come on Ellie, it's not your fault. This is a terrible, terrible accident. No one blames you, but please just tell me...are you sure Valentino got out?"

Ellie nodded her head, thankful to be able to deliver at least one fragment of good news.

"Positive. You know what he's like, 'Houdini horse' we always called him."

"Yeah, I know. He could undo the bolts and get himself out of any stable. The times he's been found wandering around the yard, helping himself to hay and carrots and winding the others up…," I trailed off, remembering the other beautiful horses who would not be there for him to wind up ever again.

"He definitely wasn't in his stable so he must have run off up the field in a panic. I'll grab a head collar and some first aid stuff, just in case."

I could hardly bear to look at the faces of the people we passed as we trudged through the yard to the fields. A strange and surreal calmness seemed to have descended on the whole place. The horses in the nearest field were mostly together in the top corner, grazing quietly as if they had already accepted that life had to go on. Some were being led back down to their stables in the two barns untouched by the fire on the other side of the yard. There was no sign of Valentino in the early dawn light and I began to feel increasingly uneasy. I called his name, but there was nothing. Then I saw the smashed fence at the top of the field and the trailing electric wire. On the far side of the next field, I could make out the shape of a horse and knew instantly it was my beautiful boy. He was facing us, head hanging down with his front leg resting awkwardly and, as we slowly walked closer, it became clear that he was tangled in wire. He threw his head up as we approached and began to squeal and struggle, making it worse for himself, but clearly not willing to trust us to help him. His rug was ripped to shreds, there was a deep gash on his chest, from which blood was running down his legs and his face was burned on one side, not to mention the damage he had potentially done to his leg with the wire. We stopped and crouched lower, making soothing noises to try to calm him down.

"Christ, Ellie, he's in a mess," I said, tears springing to my eyes. My boy may have survived the fire, but he had certainly not come out of the nightmare unscathed. "Let me try on my own."

I felt in my pocket for the treats I had shoved in there and offered them to him on my outstretched hand, whispering gently as I began to limp forward, desperately trying not to spook him again. There was a flicker of recognition in his eyes and he flared his nostrils and snorted in anticipation of the treats. Clearly exhausted and in pain, he gave in and allowed me to go right up to him. I stroked his neck gently and kissed his nose, murmuring words of comfort to him as he munched and I tried to assess the damage. Ellie and Sam joined me and between us, we managed to unwrap the wire from his legs, but it was clear that one leg was badly damaged where the wire had cut into it. We set about wrapping makeshift bandages with thick pads underneath to cover the wounds on his legs and chest and stop the bleeding. His poor burned face was too sore for him to allow us anywhere near with the head collar, so I threw the lead rope loosely around his neck and the three of us began to coax him gently back towards the stables, where the vet was already on site and treating the injured horses. Ellie had phoned one of the yard hands from the field and told her to get a stable ready in the block furthest away from the fire. As a crippled Valentino hobbled his way valiantly across the yard, several people came over to fuss him and help guide him to his new stable, all of them relieved and grateful beyond words to see another survivor of the terrible fire.

The vet came over within a few minutes of us getting him into the stable and began undoing the bandages to see what we were dealing with. He was happy that the burn to his face, although clearly sore, would heal well given time and it was a similar story with his chest wound, despite the amount of blood. There were a number of other superficial lesions, probably caused by him crashing through the fence at the top of the field in a blind panic, but the vet assured me they were nothing to worry too much about either. He was less positive about the leg injury.

"I am concerned about the depth of the wound and whether the coffin bone or the pastern joint have been affected," he said, delivering his crushing words with matter-of-fact professionalism.

"Injuries that are deep enough to cause damage to those structures can result in long-term lameness and other complications further down the line, such as osteoarthritis. And of course there's the risk of infection. It's only fair to warn you that, worst-case scenario, it may be...."

"No!" I interrupted, refusing to let him say those words. "No, I don't want to even think about that. You need to do everything, and I mean everything you can to put him right. I don't care how much it costs," I added somewhat recklessly, but knowing I would sell everything I had, including a kidney if necessary, to save my horse of a lifetime.

"I'm sorry if I'm upsetting you, I just have to be sure you understand that this is serious. Obviously I'll do everything I can to make sure it doesn't come to that. I've cleaned the wound now, so I'll stitch it, bandage it and then we start by giving him some time to rest and hopefully it will heal. I'm going to show you how to dress the other wounds on his face and chest and remember, the most important thing is to keep everything clean to avoid any infection. I'll give him a shot of antibiotics as well and we'll keep him on bute for the pain until I see him again in a few days. Oh, and don't underestimate the psychological effect on him of what he's been through tonight."

"I won't. And thank you for all you've done for him."

I looked Valentino in the eye as the vet left and promised him he would be okay. I stood there while he rested his sedated head on my shoulder, gently blowing into his nostrils and stroking his velvety nose. Sam and Ellie had gone off to help in the clear-up operation of the yard, so it was just the two of us.

"We'll get through this together, sweetheart. I know you can do it, my brave, clever boy," I whispered, salty tears running down my cheeks and onto his face. My heart was breaking and I felt his pain a hundred times more acutely than if it were my own.

Guilty Pleasure

Daniel

Daniel's guilty pleasure was inflicting pain on others. It always had been, ever since he was a kid, ripping the wings and legs off insects and watching them writhe around in confusion before brutally stamping the life out of them. It was only a matter of time until he moved on to human targets and never tired of finding new and inventive ways to torture his victims, then sitting back and watching the carnage unfold. He quickly worked out that the most satisfying form of torture, both psychological and physical, was when the victim had no idea who the perpetrator actually was. The ultimate achievement in his eyes was when they actually believed the tormentor was on their side, helping them, comforting them. It made the game so much more interesting. Daniel had always despised people, especially women, who went through life following the rules of society like sheep and abiding by conventions imposed on them. They deserved everything they got in his opinion. Grace had temporarily got one over on him and he was naturally furious about that, but he had to admit it made the game more exciting and so much more of a challenge now that she had shown a bit of backbone.

Caitlin 'nice but dim' was out at work, having polished her halo in readiness for a day at the health centre, caring for the sick and needy folk of the area. On the plus side for her, however, she had scored a solid nine out of ten in the laundry category on his spreadsheet last time he was away. He had been forced to deduct a point for failing to iron his boxer shorts, but hopefully she would remedy that, now that he had told her about it.

Daniel settled himself on the sofa in front of the fire with his feet on the coffee table, knowing how much Caitlin hated that habit. Now that he came to think of it, all the women he had ever known, with the exception of Jane, hated him putting his feet on the table. Screw them. The whole day stretched ahead of him and he intended to enjoy having some time to himself at last.

Daniel sniggered to himself as he opened Aidan Flynn's Facebook page on his laptop, using the password he had found written in the little notebook at the back of the bedside table drawer and checked Messenger, only to find Grace had continued to ignore his latest flirtation. He supposed that was understandable, given all the recent drama in her life, but he also knew how her mind worked and the way she always had to spill her guts to her friends in a crisis. He switched to Grace's profile and scrolled through all the recent posts. Yet again, it appeared she had dodged a bullet, or rather that evil bastard of a horse had. Daniel had never forgiven Valentino for biting him on the neck when he went to see him with Grace one day and didn't mind him being collateral damage in his game plan one little bit. In fact it was a bonus. In some ways, it actually worked out better and would destroy Grace more completely if the horse suffered for a few weeks, *then* had to be put down. His contact had done well.

The skiing accident and the ensuing broken leg had been a bit of an unexpected treat if Daniel was honest. When he messed with the bindings in a temper before dropping the skis off to her, it had been a peevish stab in the dark. He had half assumed she would be bright enough to check them and find out what he had done, but apparently not. Knowing how much she loved skiing, with a bit of luck that would be her days on the slopes over. The yard fire on the other hand had taken a lot of thought and careful planning, not to mention money, but he was satisfied with the result. Daniel knew that people felt pain far more acutely when it was not their own pain, but rather that of someone close to them, which was why he had decided to get the ball rolling by hurting Grace through the medium of her beloved horse.

The late Aidan Flynn, lifeboat hero and all round good guy, risen from the dead like Lazarus, was now providing Daniel with the perfect cover to be able to reach out and comfort Grace in her hour of need. Daniel began typing.

I've just seen your post about the stable fire. Absolutely horrendous! You must be beside yourself with worry about your beautiful horse, but I'm just so glad he survived the fire. How is he doing now? How are you, more to the point? Xx

He added the red love heart, followed by a sad face emoji and hit send. To his delight, Grace responded almost immediately.

Utterly devastated. Lost 3 horses. Tino is hanging in there…vet says he's done all he can and we just have to give him time xx

Daniel was pleased to note the two kisses.

Do they know what caused the fire? Xx

Seems to be accidental, started by a kerosene heater left on in the chalet, but a few things not adding up…not ruling out arson.

(Shocked face emoji) Seriously??? What kind of sick bastard does something like that, knowing that innocent animals could die? (two angry face emojis) xx

As Daniel hit send on that last one, he silently congratulated himself on the brilliance of his new deception. Even in the event that they did decide it was arson, there was absolutely nothing to link him to it and he was confident his contact would have covered his own tracks. He was a professional at the end of the day. All

93

roads would lead to a big, fat nothing and the case would have to be closed.

Grace had not replied, so Daniel tried again to engage with her.

Are you ok? xx

After a little pause, she came back to him.

Yeah fine… just a bit busy. Thanx for the message. I'll let you know how he's doing xx

Daniel pulled a face at 'Thanx'. He was not a fan of the whole 'dot dot dot' thing either. He hated all forms of text speech and made a point of always composing his messages in full sentences and with correct punctuation. He didn't want to frighten Grace off by being too pushy, so he left her to it for the moment and turned his attention to Roisin.

Unlike all the other women in his life, past and present, Roisin did not constantly pester him when he was away from her with a load of needy texts and emails. Daniel found the fact that she didn't really seem to care what he was up to strangely perturbing and he wasn't sure he liked it. He liked it a whole lot less when, three hours after sending her a message, leaving a voicemail and sending an email, he received no response from her. When the reply eventually came, with some sort of excuse about leaving her phone at home and only just having seen the messages when she got back from work, he decided to teach her a lesson and ignore her until the following day. It was important to establish who was in control of their relationship and Daniel had no intention of it being her.

Being a great believer in keeping his options open he devoted a large part of the afternoon to trawling through the various profiles that came up as matches for his alter ego Patrick Salenden on the numerous dating sites he still frequented. He had no wish to overstretch himself at the moment, given all the stuff going on with

Grace, but there was no harm in window shopping and he had always felt that variety was the spice of life. To his great amusement, two of the matches that came up were Jane and Lorraine, both of them obviously putting it out there again, sad old tarts. He was sorely tempted to start chatting with them, just for a laugh, but thought better of it, given that the potential for it all to get messy was huge. The pair of them had done very nicely out of his 'death' so far as he could see from their social media posts. He clenched his fist at the thought of the cars that had been transferred into Jane's name during the divorce, the trust fund paid for by Jupiter Holdings for Aaron's private education and the house in Oxfordshire he had renovated with Lorraine. As for Anita, she had plenty of money of her own from her inheritance to keep her and Tara very comfortable out there on Rhode Island. His conscience was clear. In fact, he was the real victim in all this, so far as he could see.

Daniel jumped as he heard the sound of someone trying the door handle, then the key in the lock. Caitlin was home early.

"I have no idea why you always insist on locking yourself in the house, Patrick," she laughed as she kicked her boots off in the hallway. "No-one ever comes out here uninvited."

"Force of habit I guess," he replied, shrugging his shoulders.

And of course, the locked door acted as an early warning system to make sure she didn't catch him off guard.

Daniel closed his laptop and reluctantly got to his feet to greet her.

"I didn't realise the time, to be honest. I've been working all day since you went out and still haven't finished my report for the guy in Dublin. I'll be up there with him most of next week I'm afraid."

"No problem," she replied cheerfully. "I've got a busy week myself. And besides, we've got our holiday to look forward to. I think I've found the perfect place, so I'll get it booked next week," she announced.

"Great."

Daniel put on his enthusiastic face and made a mental note to prepare the ground with Roisin. He should get in early and give her a plausible reason for being away over Christmas. Lord knew he had had enough practice at that in the past and Grace had always seemed to buy it. A particular favourite of his was a half-truth about factories shutting down production over the Christmas period, making it the perfect time for them to have new machinery installed. It was a known fact in the engineering world and provided him with a reasonably plausible reason to be away from home. On numerous occasions, he had been able to happily tuck into his Christmas dinner on the other side of the pond, far away from Grace, fully immersed in another life altogether.

He paused for a moment to consider whether he should use his excuse on Caitlin instead and opt to spend Christmas with Roisin. He realised he had some important decisions to make.

The Truth will Out

Caitlin

Caitlin was not the pushover 'Patrick', or whoever he really was, took her for. She did not like being made a fool of and had learned over the years that the only person she could truly rely on was herself. Everything always seemed to go wrong for her and she was sick and tired of being dealt such an unfair hand in life. She was not entirely convinced about the trips to Dublin and what he was up to there, but she intended to find out what was going on and if he thought he was going to leave her high and dry after all she had done for him…well, he was sorely mistaken. Patrick Salenden would see a very different side to Caitlin Flynn if he chose to go down that particular route.

The fact that she had not been able to find out anything at all about his past life was torturing her. She lay in bed alone, while he was away working in Dublin, racking her brains for some kind of clue. She had been through every single item of clothing he owned with a fine-tooth comb, even checking for concealed pockets that might contain a bank card or a passport, but she found nothing. A thorough examination of his briefcase while he slept one night also produced a blank. As did a search of all other potential hiding places, such as between the mattress and the bed frame, behind the heavy oak wardrobe, behind the radiator. She even explored the possibility that he may have created a false floor in the wardrobe or unscrewed a mirror from the wall to place something behind it, but all to no avail.

The answer came to her out of the blue one night and it was so obvious that she cursed herself for not having thought of it before. Patrick had told her his company was called Jupiter Holdings, registered in Delaware for tax reasons a couple of years ago. She had already tried searching for information there and found nothing, but he had told her he had been in business for many years, so what if the company had originally been registered in the UK? Companies House was obliged to make all information freely available in the public domain, including names of directors, so maybe she would find out what she needed there.

At two-thirty in the morning, having had her light bulb moment, Caitlin padded downstairs in her slippers, made herself a cup of black coffee and settled down at the kitchen table with her laptop in front of her and Bentley at her feet.

And there it was. Jupiter Holdings UK. Directors: Patrick Salenden and Daniel Callaghan. Caitlin almost choked on her coffee in excitement. At last, she had a name.

Three hours later, as dawn broke, she had a lot more than a name. Now, she had the much more difficult task of deciding what exactly she was going to do with all the newfound information.

A Time to Shine

Open your heart and soul to every new adventure, because if you do not challenge yourself, you may never know the person you could become.

Grace

"*I still can't* believe this is actually happening," I said, talking to Sam's image on my iPhone.

Born in South Africa, Sam had decided to take the opportunity of stopping off there to visit family before the rally, so we would be travelling separately.

"Don't forget your yoga mat so we can do some stretches and stuff. We'll need it after all the driving," she reminded me.

"Already packed," I said, laughing. "I can't wait."

"I know; me too. And remember we deserve this. It'll be amazing. Safe flight and I'll see you in Tana."

She blew me a kiss.

"Yep, see you Tuesday," I replied, blowing a kiss back and ending the call.

In just two days' time I would be on a plane to Paris, where I would have a short wait before boarding the eleven-hour Air France flight direct to Antananarivo, Madagascar. I had planned my five weeks away like a military operation where Valentino, Lola and Mum were concerned, but I still couldn't help fussing around and fretting about them all. I had to admit it was nice for me to feel needed, but in reality I wasn't as indispensable as I liked to think and the world was certainly not going to stop turning just because I went away for a few weeks.

Mum was doing amazingly after the stroke and her speech had come on in leaps and bounds, although life was obviously not without its challenges. She would be in safe hands with Jeremy and Phoebe, not to mention the fact that she would have my adorable Lola for company. Luke and the girls had promised to take it in turns to walk her each day with their own dogs, so she would undoubtedly be living the dream, spoiled rotten and wasting no time in getting them all wrapped around her little paw.

That just left Valentino. Since the fire he was still not back to his old self and I was beginning to wonder if he ever would be. The injuries to his face and chest had indeed healed well without leaving any ongoing problems other than some scarring, but I had to remember the vet had warned me I was in it for the long haul and it was possible I would never be able to ride him again. He was still not sound and the internal tendon damage to his leg meant several months of box rest with only a little light exercise in the form of in-hand walking around the yard. That didn't matter to me and I vowed he could take all the time he needed to recover. I spent time with him every day, grooming him and pampering him like the superstar he was, counting my blessings he was a horse who enjoyed the comforts of his stable rather than being turned out in the field. Ultimately, if he had to live out the rest of his days in happy retirement, that was fine by me.

Ellie was still working at the yard and was more than happy to care for him while I was away, although she had come close to being sacked after the fire, unfairly accused of negligence. Forensics established that the fire had indeed started in the chalet office when the kerosene heater was left on unattended and somehow fell over.

The investigations also revealed that the door had been locked, with no sign of forced entry, which immediately pointed the finger at Ellie and the other girls as the only ones who could have been responsible. Added to that was the fact that they had apparently failed to store a can of flammable fuel properly, allowing the fire to spread rapidly across to the barn.

It all seemed so cut and dried to an outsider, but I knew for certain there was no way that Ellie or any of the other girls could have been so stupid. She was utterly distraught when she came to see me after the fire investigation report.

"Someone has done this and made it look like I was responsible because I promise you, there is absolutely no way I left that heater on. The only time I ever used it was when there was a power cut in the middle of winter. So far as I knew, it was still in the bloody cupboard," she sobbed. "I just can't bear the fact that people actually think I killed those horses. I would never, ever do something so stupid, please believe me."

"Of course I believe you, so stop beating yourself up. But we can't get away from the fact that *somebody* left it on and *somebody* spilled fuel everywhere. If it wasn't any of you guys from the yard, then we have to face the fact that someone else got in there and started the fire deliberately. Someone actually went there with the express intention of harming those horses and maybe even people as well."

The overturned can of kerosene outside the chalet was particularly suspicious and meant that the fire investigation team did not rule out arson at first, but a full sweep of the area revealed no evidence of outside involvement: no footprints, other than those of yard staff and clients, no fingerprints, no tyre tracks, no leads at all for them to act on. In the end, the cause of the fire was deemed to be accidental, but I was left with the disturbing feeling we would never really know the truth about what happened that night.

Little by little, things returned to normal at the yard and people began to trust each other again. A full CCTV system was installed and a night watchman was employed to give everyone peace of mind, at least for a while. When Ellie told me she had split up with her boyfriend and was looking for somewhere to live, it seemed the perfect solution for her to move in with me temporarily as my lodger. That would pay for the cost of livery for Valentino and it would also mean that she could look after the house while I was away travelling. All of a sudden, although I hardly dared believe it, it seemed like things were falling into place for me.

I turned my attention back to the holdall on the bed and the final bits of packing ready for the trip. We had decided on outfits mostly revolving around shorts, tee shirts and the trusty Timberland boots, with several layering options for cooler weather and of course a couple of dresses and a pair of sandals to glam things up in the evenings, should the opportunity arise. We had been warned it could be cold in the mountains and the rainforest, so I stuffed several pairs of leggings in, together with some long-sleeved tops and jumpers and was planning to travel in jeans and a hoodie. I surveyed the bulging holdall, establishing with some dismay that it was on the limit of my baggage allowance weight and wondering what happened to my 'travelling light' resolution. My phone pinged with a message and I smiled to myself as I saw Aidan's name on the screen.

You must be ready for off, I guess. I just wanted to say I hope you have an amazing time on holiday with your friend. Take care of yourself and don't forget about those of us stuck here doing the boring stuff like work (sad face emoji) xx

I smiled, thinking how nice it was to have someone who cared about me and wanted me to stay safe. Then I reminded myself that I didn't really know this man and our 'relationship' was based purely on a bit of meaningless online flirtation. I considered unfriending him, but couldn't bring myself to do it as it felt rude somehow. That was the ridiculous thing about Facebook, the way it could make you feel guilty about upsetting someone who was effectively a complete stranger. On the other hand, maybe he was waiting for me to make the first move and suggest meeting up in person. I made a spur-of-the-moment decision to take the bull by the horns and put that at the top of my 'to do' list when I returned home after the rally. In the meantime, I settled for a brief reply to end the conversation, but left the door wide open for further interaction.

Aww, poor you! Sorry no time to chat now…msg soon Xx

Of course, if I had met him in the flesh, I would have known that the real Aidan Flynn hated texting and always preferred to speak on the phone. I would also have known that, on the occasions that he did send a message, he never used the stupid emoji things and never stuck random, pointless kisses on at the end.

Most importantly of all, I would have known that messaging in any shape or form was no longer an option for the real Aidan Flynn.

Part II

The Journey

par·ou·si·a

An ancient Greek word meaning presence, arrival or official visit. More especially it may mean 'presence after absence' and is often used as an alternative word for the second coming.

A Different World

Do not travel to escape painful memories, do it to create wonderful new ones.

Grace

I closed my book on Madagascar and fastened my seatbelt in preparation for landing, a mixture of excitement and nerves making my stomach churn. It would be eight-thirty in the evening on the island, just two hours ahead of the UK, so no jet lag to worry about. Sam was due to arrive earlier in the day, so she should already be in the hotel if everything had gone to plan. I had no idea what to expect at the airport but hoped to goodness that someone would be there to meet me as promised. This was already way out of my comfort zone, given that I never travelled alone if I could help it. I was the sort of traveller who liked to hand over my tickets, passport and money to a friend for safekeeping when navigating the airports, happy that, in doing so, I had given my documents the best possible chance of arriving at the same destination as me. The plane shuddered as the pilot lowered the undercarriage and instructed the cabin crew to take their seats for landing. This was it.

Half an hour later, as I trailed along behind the hordes of passengers piling in through the doors of the airport building, it quickly became obvious that chaos reigned supreme. There were people milling around everywhere, all trying to get through the passport and visa checks at the same time. When I eventually made it through the pandemonium and into the baggage reclaim area, my heart sank once more at the sight before me and I immediately abandoned all hope of ever seeing my bag again. The place was packed and bags were piled high all around, having either fallen off or been thrown off the carousel. Panic was beginning to set in as I realized it was already after ten at night and I still had no idea how I was going to find the people I was supposed to meet up with. What if they had got fed up waiting for me and gone home? I forced myself to take a deep breath and get a grip. I had been to Africa three times before and survived the experience, so surely it was not beyond my capabilities to organise a taxi to get myself from the airport to the hotel if needs be. Suddenly, against all the odds I spotted my blue holdall on the carousel and, shamelessly shoving people out of the way, I pounced on it, dragged it to safety and offered up a silent prayer that I had at least been reunited with my clothes. Feeling considerably more optimistic, I marched purposefully towards the exit, dragging the bag along the floor behind me as it was too heavy to carry. It was impossible to get Malagasy currency in the UK, so we had been advised to take euros or dollars in cash and make sure we changed money at the airport, as the ATM situation was not quite what we were used to in Europe. The exchange of money was an experience in itself and seemed to all take place in little kiosks at the airport entrance, run by people who looked more like loan sharks or ticket touts than bank employees. With some trepidation, I approached one of them, who immediately beckoned me over with an encouraging smile. A few minutes later, I nervously handed over three hundred euros and received over one million Ariary in a slightly tatty and well-used brown paper envelope in return. The local currency was clearly going to be a challenge and it looked dangerously like toy money.

"Grace King?"

I turned round in the direction of the person calling my name and all worries vanished as I established that the voice belonged to a friendly, youngish man holding out his hand to me in greeting, an infectious smile spread across his features.

"Welcome to Madagascar!" he said, taking my bag in one hand and guiding me out towards the car park with the other. "You must be exhausted after your journey."

I smiled back at him and followed obediently, delighted that someone else was now responsible for me.

"It wasn't so bad, to be honest. I'm just happy to be here at last."

The man introduced himself as Mika and told me proudly that he would be one of our local guides for the duration of the rally, together with his father, Andry, and a whole entourage of drivers, mechanics and general hangers-on, whose names he reeled off for me with the apparent expectation that I would somehow be able to remember them all. It seemed our rally was a huge deal for the country and people were falling over themselves to get a piece of the action. He chatted away happily to me, imparting various bits of tourist information as we made our way through Tana, up and down streets and alleyways that looked as though they were never intended for cars, horns blaring as people and animals wandered all over the road, completely oblivious to traffic. Also in the mix were the motor scooters and bikes, weaving their way in and out of the lines of cars with a dangerous lack of any caution whatsoever. Every junction we came to was a free for all, with a total absence of functioning traffic lights or any other form of effective control to establish right of way. I began to sweat at the thought that Sam and I might actually have to drive through the town at some point because in all honesty, I couldn't see it ending well.

It was after midnight when we eventually pulled up outside the Carlton Hotel and Sam came running out to meet me at the entrance.

"What took you so long at the airport? I was beginning to get worried about you in case you'd been arrested or something," she laughed.

"It was pure carnage in the baggage hall and don't even get me started on the visa check situation…but hey, I'm here now, so it's all good. May the adventures begin!" I announced dramatically, having watched The Hunger Games on the flight.

Ten minutes later we were up in our room, which felt strangely detached from the reality of the bustling streets in the capital below. Sam was clearly exhausted and, after raiding the minibar for a quick nightcap, she could no longer keep her eyes open, but I was far too excited to sleep. I lay awake for ages, thinking about all the strange twists of fate that had brought me to that point.

I couldn't help my thoughts returning to the anguish of the night I received the email from Lorraine and all the heartache and pain that ensued. And yet without that email, I would still have been living a lie, frighteningly oblivious to the fact that I was trapped in a toxic marriage, my life effectively on hold while my husband was busy making memories with countless other women. I was determined to focus on the future and stop dwelling on the past, but somehow, especially at night, Daniel still managed to slither his way into my thoughts. Another lifetime, another me, but as I finally drifted off to sleep, I wondered if I could ever truly be free of him.

Sam and I had decided to fly out three days early for the rally, just in case there were any problems and to give us chance to see the capital Antananarivo, known as Tana. I eagerly threw back the curtains on that first morning in Madagascar to be greeted by bright sunshine streaming through the window and over the city below us, where daily life was already in full swing. George Coulthard, the owner of Venture Rallies and his assistant Suzie Aston had flown in the same day as us and were already downstairs having breakfast when we sauntered into the restaurant at about ten. George immediately called us over to introduce himself and had an air of calm authority about him, which told me that this rally had been meticulously planned down to the last detail, but I also noticed there was no mistaking the mischievous sense of humour behind his organiser's face. Suzie was equally calm and professional, but with a dazzling smile and a wicked glint in her eye that made it obvious she would be great fun to hang out with. They had work to do in the morning, but the four of us arranged to meet up a little later for a tour of the city and a bit of shopping, during which it was quickly established that we would become firm friends. The city was manically busy again when we ventured out, with people, cars and motorcycles everywhere and no apparent rules for driving, but somehow it all just seemed to work and I already felt as if I was becoming acclimatized to the chaos, learning to relax and go with the flow.

Throughout the day, our fellow rallygoers arrived in dribs and drabs at the hotel and the plan was that everyone would meet up for pre-dinner drinks in the bar that evening. So far, all I had to go on was a list of names, so I was both curious and nervous to begin putting faces to names, knowing that these people inhabited a world I had no prior experience of whatsoever. They had all done countless rallies before this one, shipping their wonderful classic cars all over the world to some of the most exotic and at times dangerous places on the planet and I was acutely conscious of the fact that their lives seemed infinitely more interesting and exciting than mine. Even Sam had done several rallies before with Charles, so I felt more than a little out of my depth as I walked into the bar, trying my best to give the impression I was confident and relaxed.

The first to break the ice and introduce themselves were Ross, Greg and Brad, the three amigos from Australia, and within minutes we were laughing and joking with them as if we had all known each other for years. It turned out that Greg shared the same birthday as me, the day before the rally started and I had a feeling it would be a joint Aussie-style celebration I would never forget, given that he was already making preparations by stocking up on the local vanilla rum.

A man sitting on a bar stool turned towards me and immediately extended his hand in greeting, giving his name as Richard Alder. I remembered his name from the list of participants we had been given. This was Sir Richard Alder and the elegant Chinese lady at his side was his wife, Lady Meili Alder. As I shook his hand and told him my name, I noticed he had the most wonderfully engaging smile, as did his wife, and they both emanated a zest for life that drew people into their orbit. As first impressions went, I honestly couldn't have imagined a nicer bunch of people to spend the next four weeks with.

The morning of my birthday was the day of the rally briefing and also the big day when we got to meet our cars. A fleet of shiny white Ford Explorers awaited in the hotel car park and Sam and I were delighted to be given the keys to car number 7, a lucky number for both of us. We were handed a form and told to do a thorough inspection of the car, marking any dents or scratches on the diagram with a cross, so that there could be no arguments over returning our deposits after the rally. We were taking no chances there, so I promptly obliterated the picture of the car on the form with crosses, just to make sure, while Sam took a video. With the help of Ross, we even managed to check the oil and coolant level and I secretly vowed to learn more about basic car maintenance on my return home. Once the serious business was out of the way we headed off to the pool for a birthday cocktail in the sun, settling on a 'Gasikara' for the exorbitant sum of seventeen thousand Ariary, which we worked out was actually about a fiver. We sat down on the loungers by the pool to catch the last of the afternoon sun and had just raised a toast to new beginnings for both of us when my phone pinged with a message.

Happy birthday, gorgeous. Hope you're having fun xx

Aidan. I smirked at the 'gorgeous' in spite of myself and, even though it was cheesy in the extreme, I couldn't help feeling flattered.

Sam rolled her eyes and I laughed, putting my phone on silent and shoving it into my bag. This was our sisterhood adventure and I had no intention of letting Aidan gate crash the party. His time would come when we got home and he would just have to be patient until then.

It was a confident, happy me that walked into the bar that evening, bubbling with enthusiasm and high on life. I looked around me, soaking up every detail of my surroundings and loving the buzz of excitement and anticipation in the various conversations of my new travel companions. The official rally briefing and gala dinner that followed reminded me of the many sailing regattas I had done and I began to feel the wonderful bond that comes from being part of a team, as I listened to people reminiscing about their many previous adventures and wondering what tales they would have to tell about this new one. At the end of the evening, the lights were suddenly dimmed and a huge cake for me and my 'birthday twin' Greg arrived, covered in flowers with a giant sparkler in the middle. Serenaded by the assembled crowd with a resounding chorus of 'Happy Birthday', we stood up and cut the cake together for a joke, as if we were at a wedding. It was a perfect end to a perfect birthday.

My stars were finally aligned and my heart was full of optimism for the start of a journey that I felt sure would change the course of my life forever.

Out of Reach

Daniel

To say Daniel was furious was an understatement. That cheeky bitch Grace had not even had the decency to acknowledge his, or rather Aidan's birthday message. Then he found out what she was actually up to. A fucking car rally in Madagascar! What the hell was that all about? He had assumed she was off for a couple of weeks in Tenerife. What did *she* know about cars anyway and when had she ever shown any interest in doing anything like that? More to the point, where the hell had she got the money from to do it? This was not at all the life he had envisaged for Grace after the bankruptcy and he had a nasty suspicion that he was the one indirectly paying for it all somehow. If there was any justice in the world, she would now be living hand to mouth, struggling for every penny to try and make ends meet, forced to sell all that she owned in order to survive, especially that vicious nag she was so attached to. Yet there she was in sodding Madagascar, apparently 'living the dream'.

Unbelievable.

During the divorce proceedings, he had fully expected her to see the error of her ways, realise she was going to get nothing if she went ahead with it and accept that she needed to toe the line and do things *his* way, but to his utter disbelief and fury, she had steadfastly refused to listen to anything he said. She had acted like a woman possessed, hell-bent on robbing him blind of all that he had worked so hard to build up, even if it meant her losing everything (and he was arrogant enough to include himself there) in the process. What pained him the most now was that, even though she had ostensibly fallen flat on her face in the shit with the Trustee, it looked very much to him as if she had somehow managed to come up smelling of roses. He was not happy about that at all.

As he scrolled through her Facebook page, the recent posts and photos did nothing to improve his mood. Her and Sam sipping cocktails on sun loungers by a pool, her and Sam in front of a white 4x4 with a big number 7 sticker on the bonnet, her and some random guy cutting a massive cake together as if they were getting married. Seriously, what the fuck was she playing at? It felt like she was taunting him, laughing at him, shoving it in his face about what an amazing time she was having, while he was forced to skulk around in the shadows and play dead.

Daniel forced himself to take a deep breath and reminded himself she couldn't possibly be having a go at him, as she had no idea he was even alive. He consoled himself further by remembering the tidy sum he had finally netted in compensation as a result of the A&E doctors' ineptitude when he was brought into hospital following his helicopter crash and his face softened into a smile. He had got one over on her there, big time. Grace had been utterly convinced he had received a pay out after that whole balls-up, but he had vehemently denied it and she had failed spectacularly to find any evidence to prove otherwise. One day he would take great pleasure in letting her know just how much money she had missed out on and how ingenious he had been in hiding it. He began to feel calmer as he told himself he was still the one on top. That wasn't entirely the point, however. She had managed to cause him a lot of problems one way or another and he fully intended to return the favour. With bells on.

He snapped the lid shut on his laptop and picked up his phone. He had a call to make before Caitlin got home.

The woman who answered emitted a low, gravelly laugh before speaking.

"Well, well, well. I wondered how long it would be before you resurfaced, pardon the pun."

Daniel disliked her cocky attitude and was beginning to think she may have outlived her usefulness.

"This is not a social call. Just a gentle reminder that I do have people looking after my interests while I'm away. I'm sure it's just a blip, but takings seem to be down. I assume you know better than to attempt to swindle me."

The last bit was loaded with menace and Daniel paused for a moment to allow it to sink in, then ended the call with a curt "I'll be in touch".

He had always found that the best way to ensure the continued loyalty of his employees was to hold something over them and keep them indebted to him. The woman on the end of the phone was no exception and he had enough on her to put her away for a very long time. That said, she had made an enemy of a whole host of unpleasant characters in the course of her dealings and he knew it was not the long arm of the law she feared most. A bit like him really, so he had to tread carefully.

The Big Sexy Superstore was one of the many subsidiaries of Jupiter Holdings, safely out of the Trustee's reach now that Daniel was presumed dead. Its interests were being looked after by the fictitious 'other directors', one of whom was Patrick Salenden of course. They would all realise soon enough that it would take them years and cost them a small fortune to track down those directors, following up leads far and wide across the globe, which would all come to a dead end. They would eventually be forced to give up and he could get back to business as usual. He did miss his entertaining and highly lucrative niche parties, but once everything died down he would start up again, maybe even branch out with a new venue in Ireland. He already had a few ideas about that and he also had an inkling it might be right up Roisin's street.

Daniel felt himself grow hard as he remembered the last time he had sex with Roisin. Armed with a paddle whip and a feather tickler, dressed in a PVC outfit of crotch-less panties and peephole bra, she strutted into the bedroom in a pair of killer heels, ready to make full use of the impressive array of dildos in a variety of sizes and shapes on the bedside table. To his delight, she had no objection to sharing her toys, nor did she mind him filming the proceedings. He had a feeling there were a lot more avenues to explore where she was concerned and he was just the man for the job.

With brilliant timing as ever, the door opened and Caitlin arrived home, putting an end to his potential R&R session with his home video collection. The ever-enthusiastic Bentley leapt into action and bounded over to the door to greet her.

"You haven't managed to tire him out then?" she called to Daniel, laughing as she bent down to ruffle the dog's ears.

"You must be joking. We walked for miles this morning, but he's no sooner back home than he's ready for off again," Daniel lied, having spent the morning lounging in bed, stalking Grace. Bentley had barely been through the door since Caitlin let him out first thing.

"I'll take him down to the beach then. I could do with a walk to blow the cobwebs away. Are you coming with me?"

"No, I've still got a pile of work to get through for the guy up in Dublin. He's the bane of my life at the moment, always on my back moaning about something. But I guess he's paying me well enough for the privilege."

Caitlin wandered through and put her arms around his neck from behind him, noticing how he closed the laptop lid irritably before she reached him.

"Okay, but don't work too hard. All work and no play makes Patrick a dull boy," she chided, a playful glint in her eye. "I'll be about an hour, then no more work and no more laptop for the evening. Deal?"

"Deal," he replied to shut her up, his mind on other things.

Caitlin hummed a tune as she changed into her boots and dog walking gear, then headed off towards the beach, wondering to herself what Patrick, aka Daniel, had really been up to all day.

As soon as she was out of the way, Daniel picked up his phone again. He had got himself a bit distracted thinking about Roisin, but there was someone expecting to hear back from him with a piece of information and that someone did not like to be messed around. He dialled a familiar number and waited. The call was answered with silence as usual, which Daniel found unnerving and slightly intimidating. Every communication between them was a business transaction pure and simple, straight to the point, with no place for meaningless and unnecessary small talk.

"Number seven," said Daniel, waiting for a response.

The information was met with continued silence and after a few moments, he realized the call had ended.

"Tosser", muttered Daniel to himself, but nevertheless, he had to admit the man was an extremely useful tosser for the purpose he had in mind and most definitely not the sort of tosser you would want to be on the wrong side of.

With time to kill until Caitlin returned, he wandered to the kitchen and poured himself a stiff rum and coke before opening his laptop to check on Grace again. The more she refused to engage with him through the persona of Aidan and the more she enjoyed her life, the greater his obsession with her grew. The irony was not lost on him that he was spending far more time on her and was considerably more attentive now than he had ever been in his twenty years of marriage to her. Her latest Facebook post was a long one, with ten photos attached, the first being enough to cause his lip to curl involuntarily. It was a photo of Grace and Sam in the car, with what he assumed was the flag of Madagascar draped across the bonnet as they set off on the start of the rally, like they were in the bloody Monaco Grand Prix. He began to read the post.

First day of the rally! Andry with us today to make sure we get out of Tana in one piece. Drove through town of Moramanka, which means 'where slaves are cheap' – a sober reminder of the country's past history. Long drive of 272 km, with last 7 off road. Seriously muddy and rough track, but the car is definitely man enough for the job and just keeps trundling on! Most nerve-racking part was the makeshift wooden bridge at the end consisting of 2 wooden planks…Andry got out to guide us over, or maybe he was just too scared to cross it in the car with us! Parked up, then an hour long boat trip to the Palmarium hotel on the edge of a natural lagoon, only accessible by boat – reminded me of films I had seen of the Amazon, with maybe a hint of Deliverance in there (have to watch out for any banjo-playing locals!). Up some steps from the beach to the hotel…little semi-detached bungalows which are gorgeous – high thatched roofs and terrace with hammock. Perfect! Saw our first lemurs at dinner…soooo cute with their little black and white faces, but they do make seriously scary, very loud noises. Love, love, love it here!!!

There were several photos of lemurs, one of a group of women doing yoga on the beach and one of Grace laughing as she tried to balance a vase of flowers on her head, accompanied by a load of people in local dress at what looked like some kind of party. Daniel sneered as he remembered how she always liked to be the life and soul of the party and never missed a chance to be first up on the dance floor.

The last photo was in a forest and Grace was holding out her upturned palm to a lemur in the lower branches of a tree with a baby on its back. The lemur was leaning out towards her with its outstretched hand, looking into her eyes, their fingertips touching. The photo was strangely poignant and Daniel wondered for a moment how things would have turned out if he and Grace had had a child together. It had never been on his agenda, but he did acknowledge that she would probably have made a very good mother. He still couldn't really understand why she hadn't gone for the whole stepmother idea with his two children when he tried to sell it to her that it was in both of their best interests to stay together. In his opinion, she could have had the best of all worlds that way and she would have been able to teach his kids to sail, ski, horse ride, all the fun things. It really was a shame she was so irritatingly stubborn and so determined to cut her nose off to spite her face.

Daniel jumped as the door opened and Caitlin and Bentley were back.

"Perfect timing," he shouted to her. "I've just this minute finished that report, so I'm all yours for the rest of the evening."

"Great. I'll have a quick shower and then get dinner ready. We're having steak tonight."

Daniel shut the lid on his laptop and went to top up his drink. Caitlin was certainly ten out of ten on the cooking front and she was shaping up nicely in the laundry department, now that he had set out his expectations more clearly with regard to the ironing of boxers. She was a quick learner and eager to please, he thought to himself as Bentley dropped a ball at his feet and looked up at him expectantly. All things considered, it probably wouldn't be too difficult to train her up in the bedroom and persuade her to be a bit less conventional.

If Daniel had been a touch less arrogant, maybe he would have listened more attentively to what Caitlin said. Watched what she was doing a bit more closely. Remembered a little more vividly what happened the last time he underestimated someone and how he got his fingers burned not so very long ago.

He may even have noticed the little spy cam hidden in the wall clock on the mantelpiece.

Destination Unknown

The man lingered at the Patek Philippe counter at Charles de Gaulle Airport, trying to decide whether to add another watch to his already impressive collection, which included pieces from the houses of Panerai, Rolex, Lange & Sohne and of course Cartier. He was currently wearing one of his favourites, the Seamaster from Omega, the preferred brand of James Bond no less, but there was always room for another one. The immaculately dressed sales assistant was making her way over to him when his phone buzzed in his pocket. He looked briefly at the message from the bank to say that funds had been deposited into his account, then left the shop, to the obvious disappointment of the young woman, who saw her whopping great commission evaporating into thin air before her very eyes. There was still no boarding gate up for his flight, so he found an empty stool at the Sushi bar and ordered a selection with a San Pellegrino sparkling water. He opened the Times in front of him, more to discourage conversation than out of any real interest in the information it contained. Staring steadfastly at the print, he could sense the woman next to him looking curiously in his direction. It was his job to notice and observe both people and his surroundings, so he already knew she was blonde, although not natural, late forties, smartly dressed, no wedding ring.

"Travelling alone is so boring," she ventured, then paused briefly before trying again. "Are you travelling for business or pleasure?" she asked, apparently undeterred by his lack of response to her previous comment.

"Business," he replied tersely, without looking at her and hoping he was making it clear by his body language that he had no wish to engage in small talk.

"Oh me too," she said, probably having noticed his watch and earmarked him as potential 'boyfriend' material. Her over-enthusiasm screamed desperation and was extremely unattractive. He could barely resist a smirk as he thought to himself that, if she knew how he paid for that watch, she would choke on her Sushi as she legged it as fast as possible to get away from him.

"Where are you off to?" she persisted, her voice buzzing in his ear like an irritating mosquito.

"New York," he replied as the food arrived. It never ceased to amaze him how some people were so utterly incapable of reading even the most basic signs of human interaction.

"Oh I love New York. Such a great vibe about the place. I go there a couple of times a year myself and always try to catch a show on Broadway. Will you have time for anything like that."

"No," he replied, concentrating on the food.

"That's a shame. What is it you do?"

The man sighed and put down his fork, dabbing his mouth with a napkin. She was really starting to piss him off. He looked pointedly at the information board above them and finished off his water.

"My flight is boarding. Have a good trip."

Making it very clear the conversation was over, he stood up, picked up his laptop case and left, without giving her a chance to point out that the New York flight was not in fact boarding for at least another hour. He strolled over to another information screen, scanned the list of destinations, then made his way to gate forty-one and boarded the flight to Ivato, Madagascar.

Cursed

Superstition is born of fear and has the power to wreak havoc in our minds.

Grace

The Palmarium hotel on the lagoon was our very own little slice of Heaven. As Sam and I walked down the steps to the beach with our yoga mats, I couldn't help thinking how perfect it was and how sad I felt that we had to leave the next day. We had promised ourselves we would try to do a yoga session each day for stretching and relaxation and it seemed we were quickly building up a dedicated following of like-minded people. Who could resist the tranquil setting on the white sand, overlooking the lagoon in the late afternoon sun? I found myself a nice spot on the back row, conscious of my lack of flexibility and in awe of those like Meili, who was already sitting on her mat, bending forward at the waist to grasp both feet and resting her head on her knees as if it were the most natural thing in the world. I had some work to do before I got to that stage, but I was determined to see an improvement by the end of the rally. My hamstrings burned and I could practically hear them screaming in pain as I reached determinedly for my feet, making a superhuman effort to maintain an expression of calm

121

serenity in keeping with the image of yoga. The metal work in my right leg was not doing me any favours, but I had to persevere in the interest of creating the new me. Under Sam's instruction, we got to our feet and adopted my favourite warrior pose, with one arm outstretched towards the lagoon and feet spread wide, front knee bent at a right angle. I breathed deeply and tried to feel the power and strength coursing through my body and out through my fingertips. I was genuinely beginning to understand why Sam was such an advocate of the benefits of yoga.

Half an hour later, after a swim in the lagoon, we were back at our little bungalow to get ready for a boat trip to a local fishing village and a night walk to see the notoriously elusive Aye Aye lemur before dinner. I picked up the rally Roadbook and settled down in the hammock on the terrace, turning to the page with the list of cars and names. Sam came out to join me with a little pot of nail varnish to paint her toenails, determined to keep up standards.

"We need to get to grips with who everyone is. Let's have a look at the list now while we've got a bit of time," I suggested.

"Okay, go on then. Car 1 is easy, that's the Aussies, the three amigos."

"They're great fun, aren't they? Ross was telling me they've done loads of these rallies together, but they all live in different parts of the country. I bet they've got a fair few stories to tell about their adventures on the road together!"

Sam laughed.

"We need to get them talking over a few beers one night."

"I don't think that'll be a problem, do you? Car 2 is Joanna Laithwaite, Hugh Sheldon and Theo Sheldon. That's a mother and her two sons apparently; the sons are doing half the rally each. Suzie told me she's an awesome driver and has done loads of these rallies before. She seems lovely, just adores travelling and has been all over the world, so I'm looking forward to getting to know her better. I get the impression she's a very independent and capable lady though, so I'm thinking we should maybe keep it to ourselves that we had to be shown how to get the car into four-wheel drive mode on the way here."

"Probably best," Sam agreed, laughing. "Oops, have you seen the time? We need to go," she said suddenly, looking at her watch.

On the boat, I found myself sitting opposite the Portuguese couple, Alberto and Luisa da Silva. I loved the name 'da Silva' as soon as I saw it on the list; it sounded so exotic. I knew they were good friends with Joanna and they'd all done lots of rallies together, including the Peking to Paris a couple of years ago. Suzie also told me Luisa had danced at the Rio Carnival in Brazil and I was hoping we might persuade her to do some dance classes with us.

"I hear you have a Lusitano," Luisa said to me, with a smile that oozed Latino charm. "The royal horses of Portugal. Stunning," she added.

My face lit up at the chance to tell her about Valentino.

"That's right. He's actually from Brazil, so quite rare over here."

I took out my iPhone and showed her a few pictures of my boy in his traditional Portuguese tack.

"He is beautiful. You must be very proud. We have friends who own a stud farm back home in Portugal. You and Sam must come to visit one day."

As one door closes, another one opens, I thought to myself.

It took us about an hour in the boat to reach our destination. One side of the fishing village overlooked the lagoon and the other side backed onto the stunning Indian Ocean, waves constantly rolling in, breaking and crashing loudly onto the shore. The houses were built from wood with thatched roofs and raised up on stilts in the traditional style, presumably because of the danger of flooding in the rainy season. The villagers were all friendly and eager to engage with us, especially the children, who entertained us with their singing and dancing routines in return for a few Ariary. Our lives were poles apart and I couldn't help wondering whether all our first-world materialism and possessions really made us any happier in the end. I began to imagine what it would be like to simply walk away from the rat race and start a new life somewhere like that little village, but I knew I was being naïve. A few moments later my thoughts were interrupted by our guides, who reappeared to shepherd us back to the boat and off to the little island reserve in the hope of seeing the elusive, nocturnal Aye Aye lemur.

It was dark by the time we reached the island and there was a full moon lighting our way with its shimmering silver beam as we trudged after the guides, up a little path and into the woods. Everyone trod carefully and no one spoke more than the occasional whisper, as we kept our eyes peeled and finally gathered in one spot to watch and wait. The guides had placed coconuts in the lower branches of the trees to encourage the lemurs to show themselves and we didn't have to wait too long before one of the strange-looking creatures began to creep its way warily down towards the food. It had a bizarre appearance, with a long bushy tail, overly large ears, wide staring eyes and an extra-long, almost skeletal middle finger. We were all utterly mesmerized by it as it approached the coconut. The guide explained that it would, first of all, gnaw a hole in the top using its strong incisors, then insert its specially adapted finger to scoop out the flesh in a truly unique manner of feeding. As we watched, the creature abruptly stopped eating and turned to face us, suddenly aware of its audience. It remained motionless, staring, then slowly it stretched out its little arm towards us and pointed its long, thin middle finger directly at me, sending a shiver down my spine. The guide looked at me strangely, then made a sudden loud noise, which broke the spell and sent the weird little animal scuttling back up to the cover of the higher branches.

Later on, back at the hotel, I found a book on all the different Lemur species and I learned that the locals believed it was a bad omen and a symbol of death if the Aye Aye points at you. That explained the guide's reaction and horrified expression. I shivered again, at the same time chiding myself for being spooked by a silly superstition. Nevertheless, I couldn't help wishing it had pointed the finger at someone other than me.

Later that evening Sam and I were the last ones left in the bar, chatting with Suzie and George.

"You're very quiet tonight," said Sam, turning to me. "You're not still thinking about that lemur story are you?"

"No, of course not…well…maybe a bit."

"I don't think you've got too much to worry about," George laughed. "The poor old Aye Aye has got itself onto the endangered list because of its strange appearance and that habit of pointing at people with its long bony finger. Apparently, the locals have been killing them because of the supposed curse for years, so the only one it really brings bad luck to is itself."

"That's such a shame. It seems a timid, harmless little thing and it can't help the way it looks at the end of the day," I said, feeling suddenly protective of the strange little soul that had been vilified through no fault of its own.

"The island is a sanctuary," said Suzie. "They're trying to educate the locals and protect the lemurs, so at least something is being done to help them."

"Who's driving tomorrow then?" asked George, changing the subject.

I put my hand in the air, feeling a mixture of trepidation and excitement at the prospect of the long drive ahead.

"You'll be fine, but there's been a fair bit of rain the last couple of nights, so use four-wheel drive to get through the ford and then keep it going steadily all the way up the mud track to the road. If I were you I'd try to be one of the first out, before the tracks all get too churned up."

I was glad of any advice I could get, but the barman was making it very clear he wanted to get rid of us and go to bed so we reluctantly decided to call it a night, wandering slowly back along the path to our little bungalow.

I lay awake for a long while, listening to the sounds of the forest outside, thinking about how much my life had changed in the most unexpected ways and wondering what the next few days would bring. My heart ached for the little Aye Aye lemur, persecuted and misunderstood, wanting nothing more than to be left alone to get on with its life in peace.

Friendly Advice

Roisin

"*Kate, I'm so* sorry, but I'm going to have to cancel tomorrow night. Something's come up. I can do this evening if you're free by any chance?" Roisin offered, a hint of desperation in her voice as she sensed the intense disapproval of her friend.

"Look Roisin," began the curt reply. "Maybe you need to start thinking about your priorities. This is the third time you've done this to me in the last few weeks and I'm beginning to feel like our friendship means nothing to you these days."

Roisin winced at the criticism and the prickly tone, knowing it was wholly justified and understandable. She and Kate had known each other since school days and had shared a lot together, both good and bad, but right now Roisin knew she was really not treating her friend very well at all.

"Let me guess," Kate continued, "Patrick is coming back."

Of course, that was it and she had every right to be pissed off at being kicked into touch yet again. Roisin had been seeing Patrick for a few months now, having met him on an internet dating site. Her girlfriends had given the initial seal of approval when she came clean and showed them his dating profile one night, but the general consensus of opinion was that she was coming across as a bit too keen.

"You're too much of a pushover, Roisin," Kate had said over a couple of bottles of Prosecco. "Whatever happened to 'treat 'em mean'? Stop answering all his messages within a nanosecond, or he's going to think you're desperate and have no life of your own.

You need to keep him dangling sometimes, so he feels he has to work at it a bit. And you should *never* forget your girlfriends; 'sisters before misters' is the golden rule," she chided.

Roisin had kept it up for a while, forcing herself to ignore his messages, sometimes for a whole day, before sending a light-hearted reply to keep him on his toes. Unfortunately, to her great dismay, it appeared to have the exact opposite of the desired effect and she soon feared Patrick would lose interest completely if she didn't get her act together and change tactics. Sometimes she would hear nothing from him for days, despite her sending numerous texts, followed by emails and voicemails in an attempt to make contact with him. When he eventually did get in touch, she was always so relieved to hear from him that she replied immediately and promptly changed any plans she may have had in order to accommodate him.

Roisin's biggest weakness was her unusually high sex drive. In fact she was probably what people would call a sex addict, which was how she came to be on several 'hook up' dating apps in the first place. She had developed a taste for bondage and light S&M over the years, which was not to everyone's taste, so with Patrick, she felt she had hit the jackpot. Not only was he more than happy to indulge her fantasies in the bedroom, he had more than a few of his own ideas to bring to the party. The fact that he was also a successful businessman, charming and charismatic, made him quite a catch in her opinion and she had no intention of allowing him to slip through her fingers by playing stupid games, whatever her friends thought. In spite of that, she was slightly uneasy about the fact that they had fallen into a routine of him turning up whenever he felt like it and staying as long as it suited him, with no regular pattern to his comings and goings. He had a key to her apartment and appeared to have moved himself in, although he was quick to warn her that he was never going to be a 24/7 kind of guy and would often have to be away for his consultancy work, sometimes for weeks at a time. It was all on his terms.

The reason Roisin was letting Kate down again was that Patrick had been away on business in Morocco for the last two weeks, apparently working on a project in the middle of nowhere with unreliable internet access. When he eventually texted to say he was coming home the following day, couldn't wait to see her and was bringing a 'special present' with him that he was sure they would both enjoy (winking emoji), all her anger at his lack of communication evaporated. Kate would get over it; she always did. Roisin made a concerted effort to sound placatory with her friend.

"I really am sorry and you mean the world to me, you know you do. It's just that I haven't seen Patrick for two weeks and I don't think it's fair for me to be out the first night he's home."

"Okay, okay," Kate conceded at last. "As it happens, I *am* free tonight, but you really can't keep doing this to me. And for the record, I don't think it's very healthy for you to be so dependent on him either. You're dancing to his tune just a bit too much for my liking."

Roisin ignored that last comment, smiling happily as she realised she had got away with it again and quickly arranging to go round to Kate's house for seven o'clock before she could change her mind. They would have the place to themselves for a proper girlie catch-up, as Kate's partner Michael was out with his mates for the evening.

A few hours later, she was sitting at her best friend's dining table in her apartment at the other end of town. Kate came through from the kitchen with two delicious-smelling plates of food, which made Roisin wish as she always did that she could cook as well as her friend.

"It's only Spag Bol I'm afraid. I wasn't planning on entertaining," said Kate pointedly.

"It's absolutely perfect," replied Roisin, pouring them each a glass of the Rioja she had brought with her.

By the time they had finished the meal and were onto their second bottle of wine, the atmosphere was thankfully more relaxed and the earlier tension between them was forgotten.

"Do you realise it'll be ten years this weekend since Craig's funeral?" Kate asked suddenly. "It came up in my calendar today."

"God, I can't believe it's that long already. Do you ever wonder what happened to Sophie? I mean it was just so weird, the way she disappeared like that, cutting us all off completely," Roisin said, shaking her head. "Mind you, if I'm honest, I always thought she was a strange one."

"I know what you mean. I've thought about it a lot over the years. I tried to track her down for a while, but it was as if she simply vanished into thin air. My guess is she had some sort of breakdown after it happened and maybe the only way she could cope was to sever all ties with the past and the people who knew her and Craig. I mean, it was bad enough for us, but it must have been ten times worse for her, losing the guy she was going to marry in such tragic circumstances. I really hope she's okay and has managed to find happiness, wherever she is. She was always such a troubled soul."

Kate sat back in her chair and sighed, remembering that awful morning when she opened the cabin door on the boat to find Sophie screaming hysterically and Craig lying dead beside her. It wasn't as if she had never seen a dead person before, having completed three years at medical school, but when that dead person was a friend, the guy you dated all those years ago…well that was a whole different ball game.

"Anyway, enough of that," said Kate quickly, regretting dredging up all the painful memories and changing the subject. "Do you think Patrick really is 'The One' then? I must say, things certainly seem to be moving fast with you two. I just worry a bit about you, you know."

Roisin laughed at her concerned face.

"I'm a big girl now, forty-six years old to be exact. I know what I'm doing. He makes me happy, he spoils me…and between you and me the sex is fantastic! What more could a girl ask for?" she said, a defiant expression on her face as she raised her glass to Kate's.

"Well, I suppose if you put it like that…," said Kate, shrugging her shoulders, but clearly not convinced.

Kate had in fact only met Patrick once, when she was out with friends in Temple Bar and bumped into him and Roisin. She didn't take to him at all, but couldn't quite put her finger on the reason why. On the face of it, he was charming, polite, interesting, but there was just something about him, something that she didn't trust. For a start, the second Roisin went to the toilet, Kate got the distinct impression he was coming onto her with his suggestive little comments disguised as banter and she didn't care one bit for the way he looked at her, practically undressing her with his eyes. She didn't say anything to Roisin about it at the time, because there was nothing concrete to tell her, but she could at least try to urge caution now and hopefully make her think twice about diving in at the deep end quite so quickly.

"Don't you think it's a bit odd that you don't know anything about his past, his family, or any of his other friends?" she began. "I mean, that's usually the stuff you talk about when you first start dating someone isn't it? I have to say I found him really evasive when I tried to chat to him that evening we all met in town and it made me a bit uneasy, like he might be hiding something from you. He didn't seem to want to tell me anything about himself, just kept turning every question back on me. From what you've said, he doesn't talk to you about any of that either. I mean, what if he's married Roisin, with a family somewhere else? You do hear about that sort of thing happening."

Kate looked at her friend anxiously, trying to gauge her reaction. Fuelled by the wine, she had already said more than she really intended to, but to her relief, Roisin laughed and reached out to grasp her hand across the table.

"I love you for always looking out for me and I know I am lucky to have a friend like you, but you honestly don't need to worry this time. Patrick's the real deal, I know he is. He has his own reasons for not wanting to dwell on the past. And you're wrong about him not telling me anything about himself. He *was* married actually, but his wife died a few years ago in a car crash and he never met anyone else he wanted to be with until me, which is why it all feels so special. As for his family, his parents are both dead now and he doesn't have any brothers or sisters. He told me he had an unhappy childhood and implied some sort of domestic abuse, but it was obvious he really didn't want to talk about it and found it all very painful. I didn't push, because to be perfectly honest it was starting to feel like I was counselling one of my patients. And remember, if anyone should be able to spot a psycho, surely it would be me, wouldn't it?" she laughed, trying to lighten the mood.

"Hmm. The man with no past and no family," chipped in Kate, a little too sarcastically for Roisin's liking, with a clear implication that it was all a bit too convenient.

"Well, at the end of the day, we all have secrets and skeletons in the cupboard that are better left alone. Don't we?" Roisin said, looking pointedly at her friend.

"That was totally different," said Kate, suddenly feeling stone-cold sober at the inference. "I didn't do anything wrong. I just tried to protect…."

Kate stopped short, drawn back to that awful morning on the boat. She was the first one on the scene when it all kicked off and she remembered vividly how she pushed Sophie, clearly in shock and no use to anyone, out of the cabin and up onto deck with Roisin. Left to her own devices, she did everything she could to resuscitate Craig, but in reality, she could see he had been dead for some time and was eventually forced to admit there was no point in continuing. He was not coming back to them. Not ever. She sat back to collect her thoughts, trying to make her brain accept what had happened and it was then that she saw it. The syringe. Wedged between the bunk cushion and the hull. Without really knowing why, she snatched it up and shoved it into the inside pocket of her fleece, wrapped in one of her sailing gloves. She said nothing about it to the paramedics or the Guards, not even to Michael. She wanted to ask Sophie about it first because the truth was it looked bad, even though she was certain there would be an innocent explanation. There had to be.

Kate knew Craig and Sophie were having problems before the boat trip, not because Sophie confided in her, but because Craig and her partner Michael were friends. Craig was having an affair and wanted to end things with Sophie, but he told Michael he was worried about her mental health and explained how she had threatened to harm him as well as herself if he ever left her. In Kate's opinion, the relationship was toxic and the two of them would be better off without each other, but Sophie was adamant she was prepared to forgive the infidelity, determined that she and Craig should stay together, whatever the cost.

When she found that syringe, Kate had to admit her imagination began to work overtime. Had the pair of them been doing drugs? She knew for a fact Craig had dabbled back in their student days. Was it some kind of weird suicide pact? Had Sophie injected Craig with something to kill him, intending to kill herself afterwards, but then not been able to go through with it? She told herself she was being ridiculous. When Kate broached the subject the following day with her friend, Sophie denied all knowledge and looked at her as if she were completely mad, making her feel both guilty and disloyal. There was nothing more to be done except wait for the results of the autopsy. Kate had to admit she breathed a huge sigh of relief when she found out that Craig's death was being recorded as 'accidental' because that meant she was exonerated in saying nothing about what she found to anyone else; except Roisin of course. Sophie was clearly innocent and the syringe had nothing to do with his death, although she still had no idea how it came to be there or why. The next day Kate put an end to any further speculation by dropping the offending article into the sharps box in another department of the hospital where she worked and vowed to forget all about it.

Roisin interrupted her thoughts.

"I know you were only trying to protect her and I know what the Coroner's report said, but there was something very off about the whole business. I still think you should have spoken up. And I think you do as well if you're honest about it. It was not normal the way she just disappeared after the funeral and I was never convinced she didn't know more about what happened than she let on. You have to admit Sophie was always slightly unhinged. Technical term," she laughed.

Kate remained silent and Roisin paused for a moment before continuing in a matter-of-fact tone.

"Anyway Kate, that was all a long time ago. I'm not having a dig at you, I'm really not. The point I was trying to make was that we all have secrets from the past that we'd rather not talk about. Patrick is no exception and I for one intend to respect his privacy."

"I suppose you're right," said Kate, clearly still distracted by thoughts of the past. "Anyway, who am I to give relationship advice? Michael and I have been on and off more times than a light switch."

She gave an ironic little laugh to diffuse the tension and Roisin smiled back at her friend.

"Oh come on, you guys are meant to be together. You always go back to each other in the end."

Later that night, Roisin lay in bed thinking about Patrick. She could not deny that some of what Kate said had struck a chord with her, although she was never going to admit that. Of course she found it odd that she knew so little about his past, but she had made a conscious decision to trust him and take him at face value. In her opinion, there was a lot to be said for living in the moment and looking to the future rather than dwelling on the past, which can never be changed. She remembered his words the last time she tried to get him to open up to her about his wife and family.

"Let's make a pact. I don't care about anything that happened in your past. I don't want to know about it and I certainly don't need to know about any of your other relationships before me. But the same has to apply to my past. Can't you see that it's all irrelevant? From now on it's just you and me against the world."

Roisin smiled to herself, thinking how romantic that last bit sounded, blissfully unaware that the words were in fact empty and meaningless, nothing more than an echo of a conversation many years ago with another woman, a young wife full of hope for the bright future ahead with her new husband.

Unfortunately for Roisin, despite being an intelligent woman, who had built a career out of analysing other people's complex psychological disorders, she could be extremely naïve when it came to her own affairs of the heart.

A Friend in Need

At the heart of every betrayal is trust.

Grace

Eight days into our rally adventure, despite living in each other's pockets and sitting in a car together for many hours each day, Sam and I had managed to remain best friends and our bond was stronger than ever.

After an extremely wet and cold few days in the rain forest, which had certainly lived up to its name, we were due to head west with the promise of warmer weather, sunshine and turquoise blue waters. As we left the rainforest behind, my mind was on the lemurs. I had no idea before our visit that there were so many different species, but apparently no less than a hundred and five of them were in danger of extinction and I thought to myself that human beings had an awful lot to answer for.

Sam was driving, so I had time to flick through the photos on my phone and found my favourite one of her, a horrified expression on her face as a lemur perched on her head and pulled curiously at her hair. The lemurs on the island reserve had no concept of personal space and were more than comfortable with their human visitors, but in spite of their somewhat forward approach, they were always

136

very gentle and it was a moving experience to be able to have such close contact with them. The confident 'meet and greet' lemurs near the entrance were eventually enticed away by the guides with pieces of banana and we were led on through the woods to see the more reticent Sifaka, or 'dancing lemur', which had a strikingly human appearance and earned its name by skipping around upright on its hind legs. I laughed out loud as I came to a photo of a beautiful, velvety blue flower that we kept seeing everywhere, remembering how I asked our guide about it, then immediately regretted it as he informed me with a smirk that it was called the 'clitoria' flower. On closer inspection, it was easy to see how it got its name. I thought of my friend Eva at home, who was expecting a baby and wondered if she had started thinking of names yet. It was certainly a popular choice these days to name girls after flowers: Poppy, Lily, Rose, Daisy, but I somehow doubted Clitoria would make it into the top ten.

The long drive to our next destination in the Tsaranovo Reserve took us through dramatic mountain scenery and paddy fields, then a good hour off-road across dry river beds and rough dirt tracks. Sam and I always seemed to be bringing up the rear, as we stopped numerous times to take photos, chat to local people or buy stuff from street stalls. I was fascinated by the way everything changed as we drove from region to region; not just the scenery, but the weather, the style of the houses, the appearance of the people, their clothes, their food. By the time we arrived at Camp Catta, which consisted of little wooden chalets nestled in the foothills of the mountains, the skies were beginning to darken again, but the dramatic storm clouds gathering overhead meant that we were privileged to see the most breathtaking sunset of the trip so far, as the sky seemed to explode into a blaze of fire, crowned with an exquisite double rainbow.

The following morning we awoke in camp to the bitter sweet combination of blue skies, sunshine and cold water showers, but the wild beauty of the place more than made up for that and Sam and I loitered for a while after breakfast, watching groups of ringtail lemurs playing in the sun, before finally leaving in last place as usual. Joanna loved to be on the road early and the Three Amigos were always chomping at the bit to be on their way. They would more than likely reach the next destination by lunchtime, having set a blistering pace on the road. When we finally wandered down to our car, we saw that someone had written 'Les Girls' in the dust on the back window, surrounded by a heart. From then on, that was how we were known.

The only cars behind us on the road to Isalo were the support car containing the team of mechanics and guides, driven by head man Jerome, and the 'sweep car', driven by Ted with his wife Francesca. Jerome was also the representative from the company we had hired the cars from and was ultimately responsible for making sure they were all running properly. Ted was our rally mechanic from the UK and had reportedly got people out of many a scrape in past rallies. He was a larger than life character with a wicked sense of humour and plenty of tales to tell, rarely seen without his bush hat, except when he was underneath a car.

We took our time, climbing up into the mountains and then across a plateau with a vast expanse of grasslands and a road that appeared to be winding its way to eternity. Our chosen lunch stop was in the middle of nowhere on the plateau, sitting on the roof of the car and feeling like tiny specs in the universe as we absorbed the view that would stay in our memories for ever.

I was back in the driving seat for the final leg of the journey when we had our first experience of mechanical failure, the first hint of trouble in Paradise. Coming up behind a wagon, I prepared to overtake, tooting my horn to let the driver know I was there, then waiting until he indicated to tell me it was safe to go, following the unwritten rules of the road we had been told about. As I drew level with him, I felt the car die on me and lose all power. Despite my foot being pressed flat to the floor, there was no way I was getting past before I collided with the oncoming vehicle that had appeared out of nowhere, so I slammed on the brakes and slipped in behind him again, heart thumping.

"Jeez Grace, put your foot down next time," shouted Sam, looking at me accusingly. "I'd quite like to make it to the hotel in one piece."

"I did," I replied indignantly. "I thought I was going to push the pedal through the floor, but there was just nothing there. I don't know what happened. To be honest, it hasn't felt quite right all day, but I thought I was imagining it. It's been harder and harder to get into gear as well, so I couldn't even change down to get more power."

I drove the last few miles considerably slower, unwilling to push the car at all and very aware of the fact that we needed to look after it if it was to get us around the country safely. By the time we limped into Le Jardin du Roy hotel the others were all there, some of them relaxing on the loungers by the pool, others taking full advantage of the rooms, which had the welcome luxuries of electricity, wifi and hot water. We checked in, dumped the bags in our room, then went immediately to find Ted and Jerome to explain what had happened with the car. To my relief, they both seemed unfazed by the description of the problem and assured me confidently as I handed over the keys that it would all be easily sorted. Once again I made a mental note that I needed to be more self-sufficient and more capable of sorting at least some of my own problems out if I ever did a rally again.

The atmosphere was happy and relaxed at dinner that evening. It turned out Richard Alder was renowned from previous rallies for his after-dinner stories, which had become something of an institution; often surprisingly naughty, but always highly entertaining. There was the occasional disapproving look, but I got the feeling from the mischievous glint in his eye as he told his tale that he rather enjoyed shocking his audience a little, just as I did. In fact I was beginning to look forward to regaling everyone with my own bizarre story one evening. 'The Cautionary Tale of Dickhead Daniel' had a certain ring to it, I felt.

Luckily we had a rest day at Isalo, which gave Jerome and his team time to fix our car while we headed off for a walk in the mountains. The view from the top was jaw-dropping and, as we sat there on the rocks watching the birds flying around below us, it was liberating, almost like we were flying ourselves. On the way up we walked past several small caves with stones piled up outside them and I was curious.

"They are temporary cave tombs," our guide explained. "It's the burial custom of the people who live in these mountains. When someone dies, their body is laid to rest in the caves you saw, with small stones sealing the entrance. Then, after a few weeks the body is exhumed and the remaining bones are placed in a small coffin. Because there are only bones left, the coffin is much lighter and can be more easily carried to the very top of the mountains. Once up there, a young man from the village is lowered down the cliff by rope, carrying the coffin and placing it in a totally inaccessible natural cave, where it remains safe and undisturbed forever."

I was intrigued, thinking to myself how incredibly well thought out and dignified the process was and how peaceful the final resting place of the dead would be. At the same time, I shivered as an unwelcome vision of Daniel came into my mind and I wondered whether his soul could ever truly be at peace in the final resting place I had given it.

I doubted it very much.

Back at the hotel, I took advantage of the good wifi access to send photos and an email to Mum, then I put a long post on Facebook with loads of photos of the last few days to keep all my friends in the loop. I was really happy to see a message from Ellie and a few photos of Valentino, who was apparently doing well and enjoying his rest time in the field with his sheep friends. Valentino did not usually go out in the field with other horses, as he tended to be too aggressive with them, but it seemed the sheep were subservient enough for him to tolerate their presence. There were a couple of messages from Aidan, hoping we were having an amazing time and asking me to let him know how we were getting on. I felt a twinge of guilt that I hadn't bothered to reply to him. Then I saw his latest message from two days earlier:

I could really use a friend right now. Just lost my dad after a long battle with cancer. He was my rock. I can't imagine life without him to be honest (sad face emoji). Hope you're ok and having a great time xx

"What's up?" asked Sam, concerned by my sudden tears. "It's not your mum is it?"

"No, no, it's nothing to do with me. It's a message from Aidan and, before you do your eye roll thing, his father has just died of cancer."

"Oh, poor guy. That's tough," she said, nodding her head sympathetically. "I know that will bring back a lot of memories for you Grace, but seriously, you have to remember you don't really know this guy. To be honest, I don't get why he's wanting to cry on your shoulder about it. Surely he has friends and family at home who can support him?"

"I'm sure he has. It's just that sometimes I think it's easier to offload on someone you don't know so well. I feel really guilty about ignoring all his other messages now."

"Does he know what happened to your dad?" Sam asked suddenly, her eyes narrowing in suspicion.

"No, I don't think so. I've not told him much about myself at all. Look, I'll just send a quick message saying I'm sorry to hear his news and I understand what a horrible time it will be for him. A bit of compassion won't hurt me at the end of the day."

I sent the message, then turned off my phone, but Aidan dominated my thoughts that evening. Which of course was exactly what his alter ego Daniel wanted to happen.

The following day did not start well. After a restless night of very little sleep, Sam and I were late to breakfast, still in our room and panicking because the car keys were missing. We had turned the room upside down several times, but to no avail and I was starting to think I was going mad. I was the last one to have seen the keys since Jerome gave them to me after fixing the car, but I was absolutely certain I had put them straight back into the pocket of the navigator's bag where we had both agreed we would always keep them. In the end, we had to admit defeat and wandered somewhat dejectedly up to the breakfast room to confess our sins to George and Suzie.

"Don't worry, I think Jerome might be able to help you," George said with a knowing smile. "He's in reception waiting for you."

A few minutes later we found Jerome and followed him to the car park, where he calmly pointed out our car keys on the back seat of car number 7. So near and yet so far, given that the doors were all locked. Sam turned to me, eyebrows raised accusingly but refrained from saying anything. I was utterly gobsmacked.

"But...how the hell did they get there? I swear I didn't go anywhere near the car after you gave me the keys back yesterday. Why would I? All our stuff was in the room and we didn't need to drive until this morning."

It was clear no one believed my protestations and even Sam assumed I must have had some sort of temporary brain freeze, causing me to forget where I had gone after being given the keys. There was no point in arguing, so in the end I laughed it off and left Ted and Jerome to sort the problem out with a wire coat hanger and I suspected a lot of swearing. We had been warned about the fact that you could easily lock the keys inside these cars, but I was certain that wasn't what had happened. For all my bravado, I couldn't get rid of the feeling that someone had been in our room, taken the keys and meddled with our car. Or maybe I was overthinking it all and being paranoid. I told myself I needed to get a grip.

When we got back to the breakfast room there was a man we hadn't seen before talking with George.

"Who's that?" I asked, nudging Sam as we sat down.

The man immediately looked over and caught my eye, smirking at my discomfort as my flushed cheeks betrayed the fact we were talking about him. I attempted to regain my composure, smiled politely and then turned away, giving the croissant on my plate my full and undivided attention until George looked across and beckoned us over.

"Sam, Grace, let me introduce you to Maxim. He owns the Ecolodge Delphine on the west coast, where we'll be staying in a few days' time. He also runs a 4x4 adventure tour company and is keen to get involved with us on more rallies, which will be great. He knows this area like the back of his hand and he'll be travelling with us now for the next few stages to see how we do things."

Maxim stood up and greeted us with a kiss on each cheek.

"Enchanté," he said in a perfect French accent, then switched to equally perfect English. "And please call me Max. How do you like our country so far?"

"I love it," I blurted out, somewhat over-enthusiastically. "I can't wait to try driving in the sand dunes as well. I've never done anything like that before."

Max looked amused and I immediately felt like Baby in Dirty Dancing when she utters her cringe-worthy words "I carried a water melon". I couldn't help noticing how his steely blue eyes crinkled at the corners in a very sexy way and I wished I'd made a bit more effort to tame my wayward curly hair that morning.

"Sorry, I need to take this," said Max, standing up quickly as his mobile rang.

I caught a brief glimpse of the screensaver photo on his phone: a little baby girl in a pink flowery sunhat, with the biggest brown eyes, long dark lashes and an adorable smile. I had to assume the call was from his wife back at home and felt more than a slight twinge of disappointment to learn that he was off-limits.

See no Evil

The man strolled through the hotel lobby unnoticed. He had made a career out of blending into his surroundings and being invisible. The trick was not to attempt to hide in the shadows and sneak around with a furtive expression on your face, but rather to walk around in plain sight, to go about your business with the utmost discretion, to become a part of the scenery. It was no easy feat and there was a careful balance to be struck. If you avoided all eye contact or did not return a polite greeting when passing by someone, for example, it would inevitably arouse suspicion. On the other hand, it would potentially be a disaster to engage in any kind of meaningful conversation with strangers.

It took a certain degree of arrogance to do what he did for a living and he prided himself on having perfected the art. Of course people saw him in the lobby, in the bar, in the car park, but they never remembered him as a person of any significance. He dressed carefully and made subtle changes on a regular basis so that people would not be able to recall afterwards what he was wearing, what colour his hair or eyes were, or how tall he was. Consequently, he was able to walk around as he pleased; observing, listening, memorizing all the little details that may come in useful later.

He particularly liked jobs like this one because they gave him the freedom to be creative and have some fun. He had to admit, the client paying his fees was clearly harbouring some fairly major grudges against the target, but that was none of his concern and he never asked for details. Kill, maim, torture, intimidate: it was all the same to him, so long as he got his money.

A Legal High

Caitlin

Patrick was away in Dublin on business for a few days so it was finally time for Caitlin to get to know the real Patrick Salenden and find out what exactly he got up to, alone in her house for hours on end. First, she connected her laptop to the spy cam she had so cleverly hidden, congratulating herself on her ingenuity, then she made herself comfortable and began the long job of going through all the recorded footage. She had observed Patrick closely before deciding where to install the hidden camera, taking note of where he tended to sit with his laptop so that she could effectively be looking over his shoulder. It was a tedious but necessary process in order to determine how best to deal with the unfortunate situation she found herself in.

After five solid hours of staring at the laptop screen, Caitlin was beginning to see double and poor Bentley was desperate to go out. She sat back with a sigh, closed the laptop lid and looked down at the pages of notes she had written, deciding they could wait until she had been out for a quick walk with the dog to clear her head. She was furious with Patrick for forcing her to spy on him. She had so wanted to trust him and to believe he was different, but it hadn't taken him long to show his true colours.

By the time Caitlin returned from a brisk walk on the beach with Bentley bounding along beside her, the anger had begun to subside and she was thinking more rationally. She made herself a coffee and sat down again to go through her notes. A lot of the footage was not particularly interesting and showed Patrick either watching television or reading a magazine, lounging around with his feet up on the table, a habit which he knew she hated. The good stuff came when he was on his laptop and her face darkened as she zoomed in and realised just how much time he was spending on Facebook, more specifically on Grace King's Facebook.

Caitlin knew exactly who Grace King was, ever since she found out that Patrick's real name was actually Daniel Callaghan and did some digging around. Daniel Callaghan had indeed been married twice before, just as he had told her, but his recollection of both those marriages seemed more than a little distorted compared with what she had been able to find out from various sources on the internet. For instance, she discovered his first wife Julia took her own life by hanging herself, which explained why Caitlin had initially drawn a blank when she searched for anything relating to a woman throwing herself under a train. Once she knew his real name, the true story had been easy to find out, with a google search leading straight to newspaper reports of the tragedy. It was equally easy to get information on Grace, his second wife, who had divorced him relatively recently after twenty years of marriage. Unfortunately for Daniel, Grace had decided to sell her story to the press and there were several newspaper reports, as well as a couple of features in women's magazines, about his serial infidelity. Caitlin had made a note of some of the headlines:

Wife's shock on learning of husband's four different lives

Respectable businessman turns out to be devious conman and dangerous sociopath

Husband of twenty years fathered children with two other women

Caitlin could not deny she was shocked (although secretly a little bit impressed) at the extent of his deception. At the same time, she took an instant dislike to Grace, branding her a vacuous idiot who had taken her eye well and truly off the ball where her husband was concerned and allowed him to run rings around her. Women like Grace deserved all they got in Caitlin's opinion and she would most definitely not be making the same mistake. In any case, there were always two sides to every story and, for the moment, she was going to give Daniel/Patrick the benefit of the doubt and see things from his point of view.

She did not see Grace King as a threat, but nor did she take kindly to the amount of time Patrick appeared to be devoting to the activity of checking up on his ex-wife and it was clear from the video footage that he spent hours scrolling through her Facebook posts and other social media. That would have to stop. The marriage may have ended in an extremely acrimonious divorce, but it was obvious to Caitlin that Patrick was still completely obsessed with Grace, who continued to exercise some kind of hold over him. Furthermore, contrary to the sob story he had tried to feed her, she had ascertained that Patrick most certainly did not go into the water voluntarily with dark thoughts of taking his own life. Caitlin now knew from various press reports on the internet that he somehow mysteriously fell into the middle of the Irish Sea while on a boat trip with his ex-wife and was presumed to have drowned.

There had to be more to that story than met the eye and she intended to get to the bottom of it.

Caitlin saw Patrick make two phone calls, neither of which made much sense to her, as the sound quality of the recording was not great. The first one appeared to be some kind of work call and Patrick looked highly irritated with whoever was on the other end. She could make out a couple of barked instructions, but that was about it. The second call was even shorter and Patrick said just one word, "Seven", waited a moment, looked at his phone and appeared angry at realising the other person had cut him off. He then spent a good while texting someone and Caitlin deduced from the lascivious smirk on his face and the way his hand kept rubbing his crotch that the someone was a woman, undoubtedly one living in Dublin. That would account for the increasing amount of time he was spending there.

She watched as Bentley wandered into view a few times, probably looking for a walk or just a bit of attention, but Patrick shoved him away irritably with his foot and ignored him. When the poor dog became desperate, Patrick got up from the sofa and bundled him unceremoniously through the front door, closing it firmly behind him and leaving him out there whining to come back in for far too long.

His treatment of Bentley was the last straw and Caitlin could not stop the red mist from descending, her disappointment in the fact Patrick had lied to her turning rapidly to fury. Whatever was going on that Patrick thought he was getting away with, Caitlin had no intention of allowing him to play her for a fool. Nor was it her style to simply walk away and go quietly without a fight. Patrick needed to understand that there was always a price to pay for treating someone badly, especially when that person had actually saved your life. She would start by teaching him a lesson and, if he could be made to see the error of his ways and was prepared to make it up to her, there was a chance she could see her way to forgiving him. Everyone deserved a second chance at the end of the day and what she really wanted was for them to get things back on track for the wonderful future she knew they could have together, just the two of them. She smiled to herself at the image in her head of her and Patrick cosying up in front of the fire, content with each other's company, no need of outsiders.

Two more days went by before Patrick reappeared from his 'business trip' to Dublin, nicely in time for dinner and bearing a bunch of flowers with a Tesco reduced label he had not bothered to remove.

"Oh thank you, they're lovely," Caitlin murmured, maintaining an air of calm serenity and kissing him on the lips as she took the flowers from him and placed them by the sink. "I'll get a vase now. Did you have a successful trip?"

"So so," he sighed. "A bit knackering though. Lots of tedious meetings trying to finalise things for the big contract I told you about," said Patrick, rolling his eyes and looking harassed. "I won't bore you with the details. Something smells good. What's for dinner?"

"Chilli," she said, putting the flowers into a vase and adding a tablespoon of bleach and sugar to the water in an attempt to revive them, as she had seen them do once on a TV programme.

"Ooh great, my favourite," he added with genuine enthusiasm. "Would you like a drink?" he asked, walking over to the fridge. "I'll get them," said Caitlin, knowing he would be only too happy to let her do everything. "You've had a long journey and a tough couple of days by the sound of things. Go and sit down. Put your feet up."

Patrick was not about to argue with that and wandered through to the lounge to find the fire already lit and a contented Bentley lying in front of it.

Caitlin took out a bottle of his favourite Mount Gay rum and a can of coke from the fridge, half-filling a tall glass with ice and a slice of lime, then pouring a generous measure of rum, just the way he liked it. Then she reached into the back of the spices cupboard and felt in the corner behind all the other jars, taking out the bottle marked 'Tarragon'. She removed eight of the little white oval tablets it contained, crushing them on the granite work surface and sweeping the powder straight into the glass, where it dissolved without a trace. As she handed Patrick his drink with a loving smile, she had no idea history was repeating itself and she had actually laced it with a heavy dose of déjà vu, although Grace's drug of choice had borne a different name.

By the time he had downed his second rum and coke, Patrick had unwittingly ingested 400mg of Tramadol, a drug he had on prescription for pain relief from the serious injuries he had sustained in the helicopter crash a few years earlier. In reality, he rarely needed to resort to it and was aware it could easily become addictive, but on occasions, the pain could be excruciating and he liked to make sure he had a stash ready just in case.

"Dinner's ready," called Caitlin from the kitchen.

Patrick was sweating and was glad to be moving away from the fire, but as he stood up, a wave of nausea came over him and he felt the room spinning.

"Jesus Caitlin, how much rum did you put in those drinks? I feel like shit," he said, stumbling into the kitchen and sitting down at the table. "Can you get me a glass of water please?"

"Of course," she said, a concerned look on her face as she put her hand to his forehead. "Gosh, you're burning up. I think you might be coming down with something."

"I'll be fine in a minute, I just need some water."

Caitlin dutifully fetched a pint glass full of water, which Patrick gulped down in one go, wiping his sweating face with a tissue.

In the end, he only managed a few mouthfuls of his chilli, before clutching his stomach and screwing up his face in pain.

"I feel fucking awful," he snapped, gasping for breath. "I think I might throw up if I eat any more."

Caitlin looked worried.

"Poor you. You've definitely caught a bug I think. There's a virus going around. The best thing is to get some rest and try to sleep it off. If you're no better in the morning, I'll call the doctor."

"Yeah, you might be right," he panted, in between spasms of pain. "I'm really sorry, but I'm gonna have to go straight up to bed."

"Don't be silly. You can't help being poorly. I'll bring you some water up and a bowl to have by the bed in case you need to be sick."

Caitlin had done her research carefully and was testing the water, so to speak. Tramadol was usually prescribed in 50mg tablets, one tablet to be taken every four to six hours, up to a maximum of 500mg per day. She had decided to go for over half the maximum recommended dose as a starting point, to see what happened. The drug was classed as an opiate and a narcotic, from the same family as Methadone, Morphine and Heroine, equally as addictive, but with weaker physical effects. That didn't mean it couldn't kill you if you took too much of it though and any more than 450mg in a day was widely considered to be extremely dangerous. She didn't really understand why Patrick had built up such a stock pile, but nor did she care, as it suited her needs perfectly.

Caitlin pulled a face and turned up the television to drown out the unpleasant noises coming from the bathroom above, where it sounded very much like the contents of Patrick's stomach were making a violent bid for freedom from both ends. Opening the box of Lindor chocolates she had treated herself to, she closed her eyes and curled her feet up on the sofa, confident that poor Patrick would feel better in the morning, at least for a while. Just how long that feeling of well-being continued would be very much dependent on the choices he made moving forward. It was all about education, about understanding and respecting the relationship between choices and consequences.

Of course, giving someone too many of their own prescription drugs was not a new idea; in fact it was an extremely overused one, in fiction as well as in real life, but Caitlin liked to think she was putting her own spin on the technique. The thing was, she had no intention of murdering Patrick. The purpose of all this was simply to train him and, if everything went to plan, things would get back to how they should be and he would never need to be any the wiser.

The main thing was, she was in control now.

Independence Day

Sometimes the darkest challenges create the holes which
allow the light to shine through more brightly.

Grace

At last we were on the road to Ifaty, just 253 kilometres of mostly tarmac roads between us and the glorious west coast. We would be sleeping by the sea that night, hopefully listening to the waves lapping on the shore, a sound that I so loved and missed. I felt as if I was heading for the promised land and I couldn't wait to catch my first sight of the aquamarine waters and deserted white sand beaches I had seen in all the photographs. Sam was driving and the only thing dampening my mood was that I was still feeling a bit rattled about the earlier car key incident, unable to rid myself of the thought that someone may have interfered with our car.

"Just be careful when we're going down any long hills and keep checking the brakes," I said for the second time, the logical part of my brain telling me I was being ridiculous.

Sam laughed but nevertheless pumped the brakes a few times to make sure.

"See, everything's fine. Now stop obsessing about it and sort the music out please."

I flicked through our limited and somewhat random drive time selection, which included The Killers, The Corrs, Mike & the Mechanics and The Bay City Rollers, opting for our old favourite Mike and the Mechanics. We drove over the river where workers were mining for sapphires, then on into Tomb Country, where the often impressive and ornate ancestral tombs, considered to be sacred places, showed the importance of the dead for the Malagasy people. I read in the guidebook about a tradition known as Famadihana, or the 'turning of the bones', when the family would hold a celebration in honour of the dead, exhuming the body of their loved one, wrapping it in silk cloths and dancing around to live music with the corpse held above their heads. I couldn't see it catching on at home somehow, although the idea of dancing around Daniel's corpse did have a certain appeal for me.

When we were about halfway there, Sam pulled over to swap drivers as we usually did and, to my horror, I was immediately plunged into the scene of my worst nightmare. No sooner had she switched off the engine than a thick plume of whitish smoke rose up from the bonnet, accompanied by a violent clunking sound that shook the whole car.

"Get out now, get out! It's on fire," I screamed, wrenching at the door handle and practically falling out of the car as I scrambled away from it.

Sam was not far behind me and we both stood at the roadside in silence, staring at our car from what we considered was a safe distance.

"Possibly a slight overreaction," she said, beginning to laugh and putting a hand on my shoulder as I bent double, hands on knees, unable to breathe. "It doesn't look like smoke to me. I think it might just have overheated," she added.

Another car drew up behind ours and I had never been so glad to see Ted and Francesca in the sweep car, clearly recognisable by the brush they had strapped to the roof as a joke. Ted was out of his car in seconds, a broad smile on his face as he walked towards us.

"Oh dear, whatever have you been up to now?" he shouted. "Keys please," he said, calmly opening the driver's door and switching on the engine again. "Now here's a top tip for you girls. If you overheat again, switch off the AC and turn up the heater full blast, but keep the engine running. It should cool down quicker like that. Switching off the engine is totally the wrong thing to do I'm afraid."

"Oh God I'm so sorry, I thought it was on fire," I told him, feeling like a complete idiot.

"Nothing quite so dramatic, but don't worry about it, that's what I'm here for. We'll have you back on the road in no time," he reassured us.

I was annoyed at myself for not keeping a more careful eye on the temperature gauge. A few minutes later Jerome arrived on the scene with a couple of his mechanics, then Max pulled up just after him to complete my humiliation.

"Is it going to be okay?" I asked Ted nervously.

"Yes of course, don't worry. It's really no big deal. Have you calmed down a bit now?"

"I'm fine, it's just…I was trapped in a car that was set on fire once. Long story, but I guess it's made me a bit paranoid," I explained, a sheepish expression on my face.

"Well it would do!" replied Ted, eyes widening. "You'll have to tell me that story in the bar one of these evenings. Look, I can see you're still a bit shaken, so how's this for an idea? We let Jerome drive your car the rest of the way to Ifaty and you two can travel in style with us? Grab your bags and sling them in our car so you have everything with you, just in case there are any more problems with yours and he has to stop again."

I didn't want to look like a wimp over something so insignificant, but I was secretly relieved to hand over the keys and climb into the back of Ted's car with Sam. Jerome looked for a moment like he was about to protest, but a look from Ted silenced him and he took the keys from me with a mildly irritated sigh. He topped up the water after allowing our engine to cool then set off just ahead of us. After a few more kilometres, we began the winding descent from the mountains down towards the coast. The scenery was spectacular, but the road was tricky, with a sheer drop to one side and only occasional barriers. Ted, who liked to drive at a steady pace, was the first one to notice a problem.

"Jerome is caning it a bit on these roads," he remarked, a hint of concern in his voice. "Bloody idiot needs to slow down. He always drives too fast. What the hell's he playing at?"

We watched as our car continued to pick up speed, veering alarmingly to the outside edge on the corners and kicking up a cloud of dust behind.

"There's something wrong here...I think he may have lost his brakes," said Ted suddenly, a concerned frown on his face. "He needs to use his gears to slow down...why the hell isn't he changing down?"

We stared ahead in terrified silence, unable to offer any words of wisdom or any practical help as the full horror of the situation unfolded before our eyes. Jerome appeared to be trying to use the rough ground on the inside of the road to slow the car and for a moment it looked like it might be working, but when his wheels suddenly hit a pothole, he was travelling far too fast to avoid losing control. There was a loud screech of tyres and the car was sent spinning across the road towards the edge, where it ploughed head-on into the barrier. It was like watching a scene from a disaster movie, the sort of thing you always think never happens in real life, never happens to you.

Except it *was* happening to us.

The flimsy metal barrier offered barely any resistance before it simply gave way and we were powerless to do anything except watch in utter disbelief. Our beloved car 7 plunged straight over the cliff and disappeared from view completely, as if it had never been there in the first place. The whole thing seemed to happen in slow motion and the muted crunching noises as the car made contact with the ground, over and over again, seemed to come from very far away, as if the whole thing was somehow nothing to do with us.

For a moment there was nothing but silence. Time stood still. Then all hell broke loose as Ted slammed on the brakes and jumped out, running over to the edge of the road where we had seen the car leap to its certain destruction. Almost immediately Max pulled up behind us, grabbed a rope from the boot of his car and ran over to us.

"The car's gone, but I can see Jerome," Ted shouted. "Looks like he wasn't wearing his seat belt and was thrown out on impact. We have to get down to him. He might still be alive."

"I'll go," said Max, already tying one end of the rope around his waist. I grabbed the other end, suddenly galvanised into action. Pulling it quickly through the secure towing point on Ted's car, I tied a bowline, as I had done so many times on the boat, knowing it to be the strongest and safest knot to use. Max wasted no time in lowering himself down towards Jerome, while the rest of us kept a tight grip on the rope to help control his descent. Nobody dared speak as we watched and prayed for it all to be okay. Jerome was lying on a small rocky ledge about 15 metres down and Max was already kneeling by his side, checking for vital signs.

"Max, what's happening? Is he alive?" shouted Ted, but there was no reply.

I felt my stomach knot in panic as I watched Max begin CPR on Jerome, hands clasped as he pumped up and down hard on his chest, stopping only to breathe air into his lungs. Again and again he repeated the sequence, pausing regularly to check for signs of life, however slight, but we could all see there were none. After what seemed like an eternity he stopped and sat back, clearly exhausted and defeated. Then he rubbed his hand across his face, looked up at us and shook his head sadly. There was nothing more to be done.

I began to shake as the reality of the situation struck home and clutched at Sam's arm for support, hesitating to say what I knew we were both thinking: that it should have been us in that car.

The next few hours passed in a blur. There was what seemed like an interminable wait for the police to arrive, but when they did they took charge of everything, treating us with undisguised suspicion. They wanted individual interviews and statements about the incident as well as contact details from all of us. Then there was the matter of the recovery of Jerome's body. Jerome, who earlier that morning had been laughing and teasing us about locking the keys in the car. Jerome, who had unwittingly taken a bullet for us. I wondered where his family were, whether he had a wife and children at home, realising suddenly that I knew virtually nothing about the man who had saved our lives.

The police eventually released us to continue our journey, but barely a word was spoken in Ted's car for the six hours it took us to reach the coast. When we finally pulled into the Hotel Dunes d'Ifaty, I was grateful to see an anxious George and Suzie come running out to meet us.

"Thank God you're all safe. I couldn't believe what had happened when you rang me. Still can't to be honest. Jerome dead. I just can't get my head round it," said George, hugging me and then Sam as the four of us climbed out of the car. Max drove in behind us a few minutes later and a couple of the others came out to help carry our bags in as we trudged despondently along the path towards the reception of the hotel. Suzie put her arm around my shoulder.

"Come on. You're all obviously in shock after what has happened. I think we need to get you to your rooms, let you have a shower and change, then we'll call a meeting with everyone. Does that sound okay?" she asked.

I nodded gratefully and ten minutes later we were in our own little piece of paradise, a beautiful wooden chalet with its own private deck and view of the Indian Ocean, a million miles away from the horror of a few hours ago. After our shower we dressed and headed over to join the others in the reception area, where a 'money changer' was apparently due any minute with, I imagined, suitcases full of Ariary for those of us who needed more cash. It seemed disrespectful, but practicalities had to be addressed. I thought to myself how strange it was, the way life simply carried on after someone died, almost as if they had never had any real significance at all in the grand scheme of things. It wasn't that people didn't care, it was simply that life had to go on for the living.

Suzie came over with a 'Passion' cocktail for Sam and me and, once the money business was concluded, we all settled down for a full debrief. The mood was naturally subdued, but to my surprise, I discovered that a number of the others, including Joanna, had suffered similar mechanical malfunctions in the course of their travels, although happily with less tragic outcomes. Rally driving, like sailing and horse riding, was clearly a potentially dangerous activity with countless risks and things that could go wrong. Of course people were shaken by the incident, but they were also pragmatic and it was decided unanimously at the meeting that the rally would continue as planned. Max would arrange for one of his own 4x4s to be brought down for Sam and me to drive and we would carry on, almost as if the whole thing had never actually happened. I knew from bitter experience that we had to find a way to put the tragic accident behind us and move on, but I couldn't help thinking about the last time I had to do that, knowing from bitter experience that it was not as easy as people thought.

Joanna came over with a knowing smile and hugged me warmly in a show of solidarity, then ordered another round of cocktails. It was not long before the alcohol began to work its magic, calming my shattered nerves. Later that night, as we sat on the beach with George, Suzie and Joanna, looking up at the myriad of stars in the night sky, I reflected on how narrowly we had escaped death that day. Another Sliding Doors moment in my life. I shuddered at the alternative version of the story; the one where Sam and I chose to continue the journey in our own car after it overheated.

The following morning we awoke to a new day with bright sunshine pouring in through the windows and a session of 4x4 training in the sand dunes for those who felt they needed it, ahead of our next drive of 140 kilometres on rough sand tracks along the coast to Laguna Blu. Life was indeed going on, regardless of anyone who dropped out along the way.

George came over as we wandered into breakfast.

"Did you manage to get some sleep?" he asked, a concerned expression on his face.

I nodded and smiled in reassurance, feeling guilty at just how well I had actually slept, but putting it down to exhaustion rather than heartlessness and lack of compassion.

"I've been onto the car hire company this morning and torn a strip off them. They may well be facing criminal proceedings if it turns out they supplied that car with a known fault," said George. "Max has spoken to the police and they are working on getting the car, or rather the bits of the car, recovered for analysis, so they can hopefully determine the cause of the accident. I have to say though, in all honesty, given how things work out here we may never really know the truth about what happened," he added.

"Do you think there's a chance somebody may have sabotaged the car?" I asked, frowning and thinking of the key incident.

George looked puzzled.

"Well, that's a possibility I suppose, but highly unlikely, given the security we always have in place for the cars. No, I think it's more plausible that there was some sort of mechanical failure or that Jerome simply drove too fast and lost control."

"Oh right," I said, still unable to rid myself of the thought that someone had taken our keys from the room that night and tampered with the car. Someone who wanted to hurt us. Or worse.

George took note of my anxious expression and changed the subject.

"It's Independence Day today in Madagascar, so there'll be celebrations everywhere tonight. I know the timing is a bit off, but… Anyway, it's a tradition here for people to hang colourful candle lanterns called 'harendrinas' in the trees, so we'll be joining in and doing that before dinner. You'll love it, it's really pretty. And we could all do with something to lighten the mood I think."

I immediately decided I would light a candle and hang a lantern up for poor dead Jerome.

Back in our room, I consulted the trusty Lonely Planet guidebook and learned that Madagascar would be celebrating its fifty-ninth year of liberation from French colonial rule. National flags were everywhere, there would be military parades and fireworks as well as lots of eating, singing and dancing. We had already done our bit by buying a flag in one of the little towns we drove through and flying it proudly from our car window as a show of solidarity with the people of the country. My face clouded as I remembered where that flag was now and thought of our car plunging down the cliff side, disintegrating into a pile of twisted wreckage.

Later that evening, as the sun went down, the lantern ceremony was every bit as magical as promised and I felt privileged to be sharing this special event with our Malagasy team. I added my lantern to the others in the tree and said a little prayer for Jerome, then went back to sit at the bar with Sam and watch the processions. In spite of myself, I felt a little flutter of excitement as Max wandered over and ordered himself a beer.

"Can I get you another one?" he asked, gesturing towards our cocktails, then ordering them before either of us had time to answer and pulling up a stool to sit with us.

I couldn't help feeling pleased I had chosen to wear my figure-hugging green maxi dress for the lantern ceremony, perfect for the purposes of seduction. Then I remembered the photo on Max's phone and told myself to get a grip. He was a married man. Surely I of all people should have seen that as a reason to walk away and not get involved, but although I knew it was wrong, I had to admit to myself that I really didn't care. Worse than that, there was actually a tiny irrational part of me that wanted to punish another woman for what had happened to me. Why should I care about Max's wife when none of Daniel's other women had ever cared about me?

Maybe the whole sorry episode had changed me more than I realised. Or maybe, I thought to myself, when it came down to it I wasn't really all that different to Jane and Lorraine.

Love is Blind

Roisin

Patrick was due any minute. He had been taken ill with some kind of stomach bug while working away and had been forced to cancel his flight home, but he was apparently over the worst of it now and getting back to normal. Despite Roisin's initial disappointment, once he informed her that it was coming out of both ends and he couldn't get himself off the toilet, she was quick to agree it was for the best that he stayed away.

If she was honest, Roisin didn't mind Patrick being away so much. Quite the opposite in fact; she felt it helped to maintain the excitement in their relationship and had come to enjoy the unpredictability of it all, at least for the moment. She supposed there would probably come a time when she would want things to be a bit more stable, but for now, things suited her just as they were. After all, she had been there and done that with the whole marriage thing and, in her opinion, it was extremely overrated. She had grown to like her own space and the freedom to do what she wanted, when she wanted, without having to answer to anyone else.

Her marriage to Mark had only lasted five years, but that was more than long enough for her to realise she had made a catastrophic mistake. She quickly felt suffocated by her jealous and overly possessive ex-husband, who demanded to know her every move and clearly didn't trust her an inch. Worse than that, once the so-called honeymoon period was over, their sex life became increasingly boring and he made no qualms about the fact he thought she was weird if she ever dared to suggest they try anything a little more unconventional in the bedroom. She never discussed her patients with him in any detail, but she was pretty sure she had seen and heard it all over the years and she often wondered what he would have made of some of their more unusual penchants. The various psychological disorders, not to mention sexual deviancies of the people who walked through her door had long since ceased to either surprise or shock her, but Mark was sadly not so broad-minded. Not like Patrick. As she expected, he had been utterly devastated when she announced that the marriage was over, but by then she had made up her mind and was not one to waver. If there was one thing she had learned in her professional capacity, it was that life was too short to waste it with someone you were fundamentally incompatible with and it was time for her to heed her own advice. There was sadly a lot of truth in the old saying: 'Marry in haste, repent at leisure'.

She had endeavoured to make sure the split was as amicable and clean-cut as possible so that they could both get on with their lives and maybe even stay friends. Mark, who was earning big money as a financial consultant, reluctantly agreed to buy her out of their house in Dalkey, giving her the financial independence to be able to move on and buy the apartment in Dun Laoghaire without a mortgage, which suited her perfectly. Money was at least one thing she did not have to worry about going forward. At first, she found the sexual freedom of her new single life very liberating and she enjoyed some great hook-ups with some very obliging and adventurous partners, but she was beginning to crave more. When she met Patrick that night in Temple Bar, everything changed and all of a sudden she found herself thinking about building a future with him.

There was a lasagne in the oven and she had restocked the wine rack with Barolo, Rioja, Sauvignon Blanc and even a bottle of his favourite Chateau Musar, although she had baulked a bit at the price of that last one. A smile played on her lips as she imagined his face when he saw what she was wearing. She had it all planned. She would go to the door in her raincoat, as if she had just come in from work, but underneath she would be wearing the skimpy 'naughty nurse' outfit she had bought on the internet to surprise him. The little white dress clung to her curvaceous body, barely long enough to cover her modesty, with special cut-outs allowing her nipples to poke through, which she had to admit she herself found extremely erotic. The ensemble was finished off with stockings and a red suspender belt, but no panties to inhibit proceedings and of course she was clean-shaven down there, just as she knew he liked it. She took a moment to admire her reflection in the mirror, put on her favourite Chanel Rouge lipstick and tweaked her already pert nipples. She could not resist sliding her hand up the inside of her thigh and allowing her fingers to caress the warm wetness of her arousal in anticipation of what was to come. She let out a low moan of pleasure and her gaze lingered on the bedside cabinet containing her collection of toys, but she forced herself to wait, knowing it would be worth it. She heard footsteps outside and went to greet Patrick at the door, hurriedly putting on her jacket and tying the belt.

"I've missed you so much," she declared, throwing her arms around his neck before he was even through the door.

"Whoa, let me get in," he laughed.

"That's exactly what I'm going to do," she purred suggestively, allowing the coat to fall open slightly to reveal a hint of what was underneath.

"I've missed you too," he said, grinding against her hip to let her feel his erection and show her he was fighting fit and ready for action, courtesy of his little blue pills.

Patrick sniggered lasciviously, eyes growing wider as Roisin took his hand and guided it up under her coat, running her tongue slowly over her lips.

"Well Nurse, I think I'd have got better a lot quicker if you'd been looking after me these past couple of weeks. Maybe you could give me a bit of an examination now though, just to make sure I'm okay…" he added, throwing himself into the role play.

Roisin wriggled out of her coat, then turned around and bent down with straight legs to pick up the pen she had theatrically dropped on the floor, exposing her buttocks to Patrick's obvious delight. She stayed there for a moment, allowing him to admire the view, then sashayed towards the bedroom with him trotting expectantly behind her. She stopped him at the side of the bed and deftly undid his belt, then the button and zip of his chinos, allowing them to fall to the ground as she helped him to step out of them like a child. Dropping to her knees in front of him, she pulled on the waistband of his silk boxers, allowing his erect penis to spring to attention.

"Everything seems to be in order here," she said, looking up into the camera of the iPhone he was already pointing at her face. "Just one more check I need to do though," she murmured as she took him in her mouth, obliging him with her very best performance for the camera.

Alternating between expert flicks of her tongue and allowing him to thrust deep into her mouth, she brought him to the brink of orgasm but recognized just the right moment to pull away.

Getting slowly to her feet, she stepped out of her stilettos and climbed onto the bottom of the bed. She then proceeded to crawl slowly up it on all fours, wiggling her bum at him provocatively, before turning over and lying back on the pillows, parting her legs to tease him. She knew by now exactly what did it for him and set to work with her fingers, writhing around on the bed as she pleasured herself and allowed him to film the proceedings in close up. Above all, Patrick liked to watch. Roisin was not one to hold back and quickly reached a noisy climax, head thrown back in ecstasy, before allowing a red-faced and sweating Patrick to enter her. It was all over in a few short moments, which was probably for the best, as it crossed her mind that he looked worryingly like he might have a heart attack.

An hour or so later, they were sitting at her round glass dining table, tucking into the lasagne she had made and already on their second bottle of Rioja.

"So how's life been in Looney Tunes-Ville?" Patrick asked, snorting disdainfully. "Any good stories to tell me? I bet you see some real psychos in that office of yours…just make sure they never find out where you live," he added, eager to see just how far he could run with this.

He accompanied the last comment with a mock knife stabbing action, like Norman Bates in 'Psycho'. Roisin bristled slightly, feeling suddenly disloyal.

"Don't talk about my patients like that, Patrick. They're just ordinary human beings like you and me. They have problems that are often ruining their lives and they are usually desperate, at rock bottom when they come to me for help. Have a little more respect for what I do please."

"Okay, okay I'm sorry," he laughed, holding up his hands. "I was only teasing you. I know what you do is important and I think it's great that you can help people to conquer their demons, really I do."

Patrick made an effort to look remorseful, careful not to show his irritation at her 'holier than thou' attitude. He reached over to refill Roisin's glass.

"Am I forgiven? I think you need to chill out a bit. Maybe we should take our wine into the lounge, get ourselves comfortable and watch this evening's home video from our little taster session earlier to get us in the mood again, then maybe we could have an action replay…" he suggested, the master-manipulator at work.

She was easily won over and followed him happily to the sofa, bottle in hand. He had already told her he was only home for a week before he had to go away on another job, so there was no point in wasting their time together arguing when there were so many more fun things they could be doing.

The following morning was Saturday and the whole weekend stretched ahead of them. Roisin had cooked a full Irish breakfast, which was actually more of a brunch by the time they dragged themselves out of bed.

"So what made you become a psychologist then?" Patrick asked her, chewing a piece of toast.

"*Clinical* psychologist," she corrected him. "That means I specialize in *abnormal* psychology. I suppose I've always been fascinated by people and what makes them tick. You know, like what makes them behave in a certain way, what drives some people to do terrible things. The human brain is truly an amazing thing and I just love trying to unravel its mysteries. Most of my clients aren't that extreme in their behaviour to be fair, but every so often I get called in by the police as an expert witness to assess the state of mind of a murderer or a serial killer and that's when you start to realise the levels of deception people are capable of in order to hide what they are doing or get away with something. The thing is though, most of those people crave notoriety at the same time and so they start to leave clues and take more risks along the way, which usually leads to their downfall in the end. It's almost like they want some sort of recognition for what they've done."

Patrick struggled not to choke on his toast.

"Wow. I take my hat off to you. I couldn't do what you do," he said, his expression full of apparent appreciation for her skills, while in reality, he was thinking to himself that she was clearly not very good at her job.

Roisin laughed, delighted at his perceived admiration for her career. It had taken her years of study and experience to climb the professional ladder and she was proud of her achievement and reputation in her chosen field of expertise, ASPD (Antisocial Personality Disorders). She stood up and went to make another pot of coffee.

"So I was thinking," she began, looking at Patrick to gauge his reaction. "I'm due some time off, so why don't I come with you on your job next week? It'd be nice to spend some time together and I thought maybe we could make it into a bit of a holiday."

"You'd be bored out of your mind," he replied quickly, thinking to himself that Hell would freeze over before that would happen. "I'm not off on some kind of a jolly you know. I have to work ridiculously long hours, sometimes right through the night, so that the company doesn't lose any more production time than they have to. I'm usually stuck in a dusty factory, either freezing cold or boiling hot, in the middle of nowhere, not glamorous at all I can promise you. When a company calls me in as a consultant, the reason they pay top rates is because they know I'm one of the best in the world in this business, but the downside is they want their pound of flesh and it's always full-on, whether it's an installation or troubleshooting they need. That's why I'm always so knackered when I get home."

Patrick shrugged his shoulders, then continued with a sweetener.

"To be perfectly honest, I prefer to keep work and holiday separate. I just think it's better that way. Look, why don't we go on a proper holiday a bit later in the year? How do you fancy the Seychelles? I've never been myself, but one of my clients went last year and said it was amazing."

I've heard it's a popular honeymoon destination too, he thought to himself, remembering his own honeymoon there with Grace and the subsequent visits with Lorraine, but didn't bother to say that out loud. In his experience, the promise of an exotic holiday in the sun never failed to reel them in and, from the look on her face, Roisin was clearly no different from any of his other women. He doubted it would be too difficult to get her to pay for it either.

"Oh yes, that's definitely on my bucket list of places to visit. It always looks so romantic," she sighed wistfully.

"Great. Let's do it then. If you pick up some brochures and do a bit of research on the internet, we can get something booked when I get back. It'll give us both something to look forward to."

Sorted. Time to change the subject and introduce another idea while he was on a roll.

"Actually, before I forget, I've been meaning to talk to you about something," he said, ensuring he gave the impression it was nothing more than a casual thought. "I'm earning pretty good money at the moment, as you know, but interest rates on savings are so low right now, there's absolutely no point in keeping money in the bank. I've been looking into a few different options and I've decided to start buying classic cars as an investment, maybe even importing them from the US, as you can get such amazing deals over there on right-hand drives at the moment. Having money in assets rather than cash is also better with regard to the tax man," he said with a wink, careful to sound enthusiastic about the plan, but not too pushy. "A friend of mine in the UK is doing it and he says it's an absolutely fail-safe way of making money, as classic cars are going up in value all the time."

Patrick paused for a moment to let that sink in before continuing.

"I remember you told me you had a lump sum left over after your divorce settlement, so I thought it might be something you would be interested in as well. We could do it together. I'm happy to find the right cars at a good price for you if you fancy it and we could build up quite a collection between us. I can just picture you on a nice sunny day, driving around the countryside in a red Austin Healey. Look at this one."

Patrick moved in for the kill and showed her a picture of a red and cream 1959 Healey on his phone, confident that she would love it.

"Oh my God, it's gorgeous," she enthused. "I've never really thought about investing money like that to be perfectly honest, but you're right about interest rates being dire. It's certainly something I could think about. Leave it with me."

"Great stuff. You are like a breath of fresh air. I love how you are so adventurous and always open to new ideas, so completely different to any other woman I have ever known," he concluded, turning on the charm and playing the flattery card.

In actual fact, Roisin was usually quite cautious with money, but she trusted Patrick implicitly and he certainly seemed to have done his homework on the classic car idea. She knew people did stuff like that, putting money into assets to make it work for them, rather than letting it fester in a bank. It was certainly worth looking into and she was already struggling to get the image of the little red sports car out of her mind. Even more importantly, she loved how he talked about them investing 'together' and kept using the pronouns 'we' and 'us'. It gave her butterflies in her stomach to realise what that meant; he was seeing a future for them as a couple and was as committed to her as she was to him.

Patrick noted the look on Roisin's face and smiled, knowing he had played a blinder and silently congratulating himself on taking an important step towards building up his pension pot again.

A Voice from the Grave

We are not haunted by ghosts, but by the memories we refuse to let go of, too strong in our minds to be obliterated with the passing of time.

Grace

I sat alone on the wooden stage outside the nightclub, listening to the noise of the people out celebrating Independence Day on the crowded streets of Ifaty, feeling strangely detached from it all. A few metres away, inside the club, a DJ was churning out a bizarre mixture of local and western dance music. Several of the town's hookers were up dancing, while others had abandoned the dance floor and were swarming like flies round the group of Europeans that had turned up, hoping to extract some money from them one way or another. I was too hot and leaned forward with my head in my hands, feeling as if I might pass out, or throw up. I waited for one of the others to notice I was missing and come out to help me, but no one came. Max, Sam, George, Suzie...I could see them all in there, laughing and joking together, but they didn't seem to notice me trying to attract their attention with a feeble wave. It was as if they were looking straight through me, as if I were invisible. I returned my head to my hands and took deep breaths, trying to blot out the noise pounding in my ears and calm the rising nausea.

Without warning, I felt someone grab me by the hair, jerking my head sharply backwards, then dragging me roughly off the staging and onto the floor, slamming my face down into the dirt. Before I could work out what was happening, I was pushed over onto my back and felt the pain of a knee pressing hard on my neck, seemingly intent on squeezing the life out of me, a large clammy hand over my nose and mouth. I could barely breathe, let alone cry out for help, and there was no strength in my body to either fight off my attacker or try to escape. A surge of fear ran through my body and I was certain at that moment I was about to die. I didn't want to give in, but I was powerless, frozen. It was a man. I could tell that much from his outline as he leaned over me, but I was unable to make out any features in the blackness, despite the fact his face was almost touching mine. His sour breath made me want to gag. Suddenly he removed his hand from my face and I thought for a moment he was going to let me go, but instead, he prised my mouth open and shoved something hard and metallic into it.

"Do you know what these are?" he hissed, as the metal ground painfully against my teeth. "Yes, I can see you do, Grace. I've been watching you for a very long time, waiting for this moment. Because I know what you did. And now I'm going to make you pay for it."

He released his hold just long enough to allow me to sit up and spit out the metal objects into my hand. I gasped for breath, retching and staring in horror at two stainless steel shackles, covered in my blood and saliva, both of them with the pins missing. My eyes were wild with terror, searching for clues in the darkness, but no matter how hard I strained them, I couldn't bring his face into focus. I opened my mouth to scream for help, but still no sound came out, nor could I move my seemingly paralysed legs. The man laughed, a harsh, cruel tone to his voice. In a split second, I was back on the boat that night in the middle of the Irish Sea.

"Everyone has choices and those choices have consequences," he said, raising his arm high.

Then his fist made contact with my face and everything went black.

"Grace!"

I heard the shout from far away, a familiar voice dragging me back into the world of the living.

"Grace! It's me. You're okay. You're safe."

Slowly my eyes began to adjust to the bright light and allow my brain to make sense of my surroundings. I was sitting on the floor of our bedroom and Sam was on the edge of the bed beside me, her hand on my shoulder, shaking me gently.

"You fell out of bed, you idiot," she laughed. "What the hell were you dreaming about? You look like you've seen a ghost."

"Sam, it was awful. So real. I had a dream about Daniel. At least I think it was Daniel...I couldn't make out his face. He was *here*, in Madagascar. He followed us to the nightclub Max took us to, then attacked me and tried to kill me. I swear I thought I was dead," I whispered, close to tears.

"Well for starters, anything involving that arse-hole is a night terror, not a dream. Just as well he's in a watery grave at the bottom of the ocean. Are you sure you didn't have any of that whacky baccy that was being passed around in the club we went to?" asked Sam, in an attempt to lighten the mood. "Come on, forget it and try to get some sleep. It's three in the morning. Everything will look better in the daylight."

I sat up in bed for a while and drank my bottle of water, trying to remember all the details of the terrifying scene my imagination had conjured up, but it was like staring at a picture in the dark; no matter how much I squinted, I just couldn't see it properly. When I eventually lay down, I remained wide awake, fearful of allowing myself to drift into sleep in case the nightmare returned to plunge me once again into that parallel world of chaos, evil and hatred. A world in which my secret was out and Daniel was hell-bent on revenge, determined to make me pay for my sins.

I must have slept at some point because I awoke the next morning to sunlight streaming in through the shutters and the sound of waves breaking gently on a beach. A sense of peace and tranquillity flooded into my soul, banishing all the demons and dark thoughts of the previous night. When we wandered into breakfast after a swim in the sea, I saw Max coming over to greet us and there was no mistaking the butterflies in my stomach again. After the customary French greeting of a kiss on both cheeks, he proudly held up a set of car keys.

"Voila! The keys to your new car," he announced. "Only the best for you."

"Ooh thank you. I knew you'd look after us," I flirted, pushing all thoughts of his baby and wife very firmly to the back of my mind. So long as I didn't mention them or ask him anything about them, I could tell myself they didn't really exist. Classic avoidance technique. To my disappointment, he only hung around long enough to tell us it was the silver Toyota in the car park, then announced he had 'stuff' to do and would see us the following day.

"He fancies you," said Sam as soon as he had gone.

"He barely said two words to me," I laughed. "Hardly a declaration of love."

"No, but I'm not just talking about now. He couldn't take his eyes off you when we went out to that dodgy nightclub and was clearly jealous of you dancing with anybody else. Seriously, you should go for it with him. You deserve a bit of fun. And he's hot," she added, raising her eyebrows.

"Okay, okay," I laughed. "I admit I do fancy him and there's definitely a little spark there, but I'm pretty sure he's married. I've seen a picture of his little girl on his phone. I can't deny there's a part of me that thinks 'what the hell?', but at the end of the day, I just can't be that person Sam. Not after everything that happened to me and all the pain it caused."

I said it and of course I meant it, but even as I polished my halo, I was not so sure I intended to stick to my resolution.

The 140km drive from Ifaty to Andavadoaka that day was our first taste of serious off-road driving on the dirt and sand tracks, which wound their way along the stunning western coastline. It had not gone down well in the bar the night before when I said to Max after a short sand dune training session that I thought driving on the sand was like a cross between dodgem cars and a video game.

"Remember Grace, you get three lives in a video game, not so many in a real car. Be careful," he warned, genuine concern etched on his face.

The ocean views as we drove through the dunes were incredible. The dazzling aquamarine colour of the water with the sun sparkling on it, set against the pure white sand of the deserted beaches was perfect and made my heart soar with joy. The only people apart from us when we stopped were a couple of local fishermen, dragging their little wooden pirogue ashore and, as I watched them, it felt like I was looking through a window at a different world. As we drove on, there was a bit of everything to deal with: rocks, dirt tracks, dry river beds, fords to cross and deep sandy tracks, which threatened to stop the car dead if you were not careful. The driving was going surprisingly well until we rounded a corner and came up behind one of our team blocking the track completely, wheels spinning wildly as the car buried itself ever deeper into the sand. Andry was there, running around collecting branches to pack under the wheels, sweat pouring down his face in the heat of the sun. There was already a large and ever-increasing band of local villagers on the scene, who always seemed to materialize from nowhere out of the bush in a crisis and of course it wasn't long before our own cavalry arrived behind us in the form of Ted and Francesca.

"What have you done this time, you naughty little foxes?" boomed Ted as he strode towards our car.

It was impossible not to love the irrepressible Ted, with his inimitable style and mannerisms that made it seem like you had been transported onto the set of a Carry On film.

"Not us this time," I laughed, pointing towards the car in front.

The villagers were obviously keen to engage with us, so Sam and I turned our attention to entertaining them with our limited choice of music from the car and teaching them a variety of formation dances, or at least our version of them. They spoke neither French nor English and our Malagasy was non-existent, so the medium of music and dance seemed as good a way as any to communicate.

I thought afterwards how strange it was that there was a little group of people living deep in the heart of rural Madagascar, who now knew the actions to the Macarena and had been introduced to some of the iconic sounds of our teenage years, such as the Bay City Rollers. We undoubtedly left them with a lasting impression of the strange 'vezo' or foreigners that crossed their path that day, even more so when, after a sign language conversation with a couple of the girls, they also became the proud owners of a random selection of our underwear and clothing.

There was a loud cheer as the stricken car in front finally slithered and slipped its way forward out of the deep sand and we were all able to continue northwards into the land of the majestic Baobab tree. We stayed in convoy with the other two cars from the bush incident, stopping for lunch among the iconic trees, where Andry, a true font of knowledge, who could talk for hours about the flora and fauna of his beloved country, was in his element.

"The Baobab tree is known as the 'Tree of Life' because it absorbs and stores water in its trunk during the rainy season and then produces a fruit which is rich in nutrients in the dry season. The bark can be made into rope and clothing, the seeds can be used to make cosmetic oils and you can even eat the leaves," he laughed, sweeping his hand out as if to present the magical tree to us. "From now on you will see health and beauty products containing Baobab oil everywhere. You should try some," he added, with his characteristic infectious enthusiasm.

He didn't need to persuade me. I was already sold on the idea, having read that the Baobab produced collagen to give a glowing complexion and help fight the signs of ageing. Like most women I knew, I was on a never-ending quest to find the elixir of youth, the miracle product that would actually deliver on its promise of younger-looking skin. Baobab oil was definitely worth a try.

"Have you seen anything of the others? Is everyone okay?" I asked Ted nonchalantly, wondering where Max was.

"At least three of the cars have overheated and another couple have been stuck in the sand dunes. Max has been on the phone several times ranting at me, as it was his turn to 'sweep up' at the back today and he's had more than his fair share of incidents," Ted said with a wicked grin. "He's had a bit of a Gallic sense of humour failure, I'm afraid. I'm sure he's just cross because he'd far rather be up here with you," he added, winking as I blushed.

"Could you take a photo of us please?" I asked quickly, to change the subject.

Sam and I scrambled up onto the roof of our car and the photo Ted took of us in our shorts and 'Girls just wanna have fun' t-shirts, arms thrown up in the air as if we had not a care in the world, became the photo that summed up the whole trip for me.

The last bit of our journey involved navigating our way across a vast expanse of salt flats, before finally arriving at the hidden gem that was Laguna Blu. Our accommodation was in charming individual cottages and I was delighted to find that we had the most fabulous outdoor shower with gorgeous, brightly coloured murals and mosaic tiles. The Italian owners had built a spectacular deck overlooking the ocean and we all gathered there for sundowners, chatting animatedly about the day's highlights and misadventures. Sam chose that perfect setting for a little tribute to Charles, asking us all to raise a glass as she recited the South African toast he would so often say before a meal:

Here's to the blood of your health
And here's to the health of your blood.
If your blood is good and your health is good
Here's to your bloody good health!

At the end of the evening, when everyone started to peel off to bed, I lingered in the bar talking to Max. The conversation flowed easily and the connection between us was undeniable, as if we had known each other all our lives. He sat close enough that our knees were touching and his hand brushed against my arm occasionally as we spoke, sending little shivers of excitement through me. I struggled to concentrate on what he was saying, as I began to fantasise about his hands on my body, the taste of his lips on mine…

"Come on Grace, I'll walk you home," he said suddenly, taking my hand and pulling me to my feet. Before we reached the cottage, he stopped and turned to face me.

"Close your eyes, I want to show you something," he said, smiling at my expression.

"I bet you say that to all the girls," I quipped nervously.

"Trust me."

There they were, those two little words again. I had heard them so many times before and they had only ever led to heartache and betrayal, but nevertheless, I did as he asked.

Max moved to stand close behind me, his body against mine, his arms enveloping me, creating a little cocoon of safety.

"Now open your eyes and look up. Isn't that the most beautiful thing you've ever seen?"

There were no lights on anywhere around and I opened my eyes to the pure and natural beauty of the millions of stars and constellations glittering in the night sky, the pale shadow of the Milky Way stretching into infinity and beyond. I turned to face him, my heart thumping in my chest as he cupped his hands round my face and kissed me full on the lips, a long and tender kiss that truly meant something, not the sort exchanged by friends. They say the eyes are a window to the soul and, as he looked into mine, I wanted him to see it all: the hurt, the vulnerability, the strength, the fire. I wanted to shut the world out, to think of nothing except losing myself in his embrace, but I had seen the photo on his phone and forced myself to pull away.

"Max, who is the little girl in the photo on your phone?" I asked abruptly, holding his gaze.

He sighed and kissed me gently on the neck, sending shivers through me all over again, then he took out his phone to show me.

"This is Delphine, my daughter. She's nearly two. I named the ecolodge after her."

"She's adorable," I said, looking at the huge dark eyes, long lashes and soft dark curls. "I wonder what her mother would think about you kissing me like that," I added in a bristly tone, annoyed with myself and irritated with him for turning out to be no better than Daniel.

Max looked at me a little strangely.

"Grace… my wife and daughter are in Tana. We're getting a divorce. She almost died giving birth to Delphine and, when things go wrong out here…well let's just say there tends to be no plan B," he said quietly. "She hates the isolation here and prefers the town. And her new boyfriend of course."

"Right. How do you feel about that?"

"I have a life here and I'm happy for her," he said simply. "Sometimes you have to follow your heart and be true to your own dreams. It's not like I never see them and I will always provide for Delphine and be there for her, but Talia and I were not meant to be together. We hurt each other too much and we wanted different things."

It was certainly not my idea of a perfect family life, but maybe I was the one who needed to re-evaluate. An unwelcome memory of something Daniel once said found its way into my thoughts:

"We don't have to be conventional, Grace."

I couldn't help wondering how the conversations between Daniel and his other women had gone when they found out he was married. What lies did he tell them to explain me away? Did they believe what he told them, or was it simply that they didn't care about me? More to the point, was Max doing the exact same thing now? Explaining Talia away with a few carefully chosen lies? Telling me what he knew I wanted to hear?

An unexpected twist of fate had put me on the other side of the fence with a married man and all that mattered now was whether or not I chose to believe what Max was telling me about his wife.

A Dangerous Obsession

Daniel

Daniel was starting to enjoy life again. He had his bolt hole in the south with Caitlin, Queen of the Laundry Basket, his Dun Laoghaire apartment with Roisin, the Nympho Shrink and he was even thinking about branching out in the States again, variety being the spice of life and all that. He could not deny he missed his old life in Rhode Island, but going back there was obviously not an option. Not one to set his sights low however, he thought maybe he would try Cape Cod, or possibly Long Island this time. He just needed to get rid of that damn bug that was still hanging around and making him feel so lousy, then he would plan a trip out there to look at some cars. Roisin had taken the bait on that one more easily than he had expected, proving once again to him how pathetically gullible and predictable women were. Given her profession, he found it utterly hilarious that she had no idea she was being played, despite the many hints and clues he had dropped in along the way as part of the fun. He already had a few cars in his sights and thought it was probably time he closed the deal on at least a couple of them with Roisin before she had too much time to look into it all and get cold feet. He had found out she was sitting on the best part of half a million after her divorce, a discovery that brought back bitter memories of his own less than positive experience in the dissolving of his marriage with Grace. In his opinion, it wasn't like the money was really hers. She had effectively stolen it from her husband, so he felt no qualms at all about what he was planning.

Grace was still proving to be a massive thorn in Daniel's side. There was a very fine line between love and hate and he found that the more he sought to punish her and get his revenge, the more he obsessed about controlling her and keeping her in his life.

It was gone half eleven by the time he began to think about getting out of bed. Caitlin had taken Bentley out before going to work, but had clearly not remembered to shut him in the kitchen as he had asked her to do, given that the stupid mutt was now whining and scratching at the bedroom door. After waking up in a sweat again in the night, complaining of a banging headache, Caitlin had got up to fetch him some painkillers and he was beginning to feel better at last. Whatever bug he had picked up, it was certainly very unpleasant and he was beginning to worry he may have caught something from the one-night-stands he had recently indulged in. The women in question had seemed presentable enough, but you could never really tell these days, so he made a mental note to book himself into a clinic in Dublin on his next trip there to get himself checked out. Better to be safe than sorry, especially after the Herpes thing with Lorraine, when he had discovered that flu-like symptoms are a common sign of such infections.

Daniel took longer than usual in the shower, inspecting his genital area closely for signs of anything untoward. Having satisfied himself that everything was as it should be, he dressed and went downstairs, shoving Bentley roughly out of the way with his foot. He didn't feel like anything to eat, but made himself a pot of coffee and settled down for the day in the lounge with his feet up and his laptop on his knee. His first port of call was Facebook and his mood immediately darkened as he scrolled through the latest posts and photos. No mention whatsoever of her recent mechanical problems or the tragic car accident. Just a load of pictures of white sand beaches, brilliant blue sky and sunshine, Grace and Samantha doing yoga, Grace with a man looking out at the sunset, Grace with the same man, standing next to a car and laughing, Grace and

Samantha on the deck of a little wooden chalet, drinks in hand… Who the hell was the man? He wasn't in any of the earlier photos she had posted. Daniel felt the anger rising in him. What kind of a monster was she? How could she toss away twenty years of marriage as if it meant nothing, then throw herself at any random man who crossed her path, without giving so much as a second's thought to the husband she had so callously left for dead?

Daniel opened Aidan Flynn's account and saw to his intense annoyance that his last three messages had still not even been seen by Grace, let alone acknowledged. He began to type again:

I'm really worried about you as I haven't heard anything for ages. Have I done something to upset you? Please just get in touch and let me know you're okay xx

He jabbed the return key peevishly to send the message, then closed the lid on his laptop as his phone vibrated and he saw No Caller ID on the screen. He did not usually answer to unknown callers, but he had an inkling who it might be, so he swiped to accept the call and held the phone to his ear without saying a word. After a momentary pause he heard a man's voice speaking in a neutral, indistinguishable tone:

"I have completed the work as agreed and I assume you have received the photos and my report. I believe that concludes our business."

"Except you didn't, did you?" retorted Daniel. "Complete the work as agreed, I mean. Because someone else died in that *fucking* car and *she* hasn't got a scratch on her!"

There was a moment of silence before the man responded in a quiet but menacing tone.

"I strongly suggest you show a little more respect when you are speaking to me. I acted on the information *you* gave me. May I remind you that you were the one driven by your ego, determined to taunt her and drag things out so that eventually she would know it was you behind it all? If you had wanted her dead, I can assure you she would have been found by now with a bullet between the eyes. As for the other guy…what can I say? Wrong place, wrong time. That's the way the dice roll sometimes. If you want to play games you have to accept there will always be an element of Russian Roulette. Now, I'm a busy man and, as I said, that concludes our business."

Before Daniel had a chance to speak again, the caller hung up and he was left seething with fury at the arrogance and sheer rudeness of the man. He had been paid a hefty fee plus expenses to spend a week in Madagascar, so the least he could do was show some manners. On the plus side, although Grace was not dead, with a bit of luck she was well on the way to being consumed by guilt, paranoia, loneliness and fear.

There was a loud ping and the beginnings of a message flashed on the screen of Daniel's phone. He snatched it up excitedly and saw what he had been waiting for:

Hi, so sorry I've not replied to your messages. No wifi or phone signal for the last few days. All good here, having an amazing time! Photos on FB. Hope ur ok x

Daniel sneered at the 'no wifi or phone signal' comment. She had obviously learned that one from him and he did not believe it for a second, having used it on her many times in the past as his 'get out of jail free card'. He was not at all happy about the lack of reference to the 'accident', having spent a lot of money on arranging it, but he reckoned he knew her well enough by now to be sure she was just bluffing and putting on a brave face. There was no way she was not shaken by recent events, but he couldn't bring anything up himself without sounding suspicious. He would have to bide his time.

No problem. Glad you're okay. You'll have to come over and tell me all about it in person when you get back. I'd really love to meet you properly xx

He felt he needed to move things along a little with their 'relationship' and was already imagining her face when she finally came face to face with 'Aidan', the spectre from beyond the grave. He was busy congratulating himself on this latest coup to reel her in when her response came through and he practically imploded at the non-committal nature of it. A thumbs-up sign. Nothing else. No kiss, no enthusiasm or grateful words of encouragement. Nothing. Daniel inhaled deeply in an attempt to calm his temper and decided he would have to leave it at that for the moment. He needed a distraction and it seemed as good a time as any to turn his attention to clinching the car deal with Roisin.

Opening his laptop again he found the advert for the red and cream Austin-Healey 3000 on classiccars.com. It was for sale for $68,000 through Autosport on Long Island and fitted the bill perfectly. He knew Roisin had the week off, so he phoned her with the exciting news of what he had found out.

"Hey you," she answered, sounding pleased. "To what do I owe this honour? I rarely get more than a couple of texts when you're away working," she teased.

"Well don't get used to it," Daniel quipped, deadly serious, but masking it as a joke. "You know that classic car I showed you last week…the red and white one that was already sold?"

"Yes of course, the Austin-Healey," she replied, keen to show she had taken an interest.

"Well I had a couple of meetings cancelled today, so I had some time on my hands to do a bit of research and…you're not going to believe this, but it's back on the market. The sale must have fallen through. It's on at a fantastic price, probably because it's right-hand drive and nobody wants that in the States. Seriously, it's a steal at $68,000. It's absolutely stunning and it's got matching numbers and full history with it, which all adds to the value. It needs a bit of TLC in places, but I swear it'll be worth twice that amount in a year's time. Have a look at the link I've sent you."

"Whoa, steady on, that's a lot to take in all at once," she laughed but opened her laptop to take a look nevertheless.

"Sorry, sorry. I know this is all happening very quickly. It's just that I know a good deal when I see it and you don't often see a car as good as this at such a bargain price. I suppose I'm getting carried away because I know it's perfect for you."

Daniel paused to let it all sink in and for the beauty of the car to work its magic on her. He did not have to wait long.

"So it's $68,000, which is about 55,000 euros I guess," she calculated. "And you're absolutely sure it's a good investment? There's no way I could lose money on it?" she asked, tentatively.

"Trust me, there's no way. I guarantee if you don't like it we could put it straight back on the market and we'd make money on it," he promised, using the 'we' pronoun again to emphasise that they were in this together and give her confidence.

"But how would we go about buying it from the States and getting it back over here? Doesn't that cost a fortune?"

"Leave all that to me. It's not as expensive as you might think and I've got quite a bit of experience already. If you want to go ahead with it, I'll speak to the guys over there and get them to hold it until next week, when I've got to go out there on business anyway. There's a couple of others I'm interested in myself, so we could have our very own collection before you know it," he said excitedly. "We'll have a lot of fun, that's for sure."

There was a short pause and he waited patiently before hearing the words that were music to his ears.

"You know what, I've been telling myself for a while that I need to be more spontaneous, more of a risk-taker, so...hell yes, let's do it!"

Daniel smiled to himself at how easy that had been. Now for the crunch.

"There's a ridiculous amount of paperwork involved for the sales agreement and the shipping documents, but don't worry, I can sort all that out when I'm over there. I'll need to put everything in my name initially, as I'll be the one signing all the documents, but it's easy to change all that afterwards once we get it back here."

"What about paying for it?" she asked, right on cue.

"The easiest thing will be for you to do a bank transfer directly to the dealer, although…."

"What is it?"

"It's nothing really…it's just that I hate the way the banks rip you off with currency conversion fees and a load of other stuff. It's disgraceful really and should be much more straightforward than it is, especially in this day and age of technology."

Daniel paused for a moment, shaking his head and tutting in annoyance at the devious financial practices of banks.

"There is actually a way round it if you don't mind a bit more hassle," he said, eager to show how helpful he could be. "I've got a dollars account, so if you could get the money out in cash, I could put it in my US account and then pay the dealer once I've checked the car over and I'm happy with it. We can have one hell of a night out on the town with the money we'll save," he added.

Roisin looked doubtful but was clearly thinking about it.

"Why cash? Can't I just transfer the money to you?"

"Same issues I'm afraid." *And there'll be records of the transaction, you stupid cow,* he thought.

"It's no problem for me either way," said Daniel, shrugging his shoulders. "Like I said, I just don't like the way banks rip us all off, but if you're happy with it…"

"You're right," said Roisin decisively. "There's no point in giving them money for nothing. I'll get the cash out. I have no idea what that amount of money actually looks like," she laughed.

"Brilliant! You won't regret this, I promise," he said, barely able to contain his excitement. "There's nothing I like better than getting one over on the banks."

In all honesty, Daniel liked getting one over on anyone, especially women. They agreed on the sum of 80,000 euros to cover the cost of the car, shipping and other minor expenses. Not bad for a couple of hours work. And the best thing about it was that there was plenty more where that came from. Why spend your own money when it was so easy to spend someone else's?

Carpe Diem

Enjoy every moment of the path you are on, even if you have no idea where it is leading you.

Grace

Our last supper at Laguna Blu was a meal to remember, cooked by the Italian owner, who was also the head chef. The main attraction was an enormous, beautifully presented whole fish on a platter, brought in fresh by the local fishermen earlier in the day, together with oysters and the most wonderful homemade Tiramisu I had ever tasted for dessert. Max was on great form in the bar that evening and my heart melted to hear the passion and pride in his voice as he talked about his home, the Ecolodge Delphine in Belo sur Mer, where we would be staying in two days' time. We wandered outside and stood together on the terrace overlooking the ocean.

"How did you come to be here, so far from home?" I asked, curious about his decision to up sticks and leave his native Canada. "Don't you miss it?"

"Quebec is a beautiful place and of course there are many things I miss about my home country, but I needed a change and, to be fair, I was sick of the cold and snow in winter," he laughed, shrugging his shoulders. "I wanted to go somewhere I would still be able to hear my native French language, so I tossed a coin to decide between Guadeloupe and Madagascar and ended up here. I thank God every day that I did."

"I can't believe you moved halfway across the world, just like that, on a whim. I don't think I could ever be that spontaneous," I said, a touch of envy in my voice.

"It's not that difficult Grace. I just made a decision to change things in my life. Anyone can do that if they want to."

And of course he fell in love out here, which must have greatly influenced his decision to stay, but I didn't want to think about that.

"I know what you mean about this country. It gets inside your soul somehow. I think we all feel it," I said, looking back fondly at the others.

"Come on," said Max, turning to wander back into the bar. "It's a tough drive and a long day tomorrow, so be careful. I'll be going ahead with George and Suzie to meet you at the ferry," he added, kissing me on each cheek and leaving me to finish my drink with Sam.

I could only explain my feelings as some ridiculous holiday romance crush as I watched him walk away, reminding myself that in less than two weeks' time I would be leaving Madagascar, unlikely ever to see him again. This was not my real life and if I was not careful, I was setting myself up for a very big fall.

The following morning we were on the road at sunrise, trying to make sense of a highly confusing GPS route across sand flats and dirt tracks and feeling a little nervous about the drive that day, which included a ferry crossing 'unlike any other we had ever experienced' apparently. Our scheduled accommodation for the night was in a town called Manja, described by George on several occasions as 'basic' and I had to admit the name Manja did not conjure up a particularly attractive picture, but I was keeping an open mind. We reached the waypoint for the ferry around midday, where we were met by a very excitable Andry, who told us to park up in the shade and wait for instructions. It was all a bit odd, as there appeared to be no sign of a river, never mind a ferry to cross it, but I assumed all would be revealed in due course. Andry, loving his role as chief organizer and ferry marshal, was running around like a headless chicken, sweat pouring down his face as he liaised animatedly with someone on the phone, then returned to give us lengthy advice before sending us on our way down the sand dunes with an encouraging wave. The problem quickly became apparent as the car started to lose speed in the vast expanse of flat sandy riverbed we had to traverse in order to reach the ferry. Dozens of local men and boys, who were quick to capitalise on the perfect opportunity to make themselves a few thousand Ariary, were on hand to help by pushing the car until the wheels found some grip and stopped spinning. The whole process was accompanied by lots of shouting and cheering as the car began to move under its own power again and we made it to the river bank to join the queue with several more of our cars, while what seemed to be the entire male population of several villages worked on the broken down ferry. In the meantime there was the manual backup ferry, a wooden raft capable of carrying three cars at a push, which we were told would be dragged across the river by about fifteen men. It looked an awfully long way to the other side and from what I could see there was a fair current running, making me doubt the likelihood of a positive outcome. On the other hand, I had to believe the ferrymen had done this hundreds of times and undoubtedly knew exactly what they were doing.

The first challenge was getting the cars onto the ferry/raft, which involved driving them up a couple of constantly moving wooden planks, set at an alarmingly steep angle. Max laughed at my insulted face when he asked for the car keys, explaining to us that he had seen several people rev the engine so hard to get up the ramp that they drove the car straight off the other side of the raft and into the water. I had to admit that sounded like something I might do and I had no desire to see our car nosediving into the brown muddy water, so I handed over the keys without any further argument.

Once the first three cars were loaded the operatives took the rope and began dragging the ferry up river against the tide, half wading, half swimming, chest-deep in the brown muddy water. The rest of us stood on the bank watching the entertainment, trying to find any shelter we could from the sweltering heat. Gradually the shouting increased in volume and the arm waving and splashing became more frantic until it was evident that the ferry had taken control of its own destiny and was picking up speed as it headed down river, dragging the men with it on the end of the rope. Despite all the noise, it seemed they had a plan B and a few of them managed to scramble ashore, then chase along the opposite bank, wrapping the rope several times around a large tree in order to halt the progress of the runaway ferry, before finally disembarking the cars to the sound of more raucous cheers from our side of the bank.

Meanwhile, the mechanical ferry had miraculously sputtered into life, bellowing out a good deal of smoke in the process and our car, together with another six, had been loaded onto it, only to discover it was now overloaded and firmly stuck in the mud of the river bed. It was beginning to feel more and more like 'Benny Hill does Madagascar', but as there were already twenty chiefs shouting conflicting instructions and no Indians to carry out those instructions, there was nothing to do except try to find some shade and watch as the dramas unfolded. Max had been running back and forth across the sand in the blistering heat, helping to get the remaining stuck cars over to the ferry and was now staring in disbelief and shaking his head as the debacle continued. His shirt was unbuttoned and his tanned chest glistened with sweat. Sam nudged me in the ribs.

"Ooh, check out Max," she whispered. "That six-pack he's got is not bad at all. I wasn't expecting that."

"Well he told me he used to play rugby at international level and was also into boxing, so I guess it's not surprising he's kept himself in shape," I answered, averting my gaze quickly when he caught us staring at him. "Brilliant. He saw us ogling. I bet he thinks I'm some sex-starved, desperate divorcee now," I laughed. "He is hot though," I added, wishing I was down there on the bank with him.

The ferry shuddered and chains clanked, but we were still going nowhere and I couldn't help thinking it would probably have been a good idea for someone in charge of the ferry to have observed the weight limit, as it took the best part of an hour for us to actually get moving. The first stage of the laborious operation involved unloading two cars onto the little raft ferry to reduce the weight, which was a highly precarious manoeuvre in itself, dependent on the balancing of two wooden planks to enable the transfer. Stage two required the valiant efforts of twenty or so men to push and pull the ferry out into the deeper water until it could finally float.

George had gone ahead with the first cars on the raft ferry and was there to greet us when we eventually reached the other side, having successfully navigated our way onto dry land via more precarious wooden planks. He informed us happily that the rest of the journey to Manja would be a piece of cake, which we soon discovered was not entirely true, as we proceeded to drive across grassland tracks with bush fires on either side, through deep water crossings, muddy swamps and rocky river beds. I felt increasingly like Lara Croft, Tomb Raider, but in spite of the many challenges involved, the day went down in my diary as one of the best drives of the whole trip.

We were one of the last cars to arrive, having stopped off for an impromptu visit to a primary school, where we entertained the children with our own take on 'Head, shoulders knees and toes' and handed over all the stationery we could find, together with some money for the teacher to buy more. By the time we got to Manja, the others were already crammed round a couple of tables in the tiny bar of the hotel, which backed onto the dirt track running through the town, known somewhat ambitiously as the main street. There was a great buzz in the place and the camaraderie was wonderful as we all chatted and told stories of the day's adventures, laughing at the most bizarre ferry crossing most of us had ever taken. Ross disappeared into the town and returned with a huge plate of unspecified, but delicious-smelling street food for everyone to try and we all threw caution to the wind, hoping we wouldn't regret it later. Bottles of the local THB (Three Horses Beer) kept appearing on the tables as if by magic, so when we had finished a simple but tasty dinner of chicken and chips, provided by the hotel, we were feeling nicely merry and ready for another night on the town, such as it was. I went off to find Max with a beer.

"Are you going to take us out dancing again tonight?" I asked him, with what I hoped was a flirty smile.

"How could I refuse that face?" he said, laughing. "You girls will be the death of me. I'm still exhausted from the other night."

"Don't lie, you love it," I replied.

"Meet me in the bar in about half an hour. And I'd wear your boots if I were you," he added, looking down at my flip-flops and pulling a face.

The dancing bar turned out to be more like the back room of a house, with someone putting on music for a few friends and family to dance to. Our arrival caused quite a stir and I got the impression they didn't get too many foreign visitors in there, but they seemed keen for us to get involved and we had a great night of reciprocal education, increasing our repertoire of hybrid Malagasy/European dance moves. As we wandered back to the hotel under another beautiful star-studded sky, Max took my hand, entwining his fingers with mine.

"Tomorrow I will show you Belo…chez moi," he said simply.

I knew how proud he was of the Ecolodge he had built there and made his home.

"There is a boat building factory there, where they make the traditional wooden pirogues you saw the fishermen using at Laguna Blu."

Max knew I was a sailor and told me he had owned a boat himself in another life back in Canada but had lost it in a divorce years ago, a bit like me. My imagination began to conjure up images of him and me on a yacht, just the two of us, setting off on a carefree round the world trip, going wherever the wind took us. I reminded myself sharply that the reality of both our lives was a far cry from the fairy tales I always seemed to picture in my head. I couldn't keep running away from real life forever. In the interests of self-preservation, I had to start seeing this for what it was and just enjoy the moment while it lasted, but that was easier said than done. He squeezed my hand harder to keep me outside the hotel a moment longer than the others and before I could speak, his lips were on mine, his tongue exploring my mouth, his hand on the small of my back, pulling me into his embrace. The chemistry between us was undeniable and I kissed him back fervently, running my fingers through his hair, then sliding my hands up under his shirt, loving the warmth of his skin and the way his muscles tensed at my touch.

"Belo will be our time Grace," he said, pulling away and stroking my cheek with the back of his hand.

I suddenly realised it had been a very long time indeed since a man had made me feel sexy and desirable like this and I was not about to let the chance of happiness, however fleeting, pass me by.

Hell hath no Fury

Caitlin

Caitlin sat alone in the lounge, feet curled up on the sofa, staring into the orange glow of the fire, which she had lit even though it was still summer. She had been forced to punish Patrick again when he eventually returned from Dublin two days later than planned and, as a result, he was now sleeping off the unpleasant effects of a dangerously high dose of Tramadol. She had no intention of waiting around for months, however, while he continued to make a fool out of her. It was time to become a little more proactive in her approach.

When he informed her after his last 'work trip' that he would be unable to go away with her at Christmas because things had got behind on the big contract he was in charge of and he would need to be on-site over the festive period, she was naturally understanding.

Understanding on the outside and seething with fury on the inside.

Daniel patiently explained to her that the whole factory would be shutting down in order for them to install the new machine, so he had no choice but to be there as the company were threatening to sue him for breach of contract otherwise. Of course, he was devastated to be letting her down and knew how much she had been looking forward to their holiday together, but what could he do? She remembered the look of sincerity on his face as he told her how sorry he was and how he would make it up to her.

He was about to find out to his cost that two could play at the lying game.

"Don't worry about it, honestly. I know work has to come first," she reassured him with a sigh. "It'll make someone's day when I offer to swap shifts with them. Especially one of them with kids. We can plan something for Easter instead."

"You are an absolute angel. Grace would have kicked off big time and given me nothing but grief for weeks. I can't believe how different you are. I'm just so glad I found you and have you in my life, even if I don't deserve you," he gushed, enveloping her in his arms for good measure.

"I love you," she said simply, smiling serenely.

"Me too," he replied, not because he meant it, but because he knew it would be expected and it would keep her sweet.

That conversation was the turning point, the point when she decided things had to change. A hurried bit of research on the internet revealed that it was as easy to hire a private investigator these days as it was to buy a loaf of bread, even out there in the sticks. She specifically chose a woman to do the job and explained she was worried that her partner was cheating on her with someone in Dublin when he went there on his so-called work trips. The detective assured her that she dealt with hundreds of such cases every year and promised to deliver photographic and video evidence following a two-man surveillance over a period of twenty-four hours for the modest sum of 1500 euros plus expenses. Caitlin needed to know exactly what and who she was dealing with and had no hesitation at all in hiring her.

She got up, opened the little cast iron stove and put another couple of logs on the fire, watching the flames leap and dance as she sat back down to plan her next move. There was no need for her to look at the photos or videos again. She had been over them dozens of times already and they were etched indelibly on her memory.

The detective looked apologetic as she handed over the brown envelope of information in return for her money, assuming she was delivering the death blow to yet another relationship and expecting tears, but she found Caitlin surprisingly upbeat, almost excited. As soon as she had gone, Caitlin retreated to the privacy of her kitchen to study the precious contents of her package in peace, secure in the knowledge that Patrick was still holed up in his love nest in Dublin and would not be disturbing her. Her face remained impassive as she watched her lover park his car on the street outside a smart-looking apartment block overlooking Dun Laoghaire harbour and head up the steps to the entrance, carrying the holdall she had bought him only a few weeks earlier. The sight of the harbour brought memories flooding back and for a moment she was back on the boat in the marina with Craig and the others. Her eyes narrowed and she pushed those unpleasant memories to the back of her mind where they belonged, forcing herself to concentrate on the task in hand. Up to this point, Patrick had done nothing wrong and she could almost believe that he had innocently rented an apartment there while he was working, rather than stay in a hotel. But she knew that was not really the case. As he reached the entrance he held up a card and the door clicked open to allow him in, without any need to use the buzzer. Clearly, he was more resident than guest. Patrick moved with easy familiarity and knew exactly where he was going as he took the lift up to the third floor, then strode purposefully to his final destination, apartment 307, on the expensive side of the building with fabulous views over the water. Caitlin gave a little gasp of surprise and paused the video as the door was opened and she saw the woman's face, then flicked frantically through the corresponding still photographs until she came to the ones she wanted. Staring at the enlarged photo of her enemy, the woman Patrick was cheating on her with, she sat back and laughed ironically, shaking her head in disbelief.

"Well, well, well," she said quietly to herself. "Aren't you the dark horse?"

It had been a long time, but there was no way she could fail to recognise that face immediately and of course it changed everything. Caitlin returned to the video and pressed play, watching as Patrick leaned in to kiss the woman, his hands pawing at her breasts before they had even got inside and shut the door. She saw her slip off the coat she was wearing to reveal a ridiculously short and clingy mock nurse uniform, with her nipples poking out provocatively through two holes in the top, to Patrick's obvious delight. She heard him snigger lasciviously as his hand groped between her legs, then watched her turn around and bend over, exposing bare buttocks which Patrick immediately thrust himself against, making the woman giggle. Finally, he shoved the door shut behind him and the show was over, but Caitlin had no trouble imagining what happened next. Her face hardened as she rewound to the bit where the woman took off her coat. She looked like a cheap, dirty whore. The whole thing was disgusting and Caitlin felt physically sick as she replayed the spectacle over and over again, unable to stop herself. Slowly she tore the photo into little pieces and threw them on the fire to put an end once and for all to the other woman staring at her, mocking her. She now had all the information she needed, so she put everything back in the envelope and hid it in her secret place, under the false bottom of the kitchen drawer, a smile playing on her lips as an idea began to form in her mind. She inhaled deeply to calm herself and recited her favourite mantra over and over again:

"Don't get mad, get even, don't get mad, get even…."

The next morning, Patrick eventually made it down to breakfast at around eleven.

"Well I must say you look a lot better than you did last night," she said, smiling. "I'll get you some breakfast. I bet you're starving now after spending half the evening in the toilet."

"Ugh, thanks for reminding me," said Patrick, somewhat groggily. "I'll just have some toast and coffee for now thanks."

"I'm worried about you. I really think we should get some blood tests done to check everything is okay. I know you hate doctors, but

I could do it here so you wouldn't even have to go into the surgery," she offered, a concerned look on her face.

"Yeah, maybe, but I'm sure it's just a bug I've picked up. If I still feel bad next week I'll do it."

"Okay, but I won't take no for an answer. To be honest, I think you're working too hard, running backwards and forwards all over the place to see different customers. All the travelling is stressful and it's obviously taking its toll on you. You need to be at home more and give yourself time to relax and recharge your batteries. It's getting ridiculous."

Caitlin handed Patrick his toast and put a pot of coffee on the table.

"I suppose you're right and I will try to scale things down a bit and be around more, but you wouldn't want me to leave people in the lurch, would you? I've made commitments and people are relying on me. Jobs are at stake," he added, a serious look on his face. Caitlin could almost see the halo shining above his head.

"Of course I understand that," she replied. "Just promise me you'll look after yourself a bit more."

"Okay, I promise. Now stop fussing, I'm fine. Aren't you working today?" he asked, keen to get rid of her.

"I took the day off to look after you. We should make the most of it if you're feeling better. Maybe take Bentley for a long walk on the beach to blow the cobwebs away?"

The suggestion met with a less than enthusiastic response and Patrick pulled a face as he stood up.

"I still don't feel great actually. And I do have some work to catch up on after missing a whole day of my life yesterday. Maybe later."

Patrick wandered into the lounge with his laptop, leaving Caitlin to clear away the breakfast things and hopefully deal with the pile of dirty laundry he had brought back from Dublin. It was her birthday in a couple of weeks and, after some deliberation, he had found the perfect gift: red satin suspender belt and stockings with matching bra and French knickers, together with the pièce de résistance, a neat little gold vibrator. He was confident he could loosen her up a bit and intended to have some fun doing so. It was also probably time to think about tapping into the reserves of Aidan's life insurance policy, which he knew had left Caitlin in an extremely comfortable position financially.

Caitlin had bought steaks for dinner that night and was singing happily to herself as she prepared everything, putting the homemade chips in the oven, opening a nice bottle of Barolo to breathe and lighting a candle on the table. She had enjoyed a whole day of it being just the two of them at home together and hopefully, Patrick had seen how good life could be if he just behaved himself. She had booked the weekend off as well, so another two wonderful days stretched ahead of them and she intended to make the most of their time together to show him he didn't need that slut in Dublin and her ridiculous dressing-up outfits. Unlike many other women she knew, Caitlin actually enjoyed looking after her man, doing the cooking, the washing, the ironing, the cleaning. It felt good to be needed and she loved seeing the appreciation on his face when she put his favourite meal on the table or he walked into the bedroom and found a neat pile of freshly washed and ironed clothes waiting for him on the chest of drawers.

What Caitlin took to be appreciation could equally well have been interpreted as smug satisfaction at getting one over on someone, but she was determined to see the best in him in order to maintain the illusion of the perfect life she saw for herself. A life that included him. She was trying so hard, she really was, but in her heart of hearts, she knew it was only a matter of time until he left her, just like all the others.

She sighed, regret etched on her face, knowing she could absolutely not allow that to happen. Caitlin Flynn had been here before and she knew exactly what had to be done.

Clarity

Sometimes you have to walk away from what you want in order to find what will make you truly happy.

Grace

"I built the Ecolodge on land above sea level, but there is still a very real danger of flooding at certain times of the year," Max told us, as he showed Sam and me to one of the beautiful two-bedroom wooden bungalows, raised up on stumps or pillars among the sand dunes with commanding views of the ocean. "The reason for the stumps is to allow flood water and debris to flow under the buildings during the cyclone season and minimise damage," he explained.

It was a wonderful feeling to be able to kick off our boots the moment we stepped out of the car and walk around in the sand in bare feet.

"The place is idyllic Max," I said, understanding in a heartbeat why he had chosen to settle in this little bit of unspoilt paradise, where time appeared to have stood still.

"If you look along the beach there," he said, pointing to a group of low-lying buildings, "you can see where they build the boats the village is famous for, the big wooden schooner rigs called 'boutres', like that one coming back in."

I followed his gaze and saw a boat heading gracefully up the channel towards the open water. It was followed by two of the smaller 'pirogues' as the fishermen returned.

"Aren't they beautiful?" asked Max, full of admiration. Each one is built totally by hand in the traditional way and takes between four and six years to complete. It's truly a labour of love."

"Can we visit tomorrow?" I asked.

"Yes of course. And if you want to try sailing on a pirogue, the fishermen will be happy to take you out to the islands over there. The snorkelling on the coral reefs is superb," he added, smiling at my enthusiasm.

"Wow, the islands look amazing," I said, shielding my eyes against the glare from the white sand and the sun sparkling on the turquoise water. "Like something out of Robinson Crusoe."

"The best bit of all is that we manage to hold off any serious tourist invasion due to the place being so difficult to reach," laughed Max. "The road you came in on is only accessible during the dry season, from around June to late October. After that, the river levels are too high and you can only get in and out by sea from Morondova."

I loved the fact that places like Belo sur Mer existed.

"This place is really something special, isn't it?" I said to Sam when Max had gone. "Can you believe we're nearly at the end of the rally? We've been planning it and looking forward to it for so long…and now in a few days it'll all be over. I'm going to miss everyone so much."

"I know, we've become like a family. A bit of a dysfunctional one at times maybe, but that's families for you," she laughed.

That evening seemed the perfect opportunity to get dressed up for dinner and I took my favourite green maxi dress out of my bag while Sam was in the shower. As I pulled it over my head and down over my hips, I could tell that something didn't feel right, but

I only understood the problem when I looked in the mirror and was left staring dumbfounded at my reflection. There were large holes cut out of the material, two of them leaving my breasts exposed and another circle leaving nothing to the imagination in the crotch area of the dress. It was ruined.

I felt suddenly cold and shivered as I remembered how I had done pretty much the exact same thing to Daniel's dinner suit trousers in a fit of temper and how delighted I had been as I imagined the look of shock on his face when he went to put them on. I was beginning to think I was going mad, because the things that kept happening to me always seemed to be linked to him in some weird way, as if he were haunting me from beyond the grave, punishing me.

I dragged the torn dress angrily from my body, stuffed it into a plastic bag and dumped it in the bin. I refused to allow Daniel to get inside my head like this. Someone had played a spiteful trick and I told myself sharply that in all honesty, it could have happened at any point on the rally. Maybe a jealous cleaner at one of the hotels, who thought we didn't tip well enough? It was pure coincidence that I had done the exact same thing to Daniel. After all, I was hardly the first person to have cut up someone else's clothes to get at them and I would undoubtedly not be the last. I was determined not to allow it to spoil the evening and decided to say nothing to Sam or the others, rummaging quickly in my bag for something else to wear. I refused to allow myself to be tortured by the nagging feeling that someone was watching me, someone who knew all about what I had done.

As we walked up the wooden steps to the decking of the bar and restaurant to watch the sun set, I was struck by the warmth and easy camaraderie emanating from our little family and I immediately felt safe again. Some of them were playing Bridge, while the three Aussie amigos were entertaining others with stories of their various escapades together. We went over to sit with Suzie, who looked effortlessly chic as usual and, as I looked around at the smiling faces, I wished I could have bottled the atmosphere to keep with me forever.

The following day the local fishermen took us out as promised and managed to get us so close to a family of whales that we could almost have touched them. There was something incredibly special about being among those majestic creatures, watching them rise to the surface and exhale noisily from their blowholes, before diving down again, treating us to a theatrical flick of their powerful tails. I could happily have stayed there watching them forever and found myself imagining what it would be like to live on one of the little desert islands we sailed past, your life governed by the tides, the weather and the daylight rather than the hands of a clock.

After dinner that evening I sat for a while on the terrace with Max, chatting in French as we often did and he listened in silence as I told him the story of my life in answer to his simple question of why I split up with my husband. I was pretty sure he got a lot more than he bargained for and I searched his face for the usual reaction of shock, then sympathy and maybe even outrage at the way I had been treated by a man. In a strange kind of way, I liked to hide behind my story where men were concerned, using it as a shield to protect myself and an excuse for being unable to let my guard down or trust anyone. Max shrugged his shoulders and didn't appear to be shocked in the slightest, which was somewhat perturbing and not at all the reaction I expected. It made me question his morals again and whether he was telling the truth about his own wife.

"I can see how much he hurt you, Grace," he said simply. "But the fact is, everyone has their cross to bear in life. Sooner or later you have to let it go and allow yourself to trust that there are good men out there, in the same way that there are bad women. Let yourself be happy. Forget him."

He shrugged his shoulders and smiled.

Easy for him to say. I wondered briefly what he would make of my full story if I told him how I had taken my revenge on Daniel that night in the Irish sea, calmly engineering his fall overboard and then leaving him to drown without a backward glance. But I also knew there was no way I would ever tell him anything other than the edited version. That particular secret would go with me to the grave.

Sam and Suzie wandered over to join us with George.

"Do you guys fancy heading along the beach to the neighbouring lodge for a couple of drinks?" asked Max. "It's the owner's birthday and believe me, he knows how to party," he laughed, lighting a cigarette. "It'll be fun for your last night here."

The owners of the Mangrove Lodge were a gay French couple, who had come to Madagascar some eleven years ago on holiday and never left. I envied people like that. They had bought the storm-damaged lodge and done most of the building work themselves, creating the 'wow' factor with a bar constructed like one of the fishermen's pirogues and a high vaulted ceiling. The birthday boy was intent on trying out his increasingly outrageous dance moves on Sam, Suzie and me and before long we were all up on the boat bar, inhibitions out the window. I caught Max's eye and it felt good to know he was watching me, wanting me. I was dancing for him, caught up in the intoxicating atmosphere of the place (and fuelled by the numerous rum and cokes I had unwisely downed in rapid succession). Someone changed the music and I heard the Eagles song 'The Last Resort', one of my all-time favourites. I held out my hand and Max came straight over to the bar, giving me a fireman's lift down that started me giggling, then taking me in his arms and pulling me close to dance. In the real world, my descent from the bar was probably not the most dignified, but in my alcohol-skewed version, I was Debra Winger being swept off her feet by Richard Gere in 'An Officer and a Gentleman'. As we swayed gently to the music I rested my head on his shoulder and everyone else in the room melted away.

"Maybe we should just walk away from everything and make a new life out here together, Grace. What do you think?" Max whispered, his lips brushing my ear.

"Mmm, I'd love that," I answered dreamily, knowing it was impossible. Maybe in another time, another life, but not this one.

"Stay with me tonight Grace," he said simply.

There was an inevitability about our union that meant no answer was needed because at that moment I loved him and knew he loved me. It didn't matter that there was no future for us, or that it wouldn't last, because I suddenly understood that it was okay to live in the present. I had come to realise that I owed it to myself to make every minute, every second of my life count.

The spell was broken by an abrupt change of music and tempo, as the Gypsy Kings blasted out their uplifting song Bamboleo. Sam grabbed my hand and pulled me away to dance, both of us laughing at the random selection of music our hosts were churning out. All the shimmying we had practised at our Zumba classes at home was, at last, being put to good use and I threw myself into it with the carefree abandon that alcohol always tends to encourage.

As we wandered home along the beach at the end of the night, Max and I hung back from the others, who tactfully went ahead and left us to it. He took my hand in a simple gesture of affection that made me want to cry. It felt as if we were in our own little bubble, where everything was perfect, as if the stars had somehow aligned and Fate had intervened to create an open door for us to walk through.

In spite of all my bravado, I felt suddenly self-conscious and nervous once we were alone in Max's simply furnished and uncluttered chalet. He was quick to notice the change in my body language and gently pulled me close, enveloping me in his arms and kissing my neck to reassure me.

"I've wanted this since the first time I saw you, but I don't want you to do anything you don't want to," he murmured into my ear. Then he took my face in his hands and rested his forehead against mine.

"Promise me that you will always smile when you think of me and remember our time together, Grace. I never want to be the cause of any regret or sadness in your life."

"I want this as much as you do Max. I am choosing to be here with you. No regrets, I promise," I replied, turning my face into his hand and kissing it.

A moment later he took me by surprise, picking me up as he had done earlier in the bar, then spinning me round and throwing me onto the bed, making me giggle like a child as all my apprehension vanished. Then he sat beside me and slowly undressed me; stroking, kissing, exploring every inch of my body, bringing my senses alive with expert flicks of his tongue until every nerve, every fibre of my being was tingling with desire. I threw back my head and arched my back, a low moan of ecstasy escaping from my lips as his mouth moved down over my throat, across my breasts, stopping to lick and suck my nipples, then tracing a line down my stomach, gently pushing my legs apart with his knee. I could hardly bear it anymore and wanted to cry out with the excruciating pleasure I was feeling.

Max's love-making was tender, but with an electrifying passion burning just beneath the surface. The touch of his hands on my skin was thrilling and I ached to feel him inside me, almost ready to beg him to make love to me properly. He stopped for a moment, holding himself above me on his hands, his steely blue eyes piercing my soul. Then finally he lowered himself down and our bodies became one, his warm skin melting into my own as he entered me, pressing his lips hard to mine, his tongue exploring my mouth. He let out a long sigh of pleasure as the slow rhythmic movement of our hips became increasingly urgent and he pushed deeper and deeper inside me. I held nothing back, giving myself to him unconditionally until the exquisite moment of climax when we both found the release we craved.

Before Max, the last man who made love to me was Daniel, and I had been tortured by all the memories of that and the other hideous images of him with other women that filled my head. Now at last I had a new and precious memory to focus on, one which was powerful enough to force the others out. It was as if we had performed a kind of exorcism.

We lay together in contented silence, arms and legs entwined, listening to the sound of waves lapping gently on the shore. I felt a huge sense of happiness and peace as if a weight had been lifted from my shoulders. I closed my eyes and smiled, the taste of him still in my mouth as he turned to me, wrapping his leg around my hip and pulling me a little closer to him.

"I'll never forget you Grace," he whispered. "I'll always be here for you if you need me. I mean it."

I caressed his chest absent-mindedly and pressed myself into him, savouring the feeling of his warm, damp skin against mine.

"You'll always be part of my life," I said simply.

The connection between us was hard to explain, but it felt as if we had known each other forever. Max propped himself up on one elbow and looked into my eyes, then lowered his face to kiss me, stroking my face and hair.

"Promise me you'll open your heart up to the right man when he comes along. Let him in, because you deserve to be with someone who can make you happy. You have so much to give."

I snuggled closer to him and smiled to myself as I thought fleetingly of Aidan, who kept tentatively reaching out to me with his flirty little messages. Max eventually drifted off to sleep, but I lay awake in his arms for most of the night, a whole myriad of emotions racing through my mind as I listened to the comforting sound of him breathing beside me and the rhythmic sound of the waves outside.

No matter how hard I wanted to stop it, time was marching on and the next day we were due to head up the coast to Morondova, then back to Tana, where we would all go our separate ways. I had made friends for life from all over the world on this rally. I had visited some incredible places and experienced things I could only previously have dreamed of, driving nearly five thousand kilometres through stunning and ever-changing scenery, from the rain forests of the east, across spectacular mountain ranges to the deserted beaches of the beautiful west coast. I had learned to drive off-road through rivers, over sand dunes, across rocky, dry river beds and along sand tracks. I had met the local people, partied with them for Independence Day, been out with the fishermen, seen whales, danced on bars and learned to love THB beer. I had even become a football fan, caught up in the infectious enthusiasm of the country for its national team, flying the Madagascan flag from the window of our car in honour of the 'Bareas', who had qualified for the Coupe d'Afrique for the first time in history and made it all the way to the quarter-finals!

As I relived every wonderful moment in my mind, I smiled to myself, realising I had reached a turning point in my life. Somewhere along the way on our amazing adventure I had changed. My eyes had been opened to a whole new world and I felt truly alive, high on life itself and ready to embrace everything it had to offer me.

Madagascar had worked its magic on me and I knew I would be leaving a little piece of my heart there when I went home, but I also knew I was more sure of my path in life than I had been in a long time. Saying goodbye to Max would be painful and I felt a momentary panic at the thought that he would not be travelling with us when we left Belo, but I would not allow our time together to be tainted with sadness. I would always smile when I thought of him, just as I had promised.

His gift to me was the confidence to be with another man. To love and allow myself to be loved.

The Hustle

Daniel

Daniel Callaghan, aka Patrick Salenden and a few other things over the years, was a man at the top of his game. He heard the pilot of Aer Lingus flight EI 105 tell the crew to prepare for landing at New York's JFK airport and smiled contentedly. He hadn't realised how much he had missed his frequent trips to the States. He felt energised, liberated, invincible. If only Grace could see him now, he thought to himself. The old Daniel was gone, with this new version of him rising like a phoenix from the ashes, in control of everything; including Grace. She just didn't know it yet.

Daniel looked out of the window at the afternoon sunshine as the plane taxied along the runway, remembering with a smirk a quote from somewhere or other:

'The sun shines on the wicked and righteous alike'.

He was a great believer in travelling light and strode purposefully through the airport with his hand luggage, which contained his laptop, a few items of essential clothing and toiletries. It was only a four day visit after all, but that should be more than enough time to clinch the deal on the classic car he had his eye on and hopefully celebrate with Allegra, divorced 51-year-old real estate agent, looking for love, according to her profile. Daniel always took great pains to ensure he chose wisely on sites like mingle2.com. He searched for women of a certain age, divorced or widowed, no kids or kids grown up and gone, a job that suggested a comfortable financial position, presentable but not too attractive, a little overweight maybe…these were the criteria that, in his experience, added up to a perfect match, or at the very least something he could work with. He had high hopes for Allegra. They had been messaging for a while and were both looking forward to meeting up on this business trip so that they could get to know each other better and she could hopefully help him to find a suitable property on Long Island. He had been away from home for too long now and it was time to move back to the States, where so many of his clients were based and where his heart was.

Or at least, that was what he told her.

It wasn't so much that he was bored with Roisin. Or Caitlin for that matter, who fulfilled his needs in a different way. It was simply that he didn't like to put all his eggs in one basket. He also felt it would be wise to set up an escape route to the States, should he need it. The buzz he got from juggling the various relationships he had on the go was an added bonus and he found it a massive turn-on to know that each one of his women was oblivious to the others' existence, each believing herself to be the centre of his world. He was the first to admit that his behaviour pattern was a kind of addiction. Roisin, in her professional role as a clinical psychologist, would have a field day analysing him if she ever got wind of what was going on. Not that he intended to allow that to happen, of course.

As soon as he was through security, Daniel wasted no time in heading out to Long Island and it was around 4.30 pm when he walked through the door to the showrooms of Autosport Traders. Even after everything that had happened to him he remained a creature of habit. In spite of the obvious risks, he was determined to rebuild his old life, given that it had been taken from him very much without his consent. The classic car collection was the biggest sore point, in particular, the E-type jag Grace had 'sold' to her mother and hidden in her garage. It was disgraceful the way the courts had allowed her to get away with that, the conniving little bitch. Daniel took a deep breath and forced himself to concentrate on the here and now, secure in the knowledge that Grace would get what was coming to her, sooner rather than later if he had anything to do with it.

Jake, the salesman at Autosport, was expecting him and greeted him in a suitably gushing manner, confident of his impending commission. The price on the car, a fairly tidy Corvette, had already been agreed subject to viewing and was the perfect vehicle for his forthcoming trips to the States. As for the Healey he had told Roisin about, that was way too expensive to be worth the money and hassle of importing it to Ireland. He would get her a nice little MGB instead for a fraction of the cost and come up with a suitable story to fob her off regarding the Healey. Jake was on the lookout for an E-type to replace the one Grace had stolen and he was confident he would have something for him soon.

Allegra the real estate agent was pleasant enough, but sadly did not live up to her name and turned out to be more of an 'andante' kind of girl, laying her cards on the dinner table before they had even been served the starter.

"I never sleep with anyone on a first date," she stated. "I just thought I should tell you that straight away, so you know where you stand."

Daniel summoned up his best injured expression, with a touch of horrified thrown in for good measure.

"What do you take me for? I would never expect that from a woman, especially not one I like as much as you," he said, looking her directly in the eye. "I'm more than happy to take things as slowly as you like because I really feel we have a connection and I'd like to get to know you properly."

"I'm so glad you feel that way", she laughed, clearly reassured. "I don't mean to be blunt… it's just that I've met some real scumbags on this dating site, men who are only interested in one thing."

"Well I promise you, that's not me," Daniel said emphatically. "I've met my fair share of unpleasant women as well, I can assure you. Out to get whatever they can from me," he said carefully, hinting at a suitably impressive bank balance. "I even married one of them, then she left me for a property developer around five years ago. Sadly for her, he went bust, while my company really took off the year after we divorced."

Allegra laughed, raising her glass to his.

"Wow, she must have been pissed! My ex-husband got the au-pair pregnant. She was nineteen years old, barely legal. God knows what she saw in him, apart from the money obviously," she said wryly.

Daniel pricked his ears up at her last comment.

"Well I hope you took him to the cleaners," he said with a broad smile, showing her he was on her side. To his annoyance, she refused to elaborate any further and he was forced to spend the rest of the evening making up answers to her ridiculous questions about life in the UK and listening to her droning on about nothing of any real interest. Daniel resigned himself to spending the night in the hotel he had provisionally reserved, with nothing but a bottle of wine and his home videos for company.

By their second date the following evening, however, things were looking up and Allegra seemed to have forgotten all her earlier inhibitions and chaste resolutions. They spent the afternoon looking at properties in the Huntington area near where she lived, although Daniel had no intention whatsoever of spending his hard-earned money on buying a house when he knew she had a perfectly good place he could use as his base in America for the moment.

Allegra, good Catholic girl that she was, came up trumps after dinner and was only too happy to drop her pink and black lacy French knickers for him. Daniel squeezed her ample buttocks in his hands and sighed appreciatively as she writhed around on top of him, huge breasts jiggling up and down as her movements became increasingly frenzied. He allowed her to reach a noisy climax, then made it clear it was his turn and pushed her off him a little too roughly, signalling to her to take him in her mouth as he began to film the performance.

'Rotorvator', as he liked to call himself on various platforms, had built up a good following over the years on Porn Hub, where he regularly posted his amateur videos. The one of Jane pleasuring herself in the schoolgirl outfit had gone down a storm and he was now looking forward to introducing Allegra to his fans, as he suspected there was a lot more to come where she was concerned.

"I'm going to need something to fall back on when I get horny on my own, miles away from you," he coaxed when she hesitated about the camera, knowing from experience that flattery always worked.

Daniel suspected from Allegra's enthusiasm and willingness to comply in the bedroom that she had not seen any action for a while and was clearly grateful for his attentions. That was all well and good, but what he was really interested in was the Huntington address he intended to use for his own purposes.

"It's just until I find somewhere of my own," he assured her, more than a little disappointed to find she lived in a two-bed apartment in the centre of town and not one of the smart, waterfront properties lining the shores of Oyster Bay or Lloyd Harbor, as he had hoped.

A point in Allegra's favour was that she had a garage he could keep the Corvette in, so she would do for the moment until he could find something better. To be fair, she had provided quite a pleasant distraction for a couple of days, but he sincerely hoped she did not fancy her chances of him being some sort of meal ticket, because she would soon find out she was barking up the wrong tree there. Once bitten, twice shy and all that. It had transpired in conversation that her well-heeled ex-husband had pulled out the big guns in the divorce and succeeded in saving most of his wealth from her greedy clutches. Consequently, she was less of a keeper than he had hoped, but he knew from experience there were plenty of other fish in the sea. He could afford to be patient.

Daniel managed to blag himself an upgrade to business class on the flight home, courtesy of the doctorate he had purchased some time ago from Nigeria. Stretching out his legs and pulling on his eye mask to try to get some sleep, he congratulated himself on what he had achieved in such a short time. He felt invigorated. He had meticulously arranged all his ducks, new and old, in a very neat row and it would soon be time to hammer the final nail into Grace's coffin, literally if he had anything to do with it. Feeling himself grow hard, he squirmed in the seat, realising he got as much sexual gratification from screwing her over metaphorically as he did from screwing his other women physically. She was due back from Madagascar imminently and Daniel's alter ego Aidan was just dying to meet her.

Daniel planned to head straight for Roisin's apartment when he landed, having informed Caitlin he would be spending the night in Dublin and travelling home the following day after sorting out some 'work stuff'. It was never any problem to pull the wool over her eyes. Daniel knew every trick in the book to keep all the plates spinning in the air and was actually finding it even easier than last time. Obviously, he had learned from his mistakes there.

In all honesty, he simply couldn't understand the mentality of men who limited themselves to one partner for life. In his opinion monogamy was a ridiculously outdated, overrated concept and one that should be reserved for those totally lacking in imagination.

Mind Games

Roisin

Roisin sat at a window table in Harry's Café Bar in Dun Laoghaire, waiting for Kate to arrive. She was looking forward to lunch and a catch up with her best friend, especially after the morning she had just had. She was usually pretty good at switching off from work, but the client she had spent the last hour with had got under her skin. He was accused of the violent assault and rape of three women and the attempted murder of one. That was what they had managed to pin on him, but Roisin thought it highly likely there was a hell of a lot more he was getting away with. His defence lawyers were typically going for the insanity plea, claiming he was mentally unfit to stand trial, but she wasn't so sure. Her job was to give her professional opinion and a formal assessment. Today was just the beginning, a preliminary session during which she had asked him to fill out a short questionnaire as a kind of self-awareness exercise. She had observed him as he wrote, a hint of a smirk on his lips, but when he looked at her, there was a kind of detached coldness, as if he were dead behind the eyes. His answers to the questions all suggested ASPD (Antisocial Personality Disorder), but he was smart and she would put money on the fact he was simply playing the game, trotting out bare-faced lies to hoodwink them all. Her job was to look beyond the mask he wanted everyone to see and break down the barriers. She was fascinated by characters like him and felt compelled to get inside his head, to find out what made him tick. That was what she prided herself on being good at.

"Hey, sorry I'm a bit late," said Kate, out of breath after running most of the way from the Dart.

"No problem at all…it's so great to see you," said Roisin, getting up to hug her best friend tightly.

Kate had messaged her earlier to see if they could meet up for lunch and Roisin now understood the urgency.

"Oh my God, is that what I think it is?" she demanded, grabbing Kate's left hand.

Kate beamed happily and nodded.

"Michael came over last night and asked me to marry him, totally out of the blue. Got down on one knee and everything," she laughed.

"Oh Kate, I'm so happy for you," said Roisin, genuinely meaning it. "I always said you two were meant to be together. I just have no idea what took you both so long to realise it. So when are you getting married?"

"Well, neither of us wants to waste money on a big wedding, so we thought maybe next spring. There's not really much point hanging around at our age," she laughed, clearly ecstatic. "Will you be my matron of honour?"

"Oh God, that makes me sound about ninety, spinster of the parish," Roisin laughed. "But yes, of course I will! I'm so happy you asked me. Please don't make me wear an over-the-top dress though," she added quickly, pulling a face.

"I promise," said Kate solemnly. "We can go dress shopping together, proper girlie time like the old days."

"Have you got to work this afternoon, or shall I order us a bottle of fizz to celebrate?" asked Roisin.

"No and yes, definitely order fizz!"

Roisin looked at her friend, bubbling over with excitement and happiness, and remembered how happy she had felt when Mark proposed to her. She had fallen head over heels in love with him, and he with her, and she honestly believed they would spend the rest of their lives together, grow old together…but then, she supposed everyone believed that when they were first married. Her face clouded slightly as she remembered how quickly the magic had faded, both of them seemingly powerless to stop the inevitable happening. She reminded herself that she was the one who instigated divorce proceedings and wanted out, but she couldn't help feeling that she had somehow come off worst. Mark was still living in their beautiful house overlooking the sea in Dalkey, with his new (much younger) wife and two kids. He now had the perfect family, while she on the other hand boasted a string of failed relationships, usually lasting no more than a couple of months and always ending in heartache. She was beginning to think she was destined to grow old alone, a sad and lonely divorcee. Then she met Patrick…

"Are you okay?" Kate's voice interrupted her thoughts.

"Yes, sorry, I was just daydreaming. I had a bit of a tough morning. Let's order food."

Roisin thought to herself guiltily that, although the whole marriage thing hadn't worked out for her, she had no wish to rain on Kate's parade.

"I've been thinking…," began Kate. "Maybe I've been a bit unfair about Patrick. After all, I don't even know the guy, not properly, so maybe I need to make a bit more of an effort for your sake. I was thinking perhaps the four of us could go out for dinner one evening. Just let me know when is a good time, as I know he has to work away a lot."

Roisin was beyond grateful for this olive branch, knowing Kate's reservations about Patrick. "Thank you, Kate. I really mean that. I just know you and Michael will both like him once you get to know him. He's a big part of my life now and I can't see that changing any time soon. Without wanting to sound too cheesy, I think he's The One," she stated decisively.

"Wow! I never thought I'd hear that from you, Miss Commitment-phobe," laughed Kate, raising her glass. "Here's to true love then. For both of us."

"To true love! He's actually due back from a trip to the States today, so maybe we could go out together on Friday?" she suggested eagerly, hoping she could persuade Patrick to go along with the idea.

It was almost three o'clock by the time they left Harry's, having made plans to meet for dinner on the Friday night. Roisin couldn't wait to tell Patrick, who was already sitting on the sofa with his laptop open on his knee when she got back to the apartment.

"Hey you," she called out happily, a little bit the worse for wear after drinking at lunchtime.

Patrick shut his laptop and stood up to greet her, but she felt him stiffen awkwardly, as he always did when she threw her arms around his neck to hug him. That was just how he was, she told herself, not a touchy-feely kind of person, but she couldn't help wishing he would be a bit more demonstrative with her.

"You'll never guess what," she began, then continued immediately without waiting for him to speak. "Kate and Michael have finally got engaged!"

Patrick raised his eyebrows in surprise.

"Wow. I thought she'd binned that loser off. She could do so much better," he said in a dismissive tone.

"Aww come on, give the guy a break. Not everyone can be a high-flying entrepreneur like you," she teased. "Besides, you hardly know either of them," she admonished gently.

"Well no, I don't, but I've formed an opinion from what you've told me. To be honest, I didn't think you were that impressed either. They're just not my kind of people."

Patrick wandered into the kitchen and took a beer out of the fridge as Roisin persisted.

"You're right, he's messed her around over the years, but Kate is still my best friend. We go back a long way and I need to make an effort for her sake. And so do you," she added pointedly. "We can start by having dinner, the four of us, on Friday night. I want you to get to know my friends Patrick. It's part of being a proper couple."

"I can't, I'm away this weekend," he said without hesitation. "I'm sure I told you. We've got a big push to meet the deadline on that machine I've been installing in the south. We're already behind and there are some serious penalty clauses if it's not completed on time."

Roisin was irritated and didn't bother to hide it. She could already see Kate's 'knowing face' mixed with 'I told you so' if she had to cancel their plans again.

"Oh for God's sake Patrick, I know your work is important, but surely there is someone else who can hold the fort for once. You've only just got back from the States. I think it's time you got your priorities sorted and put me first for once, don't you?" she snapped, a challenging look in her eyes.

Patrick sighed wearily.

"Fine, okay. I'll see what I can do," he conceded grudgingly. "But let's not argue about it now. I hate confrontation. Such a waste of energy when there are much more fun things we could be doing," he added, moving closer to grind his pelvis against her thigh and sliding a hand up inside her top to massage her breast.

Roisin gave a low moan of pleasure as her baser instincts began to creep in. Lifting her leg to hook it around his hip, she pushed his hand down inside her lace panties and began to thrust against his probing fingers. There was a primitive sense of urgency in the way she moved, head thrown back, lost in her own personal quest for fulfilment. She came quickly and then slumped against him, laughing.

"Your turn now," she added, her voice husky as she went to unbuckle the belt of his trousers.

"I can wait till later," he said, preferring the guarantee of an erection that only the pills in his wash bag could provide. "You really are very sexy, you know," he added, wishing he had been able to capture the moment on camera.

"Okay, if you're sure. I'm going to have a shower, then I'll fix us some dinner and you can tell me what happened about the car."

Patrick watched her disappear into the bathroom, then immediately took out his phone and composed a message to Caitlin.

Hi, hope you're okay. Back safely, but unfortunately I can't come home yet. We've got big problems here with the installation I've been working on. The company is threatening to sue, so it's all hands on deck I'm afraid. I think it's nearly sorted, so hopefully I'll only need to stay one more day. I'll let you know.

He re-read the text, then added *xxx* for good measure, before pressing send. Caitlin would not be happy, so he turned off his phone to avoid any unpleasant exchanges. She'd get over it. Roisin came padding into the lounge in her dressing gown and sat down beside him, her long dark hair wet and tousled from the shower. She reminded him a little of Grace.

"So, don't keep me in suspense any longer. Did you get my car?" she asked excitedly.

"Well actually, there was a problem with the car," he began. "I'm afraid it wasn't as good as I had been led to believe and as soon as I saw it I knew it wasn't worth the money the guy was asking, so I didn't go ahead."

Roisin's expression clouded with disappointment. She had already bragged about the car to Kate, wanting to build up a more positive picture of Patrick for her friend. Now there was no car and she was in danger of looking like a mug again.

"But…," said Patrick, with a theatrical pause. "I've managed to get my hands on this little baby for you," he announced, showing her a picture of a red MGB on his laptop. "A friend put me in touch with this guy in Malahide who's selling it following a divorce and, to cut a long story short, we've done a deal over the phone. We can drive up there tomorrow and pick it up if you're free."

Roisin immediately perked up, realising that she would not have to lose face after all.

"And no arguments, this one is a present from me," said Patrick generously. "I earned a good bonus from the last job I did. Of course, I'll get your money back to you asap. Although…if you're still keen to go ahead with building our investment stable, it probably makes sense to leave it where it is in our dollars account. That way I can move quickly when the right car does come up."

He waited a moment before finishing, choosing the word 'our' deliberately.

"That is if you trust me not to run off into the sunset with all your money," he laughed.

"Of course I trust you," she replied, huddling closer to the screen to look at the MG. "That is such a cute car. I love it. Thank you so much!" she enthused, refusing to allow herself to be disappointed with the 8,000 euro price tag and not wishing to appear ungrateful. She was delighted to have something to impress Kate with as evidence of Patrick's commitment to her and, at the end of the day, Kate wouldn't know one red soft-top car from another, never mind how much they were worth. Unlike Michael, who was a bit of a closet petrol-head and would be considerably less easy to impress.

For a number of reasons, the Friday dinner date was not the roaring success Roisin had hoped. Patrick had continued to resist the whole thing, saying he preferred to have her all to himself, given that he had to work away so much. Then he changed tack, insisting that Kate disliked him and was trying to split them up (which was not entirely untrue).

"I just don't understand why you want to be friends with someone who is so obviously jealous of you and doesn't want you to be happy," he announced, leaving it very late to get ready to go out.

"That's a bit unfair Patrick. Can you please just make an effort to get on with them? For me?" she pleaded.

Throughout dinner Patrick seemed unable to resist goading Michael, particularly about his job as a geography teacher and how difficult it must be to manage on a teacher's salary in this day and age.

"I have no idea how anyone manages to live these days on less than a hundred grand a year," he said, with his customary lack of tact.

"We muddle through somehow," said Kate sarcastically, glaring at him.

Roisin turned the topic of conversation to her new car in an attempt to keep things civil. She did not much care for this side of Patrick.

"Just a little gift from me as a thank you for putting up with me," he said smugly. "It's only money and I enjoy spoiling her."

Michael predictably took the bait, making a point of raising his eyebrows in surprise.

"Nice. My dad had one, but got rid of it a few months ago when it was obvious the bottom was dropping out of the low-end classic car market," he said, emphasising the words 'low end'.

It was clear they were not going to be friends and Roisin couldn't help feeling a bit sad as they limped through the rest of the evening, knowing that when the chips were down, Kate would inevitably side with Michael and she would side with Patrick, driving a wedge between the two of them. Sometimes, you just couldn't force things, she thought to herself, feeling Kate's anger without having to look at her face.

The following morning Patrick was up and about uncharacteristically early. Roisin dragged herself reluctantly out of bed, feeling the after-effects of having drunk far too much by way of compensating for the way the doomed evening was going. They had rowed on the way home and, despite their pledge that they would never go to sleep on an argument, that was exactly what they had ended up doing. She padded through to the kitchen in her dressing gown to find Patrick drinking coffee at the table, laptop open in front of him.

"Seriously?" she yawned. "You're surely not working already on a Saturday morning? It's not nine o'clock yet."

He closed the lid sharply as she walked round behind him to look over his shoulder.

"I told you I had to make an early start to make sure everything goes to plan with that installation. I was just checking my emails, but I really need to get on the road now."

Rosin pulled a face, but noticed his overnight bag already packed at the door and realised there was no point in arguing.

"Sorry about last night," she said, feeling rubbish.

"Yeah, me too. I just hope now you can see I was right about that pair."

She decided to let it go, despite the fact that she would have given very different relationship advice to one of her clients.

"When will you be home?" she asked.

"Shouldn't be too long. I'll let you know as soon as the job's finished. It's a pain in the arse, but that's the way it is I'm afraid," he answered, shrugging his shoulders as he stood up. He gave her a quick hug and a kiss, but Roisin could tell his mind was elsewhere. As he walked towards the door, it was as if he were already long gone. She closed the door after him, hesitated for a few moments, then decided to take some painkillers for her banging headache and indulge herself in a nice hot bath. No sooner had she set the taps running and poured in a generous amount of her favourite Jo Malone 'Pomegranite noir' bath oil than the doorbell rang. She smiled and shook her head. Patrick was back. She was delighted to have the unexpected chance to make up properly before he left again and ran into the hall to greet him.

"That'll teach you to leave in such a rush. Did you forget your key?" she asked, laughing as she flung open the door.

Part III

The Coup

Ju ·das kiss

An act of betrayal, especially one disguised as a gesture of
friendship.

Double Bluff

Caitlin

Patrick would be home by now and probably wondering where she was. Served him right. She knew his flight from America had got in on Wednesday morning and he was supposed to come straight home. He promised. But instead, he chose to feed her some bullshit line about problems at work so he could go off shagging that slut of his in Dublin. Three nights he stayed there with her, only bothering to contact Caitlin on Friday morning.

Sorry, I've only just seen all your messages; the phone signal and wifi here are crap. I didn't mean to worry you. It's been crazy and we've had to work all hours to get finished, but I'll be home tomorrow. I can't wait to see you xx

She felt like everything was slipping away from her again, as if she was being dragged towards a cliff edge, powerless to resist the urge to hurl herself into the abyss. She tried time after time to ring him, only to get his answerphone message, so she tried texting, but there was no reply to those either. When he eventually deigned to get in touch she ignored him back, deciding it wouldn't hurt for him to have a taste of his own medicine. She made sure she was not at home when he returned to the cottage, wanting him to worry about her, maybe even panic about what may have happened to her.

The only flaw in Caitlin's thinking was that it required Patrick to actually give a damn about anyone other than himself and she quickly realised there was little point in playing games. Things were

227

about to get deadly serious. He had to understand that this was all on him. If only he had come home when he was supposed to. If only he had answered his phone when she rang him. Maybe then things would have turned out differently. At the end of the day, he had only himself to blame.

It was just after five-thirty in the afternoon when she walked through the door to find Patrick in his favourite position, on the sofa with his feet up, laptop open on his knee, rum and coke in hand. The television was on in the background.

"Ah, you're back. I wondered where you'd got to," he said cheerily, no doubt rejoicing at the prospect of clean underpants and some home cooking. "I've done some shopping," he continued. "I got stuff for a chilli tonight, unless you fancy going out somewhere?"

"No, chilli's fine," she answered, taken by surprise at his cheery demeanour. "I'll get it started in a minute."

"Where have you been then?" he asked.

"Oh…a friend of mine has been having a bit of a hard time lately, so I offered to stay with her for a couple of days while you were away."

Caitlin wandered through into the kitchen and saw the Tesco shopping bags and a bunch of flowers on the table.

"Turn the telly up so I can hear the news," she shouted as she began to unpack the shopping. After a quick rummage in the cupboards, she found a vase for the flowers, cut about an inch off the stems and put them in water. She noticed that they were still full price and actually very pretty, a mixture of lilies and dark pink roses. No sooner had she begun to chop vegetables for the chilli than she heard a crash from the lounge as a glass fell to the floor.

"Fuck! Fucking hell!" shouted Patrick, then there was silence.

Caitlin left what she was doing and ran through to the lounge, where Patrick was staring mesmerised at the TV screen in front of him, hanging on the newsreader's every word. Whatever it was that had captured his attention had obviously shocked him enough to cause him to knock his precious glass of Mount Gay onto the floor and he appeared to be oblivious to it.

"What's happ…."

"Shut up!" snapped Patrick, cutting her off in mid-sentence. "Sorry, it's just…I need to hear this."

Caitlin stood beside him, taking in his ashen face, looking at the screen and listening.

The woman, who has been named as Roisin Delaney, was bludgeoned to death in her own flat. Her body was discovered this morning by a close friend. The Garda are appealing for witnesses to come forward and they would like to speak to anyone who may be able to offer information. They are keen to interview a man called Patrick, with whom they believe she was in a relationship. He is not a suspect at this stage but could be a key witness, as he is believed to have been the last person to see her alive. He is urged to make contact immediately….

"Patrick?" Caitlin asked nervously. "I don't understand. I mean, I know this is awful, but things like this are reported all the time on the news. Why is this so important to you? You're scaring me."

She stopped, waiting for him to say something, but he remained dumbstruck.

"Patrick, did you know this woman?" she asked, sitting down suddenly, afraid of the answer.

"No! Well, I mean yes, but…hardly at all," he answered, attempting to regain his composure. "She's been doing some admin work for the company I'm dealing with up there. I met her a couple of times when I had to drop papers off at her flat. I was there yesterday. It's just a shock when something like this happens to someone you actually know…." he trailed off.

"Oh right, I see. But I thought they said she was a clinical psychologist. It was on the news earlier. I'm sure I heard that," said Caitlin, furrowing her brows thoughtfully.

"How the fuck should I know?" exploded Patrick, standing up and running his hand through his hair. "I just told you I hardly knew her. Maybe she was doing admin stuff on the side as a favour for the guy I'm working with. Does it actually matter?"

"Well no, I suppose not, it's just…."

Caitlin looked close to tears and didn't bother to finish her last sentence. Patrick appeared to calm down.

"Okay, I'm sorry. I shouldn't have shouted at you. I just got a shock, that's all. It's nothing for you to worry about."

Caitlin wished that were true.

The following morning, the news of the woman's murder was all over the papers. Caitlin observed in silence as Patrick read the reports and became increasingly agitated. She left him to his own devices for a couple of hours before bringing the subject up again.

"Patrick, I have to ask you something," she said quietly, noting the irritation in his manner. "Are you the 'Patrick' the Guards are looking for? Were you having an affair with this woman? Please just tell me the truth. I have to know."

The question hung in the air, then he gave a little snort of laughter.

"Caitlin, darling, don't be ridiculous. Of course I wasn't having an affair with her. Patrick is not exactly an uncommon name over here you know. It's just an unfortunate coincidence."

"But you *were* at her flat the day she died. Didn't you just tell me you dropped some papers off there? So there's a chance you were the last one to see her alive. We need to contact the Guards and explain everything to them. It could be important in finding her killer," she pressed.

"I don't think that's a very good idea, do you? I've done nothing wrong here and they need to concentrate their efforts on finding the bastard that actually did this, not waste their time poking their noses into my affairs. I mean it, Caitlin, we keep quiet on this one. I can't face all that shit from my past being raked up."

Caitlin stared at him incredulously.

"Patrick, this is *murder* we're talking about. A woman has died and you are a key witness. We can't just pretend you were never there, or you could end up in a lot of trouble. We both could," she reasoned.

Patrick began to pace back and forth, clearly agitated.

"Let me think," he said sharply, doing his 'talk to the hand' thing that she found so infuriating. "There's no CCTV in the building apart from the car park, which I didn't use as there's never any space. I never saw anyone else when I was there, so I really don't see how they can put me anywhere near the scene…all they have is the name 'Patrick'. Let's just stay out of it and see how things progress over the next couple of days. If I thought I could help by coming forward I would, but I know I would just be dredging up a whole load of pain for myself, all for nothing."

Caitlin stared at him in silence for a few moments, clearly having misgivings about the whole thing.

"Okay, you know best," she said simply, then walked into the kitchen to make dinner.

The following morning, after a restless night of very little sleep, Patrick came downstairs to find Caitlin sitting at the kitchen table, a pot of coffee in front of her and a large brown envelope opposite her.

"You look like death warmed up," she said in a flat voice. "Come and sit down and I'll pour you some coffee."

Patrick yawned loudly and sat down, picking up the envelope.

"What's this?" he asked, looking at Caitlin.

"Have a look," she replied, holding his gaze.

Patrick took out the photographs and visibly blanched as he recognised the scenes captured in the images.

"What the fuck is this?" he demanded, slamming the photos face down on the table and getting abruptly to his feet. "Where the fuck did you get these?" he shouted.

Caitlin did not flinch at his outburst. She had seen far worse.

"I think the more pertinent question is: what the *fuck* were you doing shagging this woman behind my back and lying to me about it last night?" said Caitlin, maintaining a calm and measured tone. "You were spending so much time away I began to wonder whether you were really being straight with me. So I had you followed. Simple as that. I didn't confront you about it straight away, because I wanted to give you every possible opportunity to tell me yourself last night. I gave you so many chances to just tell the truth," she concluded, shaking her head sadly.

Patrick's face was ashen and he looked like he might actually throw up. She thought to herself how alike they actually were; both of them needed to be in control and both of them played to win, no matter what the cost. Right now, she had the upper hand. And he knew it. She could almost hear the cogs turning as he searched for a way to get himself out of this one.

"Christ, what a mess," he said finally. "Okay, okay, I hold my hands up. I made a stupid mistake and things just got out of hand. I'll admit I've been a bit of a naughty boy, but I'm not the first and I won't be the last. The truth is, I tried to finish it, but she kept hounding me, wouldn't let go. She is…was…a complete nutter. I went to her apartment the night before last to tell her once and for all it was over, that I was with someone else and…."

"So is that how it happened Patrick?" Caitlin interrupted. "Did you have an argument that went too far? Is that how she ended up dead? Tell me the truth!" she demanded.

"What? No! Absolutely not. Don't be fucking stupid. I'm not a murderer. I went to the apartment and I told her it was over, which I admit didn't go down particularly well, but then I left. That's the truth."

Caitlin looked at Patrick, thinking how unlikely it was that he would be able to recognise the truth if it jumped up and slapped him in the face.

"I don't know what to believe anymore. How could you betray me like that? After all I did for you. I loved you and I trusted you," she said, beginning to cry. "I saved your life, for Christ's sake. It said on the news that 'Patrick' is now a person of considerable interest in the case. Someone else has come forward, a key witness. Apparently, she and her fiancé were out with this 'Roisin' and 'Patrick' for dinner that night. She said there was an argument and the evening ended badly. Oh God, Patrick...did you kill that woman?" she blurted out, her voice becoming hysterical.

"Oh grow up, Caitlin! How many times do I have to fucking repeat myself? Of course I didn't. I barely knew her. Someone is trying to make me into a scapegoat here," he yelled.

Daniel was clutching at straws, clearly flustered. Caitlin glared at him, then stood up and walked towards the door.

"I can't be around you right now. I need some space to get my head around everything and decide what to do. We'll talk about it when I get back," she announced, pulling on her boots and jacket and heading for the beach with Bentley.

She stayed out for a good two hours, deciding it would do Patrick no harm to sweat about things on his own for a while. When she eventually returned, she opened the door to the smell of bacon cooking.

"I thought I would make us some brunch. Are you hungry?" asked Patrick, as if everything was completely normal.

"Not really," she replied, unwilling to extend an olive branch too quickly. "Could you leave that and sit down, please? We need to talk."

Caitlin knew how much he would be hating all this, especially the loss of control, but she noted with satisfaction that he had made the wise decision it was in his best interests to get her on his side.

"I'm only going to say this once," she began. "I want you to look me in the eye and tell me you had nothing at all to do with the death of that woman."

That was no problem at all for a man who was utterly incapable of making any kind of distinction between lies and truth.

"I promise you, hand on heart, I had absolutely nothing to do with it. I've told you that already and it's the truth."

Caitlin stared at him in silence for a while, then nodded her head slowly.

"I believe you," she said simply.

There was a look of relief on his face, but she had not done with him yet, not by any stretch of the imagination. It was important for him to realise that she was holding all the cards now and he needed her.

"But there's still the problem of the Guards looking for you in connection with all this. If what you say is true, it looks like someone really has it in for you. Are you absolutely sure there's no evidence in that apartment that can link them to you?"

Patrick made a show of thinking about it, but in reality, he knew the answer immediately. After the debacle with Grace, he had learnt his lesson and made sure all his documents, laptop and paperwork went everywhere with him in his briefcase, but there was no getting away from the fact that his DNA would be all over the murder scene. He would need to act fast.

"Hundred percent sure," he answered with total conviction. "And like I said before, no one ever saw me there," he added.

"You mean you never *saw* anyone see you. It's not the same thing. But we'll have to hope you're right. If I'm going to put my neck on the line for you, that is."

"What do you mean by that?"

"I mean, Patrick, that if any questions are asked, I will give you an alibi. I will swear on my life that I picked you up from the airport after your trip to the States and we came straight back here. That's what you do when you love someone," she added pointedly. "What about the 'friend' you were out with? The one who told the Guards about your relationship with that woman. Could she be a problem?"

Caitlin could not bring herself to refer to Roisin by name and her lip curled involuntarily into a sneer at the word 'relationship'.

"She knows me as Patrick James, as did Roisin, so no, I don't think so," replied Patrick, clearing his throat and shifting uncomfortably as he noticed Caitlin's face harden at the mention of 'Roisin'.

"Right. Let's just hope this all goes away by itself then and they find whoever actually killed her before they have a chance to go delving too deeply into the lead on you. I'm going for a lie down. I hardly slept a wink last night."

As Caitlin stood up and walked away, Patrick had no way of seeing the smile of satisfaction on her face. No way of knowing that the hunter had just become the hunted.

Pastures New

Daniel

Daniel had been severely shaken by recent events. Not particularly because Roisin was dead, although obviously he was sorry about that, but more because his new life appeared to be in jeopardy, quite out of the blue. He was furious at the way Caitlin was treating him but had decided it was best to pacify her for the moment and buy himself some valuable time to think. How dare that conniving, devious little bitch have him followed? It was like Grace all over again. Who the fuck did she think she was? Miss *fucking* Marple? He hadn't seen that one coming. Well, she was about to find out she was not as clever as she thought she was. He had a few surprises up his sleeve where she was concerned.

First things first though. It was only a matter of time until the Guards tracked him down and he had no intention of hanging around waiting for the knock on the door. Given his contempt of and natural aversion to all types of authority, especially the police, his default response was to make sure he was long gone when they came calling and his immediate priority was therefore to get the hell out of there. Fortunately he had already hatched his plan to reinvent himself in the States and had lucked out big time by having the foresight to pave the way for that on his recent visit. Of course Daniel knew that 'Patrick' had not actually killed Roisin, as did Caitlin, but he was not naïve enough to think that a little thing like being innocent would stop the police from trying to pin something on him. He had learned from bitter experience not to trust them and was not about to cut them any slack. In fact, he had often been heard to say he wouldn't piss on them if they were on fire.

Speed was of the essence, given that they would undoubtedly already be on the case, sniffing around IP addresses, phone and email records. Things would have been made a bit more difficult for them, given that he always hid his IP address when using his laptop, a trick he had learned after his dealings in court with Grace, but he strongly suspected this was not an insurmountable problem for them. One thing he did need to deal with as a matter of urgency was the UK registered office of Jupiter Holdings. Most of his correspondence was done by email these days, but there were still a few extremely important things that were sent by snail mail to the flat in Stainsford, some addressed to Daniel Callaghan and others to Grace King, not that the latter had the first clue about any of that of course. It had suited him to use her name and details for certain things, one very important one in particular, but it was time to tidy up all those loose ends now. Grace was rapidly outliving her usefulness.

Daniel was used to living a nomadic life and had made sure that he could drop everything and move on at extremely short notice, should the need arise. So long as he had his briefcase with him, he would always have everything he needed. He was a man with a plan, but it would be foolish to rush things at this stage and risk making a mistake. The Guards would no doubt be on the lookout for anyone by the name of 'Patrick' trying to get out of the country, so boarding a flight or a ferry was out of the question at the moment. It was time to think out of the box and Daniel knew all about that. A quick search of yacht racing programmes for the Irish Sea revealed an offshore race scheduled that weekend from Cork to Falmouth. Daniel had spent enough time in the world of yacht racing to know that big boat skippers were pretty much always looking for crew, especially when it came to the logistically tricky offshore races and sure enough, there was a link on the Royal Cork Yacht Club website to a crew finder page, aiming to match up boats with available crewmembers. He registered as Daniel James, so as not to arouse suspicion with the name 'Patrick' and it took just half an hour to get a reply from the owner of 'Fortuna', an Elan 40, who was only too happy to sign up someone of his experience for the race. By Saturday evening, if everything went smoothly, he would be in the UK, having slipped in totally under the radar, free to do as he pleased. There was a small chance someone from the sailing crowd would recognise him, but it was unlikely, given the time that had gone by since his 'death', his carefully changed appearance and the fact that he had taken the precaution of making sure the name of the owner was not familiar to him. Once in Falmouth, he would tell the skipper there was a family emergency that meant he needed to stay on in the UK. That way, no alarms would be raised when he did not return with the boat. He would arrange for one of his 'business associates' to pick him up from Falmouth, given that it would be unwise to leave any kind of paper trail with a hire car or train ticket, then he would head north to the flat in Stainsford to put his affairs in order. After that, he would get the hell out of there on the first available plane to New York from one of the regional airports.

Daniel sat back, a grin on his face like a Cheshire cat, having gone over the plan one more time for good measure to check it was watertight. Then he booked a cottage for the next few nights in Crosshaven, where the marina and Cork yacht club were based, to make sure he was well out of the way if, by some remote chance, the Guards showed uncharacteristic resourcefulness or diligence and managed to ascertain where he had been living. He booked it in Caitlin's name and had already decided it would be best if she came with him on the first stage of his journey, mainly because he couldn't risk her blabbing and spoiling everything if they did turn up. He wanted her where he could keep an eye on her. Nothing would be mentioned about the race of course and, by the time she realised he had left, he would be halfway across the Irish Sea and she wouldn't have a clue as to his whereabouts. She had never really been his type anyway. Too needy. Easy come, easy go had always been Daniel's motto.

His thoughts turned again to Grace, who would be back from her rally by now. He had fantasised for so long about confronting her. He was irritated at having to rush things, but there was no way he was going anywhere without meeting her first. He couldn't wait to see the look of shock on her face as she thought she was seeing a ghost, changing to fear as she realised the truth, that he had been there all the time in the background, responsible for everything that had been happening to her. He imagined her expression as he delivered the final pièce de résistance and told her all about the money he had managed to hide from everyone, including her, despite all her pathetic attempts at amateur sleuthing. She had always suspected he got a big pay out after his helicopter crash injuries were misdiagnosed and she had been right, but could never find any proof. Thank God for data protection and patient confidentiality. Now at last it was time for the big reveal and he intended to savour every moment.

Most of all, he wanted her to admit he had won. He imagined her begging him to take her back, to take her with him to New York. There were actually two different scenarios in his head for the way things panned out at that stage. The first one was that he listened patiently to her pleading and grovelling, before eventually giving in, allowing her to be part of his life again, but on his terms of course. The second was that he laughed in her face, then grabbed her by the hair, dragged her across the room and smashed her head repeatedly against the wall, leaving her to bleed out unconscious on the floor as he jetted off to pastures new. Given all the trouble and heartache she had caused him since the email, the second option was the one he currently favoured.

Daniel's musings were interrupted by Caitlin coming down the stairs, a pained expression on her face.

"What are you doing?" she asked suspiciously, as he closed his laptop.

"That would spoil the surprise," he replied, raising his eyebrows theatrically and wondering how the hell he had managed to get himself saddled with her. "All will be revealed, but you need to pack a bag for a couple of nights. I'm not telling you any more at the moment, but you'll love it, I promise."

Caitlin was irritating the hell out of him and it was increasingly clear she intended to milk his minor indiscretion for all it was worth.

"You know I don't really like surprises," she said but went back upstairs to do as he said.

Once she was out of the way Daniel opened his laptop again and checked the latest news reports, happy to see there were no further leads mentioned at this stage. They had nothing on him because he hadn't done anything, at least not this time. Someone certainly had it in for him though and his money was on that bitch Kate. She had never made any secret of the fact she didn't like him and did everything she could to spoil things right from the start between him and Roisin. The situation was a mess, but thankfully one that would soon cease to be his problem. He came to the conclusion there was no point in wasting any more of his precious time and efforts on the whole sorry business, so he turned his attention to the more pressing issue of checking what Grace was up to and arranging a long-anticipated catch up before he vanished to start his new life.

Having shunned Facebook and all social media for years, it was ironic that it had recently become Daniel's best friend. Grace had predictably bombarded the internet with photos and posts about her 'trip of a lifetime' to Madagascar with Samantha, but it was her most recent post about something different that caused him to clench his fist so hard the nails bit into the flesh of his palm.

"You fucking bitch," he hissed under his breath as he scrolled through the latest photos. Photos of her with various members of her family taking turns in *his* car, the stunning red convertible E-type she had stolen from him. He became increasingly furious as he remembered how she had stood there, cool as a cucumber and lied to the judge about 'selling' it to her mother and the silly old fool had let her get away with it. Now here she was, flaunting it all over social media, laughing at him. The irony in his outrage about the lies was completely lost on Daniel. If there had been any doubt in his mind before, there was none now. Grace had to be made to pay and this time, he would enjoy doing the job himself. Time for Aidan to go phishing again:

Hi Grace, hope you got home safely. It's a bit of a long shot and very short notice, but a friend of mine has a yacht down in Cork and I've agreed to crew for him in an offshore race next weekend over to Falmouth. He needs a bowman and I thought of you straight away. Do you fancy it? It'd be great to finally meet up properly and the craic is always good on the boat. It's an Elan 40 by the way. Great boat. Let me know asap xx

Show time, he thought to himself as he pressed the send button.

A First Date

*Sometimes bad things in our lives will put us directly on
the path to the best things that will ever happen to us.*

Grace

I was missing Sam and my Madagascar rally family like crazy since
getting back to the UK. And of course I was missing Max, but to my
surprise I found I was able to think about him without feeling sad,
knowing that our short liaison could only ever have worked in that
one very special scenario. He sent funny little messages and photos
most days and it always made me feel happy that he was thinking
about me and caring enough to keep in touch. Despite us only being
together briefly, the bond we had formed was a strong one, but I
knew it was time for me to move on.

I read the latest message from Aidan on my phone again and felt
a little frisson of excitement at the prospect of going sailing with
him. I missed the buzz of racing that had been such a big part of my
old life, so this would be a perfect first date, doing what I loved
most with lots of other people around to take off the pressure and
make sure I was safe. I would be totally in my comfort zone. I began
to type:

242

Hi, got back safely and v excited to see msg. I'd love to come over and race with you. I'll check out flight times to Cork today. Look forward to it! X

I paused for a moment, then pressed send before I could talk myself out of the whole thing. Aidan suggested going over a day early, so we would at least have the chance to see each other in person before the race and avoid any awkwardness. An hour later I had booked my flight from Newcastle to Cork and an Air BnB reasonably close to the marina in Crosshaven. Who said I couldn't be spontaneous? I picked up the phone to ring Sam.

"Hey, it's me. I've done it," I announced, proudly. "I've agreed to meet up with Aidan!"

"Wow, that was quick work. I hope you listened to me and chose somewhere public at least," she said, concern in her voice.

"Don't worry, it's the absolute best scenario. He's invited me to go racing with him on a friend's yacht. There's a race from Cork to Falmouth next weekend and they need someone to do the bow apparently, so he asked me and I can't tell you how much I'm looking forward to it. I've really missed my sailing."

"I have to say I'm relieved," Sam laughed at my obvious enthusiasm. "They're lucky to have you with them and I'm sure you'll have a brilliant time. It'll be great to have other people there and I guess it does give him a lot more credibility. I was just a bit worried, because of the way you met him, but it all seems to be turning out okay."

I was happy to receive her seal of approval, given that I didn't really trust my own instincts so well these days. After all, I didn't have the best track record of success in spotting the tell-tale signs of a dodgy character. I decided not to tell her I was meeting him a day early on my own, as she would only worry.

"Keep in touch while you're over there and we need a girlie weekend with Suzie to hear all about it when you get back," she added.

"Definitely. And if he's nice, I'm sure he's got friends," I laughed. "I'll have to go because Lola is pestering for a walk, but speak soon."

I changed quickly into wellies and Barbour jacket and set off along the lane to the fields, dog whistle hanging optimistically round my neck. It was neither use nor ornament where Lola was concerned if I was brutally honest, as no amount of blowing it could get her to listen or come back to me when she was otherwise engaged with something of far greater interest. That covered a lot of things. I usually ended up with every other dog in the vicinity round my heels and no sign of Lola, but in spite of her delinquent behaviour she could always raise a smile from me and lift my spirits with her 'butter wouldn't melt' expression.

As soon as we got back from a relatively uneventful walk, I started to sort out my sailing gear and pack it all into a small holdall I had been given by one of our sailmakers years ago. It was a bit battered, but I loved it. My face clouded for a moment as I remembered how I had used it as a pattern to make a similar one for Daniel out of one of our old sails and how I had found it on the bed in Stainsford, violated and stuffed full of his dressing up gear... I pushed the unwelcome vision from my mind and carried on with my packing. Skippers were always keen to have as little weight as possible on a boat and big bags with loads of unnecessary extra clothing never went down well. I even knew some people who didn't let you on the boat with anything other than what you were wearing. I smiled to myself at the memories of racing 'Mistress' and my own rule of 'boots or shoes, never both', when I had been known to stand on the deck, monitoring the crew and what they were bringing on board. My toilet bag consisted of only the bare essentials, miniature containers of everything I needed, which included of course a little bottle of Chanel Allure perfume, one luxury I always allowed myself. I pushed in one change of clothes and zipped the bag shut, satisfied that there would be no complaints from my new skipper.

I felt a surge of optimism that this was the start of a whole new chapter for me. Sailing was a world I knew and felt confident in, a world where I could shine and be myself.

A One Way Ticket

Daniel

It was gone eleven o'clock. Time to go.

"Come on Caitlin," he shouted irritably. "We really need to go if we're going to get there at a reasonable time."

Caitlin eventually struggled down the stairs, Bentley at her heels, carrying a suitcase that looked as if she were planning on going away for several weeks, not a few days. She noticed the disapproval on his face and shrugged her shoulders.

"You wouldn't give me any details about what we were going to be doing so I had to pack to cover every eventuality," she laughed.

Daniel lugged her case outside and heaved it into the boot of the car, scowling as Bentley hopped onto the back seat. She looked so excited to be going away with him, he was once again reminded of how like her dog she was. To be fair to her, she had scored pretty highly on the spreadsheet after a bit of careful tweaking and he would definitely miss her cooking and laundry skills, but it was time for him to move on to greater things now.

As they drove along the track towards the main road, she chattered away happily, apparently having managed to put the fact of him being a key suspect in a murder inquiry to the back of her mind. Daniel had all he needed in a small holdall. His sailing gear was stuffed in the bottom, so as not to arouse her suspicion, but apart from that the only clothing he had was a couple of his signature polo shirts, a pair of chinos and a jumper. Next to the holdall was his briefcase, containing laptop, personal documents and all paperwork from Caitlin's house. He had surreptitiously made sure he removed all trace of him ever having been there and the few bits of clothing he left behind to stop her from asking questions could have belonged to anyone. He had booked a flight to New York JFK out of Manchester in five days' time and the e-tickets were stored on his phone. When the time came, he would check in online and his boarding pass would also be on his phone. He offered up a silent prayer of thanks for the wonders of modern technology, which had been both his downfall and his saviour in recent times.

"What do you think?" asked Caitlin, clearly waiting for a response to something.

"Sorry, I was miles away," he said, not sorry at all and silently congratulating himself on his ability to successfully tune out where her incessant prattling was concerned.

"I was asking you what you thought about maybe moving to the city, or at least a bit closer to it, given you have to spend so much time working there."

He had to admit she had surprised him with that one, but it was not something he intended to waste time and energy discussing.

"Maybe," he replied, then immediately changed the subject. "Are you hungry? Keep your eyes open for somewhere nice to stop for lunch."

Daniel felt no remorse for the fact he was planning to leave her high and dry with no clue as to his whereabouts, but he was not completely heartless and felt it was only fair to make their last couple of days together enjoyable for her. She had saved his life, after all.

It was late afternoon by the time they reached the cottage on the outskirts of Cork, having stopped off on the way to do a supermarket shop for provisions. They had also made a detour to a clinic, as Caitlin had absolutely insisted on him having a full sexual health check after the business with Roisin. He had objected initially, but in the end, he had given in to shut her up, deciding it was probably not a bad thing anyway. He knew the routine and at least he would be starting his new life with a clean bill of health. A small blonde woman met them at the cottage, handed over the keys and a long set of house rules, then dashed off to pick the kids up from school. That suited Daniel just fine, as he had no wish to engage in small talk or answer any potentially awkward questions.

"I'll light the fire while you make us some drinks," he announced, walking towards the wood burner. "The usual for me please."

Daniel was buzzing and could barely conceal his excitement as he opened the firelighters and piled kindling and a couple of big logs into the stove. Reinvention was what he did best and he was more than ready to embrace his new life in America, land of freedom and opportunities. He switched on the TV, then quickly switched it off again as soon as he saw the unpleasant images of a crime scene outside Roisin's apartment block and a reporter talking earnestly about the ongoing investigation. He just caught something about them following up a lead regarding a male client she had been treating, some psycho not long out of jail and being counselled as part of his rehab. That was what you got for going out of your way to spend your time with nut jobs, he thought cynically to himself. The sooner he was on that plane to the States and away from all this nonsense, the better.

"I need to take Bentley out for a little walk," Caitlin announced, as she wandered through and handed him his drink. "I'll only be half an hour or so. Then I thought we could walk into town and find somewhere for dinner."

"Sure. Sounds good to me. I'll just check my emails while you're out and then I'm all yours," he said, glad to be getting rid of her for a bit.

As soon as he heard the door close behind her, Daniel took out the pay-as-you-go phone he had bought to use for his communications with Grace and checked for messages. He knew exactly how to pull her strings and she had predictably swallowed the whole 'come sailing with me' line without question, just as he had anticipated. 'Gullible Grace' was flying into Cork airport tomorrow evening and good old Aidan would be there to meet her at the marina. He had thought very carefully about how best to ensure they had some private time to chat, away from prying eyes and security cameras. She would be alone on his territory, isolated and vulnerable. It was making him incredibly horny just thinking about it and he couldn't help laughing out loud as he imagined her reaction when she finally met Aidan. He pictured her smug, self-satisfied little face, thinking she held all the cards and firmly believing she had come out on top. She was about to be disabused of that belief, very forcibly.

No one screwed Daniel Callaghan over and got away with it.

Life after Death

Ghosts are nothing but the shadows of our past that we allow to haunt us.

Grace

It was already dusk when I got to the marina in Crosshaven at around eight o'clock, but I had sailed in many regattas there in the past and I was on familiar territory. There was a raucous party in full swing and posters everywhere about the 300th birthday celebrations of the world's oldest yacht club. Loud music blared out and crowds of people spilled onto the terraces, laughing and joking, recounting tales of past adventures on and off the water. A young woman screamed and then giggled, turning to the man who had startled her and punching him playfully on the shoulder. I smiled to myself as I keyed in the numbers Aidan had already given me for the gate into the marina, then walked confidently down to the pontoons to find the boat we would be racing on, my small sailing bag slung across a shoulder. Memories of racing at legendary Cork Week events on 'Mistress' filled my head and I remembered the thrill of the competition and all the fun we had ashore in the evenings. They were good days, in spite of everything that happened afterwards. The marina was pretty much deserted and I

250

guessed everyone was up at the club partying by now, all preparations for the race completed earlier. I found 'Fortuna' without any problem, right at the far end of the marina, but she was all locked up and there was no sign of Aidan yet, so I put down my bag and wandered up to the front of the boat to check out the way the bow was rigged. I took out my phone, but before I could send a text to say I was there, I heard a voice behind me.

"You made it then, Grace."

A spike of fear shot through me and I stood rooted to the spot, staring steadfastly at the yacht in front of me, refusing to turn round, refusing to look at the man the voice belonged to. I would have known that voice anywhere. But it couldn't be him.

Daniel Callaghan. My nemesis. Back from the dead. It just wasn't possible.

Questions raced through my brain as I desperately tried to make sense of what was happening.

How was he still alive? How did he know I was here? Where the hell was Aidan? Slowly and deliberately, I took a deep breath and forced myself to look at the face of the man I once loved, but now hated with a passion.

"You seem shocked Grace. It's almost as if you'd seen a ghost," he said, a sadistic smirk on his face.

I knew I was vulnerable and completely wrongfooted, having walked straight into a trap, but there was no way I was going to show my fear like a cornered animal.

"I have no idea what's going on here Daniel, or how the hell you actually survived that accident on the boat, but I'm telling you now I don't care and I'm not afraid of you," I lied. "I'm meeting someone and he'll be here any minute now, so crawl back under whatever stone you came from and leave me alone."

"Sorry, *accident* did you say? I think we both know that's a bit of a stretch, don't we?"

The words hung in the air, then he laughed and moved closer towards me, forcing me to take a step back, closer to the edge of the pontoon. I looked past him towards the clubhouse, hoping to see Aidan making his way down to the boat.

"You still don't get it, do you? The lights are on, but nobody's home. Story of your life. I can see the little cogs turning in your brain, but you haven't got a clue, in spite of you being such a super sleuth these days."

His voice was dripping with contempt and sarcasm. He was right, I didn't have a clue how he had come to be standing there in front of me, but I was determined to keep up the bravado and refused to let him intimidate me. I could sense the threat in every word and I knew I had to get away from him, fast. I opened my mouth and screamed as loud as I could, a piercing, desperate shriek that should have signalled to anyone in the vicinity that I feared for my life, but nobody heard, nobody came running to help, because my scream of terror was lost in all the other noise of general merriment and high spirits from the party. At the same time, I stamped down on his foot as hard as I could with my heel and aimed a fist at his face, but he was too quick. Recovering quickly from the surprise of the attack, he lunged forward and clamped one hand hard over my nose and mouth, using the other one to grab my arm and twist it up painfully behind my back.

"That's enough of that," he said, forcing me roughly down to the ground. "Now, carry on pissing me off and I'll break it," he added, as I struggled and clawed frantically at his face with my free arm. "It's high time we had a good old chat about things, don't you think? Clear the air, so to speak. But you need to understand this Grace: I've had enough of your poor behaviour to last me a lifetime. So shut up. Now. And keep still. If you know what's good for you," he threatened, a cold, hard edge to his voice.

He took his hand from my face for a split second, just long enough to stuff some sort of rag into my mouth to make sure I kept quiet. Then he produced a cable tie from his pocket and secured my wrists behind my back. My eyes were darting around, searching for a way out, betraying the terror I felt. I was struggling to breathe, but

I knew I had to try to stay calm, try to evaluate the situation properly, while all the time cursing my stupidity for letting my guard down and allowing him to get the better of me.

"Good girl, that's better. You see, doing the right thing is not so hard after all. Now we can relax and talk properly," he mocked. "Oh and by the way, I should make one thing clear from the start to put you out of your misery. Don't be under any illusions that there's a hero out there, waiting to ride in on a white horse to save you like they do in those soppy romantic movies you're so fond of. Aidan Flynn was a nice enough guy, but don't pin your hopes on him, because he's gone now," he declared, a sinister expression on his face.

I was increasingly fearful of his menacing tone and I felt sick at the thought of what he might have done to Aidan, but I was powerless to do anything except listen.

"For fuck's sake Grace, get with the programme. Don't look so baffled. Do I really have to spell it out for you? It was *me* sending all those messages to you. I *am* Aidan Flynn. At least I was for a while," he declared, obviously proud of his deception. "And you were so pathetically desperate for attention from a man that you swallowed it, hook, line and sinker. Just like I knew you would. Nobody knows you like I do Grace."

Daniel paused to allow his words to sink in, then continued his self-indulgent monologue.

"How is your horse, by the way? Terrible business about that stable fire. And your poor leg after the skiing accident. Not to mention that tragic car incident in Madagascar, when an innocent man died. All because of you."

He shook his head and tutted, taunting me.

"Disaster really does seem to follow you around, doesn't it?"

He stopped again, then suddenly seemed to grow impatient at my dumbfounded expression.

"I can see from your face that you still haven't figured it out, so I'll tell you, in words of one syllable. It was me Grace. All of it," he said, enunciating the words slowly as if he were speaking to a small child. Did you really think I would let you get away with what you did to me? Surely you know me better than that," he added with a weary sigh.

I tried to answer back, but only muffled sounds came out. Daniel leaned closer, feigning interest.

"Sorry, what did you say? Oh, silly me," he chuckled. "I'll take it out so you can speak, but only if you promise to behave yourself. Deal?" he asked, a patronising look on his face as he snatched the rag out of my mouth.

"You are a sick bastard. What the fuck more do you want from me?" I shouted in his face.

"Revenge. Obviously. And keep your voice down," he warned, gripping my arm tightly and making me wince. "Not that anyone can hear you," he laughed, with a dismissive gesture towards the party.

He stared at me for a moment, appearing thoughtful, then shook his head.

"Oh Grace, what a team we could have been. If only you had kept your mouth shut after that email. I have to admit these last couple of years have been fun, but all good things must come to an end, as you know only too well."

I began to panic then and reacted instinctively. I spat in his face, catching him off guard, then leaned back and kicked out wildly, hoping to hit him in the mouth or nose, but he dodged to one side and my feet failed to make contact. He retaliated immediately with a stinging slap to the side of my head, which set my ears ringing.

"Temper temper," he said, wagging his finger. "Now, before you go, is there anything else you'd like to say to me? An apology for leaving me for dead maybe?"

I was clutching at straws, but I needed to shock him, show him he didn't hold all the cards. Tell him I knew his secrets. My words were full of hatred and contempt as I spoke, looking him straight in the eye.

"You think you're so clever, don't you? Such a stud with *all* your women. But the truth is, you're nothing but a filthy pervert. You disgust me. And what's more, I know what you get up to in that flat in Stainsford."

I stopped and waited for a reaction to that revelation, but his face gave nothing away, so I began again.

"I *know*, Daniel, because I got in there and went through everything in that seedy hole with a fine-tooth comb when you were away in America. And do you know what the best bit about it is?" I paused again, revelling in my moment of glory. "I told everyone," I whispered. "And I showed them photos. All your old sailing pals, our crew, our friends, my family… *everyone*. And they all pissed themselves laughing at you."

I looked at him with a defiant smirk, unable to avoid the blow from the back of his hand as he hit me again, hard enough this time to make my nose bleed and my eyes water.

"You never did know when to keep your big mouth shut Grace," he said in a quiet voice, loaded with venom. "That was always your problem. But you really, *really* should have kept that to yourself. You just have to press my buttons, don't you?"

I screamed again as loud as I could, in the hope that someone would recognise the difference in tone between fear and high jinks, but there was no point. One minute I was sitting on the jetty, the next I was in the water, kicking and struggling to stay afloat as the fleece-lined jacket I was wearing began to get heavier and drag me down. Daniel leaned over and grabbed a handful of my hair, keeping my head just above water. His words were strangely matter-of-fact, as if we were chatting over a friendly drink in the bar.

"You see, Grace, I thought you should know what it felt like. To experience first-hand the true horror of believing you are going to drown. Kind of a fitting ending to everything, don't you think?"

I kicked and squirmed like a fish on a hook as he pushed my head under water again and held it there. My brain felt as if it were about to explode and there was a fierce, stabbing pain in my lungs and chest when he eventually allowed me to resurface, gasping and spluttering for air. I looked up into the face of my torturer and saw the undisguised pleasure written all over it. I was under no illusion that there would be a reprieve. I was fighting for my life.

"I'm not gonna lie, Grace. It's not a nice way to go. The pain of drowning is indescribable, despite all the myths. Such a shame it had to come to this, but you know you have no one to blame but yourself. Don't fight it," he said abruptly, shoving my head under the water again.

I twisted my head sharply and bit down as hard as I could on his arm to make him release his grip on my hair, but a moment later his foot was pushing on my head and I felt myself sinking down, becoming increasingly disorientated. I wondered for a moment how quickly it would all be over if I just stopped struggling and let it happen, but then I thought of my dad, my mum, Sam, Valentino, Lola, everyone who loved me and I knew I could never give up. Kicking as hard as I could, I managed to get back to the surface, but my strength was fading rapidly and my clothes, especially the jacket, were weighing me down and working against me. I expected to feel another blow to my head the second I emerged, forcing me back under, but there was only the sound of the party up above me. Daniel appeared to have vanished into thin air. Or maybe he was just playing with me like a cat with a mouse, waiting to start the torture all over again. The cable tie cut into my wrists as I continued struggling to free my hands, but I had to keep trying. I remembered my survival courses for offshore racing and lay back in an attempt to float, snatching little gasps of air, knowing I could not afford to go under the water again. My wrists were bleeding, but I felt no pain and then, just as exhaustion and the desire to give in to sleep began to overcome me, my hands brushed against something sharp and metal on one of the jetty posts. I was crying tears of frustration at the effort of keeping my head above water, while at the same time working behind my back to saw through the cable tie on the rusty metal strip I had found. I could scarcely believe my good luck when it gave way and my hands were finally free. My flailing arms found one of the mooring ropes attaching 'Fortuna' to the jetty and I clutched it, holding on tight with every bit of my remaining strength. Freezing cold and exhausted, renewed hope gave me an adrenalin rush and I hauled myself painstakingly along the pontoon, hand over hand until I came to one of the emergency ladders I knew were there at regular intervals. I looked around desperately for any signs of Daniel, but he was still nowhere to be seen and I could only conclude he had simply left me to my fate, as I had once left him to his.

As soon as I had managed to haul myself out of the water, I began to shiver violently and I knew I had to get myself dry and warm fast. By some miracle, my sailing bag appeared to have gone unnoticed by Daniel and was sitting at the other end of the pontoon, exactly where I had put it down. I dragged myself to my feet, picked it up and took off my sodden jacket, then headed up to the marina wash block. Turning the shower on full blast I slumped down to the floor, still fully clothed, allowing the hot water to run over me as the enormity of what had happened struck me like a bullet and I began to sob uncontrollably. I felt utterly defeated as I dressed myself in the warmest things I had, then trudged up the hill to the B&B I had checked into before heading down to the marina and collapsed onto the bed in my room. Every bone in my body ached and my face and wrists were stinging, but I knew my escape had been nothing short of miraculous and I was lucky to be alive. I really did have a guardian angel looking after me. I crawled under the duvet and drifted off to sleep, not even bothering to undress.

The following morning I checked out early, feeling too sick for anything to eat and headed straight for the airport. My phone was dead and beyond resurrection, having been in my jacket pocket when I went into the water, but my purse was safe in my bag, so at least I could get a flight back home without any problems. Instinct told me there was no point in going to the Guards about what had happened. I had already learned the hard way that the law and those who professed to enforce it were no match for the likes of Daniel Callaghan. They would never find him and, even if they did, he would just deny everything. My word against his. I was certain he would get away with it like he got away with everything before. I had to deal with this in my own way, once I had given myself time to think.

And this time there would be no mistakes.

A Kiss Goodbye

Daniel

Caitlin was upstairs when Daniel got back to the cottage, still seething after what Grace had said to him about the flat in Stainsford. That was his bolt hole for precious downtime, his private place, but now it had become just another thing she had ruined. He still had no idea how the hell she had got in there, because he had always been so careful, installing the alarm and the second lock that even the letting agents didn't know about. Even more mystifying was why she had kept her mouth shut for once and not gloated about it to him. Not like here at all. After his 'death', the imaginary co-directors of Jupiter Holdings had kept it on as the registered office of the company and his long-term plan had always been to continue the arrangement of using it as his UK base. He reassured himself that there was really no need to change those plans and that, in all probability, nobody believed a word Grace had told them about the goings-on there anyway. A sadistic little smile crept across his features as he relived the way he had dealt with her earlier at the marina and he began to feel quite horny.

He steeled himself for a grilling at the sound of Caitlin clumping down the stairs.

"Where have you been?" she asked, narrowing her eyes suspiciously. "You said you would only be an hour."

"I know, sorry. Time just ran away with me."

"Okay, well you're here now I suppose, so let's have a drink."

"Whatever you want," he replied curtly, not in the mood for company.

"Is everything okay?" asked Caitlin innocently, for the sake of appearances more than anything else, given that she had managed to get a sneaky peek at the text exchange between Aidan and Grace and knew exactly what he had been up to.

Or at least she thought she did.

"Everything's fine. Why?"

"It's just, you seem a bit cross about something. Have I upset you?" she asked, noticing his rapidly subsiding erection, which she wouldn't mind betting was nothing to do with her.

"No of course not," he replied, attempting to sound nicer. I've just got stuff on my mind, work mainly. Nothing for you to worry about. Now, why don't you fetch us some drinks and a nice cheese board? I'm a bit peckish."

She headed off dutifully into the kitchen, coming back with a large glass of rum and coke for him, laced with a liberal helping of her own secret ingredient.

"Here you are. You look like you could do with this to help you relax," she said, giving him a kiss on the cheek, then disappearing again to get the cheese.

Daniel picked up his drink and pulled a face at how strong it was. Caitlin appeared to be economising on the coke. Nevertheless, he downed it quickly and began to enjoy the pleasant numbing effect of the alcohol on his nerves. He relaxed back into the cushions and put his feet up on the little coffee table, listening to her bustling around in the kitchen and smiling to himself as he relived the marina incident.

"You are an angel," he said appreciatively, as she placed a second drink on the table next to his feet.

He closed his eyes and sighed contentedly, thinking to himself that this was the Caitlin he was so fond of. The one who was always trying to please him, not the one whinging and whining about his affair with Roisin, turning the milk sour with her kicked puppy expression. It had been an exhausting evening and Daniel was struggling to keep his eyes open.

"Patrick? Wake up, sleepyhead."

Daniel was awakened by Caitlin shaking his shoulder and wondered for a moment who the hell Patrick was, before coming to his senses and rubbing his hand across his face.

"Sorry, I must have fallen asleep. I didn't realise how tired I was," he said, yawning.

A smile formed on Caitlin's lips, but her eyes told a different story.

"You were spark out. Are you going to have some cheese?"

He had to admit she was a great hostess, good enough to score the full ten out of ten on his infamous spreadsheet, although she would sadly never know she was such a high achiever.

Daniel suddenly felt incredibly weary and his head seemed to weigh far too heavily on his shoulders. All he could think about was closing his eyes and going to sleep.

"I have to go to bed," he said, feeling decidedly groggy. "I just need a good night's sleep and I'll be fine tomorrow," he added, noticing the look of disappointment on her face, presumably due to the fact that her anticipated night of passion was evaporating before her very eyes.

Daniel felt himself sway a little as he got to his feet.

"Are you trying to get me drunk?" he asked, slurring his words.

"Hmm, that must be it," replied Caitlin, without humour. "I could do with some sleep myself to be honest. I'll come up with you," she said, taking the cheeseboard back to the fridge and following him out of the lounge.

Daniel stumbled his way up the stairs and into the bedroom, where he immediately collapsed on the bed without bothering to undress. Caitlin pulled up a chair and sat for a long while just staring at him in silence, reflecting on their time together, from the fateful day she first found him on the beach to the series of bad decisions on his part that had led them irrevocably to this point. He was out for the count, oblivious to anything or anyone else, snoring away with his mouth wide open, but his vulnerability did not in any way diminish his culpability for their doomed relationship. She could not forgive him for that. He had to start taking responsibility for the way things had turned out and face the consequences of his actions. No going back now. Because unfortunately for Daniel, Caitlin was not as thick as he thought. She knew all about his plan to leave her and had wasted no time in formulating a plan of her own to put a stop to it.

Eventually, she stood up, leaned over to kiss him tenderly on the lips one last time, then she closed her eyes and said a prayer, like the good Catholic girl she was, asking God for forgiveness.

The following morning Caitlin woke early and went for a long walk with Bentley. She stopped off to pick up a few bits and pieces she needed on the way back, then crept quietly into the cottage, fed Bentley and made herself some scrambled eggs on sourdough toast for breakfast. There was no sound or movement from upstairs. Half an hour later she stood up from the table, loaded everything into the dishwasher and set it going. Taking the car keys from the hook in the hallway she put on her coat and boots, loaded her large tote bag and suitcase into the car, then closed the door behind her and opened the boot of the Land Rover for Bentley to jump in. She had planned her route carefully and had no need of a map or the GPS on her phone for assistance.

Caitlin drove cautiously through the town until she came to the end of the houses and open countryside stretched ahead. Then she put her foot down and kept on driving without a backward glance.

Daniel was not the only one with a hidden agenda.

The Long Arm of the Law

Trouble will always be there in the shadows. You can't avoid it and in the end it's how you deal with it that counts.

Grace

I was back to living with one eye permanently looking over my shoulder, fearful of footsteps behind me, trying to second guess what might happen. My thoughts turned to a conversation I had a long time ago and a black and gold business card I had been given. There was more than one way to deal with someone like Daniel and I knew there were people out there who could help me. Ruthless people, who would make sure they did the job properly and didn't screw it up as I had done. All it would take was a phone call.

The knock at the door made me jump violently as if I had somehow been caught out plotting to order a hit on my ex-husband. I went to the front door with more than a hint of apprehension, noticing it was gone nine-thirty in the evening and thinking to myself that nobody ever called unannounced this late in the evening with good news. There was a woman in a police uniform and a man in a suit standing next to her on the doorstep, both holding out their ID cards for me to see. I opened the door

263

cautiously, terrified of what they might be going to say to me, random thoughts racing through my mind.

"Mrs Callaghan?" asked the man.

"Miss King actually," I corrected him immediately. "Callaghan was my married name."

"Apologies. I'm DCI Colin Gates and this is WPC Shelly Talbot. Could we come inside please?" he said, in a voice that made it clear there was only one correct answer.

I stepped aside obediently to allow them in. Why the hell were they here? I knew it couldn't be Mum, Jeremy or any of the family, as I had spoken to them less than an hour before.

"What's this about?" I demanded, more aggressively than I intended.

"Sit down please and we'll explain everything," the man said.

Again, I did as I was told and sat down at the kitchen table with the two of them opposite me.

"I'm afraid we have some bad news for you. Your husband, sorry, your *ex*-husband was found dead two days ago."

He waited for the information to sink in, but all I could think about was that someone else had beaten me to it.

Hardly bad news, I thought to myself, but refrained from voicing it.

"Right," I said, attempting to look something more than relieved. A vivid image of my last encounter with him was etched in my memory and I thought of how he had done his very best to make sure I was the one becoming just another police statistic.

The detective was staring at me, a puzzled expression on his face.

"Forgive me Miss King, but you don't seem particularly shocked by the news," he said.

I stared at him, utterly confounded and completely lost for words, trying desperately to regain my composure.

"I'm sorry, it's just…well the last time…," I trailed off, wary of saying too much. "Are you sure it's him? The thing is, I thought he drowned in the Irish Sea when he fell overboard from our yacht."

"Quite sure. The body has been positively identified. He was found by the owner of a cottage he was renting for a few days in Ireland, in a village called Crosshaven, near Cork."

I nodded, confused and unsure of how I was supposed to react.

"How did he die?" I asked, in an attempt to sound more normal.

"He was found in bed upstairs and it appears he suffered a massive stroke in his sleep, which would have killed him almost instantly, although we will of course know more once we get the results of the post mortem."

He stopped talking to allow me to process the information, but I knew he was watching me like a hawk, assessing me, judging me.

"The strange thing is, he was found with two passports in the names of Daniel Callaghan and Patrick Salenden, so it would appear he was using a pseudonym for some reason. There are in fact a number of issues we need to discuss with you, in particular his possible involvement in the recent murder of a woman in Ireland. It's nothing for you to be worried about, but we are hoping you might be able to help us fill in a few gaps."

I felt as if my head was about to explode and I thought for a moment I might be physically sick. What the hell was he talking about? I needed to get rid of them and give myself time to think.

"Look, I have no earthly idea why you would think I can help you. I haven't seen anything of him since that night on the boat when I thought he drowned. None of this makes sense to me. It's all such a shock, I...I can't take it in," I stammered, close to tears.

"I completely understand," the detective said, getting to his feet. "I think the best thing would be for us to come back tomorrow when you've had a bit of time to come to terms with things." The policewoman smiled sympathetically but still said nothing. Her seemingly pointless presence was irritating me and I was tempted to ask her if she was an elective mute.

DCI Gates informed me they would be back at ten the next morning if that was convenient. Again, I got the distinct impression I had no choice. His parting shot took me by surprise:

"Oh, I almost forgot, we understand you went to Cork yourself recently, which means you would have been in the area at the time of Mr. Callaghan's death. Quite a coincidence, don't you think? Did he attempt to contact you at all, or did you see him while you were there?"

"No, of course I didn't. I've already told you, I thought he was dead. And even if he wasn't, we weren't exactly on friendly terms," I answered, becoming increasingly concerned that I was digging myself into a hole I would struggle to get out of.

"Okay, thank you. We'll talk more tomorrow. Good night."

As soon as they had gone, I locked the door with shaking hands, then went back into the kitchen and rang Sam. I would feel better after talking to her, but I had to come clean first. To my relief, she answered after a couple of rings.

"Hey, I didn't think you'd be back yet. Come on then, how was it and, more to the point, how did you get on with Aidan?" she asked, expecting to hear all the gossip of the fun few days I had planned.

I launched straight in.

"Sam, I need you to listen. I've just had the police round. They turned up to tell me Daniel was dead," I announced.

"What? No way! I can't believe they found his body after all this time. I did not see that one coming. Where was he washed up?"

"That's the whole point. He wasn't. He was found dead in his bed in a rented cottage in Crosshaven."

"Crosshaven? But that's where you were this weekend…" she trailed off. "Well it can't be him, can it? There must be some mistake."

"Apparently he's been positively identified, although I have no idea who did that. I'm guessing maybe Kieran? I swear this is so fucked-up I can't even begin to take it in."

I paused, then took a deep breath and began again, knowing I had to tell her the full story.

"There's more Sam, a lot more."

She listened in stunned silence as I explained the truth behind Aidan Flynn's messages and recounted the ordeal with Daniel at the marina, fighting back the tears as I spoke.

"It turns out he's been living in Ireland all this time under a false name, getting up to goodness knows what, making a hobby of stalking me and dreaming up ways to hurt me, the sick bastard. According to him, he was responsible for pretty much everything that's happened recently: the ski accident, the stable fire, even the car crash in Madagascar. And as if that wasn't bad enough, the police casually dropped into the conversation that they think he might be connected with a woman's murder over there…a *murder* for Christ's sake! Sam, what the hell had that wanker got himself into? And more to the point, why are they so interested in talking to me about it?"

"Grace, I don't know what to say, I really don't. I'm still trying to get my head around the fact that he was alive and kicking all this time. This is the sort of thing that happens in movies, not in real life."

"I haven't told the police I saw him in Ireland, or any of the other stuff," I said, feeling suddenly stupid for my rash decision to deal with things in my own way.

"Why the hell not? You need to. And do it as soon as possible. I really don't understand you sometimes Grace," said Sam, clearly frustrated with me.

"I don't trust them. It's as simple as that. If I tell them about the fight at the marina, they will jump to conclusions about me having a motive for wanting him dead. They'll try to pin something on me, I guarantee it, especially after what happened on the boat that night. There's a lot more to all this than meets the eye, I know there is, and I would put money on the fact that his death was not an accident."

I wanted more than anything to distance myself from the whole sorry mess, but it seemed inevitable I would be dragged back into the seedy underworld of Daniel Callaghan. My way of coping was very much like my initial reaction to Lorraine's email: don't tell anyone about it, because if you don't say it out loud it won't be true.

I lay awake most of the night, getting out of bed at around five in the morning and going through old photographs to distract myself. Memories of happier times. Photos of us on a boat on our honeymoon in the Seychelles. I had been meaning to sort them out for ages and get rid of all the ones he was in, but somehow I hadn't been able to do it. Maybe I needed to remember that we had been happy once. A long time ago.

When the police arrived the following morning, the silent uniformed one had been replaced by a more talkative version in plain clothes, who introduced herself as DI Gemma Ford and looked about fifteen. The three of us sat at the kitchen table again and DI Ford ("Call me Gemma") made polite conversation about the weather to break the ice. I even made coffee. Then it was down to business.

"I'm afraid to say it looks as if your ex-husband was more than happy for you and a lot of other people to believe he was dead, while he created a new life for himself over in Ireland, going by the names of Patrick Salenden and Patrick James. Do either of those names mean anything to you?"

I pretended to think for a moment before answering.

"During our divorce, he told the judge that Patrick Salenden was a director of his company Jupiter Holdings. I have no idea why he would have been calling himself that and pretending to be someone else though. Unless he was up to no good again."

"What about the names Roisin Delaney and Caitlin Flynn? Have you ever heard of them or had anything to do with them?" asked Gates.

"No, I've never heard of either of them," I answered truthfully.

"It seems Mr Callaghan was in a relationship with both of those women at the same time."

I gave a sarcastic little laugh at that, hoping he was not expecting me to be shocked.

"Well, I assume if you've done your homework, you will know that is his signature MO then?"

"One of the women in question has been found dead in suspicious circumstances and the other one is still missing," said Gemma in a waspish tone. "We are concerned for her safety," she added, a stern look on her face as if it were somehow my fault.

"And yes, we have done our homework, so we are aware of the circumstances of your divorce and the subsequent bankruptcy," she continued, a pitying look on her face.

"That's a nasty bruise you've got there Grace," she said suddenly, changing the subject to catch me off guard.

"Yeah, I was sailing at the weekend and I got hit in the face with a winch handle…a hazard of racing," I explained, looking her straight in the eye and surreptitiously pulling my sleeves down over my wrists under the table to hide the angry red marks.

"Right," she said, in an irritating tone that made it clear she did not believe a word I said. "When Mr Callaghan was found, he had with him a holdall full of sailing gear and a briefcase containing his laptop. We gained access to his computer and phone records, which showed he had booked a flight from Manchester to New York, no return ticket. Have you any idea why he would want to leave the country all of a sudden?" she asked, staring me straight in the eyes.

"Absolutely none, but my guess is he'd crossed the wrong people and was on the run. He made a bit of a habit of that. Look, in all honesty, I can't say I'm sorry he's dead and I'm pretty sure I'm not the only one who thinks that way," I concluded vehemently.

Gemma raised her eyebrows at my outburst and scribbled a few notes before continuing.

I felt an increasing urge to slap her.

"Does the name Aidan Flynn mean anything to you?"

The trouble with lies is that, once you start, you can't stop and you can't go back. One lie always leads to a dozen more and before you know it you are completely entangled.

269

"Well…yes, he was a friend on Facebook, but I've never actually met him. In fact, I wasn't entirely sure he was above board," I said, feeling like a schoolgirl in front of the head teacher. "Wait a minute, was he married to the Caitlin Flynn you asked me about before?"

"He was once. Your instincts about him were right in a sense, but the truth is the real Aidan Flynn died some time ago. It seems your ex-husband was using his account fraudulently to gain your trust and establish contact with you. We've seen the messages."

I slumped in the chair, covering my face and pressing the heels of my hands hard into my cheekbones. This day was rapidly turning into my worst nightmare.

"You had no idea it was your ex-husband corresponding with you?" she persisted.

"Of course I didn't!" I snapped, furious at the insinuations. *At least, not until he turned up at the marina*, I thought to myself.

Gemma sniffed disdainfully and changed tack.

"Have you ever been to this property in Stainsford?" she asked, pushing a photo of the bedsit towards me, with the address printed on the bottom.

"No, never, but I know he used it as the registered office of his company," I replied carefully, holding my nerve.

I had made the mistake before of being completely open and honest in court, believing that the law existed to protect and help people like me. It hadn't gone well then and I would not be making the same error of judgement again. I already disliked Gemma a lot, especially as she bore an uncanny resemblance to Corinne Burns, the barrister for the Trustee in Bankruptcy, the woman who had done everything humanly possible to ruin my life. I suspected the feeling was mutual.

"We know that Mr Callaghan's company continued to rent the property after his disappearance and it appears from various pieces of information found on his computer and phone records that he intended to go there before leaving the country. Prior to his disappearance, the property was already on our radar, with a

270

possible connection to trafficking of sex workers. Did you ever have any suspicion that he may have been involved in something like that?" asked Gates, leaning forward towards me across the table. "Do you have any idea why he would be going back there?"

I didn't like the way this whole 'informal chat' was going and decided to put them straight.

"You have to understand that my ex-husband deceived me for twenty years. He lived four different lives and fathered children with two other women behind my back. Have you any idea what it was like for me to find all that out? He was a compulsive liar and very secretive about his business affairs. I can't help you I'm afraid. As far as I was concerned, he died that night when he fell into the water," I said sharply. "I really wish he had done."

There was a pause and I could sense their frustration with me. I could tell from their faces that they believed I knew more than I was letting on and thought it highly likely that I was somehow involved in Daniel's dodgy dealings and maybe even his death. At the end of the day, I was guilty of one thing and one thing only and there was no way they could ever know about that, so they would have to realise before long that they were barking up the wrong tree with me.

"Please think hard Grace," said Gemma earnestly, opting to try a different approach and appeal to my better nature. "This is really important. Can you think of anyone your ex-husband may have kept in touch with secretly? Anyone at all who may be able to help us build up a better picture of what was going on? We're very concerned about the missing woman Caitlin Flynn. Two deaths and a missing person, all three connected and in the space of a couple of weeks. It has to be more than an unfortunate coincidence."

I shrugged my shoulders and shook my head defiantly, noticing her expression harden.

"I'm sorry, I really can't help you. None of this makes any sense to me. I can only keep telling you, I believed he died years ago when he fell off the boat. I thought I'd put all that behind me and yet here I am again, back in the middle of all the chaos and misery that surrounded him throughout his whole life," I said tearfully.

"Okay Grace, I think we'll leave it there for today. If you think of anything at all that could be of any use to us, please give me a call," said Gates, handing me his card. "We're just trying to get to the bottom of what happened. We don't want to cause you any further distress, I can assure you, but we may well need to talk to you again."

On that note, they both stood up and I showed them out, relieved to see the back of them. I had a lot of thinking to do.

I watched their car drive off, then I went upstairs and took out a little jewellery box from the back of my bedside table drawer. In it was a set of two keys with a Timpson key ring. The keys to Daniel's bedsit. I sat down on the bed, turning the keys over and over in my hand, knowing exactly what I needed to do.

A New Look

Caitlin

Caitlin Flynn knew that practice made perfect. The more you did something, the easier it became and the better you got at it. The act of killing another human being was no exception to that rule.

She stood outside on the little deck used by smokers and dog owners, watching the gentle rise and fall of the waves. The ferry would soon be pulling into the port of Bilbao in Spain and from there she would head south, maybe even go over to Morocco, although she hadn't made up her mind on her final destination yet. It had been a good crossing from Rosslare and she and Bentley had both managed to get a bit of sleep in their cabin. She glanced at her watch and decided it was time to head back to the cabin and get her things together, not that she had much luggage. This was a new start for her and it was important to leave both physical and emotional baggage behind if she was going to make a success of it. She stood in the tiny bathroom, staring at her reflection in the mirror and coming to the conclusion that she liked her white-blond, spiky hair, which was both edgy and surprisingly flattering. The ripped jeans, biker boots and leather jacket gave her a whole new look and made her feel somehow more empowered. Her eyes looked bigger, framed with a thick line of kohl pencil and several coats of mascara and the dark red lipstick was far more daring than anything she used to wear. It was a good look, she decided.

An hour later, she drove off the ferry in the little Toyota Yaris she had bought a couple of weeks earlier and left parked on a side street in a residential area near Rosslare, waiting for her to pick up on her way to the ferry. She went through customs with everyone else, handing both her own passport and Bentley's doggy one over to the man at the border check. After a few moments of studying both documents with a stern expression on his face and looking the pair of them up and down, he stamped the papers decisively and handed them back to her across the desk.

"Have a good journey Miss Sullivan and enjoy your time in Spain."

She smiled back at him and nodded, turning up the radio as she drove away. Caitlin Flynn would have been worried about doing the long journey into the unknown all by herself, but Rachel Sullivan was embracing it and loving every minute. She could never understand the people who allowed bad things in their lives to define and torture them when it was so easy to simply walk away, leave it all behind and start over.

It was barely thirty-six hours since she left the cottage on the outskirts of Crosshaven, with Patrick upstairs in the arms of the angels. Or more likely the devil. It would be another day before he was found by the cottage owner and Rachel knew the poor woman was in for one hell of a shock, but it couldn't be helped. People like Patrick couldn't be allowed to roam free, treating people like dirt and ruining lives without a care in the world. She had given him more than enough chances, but in the end, he had proved conclusively that he was completely incapable of changing. In her experience, that was sadly almost always the case. At least she could sleep easy at night now, knowing it was a good thing she had done, a kindness, almost like putting a sick animal out of its misery. To be fair, she had shown him more mercy than he really deserved, because he wouldn't have known anything about it when the end came.

Not like Roisin. That had all gone horribly wrong. In spite of her well-thought-out plan, something inside just snapped when she came face to face with the other woman, knowing what she had been getting up to with Patrick, remembering what she had seen on the video. She had gone down hard after the first blow to the head and lay there motionless on the floor, but Caitlin found she was somehow unable to stop beating her. A bit like it was with her father all those years ago.

She pushed the unpleasant images out of her mind. That was all in the past now. No point dwelling on it.

She had been on the road for a couple of hours when Bentley began to whine and she found a place to pull over and let him out. The sun was shining and she allowed herself to soak up the warmth on her face as she let him wander around on his flexi lead, sniffing all the new and exciting scents he was finding. Not for the first time she asked herself why men couldn't be as faithful and dependable as dogs were. Bentley would never let her down and loved her unconditionally. He was uncomplicated.

Her mind returned to Roisin and the look of utter bewilderment on her face when she opened the door, clearly expecting it to be Patrick, only to find her past had come to visit. In spite of her changed appearance, she recognised Caitlin immediately, although she called her Sophie, as she had known her all those years ago when they used to hang out together. They had been happy times. At least, they were until the business with Craig spoiled everything.

Getting back into the car she caught sight of herself in the rearview mirror and smiled, thinking how much her new look suited the image she had of herself as a kind of vigilante. Life experience had moulded her into the woman she was today: a woman on a crusade to force the cheats of this world, both male and female, to face the consequences of their actions. She was well aware that there were some women who thought it was perfectly acceptable to steal another woman's man and in Caitlin's eyes they were every bit as bad as, if not worse than, the men who cheated on their partners. Roisin had learned the hard way that there was always a price to pay for such duplicity, as had Patrick.

Caitlin wondered what the Guards would make of Patrick's untimely demise when they eventually found him. His visit to the STI clinic on the way to Crosshaven had been no accident. It was all part of the plan and she had thought of everything. The fact that the nurse had taken his bloods as part of the health check meant that nobody would think the small puncture wound from a needle in his arm was in any way suspicious when they conducted the post mortem. Fortunately, she had a steady hand and had practised inserting a needle into the same hole on her own arm countless times. She had even made sure the appointment card for the clinic was in his pocket as a vital clue, just to make sure the investigation did not head off in the wrong direction. They would come to the conclusion that he had suffered a catastrophic stroke in his sleep and died almost immediately. Not too far from the truth in fact.

Patrick's DNA would be all over Roisin's apartment, not to mention her body, which would hopefully enable the Guards to draw a line under her death at the same time. They were already looking for him in connection with the murder, so they would be delighted to be able to kill two birds with one stone. A lovers' tiff which went horribly wrong maybe? A violent argument because one of them was cheating on the other? A crime of passion? However they explained it, it wouldn't need to involve Caitlin. Or Rachel.

It was two days before she saw the story she had been waiting for on the internet. She read all about it on the terrace of the little apartment she had rented in a quiet residential area a few miles inland from Malaga.

It has been confirmed that the body found in Crosshaven this morning was that of Patrick Salenden. He is believed to be the same man that was wanted in connection with the murder of Roisin Delaney in Dun Laoghaire last week and may also have been using the names Patrick James and Daniel Callaghan.

The Garda are extremely concerned about the safety of another woman, Caitlin Flynn, who was apparently staying at the rental cottage with him and is still missing. They are appealing to anyone who knows her or may have information regarding her whereabouts to come forward at the earliest opportunity.

Caitlin stared at the photo of her they had circulated. No one would recognise her now, that was for sure, but she still did not like attention being drawn to her. Reporters and Guards were probably already crawling all over her little cottage. Sinead from the Post Office and Aidan's family would have a field day dishing the dirt on her, but none of it mattered anymore, because Caitlin Flynn had gone for good. Preparation was key. Weeks earlier, she had re-mortgaged the cottage up to the hilt and then withdrawn the lot in cash so she wouldn't have to worry about money for a long while. The cottage would of course be repossessed when she defaulted on the payments, but she didn't care about that as she had not the slightest intention of ever going back there.

Taking a deep breath, she closed her eyes and felt a wonderful sense of peace flowing through her body. Rachel Sullivan had so much to look forward to and was about to start a new life in Spain, where she could surely find happiness. Maybe she would, at last, meet the man of her dreams out there, her very own Prince Charming, who would sweep her off her feet and love her with all his heart, just like she deserved.

Surely that wasn't too much to ask for?

A Key to the Future

You should always trust your instincts, because they are messages from your soul and they will not let you down.

Grace

"Are you okay? What did they say?" asked Sam, when I rang her after the detectives left.

I played with the keys in my hand as I spoke.

"I'm fine, but the bastards managed to make me feel like I was a suspect for something. Apparently, they have reason to believe Daniel was coming back to the UK before doing a runner to the States. They found a one-way ticket from Manchester to New York in his name."

"Jeez, I still can't get my head around the fact he's been alive and kicking all this time," said Sam, clearly as stunned by the revelations as I was. "And the dead woman they told you about...do they really think he might have killed her?"

"Well it's certainly one of the theories they're looking into and I have to say, I wouldn't put anything past him. They also seemed pretty sure he was heading for the flat in Stainsford before leaving the country."

There was a short silence before she answered.

278

"He would have been taking a hell of a risk doing that, but I guess he was arrogant and deluded enough to believe he could get away with it without being noticed."

"Sam…they asked me if I'd ever been to the flat in Stainsford and I told them I hadn't," I blurted out.

"Why do you need to lie about that now he's dead? I don't get it. You could land yourself in a whole load of trouble. Just tell the truth about what you found. Give them a laugh if nothing else," she said with a little snort.

"The thing is, they said the flat was a place of interest to them even *before* his boat accident. Something about sex trafficking, which would certainly tie up with all that stuff I found there and those disgusting videos of orgy parties on his computer back up. The trail apparently went cold after he was presumed to have drowned, but they knew his company continued to rent it, so it stayed on their radar. The way I see it, if he was prepared to risk going back to it, there must be something in there he wanted very badly and I need to find out what it was. Before the police have a chance to get too involved. In fact, I'm going back there today," I concluded decisively, knowing she would not approve of the idea.

"Why, Grace? What's the point? You already went through everything with a fine-tooth comb and took all the stuff that could be of any use to you. I think you should just leave it and let the police do their job. Why put yourself in danger?"

"I don't think I'm in any danger. Daniel is hardly in a position to pose a threat to me now, is he? I can't explain, Sam, I've just got a feeling about it. I need to do this, but you're the only person I'm telling. No one else can know, especially not Mum. Keep your phone on and I'll check in when I get there, every half hour I'm there and when I leave. I'm relying on you to raise the alarm if there's a problem. Just make sure you send a hot guy to come and rescue me, like in the films," I joked, trying to lighten the mood.

"That's not even funny, but I'm guessing you've made up your mind and nothing is going to change it. Do you want me to come with you?"

"You know me too well," I laughed. "No, I'll be fine, honestly. This is something I have to do on my own. Like I said, I need you on call for backup if anything goes wrong. Which it won't, of course," I added.

I was actually quite looking forward to revisiting my brief career as a Private Eye. I even toyed with the idea of getting out my blonde wig again but decided, in the end, there was nothing to be gained by going in disguise. The one thing that worried me slightly was that the police may be watching me, so I took precautions by driving to the big Tesco supermarket, parking the car, then walking into the store and straight out another entrance. From there I walked the short distance to the Enterprise depot and hired a blue Ford Fiesta for the day, knowing I was probably being overly paranoid, but no harm in being careful. The route to the Stainsford bedsit was etched on my memory, despite the fact that I hadn't been there for over three years. After the court case for our divorce, I knew Daniel continued to go there regularly, but I never saw any point in returning and had to hope now that he had not put a spanner in the works by changing the locks. I drove past the little key shop on the corner and wondered casually whether the tall ginger guy still worked there, remembering how he had been kind to me when I first embarked on my career as a PI. Then I parked round the back and sat in the car for a good half hour, observing. When I was finally satisfied there was no one around, I sent Sam a text and walked confidently up to the door, clutching the keys in my latex-gloved hand. Fortunately, they were still the right keys and, with a hard shove like last time, the door opened and I was in.

Memories of my last visit came flooding back and my heart was thumping hard in my chest, but I took a deep breath and began to climb the stairs, unsure of what I expected to find. It was like stepping back in time. The bin bags full of ripped and graffiti-covered clothes had gone, but everything else looked eerily the same. A quick peep into the bathroom showed the cat mask and tail still hanging on the mirror and in the kitchen, the fridge contained several bottles of Wairau Cove like before. The bins were empty this time, as was the washing machine and I couldn't help sniggering as I wondered whether he had been wearing his favourite pink bloomers when they found him in Ireland. A cursory inspection of the bedroom revealed nothing new. There were the same stains on the carpet and wall that made me feel a bit nauseous, the same false boobs in the drawer, the same underwear and headless mannequin under the bed. It was as if the whole place had been locked into a kind of time capsule, just waiting for someone to find it in years to come. I shuddered at the thought of what Daniel might have been getting up to in that room and beat a hasty retreat back downstairs, anxious to get the images out of my mind and focus on documentation. The desk in the lounge was cluttered with envelopes and files, most of which I recognised as correspondence with the Trustee in Bankruptcy and paperwork concerning the cars, in particular the Ferrari he had tried to pass off as belonging to Jane. I pushed them around irritably, still angry at the way no one had listened to me about all that. It seemed a lifetime ago.

Then I noticed a file with the words Safety Net and an exclamation mark scribbled on the front. I snatched it up excitedly. This was something I hadn't seen before. Inside there were a couple of letters addressed to me at the Stainsford address, dated between our divorce and the bankruptcy. I realised in disgust that Daniel must have been using my name to hide something from the Trustee. Furious at the blatant identity fraud, I ripped the first one that came to hand out of its envelope and hurriedly scanned its contents.

I had gone there because of a gut feeling that Daniel was up to something again, but nothing could have prepared me for what that envelope contained and I felt so light-headed with the shock that I thought I might actually faint. I stared at it in disbelief for a long while, reading through it again and again, then slowly sank to the floor, unable to make any sense of it whatsoever.

Daniel had done it again. Pulled another rabbit from the hat. Just when I thought I had seen it all.

Hidden in Plain Sight

Two years earlier
One week before the delivery trip on Mistress

Daniel

Daniel could feel the net closing in on him and to say he was pissed off was the understatement of the year. The bitch Trustee in Bankruptcy and her bunch of Harpies were constantly breathing down his neck and, for some bizarre reason he utterly failed to comprehend, Grace had put herself firmly in their camp and was on some kind of mission to ruin everything for him, even if it meant destroying her own life in the process. He was sick and tired of trying to get her to see sense and had given her more than enough chances to see the light, but she was still refusing to listen and his patience had finally run out.

Then all of a sudden she surprised him by agreeing to his suggestion that she help him move 'Mistress' over to Ireland, supposedly to put the race yacht out of reach of the Trustee, sell her and split the profits. Like that was ever going to happen. Yet for some reason, Grace took the bait. Just like that. Daniel wasn't buying it and had a strong hunch she was up to something, but if she thought she was going to get the better of him, she had another think coming. She was about to find out just how far out of her depth she really was.

The little car park round the back of the bedsit in Stainsford was almost empty when he arrived at around ten-thirty. He parked in his usual spot and took the keys out of the glove compartment, smiling to himself as he entered the place that had become his personal haven, his safe space. The first thing he had done when he rented it was to fit a second lock that not even the letting agents knew about so that no one could ever get in there without his knowledge and consent. Daniel valued his privacy, especially there. He bent down to pick up the mail and a quick shuffle through revealed the things he had been waiting for. Closing the door behind him, he went upstairs and put the pile of letters on the desk by the window, then wandered into the kitchen to make himself a coffee. He made sure his phone was on silent to make it easier to ignore the Trustee or whoever else might decide to pester him, like Jane for example, who was always demanding money for the kid in a shameless effort to bleed him dry. They could all go to Hell, every last one of them. He was taking control again, putting the shit show of the last few months behind him and rolling out his safety net, the one they all naively thought he didn't have. Daniel couldn't help feeling smug as he sat down at the desk, knowing he had won, beaten the system again, despite all appearances to the contrary.

Grace Callaghan (and more recently Grace King) had unwittingly been extremely useful to Daniel, but never so much as right now. To be fair to her, she had found out more than he expected about what he had been getting up to and her annoying snooping phase had turned out to be extremely inconvenient. Like the fact that she 'owned' Mistress and had corresponded regularly with HMRC regarding the company for example. But she didn't know the half of it. Over the years, Grace had been given a variety of roles in his various companies, ranging from Company Secretary to Director. She used the Stainsford address to set up two different bank accounts and regularly ordered assorted items of kinky underwear and sex toys to be delivered there. She even paid some of the bills. Now it was time for her to branch out and hit the big time with an offshore bank account of her very own in the British Virgin Islands. Not that she had the first clue about any of it of

284

course. What a coup to pull off, he thought to himself as he began to open the envelopes.

The first one bore the stamp of Fisher Tait Medical Negligence Specialists. The other was A4 sized from a company called, rather unimaginatively, Offshore Solutions, which informed Grace that her application to open an account in the BVIs with the VP Bank Ltd had been successful and included various other documents such as the all-important access details to get the account up and running. The whole process had been ridiculously easy, which was why Daniel had chosen that particular location for the account after studying their sales pitch and instructions on the website:

- Fill out the application form
- Sign the opening documents and send them back to the bank
- The bank will confirm the opening of your account with minimal reference requirements
- No background check
- 24/7 Internet banking
- Strong banking secrecy
- Easy to open your account by mail
- Approval guaranteed!
- Fully usable account in just 3-5 working days with access details sent in the post
- Account cost: 550$US

It was a no-brainer. Grace's signature on the papers was no problem for him and the only documentation they apparently required was a copy of her passport, accurately specifying all the data and clearly visible. Again, it had not been difficult to obtain that on one of the nights he spent at the house. Her new passport in her maiden name of King was sitting there alongside the old one in the bedside cabinet drawer, exactly where it had always been. For someone who thought she was so clever, she could be surprisingly naive and ridiculously predictable at times.

Setting the information from the bank to one side, he tore open the other envelope, barely able to contain his excitement. The final piece of the jigsaw. Fisher Tait, the 'no win, no fee' firm of lawyers, who had been pursuing his medical negligence case against the NHS for their failure to accurately diagnose his injuries following the helicopter crash, had eventually come up trumps. He had already spoken to them on the phone, but this letter was the official confirmation that they had agreed on a six-figure settlement out of court. All they needed now was a signature from him and the details of the account into which he would like the money to be paid.

Absolutely fucking perfect.

He had to admit he had initially been irritated at the ridiculous amount of time it had all taken, but in the end it had worked to his advantage. If he had received a pay out before the divorce and Grace had got a whiff of it, it could have proved disastrous. At least now he only had the Trustee to worry about. Nevertheless, he knew he couldn't afford to be complacent and it all had to be handled very carefully indeed. Grace had already unearthed a number of bank accounts in his name, including three in the States and the Trustee was now scouring the four corners of the earth looking for any further accounts he might have stashed money away in. Goody two-shoes Grace had of course disclosed chapter and verse to the courts about her two bank accounts, so no one was interested in the little amount she had anymore. It was all about him. That was why he had chosen to hide his windfall in plain sight, so to speak, right under their noses. Opening the offshore account in Grace's name was a stroke of pure genius in his humble opinion. Nobody else, not even Grace, would ever suspect it existed or go looking for it because it was wholly and absolutely the last place on earth they would ever think he might try to hide money.

Daniel set to work immediately, following the instructions to access the new account and then setting up his own unique password, before sending the details to the solicitors so they could transfer the money he was due in their regulation five working days, less their eye-watering commission of course. Once he had finished and checked everything was working properly he put the papers in a pile at the back of the desk, ready to be destroyed on his next visit, once the funds had cleared. After that, he would not be visiting the flat for a while, as he had decided to lay low and let the dust settle with all the bankruptcy shit that was going on. The stress was not good for his health.

Opening the desk drawer he took out a passport in the name of one Patrick Salenden, whose photo was remarkably similar to Daniel himself. You might almost have thought they were one and the same person. He put the passport and a couple of credit cards into an Aquapac pouch, which he then strapped around his waist under his clothing. The situation he found himself in was volatile, to say the least, and there was no harm in being prepared for any eventuality, should the need arise for him to act quickly.

Satisfied he had everything he needed, Daniel locked up and left the bedsit. His ducks were lining up very nicely indeed. Once he had got the boat delivery out of the way and dealt with Grace, he would be back to tie up any loose ends before doing his disappearing act.

He just wished he could be around to see all of their faces when the penny finally dropped that he had royally screwed them over.

Silver Lining

---

*The greatest turning points of life tend to come at the most
unexpected times and from the most unexpected places.*

Present Day

Grace

I stared at the paper in my hand, re-reading it over and over again,
unable to believe what I saw with my own eyes. The envelope was
addressed to me, it had my name on the documents inside, but I
knew nothing about it whatsoever. There was a covering letter from
a company called Offshore Solutions (which I had never heard of),
congratulating me on the successful opening of my account, then
there were some papers from the VP Bank Ltd in the British Virgin
Islands. I had never heard of them either. And I had never been to
the British Virgin Islands. The whole thing stank of fraud and I
began to feel very nervous. Why the hell would Daniel set up a
secret offshore bank account in my name, an account that would be
wholly controlled by him? The only possible explanation so far as I
could see was money laundering from whatever seedy and
debauched niche of the sex industry he had got himself into,
although I didn't really know how all that worked. I was out of my

depth. The police already seemed to think I was more involved with his dealings than I was admitting to, so what on earth would they think once they found out about this?

I had to get a grip and pull myself together. Whatever had been going on, I had to deal with it and, in order to do that effectively, I needed to buy myself time to think. I got slowly to my feet and went through all the papers on the desk, bundling everything that bore my name into a folder. There was some other new stuff there that looked important to me, bearing the stamp of Fisher Tait LLP. Clearly, he was involved with solicitors about something and I intended to find out what it was, shoving the envelope into the manila folder with all the others. I was seething at Daniel's bare-faced cheek. He must have thought he was so clever, putting dirty money into an account in my name, knowing I would be completely oblivious to its existence. There had been no stone left unturned in the search for accounts in *his* name or in the names of his various girlfriends, but no one had bothered to look into my accounts, because I had already declared everything in the divorce court and it was clear to all involved that I had never had more than a few grand in the bank at any given point in my life. It was the perfect solution. And of course, he would have loved the blatant audacity of such a manoeuvre. It was always all about the game with him.

I had one last look through everything on the desk to be certain I had not missed anything, then I picked up my precious folder and practically ran down the stairs, feeling suddenly claustrophobic and anxious to be outside. I locked the door behind me with both keys, put them safely in the inside pocket of my Barbour and glanced nervously around me as I walked back to the car. There was no sign of anyone, but this place gave me the creeps and it was impossible to rid myself of the feeling that someone was lurking in the shadows, watching my every move.

As soon as I got back home I locked myself in, sat down in the kitchen and put the folder in front of me on the table. Only then did I feel safe. I rang Sam.

"Hey, it's me. I'm back home."

"Thank goodness for that. I was beginning to get worried."

"I know, I'm sorry," I said, realising I had forgotten to text her when I left as promised.

"So, did you find anything?"

"I did, but you are not going to believe it. I'm not sure I do. Sam, he set up an offshore account in my name and I think he was using it to launder money. I was scared the police were going to think I knew about it all along, so I took all the paperwork, everything I could find with my name on it, out of the flat and brought it back here."

"Wow," she said, clearly stunned by the news. "Shit, this is huge. How much was in the account?"

"I don't know. I still need to get access to it and read through all the other stuff I found. For all I know the account could be empty."

"Well, that's the first thing you need to find out. Because…I'm thinking out loud here…if there is any money in it, maybe you should just hang onto it and say nothing, at least for the moment. Seriously, how will anyone else find out about it?" she said, becoming more and more animated. "The account is in your name, so all you need to do is keep quiet and act innocent. Bloody hell Grace, this could actually work in your favour. Think of it as compensation," she added decisively.

I smiled to myself, relieved at her response.

"That's exactly what I've been thinking, but I wanted to hear your take on it. The thing is, if I say anything to the police, I'll probably just land myself in it somehow and that cow of a Trustee will immediately snatch any money there is to cover her own exorbitant fees," I said carefully. "I played it all above board once before and look how that turned out. I'm not so naïve now and I won't be making the same mistake again."

"Good for you. I just hope there's actually some money in the account because that really would be the best kind of justice ever."

I laughed.

"I won't be that lucky, but I intend to get to the bottom of it all one way or another. I'll ring you back later with an update."

As soon as I had put the phone down I began the slow process of analysing everything in my folder, making careful notes as I did so. The first thing I found out was that the law firm Fisher Tait LLP were medical negligence specialists acting on behalf of Daniel Callaghan. Apparently, their team had managed to negotiate a settlement out of court with the North Yorkshire Hospitals Trust in respect of their failure to correctly diagnose and treat the injuries he suffered in the helicopter crash. A settlement to the tune of just under a million pounds.

"I knew it! You lying, cheating, conniving piece of shit," I hissed under my breath, remembering his protestations that he would never sue our amazing NHS after all they had done for him, his earnest assurances that he wasn't that kind of person. There had never been any doubt in my mind he was lying, but in trying to prove it I was constantly faced with a brick wall of patients' rights to privacy and confidentiality. It had been a hopeless battle. Until now.

The question was, where had the money gone? I had butterflies in my stomach and hardly dared allow my brain to consider the possibility that he had hidden it in 'my' offshore account. I forced myself to be methodical and went through the letters in chronological order. The one that really mattered was the confirmation of the account being set up and the internet access details. I hurriedly typed the web address and access code into Safari, only to be met by the obvious stumbling block of the password. I wracked my brains for all the combinations he could have used, bearing in mind that there was usually a requirement for upper and lower case letters as well as numbers and I knew he always used key dates in some form or other for numbers in his passwords. I also knew I would only be allowed a certain number of attempts before I was frozen out and after the third failed attempt I was getting very nervous. The only other option was to reset the password, but they would undoubtedly send a link to an email address I could not access. I sat back and closed my eyes, trying to think clearly and remembering the Apple Time Capsule fiasco. I had been here before. There had to be a way. Desperation was setting in as I hurriedly went through all the papers again for clues. And suddenly I had my answer. There on the back of one of the cover letters.

RV Bday.

RV…Rotorvator, it had to be. Rotorvator was a name he used for himself on various forums and his birthday was 25th December. Born on Christmas Day. Baby Jesus himself. Or more likely the Antichrist. I carefully typed in Rotorvator1225, taking a punt on him using the American format for the date. I pressed enter and offered up a silent prayer that he had indeed been stupid enough to write down a clue for the password on the account. Miraculously the page burst into life, confirming what I had only dared dream was true. The figures were there in black and white and the ridiculous irony of it had me laughing out loud. The man who had done everything in his power to ensure he left me destitute and penniless had unwittingly made me a rich woman. Wealth is always relative of course, but in my case, where the bar had been set somewhere below ground zero, I felt like I had won the Euromillions.

I stood up and began pacing around like a cat on hot bricks, still unable to fully believe what I had discovered. With everything that had happened over the last few years, I was not used to fortune smiling on me without there being some sort of catch, but the more I thought about it, the more there simply didn't seem to be one. I sat down again and rang Sam to bring her up to speed. I finally allowed myself to be properly excited because this was real.

"Well that settles it," she said immediately. "You definitely keep the money. It's all legit and above board, nothing to do with dirty money. And I think you should leave it where it is for the moment," she added. "Just in case."

"In case of what?" I asked, laughing. "The account is in my name, I have access to it and nobody else knows about it. I can do what I want with the money, so far as I can make out."

"Exactly. So what I mean is, don't move it into your main account and don't spend too much at once, because there's a slim chance it could arouse suspicion if anyone does decide to go snooping into your affairs, what with everything else that's going on. It seems Dickhead Daniel actually did something right for once and hid the money well, so don't go spoiling all his good work," she said sarcastically.

"Yeah, you've got a point. My plan was to transfer it and close the account, but I don't suppose there's any urgent need to do that. Best to let the dust settle while the police are investigating and the Trustee is prowling around like a hyena waiting to pick the bones of the carcass," I said, pleased with my analogy and the unpleasant image of Vanessa Harding it conjured up. "Bloody hell Sam, I still can't believe it."

"I know it's crazy, but the thing you need to remember above all else is that you deserve that money. That bastard owed you big time. And I hope he's turning in his grave," she said with a little laugh. "There's one word for this Grace: Karma," she concluded.

Over the next few days, I kept looking at myself in the mirror, expecting to see a new, changed me somehow, but I was just the same. I began to realise that, nice as it was to finally have financial stability, the money was relatively unimportant in the grand scheme of things that really mattered in my life. Family, friends and health were the big ones and I would never forget that.

I didn't go to Daniel's funeral when his body was eventually released for burial after the post mortem. The truth was I no longer felt anything for him, good or bad. I did wonder how many of the other women in his life would turn up and whether any new faces would come out of the woodwork, but I decided he had haunted me for long enough. It was finally time to look forwards, not backwards.

The police came to see me before the funeral to tell me they were treating Daniel's death as suspicious, due to new information that had come to light. That didn't surprise me. Roisin Delaney's murder inquiry remained an open case and police were still searching for the missing woman Caitlin Flynn, who had become a person of significant interest apparently. A tangled web indeed, but not one that I had to be caught up in any more.

So far as I was concerned, the investigation into the suspected illegal activities at the Stainsford address was ongoing, but DI Gemma Ford informed me they were satisfied I had no involvement in that. She looked disappointed, I thought, but all I really cared about was that I was off the hook.

I waited and waited for them to find out about the account in the BVIs and come knocking at the door again, wanting to interrogate me further about my visits to the flat and accusing me of fraud. Once they started, it was only a matter of time before they put two and two together to make five, drawing their own conclusions that I had been in cahoots with Daniel all along. But the knock never came and, as each day went by, I began to allow myself to believe that it was going to turn out all right after all.

It would be a long time before I stopped looking over my shoulder, expecting something to go wrong and to have everything snatched away from me all over again, but I was determined to have faith.

This time it would be different because I knew for certain, beyond any shadow of a doubt, that I had finally laid the ghost of Daniel Callaghan to rest. Daniel, my nemesis, the man who had betrayed, tormented and haunted me, was gone from my life forever.

I smiled as I watched a boat sail across the bay from my window and told myself that the future was not simply the place I was heading towards, it was the place I got to create.

Epilogue

DCI Colin Gates was intrigued by the Callaghan case, even more so after he had spoken at some length to Grace King and learned about the bizarre story behind their extremely acrimonious divorce. He was not surprised to see that the circumstances surrounding the death of Daniel Callaghan were becoming increasingly suspicious by the minute. The man had lived his entire life entangled in a ridiculously complicated web of lies and deceit, so why should his death be any different?

A woman by the name of Kate Ryan had recently come forward with key information regarding the deaths of both Callaghan and the female psychologist murdered in Dublin. But from what she said in her statement, it appeared there could be a further link with the sudden death of another man in Dublin around ten years earlier, the common denominator in both cases being the missing woman Caitlin Flynn. The man who died a decade ago was called Craig Vardy and Caitlin Flynn was his fiancé at the time, although she was known then as Sophie Bevan. There were a number of striking similarities in the manner of death for both Callaghan and Vardy that could not be ignored and it looked increasingly likely that they would both become murder investigations.

As soon as Kate Ryan saw the photograph in the paper she recognised the face staring out at her. Different hair colour, different style, a bit heavier, but it was definitely her, no doubt about it. The woman the Guards were now searching for was her old friend Sophie. She quickly scanned the report under the photo.

...A spokesman for the Garda told reporters they were anxious to trace the woman and were concerned for her welfare. Caitlin Flynn, a nurse from Clearpoint near Baltimore, disappeared without trace after the sudden and tragic death of her partner while on holiday in Crosshaven. The man, named as Daniel Callaghan, was using the pseudonyms Patrick Salenden and Patrick James and was wanted in connection with the recent brutal murder of clinical psychologist Roisin Delaney in Dun Laoghaire. He appears to have suffered a catastrophic stroke in his sleep and died almost instantly as a result....

Kate put down the paper, stunned.

"Christ Michael, look at this," she said, pushing the paper across the table for her husband to see. "That's Sophie," she said, pointing at the photo. "Read what it says."

"Wow. It certainly looks like her, but I couldn't be sure after all these years. Weird how tragedy seems to follow some people around...if it is her, she doesn't have much luck with men," he said, returning to his breakfast with an ironic little laugh.

"Come off it Michael, it's more than *weird* and I'm telling you, it's her for sure. The way this man Callaghan died, it's exactly what happened to Craig on the boat that night. And Sophie vanished into thin air then as well."

Michael looked at her curiously.

"So what exactly are you saying, Kate?"

"I don't know. I really don't. I just feel in my heart of hearts that this is more than a strange coincidence. You know what they say: lightning never strikes twice."

Kate shivered and felt a wave of nausea come over her as her memory took her back in time, back to that morning on the boat. She could hear the blood-curdling screams as Sophie completely lost the plot in the front cabin and, worst of all, she could see Craig's face, his lips blue and his skin as cold as ice. Kate had always known deep down that something was not quite right about

Craig's death, but she had kept it to herself, feeling disloyal to her friend. She couldn't keep quiet a second time.

Picking up her phone, she rang the number for the information line and told them everything she knew about Sophie Bevan, aka Caitlin Flynn, and about what happened on the boat with Craig, satisfied that her conscience was clear at last.

Gates was working in collaboration with the Irish police and had read Kate's statement, together with all the associated reports. He had also done a fair bit of digging of his own and was beginning to piece together a full and detailed picture of the missing woman Caitlin Flynn, but it did not make for pleasant reading. He discovered a child with a troubled past, characterised by domestic abuse, bullying and various mental health issues. Things had come to a head when the teenager, known then as Megan Blackstock, stabbed her father to death in a vicious and brutal attack. In court, the judge found she had acted in self-defence and recommended long-term counselling for the trauma she had suffered. The girl and her mother moved away to make a new start, which was when she began calling herself Sophie, but reports from social services showed continued involvement with an Educational Psychologist for anger management and repeated incidents of bullying in school, where she was both the victim and the perpetrator. Tragedy struck again a few years later when she suddenly and unexpectedly lost her mother, who suffered a fatal stroke in her sleep, aged just forty-two.

Gates read over his notes again, thinking to himself that there was no wonder the girl was screwed up. But that didn't mean he thought she should get away with murder. It was too much of a coincidence that first her mother, then two different men she was involved with all died in exactly the same way, of seemingly natural causes. It just didn't add up. Something resonated in his memory and he remembered a true crime story he had read a short while ago in a book from a charity shop. After a quick search of his bookshelves, he found what he was looking for and put on his reading glasses.

In 1997 a 55-year-old doctor in Frankfurt and his nurse accomplice were tried and convicted for the murder of at least ten people by injecting air into their bloodstream. The deaths were originally recorded as being 'due to natural causes' as the patients had all suffered a catastrophic and fatal stroke or heart failure. No toxic substances were found in their bodies, except occasional traces of medication to aid sleep. Needle marks on the bodies either went unnoticed or were explained by the fact that the victims had recently had bloods taken. Suspicion was aroused due to the sheer number of similar cases linked to the same doctor in a relatively short period of time and police now fear the true death toll could in fact be over thirty.

In an interview with a psychiatrist following his arrest, Marcus Kettermann stated that he had 'actively euthanised dozens of people for the greater good of society'. He maintained that his actions would ultimately have saved lives and his victims were all individuals of dubious moral character, often known criminals involved in the sex and drugs underworld. In his opinion, he was acting out of compassion, to spare the mental anguish of people who he believed were tortured by the fact that they were a menace to society and incapable of changing.

At the trial, Professor Hans Bauer, expert witness for the prosecution, said he believed Kettermann may have taken inspiration from the outrageous T-4 murders of psychiatric patients in hospitals in Nazi Germany. After 1941, largely due to increased public awareness of what was going on, institutions were ordered to stop using gas for the murders. Instead, 'special orders' were issued, instructing them to continue secretly with the so-called 'wild euthanasia programme', using a new method of injecting air into the patients' bloodstream. Those patients who were given an air embolus died within minutes. Their deaths were recorded at the hospitals and a common and plausible diagnosis such as 'stroke' was supplied.

Bauer stated that in his opinion an injection of 50 – 100ml of air into an adult's bloodstream would almost certainly be fatal and the person would appear to have suffered a severe stroke. In order to keep his victims calm, he suspected Kettermann may have first administered a light sedative and may also have used a topical cream such as EMLA to numb the area prior to the injection. It was also possible that he hid some of the murders by inserting the needle into a previous puncture wound, if, for example, the victim had recently had bloods taken.

Bauer concluded that in cases such as this, foul play was extremely difficult, although not impossible, to prove and the cause of death was often erroneously recorded as stroke or heart failure.

Gates closed his eyes and inhaled deeply. Everything fitted. If his suspicions were correct, Caitlin Flynn was a serial killer, having murdered at least three people and quite possibly more that they didn't know about yet. It was also now looking highly likely to him that she was behind the murder of Roisin Delaney, the woman bludgeoned to death in her own apartment in Dublin. His theory was a violent and vengeful attack by Flynn, a woman scorned, having found out about the relationship between Callaghan and Delaney. He had to hand it to her, she was an extremely flawed, but very clever and ruthless woman, who had clearly got the measure of Daniel Callaghan and played him at his own game.

Karma at its best.

That said, however much of a loathsome and contemptible character Callaghan had clearly been, there was no doubt whatsoever in Gates' mind about the fact that Caitlin Flynn had to be stopped and brought to justice. The problem was, she was several steps ahead of them now and was probably already in a different country with a new name and changed appearance. *Bring it on*, he thought to himself. Because if there was one thing Gates relished above all else it was a challenge and he knew that this case, with all its many complications, could be the defining point in his career if he managed to pull it off. He began to arrange photos and make notes on the evidence board, before sitting back at his desk and settling himself down for a long night; the first of many, he suspected.

"RIP, Daniel Callaghan," said Gates to himself, staring at the photo in front of him.

But he had a strong hunch there was little chance of that ever happening.

THE END

Printed in Great Britain
by Amazon

30554866R00179